THE SON OF GOD

Sharon Lindsay

Drink This Cup

THE SON OF GOD

Series: Book 5

TATE PUBLISHING
AND ENTERPRISES, LLC

Published by Tate Publishing & Enterprises, LLC
127 E. Trade Center Terrace | Mustang, Oklahoma 73064 USA
1.888.361.9473 | www.tatepublishing.com

Tate Publishing is committed to excellence in the publishing industry. The company reflects the philosophy established by the founders, based on Psalm 68:11,

"The Lord gave the word and great was the company of those who published it."

Book design copyright © 2015 by Tate Publishing, LLC. All rights reserved.
Cover design by Nino Carlo Suico
Interior design by Jomel Pepito

Published in the United States of America

ISBN: 978-1-68028-155-2
1. Fiction / Religious
2. Fiction / Christian / Historical
15.03.24

To my husband,
Donald J. Lindsay Jr. 1947–2006
Jesus lived the sinless life
that neither of us could live.
He died the death we deserved.
He took the keys of death.
After three days, he left the tomb, alive;
and now, he sits at the right hand of God.
Jesus is coming as king of this Earth soon.
Because this is true, factual, not fiction,
I will one day enjoy your companionship
again. This time, for eternity.

Contents

Introduction

Two thousand years ago, the blood of Jesus literally poured from his body. Today, we remember that event through the symbolism of a small sip of wine or grape juice when celebrating the Lord's Supper. That little taste of his sacrifice is so meaningful to most modern Christians, but few understand its history and significance.

That sip of wine comes from the Jewish observance of Passover, the meal they eat to commemorate the Exodus. It is the same meal that Jesus ate with his disciples just before he was arrested.

In the traditional Passover Seder, during the course of the meal, the participants drink four cups of wine. With each cup, there is a specific scripture and teaching. The first cup is about sanctification and identifying with the Kingdom of God. The second cup recalls the ten plagues of Egypt, the battle God waged. The third cup commemorates the blood of all the sacrificed lambs and deliverance by an "outstretched arm." Finally, the fourth cup is a drink that celebrates the joy of deliverance.

The disciples entered into the meal, drinking the four cups, remembering the exodus of their ancestors. But as the meal progressed, Jesus used the imagery of these four cups to demonstrate the deliverance that he was about to offer.

In the garden, he prayed specifically about the third cup, ultimately drinking it by going to the cross. When he drinks the fruit of the vine again, with us in heaven, it will be the fourth cup, the celebration of our deliverance.

Drink This Cup is the final book in the *Son of God Series*. It is about the events of Passover, the first one when God became the destroyer and a Passover two thousand years later when God went to the cross to become the deliverer.

Because the *Son of God Series* has imagined characters and subplots that have been added to the biblical account, it is classified as historical fiction. Nevertheless, there is much more truth than fiction. As a strong believer in every word of the Bible, I hope I have brought both life and insight to the familiar biblical narrative. An index of characters has been provided so you can distinguish between reality and imagination.

Prologue

The First Passover

Then the LORD said to Moses, "Now you will see what I will do to Pharaoh: Because of my mighty hand he will let them go; because of my mighty hand he will drive them out of his country.

—Exodus 6:1

The daughter of Putiel who had married Eleazar, one of the younger sons of Aaron, watched her own young son. The boy was excited, eagerly tying his meager belongings into a small bundle. With a heavy sigh, she folded both hands over her heart. The gesture was a futile attempt to control her fears. Her eight-year-old son was leaving his home in Goshen and going to live in the Pharaoh's palace. How could she let him go? What would happen to her firstborn within the royal complex of palaces and temples? When would she see him again?

Keeping her distance in the small room that was their home, the Hebrew mother caressed her son with her eyes. Her tearful glances brushed the bronze smoothness of his skin. It was young flesh that had never felt the whip of their Egyptian masters. She could not bear to think of his beautiful back, ripped and bleeding.

"Phinehas?"

The boy looked up and flashed his mother a carefree smile.

"Son, be quick to please your young master. Don't let any harm come to him. Always remember, he is the son of Pharaoh. He is a few years younger than you, so you must watch over him and be a companion to him. But never forget you are his personal slave."

The woman gulped. Fear was rising in her throat again. In her lifetime, she had seen so many tragedies. "Your well-being is in a boy's hands. In a moment of childish temper, he can order—"The Hebrew mother stopped short. She could not say the words. "Just don't displease him."

Phinehas shrugged. His natural optimism did not know how to respond to his mother's anxiety, so he grinned. "Working in the palace is better than making bricks. I'll be all right." Then the boy changed the subject. "I heard Grandfather Aaron has returned and his brother, Moses, is with him."

"Yes."The daughter-in-law of Aaron chose her words carefully. "Do not speak of this in the palace. No one must know you belong to the family of Aaron and Moses."

Phinehas looked into his mother's serious eyes. With a little impudence, he countered, "You worry too much."

"Respect your mother and do as she says." Eleazar stepped through the doorway.

Phinehas bowed his head in submission to his father's authority.

Eleazar turned to his wife. In hushed, yet eager tones, he spoke over the boy's head. "Early this morning, Moses and Aaron met with all the elders of Israel. Moses performed the signs God had given him, and the people believed.

"Has the God of Abraham really seen our misery?"

Tears flowed. Neither parent could contain their emotions.

Phinehas stared silently, watching his father and mother. The boy felt unsure and slightly confused by such an unusual display of emotion.

Reassuringly, Eleazar pulled his wife into his arms. "Moses says the Lord spoke to him. It was the God of Abraham, Isaac, and Jacob. He said, '*I have heard the groaning of the Israelites, whom the Egyptians are enslaving…I will free you from being slaves to them, and I will redeem you with an outstretched arm and with mighty acts of judgment. I will take you as my own people, and I will be your God."*[1]

"I can't imagine." The Hebrew woman shook her head as she tried to wrap her mind around the wonderful yet fear-invoking message. "How? How long?" Her eyes returned to Phinehas. "Our son can't go to the palace when we are so close to freedom!"

"We have no choice." Eleazar sighed. "For now, we are still slaves." Eleazar put his work-hardened hand on his son's shoulder. "My overseer gave me this afternoon to take Phinehas to the palace. We are fortunate to have a little favor. It's because you assisted his wife when she was in labor."

The daughter of Putiel nodded, grateful that kindness still had its own reward. She bent and kissed her son. Her fingertips brushed his warm skin. Then she turned away to struggle with her own anxious thoughts.

Two weeks passed. The sun was touching the tops of the palms that grew along the Nile as the crew of the royal barge guided their vessel to one of many docks where a ship could safely spend the night. Phinehas brought the little crown prince forward so the boy could stand by his father to wish the sun a speedy journey through the underworld of the night. Phinehas placed the boy between Pharaoh and Jambres, the oldest priest in Egypt. Then the slave boy stepped back, close to the rail, respectfully waiting.

When the royal barge was securely docked, Jambres began calling to the sun, their most important deity. "Do not leave us, O blessed sun. We cannot live without you."

Pharaoh then chanted the next lines of the evening prayer. "O wonderful sun, if you must make this journey into the world of darkness where the ancestors of all people dwell, return to us quickly. We are the living who will, one day, take this journey with you."

The sun seemed to pause, a huge orange disk resting on the banks of the Nile.

Jambres bent and spoke to the little prince. "See, the sun waits. It has heard the voice of your father, and now, it is considering whether or not to continue its journey. One day, the sun will pause to listen to what you have to say."

Phinehas looked away. He let his gaze travel up and down the river. A collective gasp brought his attention back to the evening service.

A boat was approaching the royal barge, a small skiff. It seemed to be coming directly out of the sun, like a messenger from the god of daylight. Two bearded men were standing in the boat. Phinehas immediately recognized that they were wearing the garments of the Hebrew patriarchs. A much younger man wearing only a loin cloth guided the vessel.

The skiff tied up beside the royal barge. Phinehas recognized his grandfather, Aaron. He assumed the other bearded man had to be his great uncle, Moses. Phinehas caught his breath. The man guiding the skiff was his own father, Eleazar. For a brief moment, the father and son locked eyes. A silent warning passed from the elders to the youngest grandson of Aaron. There was no other communication.

Grandfather Aaron addressed Pharaoh. "We have come from the God who created all life. He is the God of the Hebrews. Before our people came to live in your land, the father of our nation was the personal friend of God. Now our God is calling all the Hebrews to leave their homes and their responsibilities to come into the desert to worship him."

Moses spoke a few stuttering words in a language that Phinehas did not understand.

Aaron interpreted. "*This is what the* LORD, *the God of Israel, says: 'Let my people go, so that they may hold a festival to me in the wilderness.'*"[2]

Pharaoh looked at Jambres for direction.

The old priest scowled and shook his shaved head negatively.

Pharaoh's lips curled into a sneer. Then he turned back to the men in the skiff. *"Who is the* LORD *that I should obey him and let Israel go? I do not know the* LORD *and I will not let Israel go."*[3]

Aaron quickly responded with a warning, *"The God of the Hebrews has met with us. Now let us take a three-day journey into the wilderness to offer sacrifices to the* LORD *our God, or he may strike us with plagues or with the sword."*[4]

Jambres laughed.

Pharaoh then added his own scoffing laughter.

The little prince did not understand, but his childish laughter mimicked that of his elders.

Phinehas felt very uncomfortable. His family had become the focus of Pharaoh's ridicule. The slave boy looked down at the deck of the barge, not lifting his eyes, only listening.

He recognized the voice of Jambres. "None of the gods have spoken to you. You are men. You are Hebrews. Tell us your names."

Phinehas cringed as he heard his grandfather's voice again. "I am Aaron from the family of Levi and this is my brother, Moses."

There was an uncertain pause. Phinehas snuck a peek at the old priest. Jambres was squinting into the setting sun, studying the two men. "Moses, I think I know you. You have said very little. Talk to me. Let me hear your voice."

Aaron responded, "My brother has been forbidden to speak directly to the court of Pharaoh. Our God speaks to him. He speaks to me in the language of our God. Then I relay the message to you."

"Humph!" Jambres grunted in disgust and turned away.

But Pharaoh did not turn away. He looked hard at both men and then in a menacingly soft voice, he said, *"Moses and Aaron, why are you taking the people away from their labor? Get back to your work!"*

"You are Hebrews, therefore you are slaves. And you have work to do!" Jambres reasserted himself.

Then Pharaoh said, "Look, the people of the land are now numerous, and you are stopping them from working.[5] Leave us and return to your responsibilities."

Phinehas looked up to see what would happen next. He watched as members of the royal guard moved swiftly to untie the skiff and push it into the current of the river. With his eyes, he cautiously followed his family downstream. Then he turned his attention back to the needs of the crown prince.

Later that day, Phinehas overheard Pharaoh give an *order to the slave drivers and overseers in charge of the people: "You are no longer to supply the people with straw for making bricks; let them go and gather their own straw. But require them to make the same number of bricks as before; don't reduce the quota. They are lazy; that is why they are crying out, 'Let us go and sacrifice to our God.' Make the work harder for the people so that they keep working and pay no attention to lies."*[6]

Phinehas struggled with a turmoil of confusing thoughts. How could his family approach Pharaoh with such an outrageous proposal, and how could they bring such trouble upon the entire nation of Israel?

That night, after the little prince had fallen asleep, Phinehas lay on his back, looking up at the stars. He tried to remember the stories of his heritage, how God had spoken to Abraham, Isaac, and Jacob. He knew about the fall of Adam and the promise of a Deliverer, but his mind was filled with doubts. And he wondered who was greater, the God of the Hebrews or Pharaoh.

One week later, Phinehas stood in the entrance to one of the inner rooms of the Temple of the Cult of the Bull. He knew better than to take another step. His back still stung from the day before when he had hurried into the sacred room to assist his young master. Jambres, the crotchety court magician, had used his scepter effectively, laying stroke after stroke across the slave's bare back. "You must never under any circumstances enter the sacred chambers of this temple!"

Phinehas moved a little and felt the crust that had formed over the welts. It caught and pulled on the light linen fabric that covered his back.

From the safety of the outer court, Phinehas kept his eyes on the young prince. Both boys longed for the freedom of childhood. They would rather play a game of hide and chase through the columns of the outer court. Yet the boy who would become the next pharaoh sat miserably in his own royal enslavement.

"Repeat!" Jambres glared down at the boy as he smacked his jackal-headed scepter on the brick floor.

The young prince stared mutely at the confusing patterns of figures interspersed with symbols.

"Your father is going to hear about this!" Jambres shouted. "You are not the student he was!"

Phinehas felt a little sympathy for the boy. The prince was not the smartest child he had ever played with, but they had become friends. The Hebrew boy casually glanced at the symbolic figures painted on the wall. He understood everything the priest had said. There were eleven gates in the underworld. Each gate was guarded by two divine beings and a dangerous serpent. The dead must pass through each gate before they could enjoy the pleasures of the afterworld.

A gong sounded. Jambres bent and hissed at his young student. "Come again tomorrow. Plan to sit in front of this wall until you can name every god and explain every symbol."

The prince kept his eyes on the floor until Jambres strode away, his scepter tapping the floor with each step. Then the royal child stood. He bowed to the deities on the wall and remained in that bent-over position, backing out of the sacred room while sweeping his footsteps away with his hand.

As soon as the royal child stood up, Phinehas took his hand, and together, they ran to the main entrance where the sacred bull was being led to the man-made lake where it bathed every day. Both boys watched as the lumbering animal with long sleek horns ambled down a series of ramps, finally entering the water.

A small crowd began to gather. It was believed that this animal could answer yes or no questions with a nod of its head and cure all illnesses with its breath. Everyone wanted to ask a question or just get close. The boys ignored the crowd. They began to run and chase each other up and down the ramps, never stopping until they heard a commotion near the lake.

The palace guard was dispersing the people. The bull was coming out of the water. Pharaoh with his advisors had arrived to make their own inquiry.

Phinehas placed a cautionary hand on the shoulder of the crown prince. He wanted the little boy to know that this was a time to show dignity and respect. The prince responded, calmly focusing his attention on his father.

To the right, Phinehas heard the steady tapping of wood hitting the brick paving stones. At first, he thought it was Jambres, walking with his scepter. But the old Egyptian priest was already listening to Pharaoh's question and positioning the bull so it could indicate a yes or no response.

Phinehas turned toward the tapping sound. His breath caught in his throat, and his heart began to pound like it was going to come out of his chest. Two bearded Hebrew men were approaching. Phinehas was certain of their identity!

The men did not look to the right or to the left. Their eyes were fixed on Pharaoh who was laying a garland of flowers over the neck of the sacred bull. Straightway, Moses and Aaron approached the royal party. At the top of the ramp that entered the water, they stopped. Grandfather Aaron spoke. "Why do you need an animal to nod its head and give you advice? The Creator God has sent us to speak directly to you."

"Remove these men!" Pharaoh ordered.

The palace guards took one step forward and then slumped to the ground, leaving Pharaoh and Jambres with only their attendants for protection.

Aaron and Moses stepped closer. "The God of the Hebrews has remembered the promises he made to our ancestors who rest in the dwelling place of the dead. Our God is calling all the Hebrews to come out into the desert to the sacred mountain of his presence."

Again, Phinehas remembered that Adam had been promised a descendant who would defeat the Evil One and restore a perfect life to God's people. Also, Abraham had been promised a fertile and wonderful land. Cautiously, the slave boy wondered, was the God of the Hebrews strong enough to change the course of history? Could he keep such promises?

Jambres whispered into Pharaoh's ear. Then Pharaoh took a confident step toward Aaron and Moses. "If you come from the gods, then you can show us something amazing, something that only the gods can do!"

Moses nodded his head, and Aaron took the long wooden shepherd's staff from his brother's hand. He raised it over his head like he was about to strike the ruler of Egypt.

Pharaoh and Jambres jumped back.

Nearby, the bull pawed the ground and snorted, angrily shaking its head from side to side.

Protectively, Phinehas pulled the crown prince close. He did not know what was going to happen next.

Grandfather Aaron violently threw the stick to the ground. It hit the paving stones with a smack. Suddenly, it became a fast-moving cobra.

Pharaoh and Jambres jumped back again! And the bull broke loose from its handlers, snorting and running away.

Jambres regained his composure first. Frantically, he gestured for his assistants to come with their staffs. "You do not have power that is beyond our power!" the old priest angrily announced as he and his assistants threw their scepters to the ground.

Phinehas heard a collective gasp. He watched all of Pharaoh's attendants scramble to put distance between themselves and nine active serpents. Nine serpents now coiled, slithered, and darted near their feet.

In the midst of the nine serpents, one serpent raised its hooded head. It looked directly at Pharaoh. Then, slowly it began to turn from side to side. With forked tongue it tested the air. With black eyes, it briefly studied the other eight snakes. Then, faster than the gasps of the onlookers, it attacked and ate each serpent. When the last serpent had been swallowed, Aaron calmly bent over and picked the cobra up by its tail.

The cobra became a shepherd's staff again, and Aaron returned the staff to Moses.

Phinehas held his breath. How would Pharaoh respond?

Pharaoh turned his head and seemed to notice his son for the first time. He then turned back to Moses and Aaron. "I am not going to let my entire labor force go. Should I bankrupt Egypt because you are clever magicians? I must turn over to my son an Egypt that is stronger and more prosperous than the Egypt I received."

Aaron turned and looked at Moses. Moses nodded his head again. This time, Aaron put his hand and most of his arm deep into the folds of his garment. When he pulled it out, it was white with leprosy. Fearlessly, he extended the infected arm toward Pharaoh. "Look! Egypt will be as ruined as this arm if you do not listen and comply with the commands of the God of the Hebrews. He is a god who can destroy and who can heal. He is the most powerful god." Aaron walked over to where the sacred bull waited in the shade of a nearby tree. He put his leprous arm close to the bull's nostrils. He could feel the breath of the animal on his skin. Then he looked back at Pharaoh, waving his infected arm toward the monarch. "Your god cannot heal this disease.

None of your gods can save you from the wrath of the God of the Hebrews." Aaron then put his hand back into the folds of his garment. He brought it out again, completely healthy. "See for yourself, O ruler of Egypt. See what the God of the Hebrews can do."

Moses and Aaron turned abruptly. Without the permission of Pharaoh, they strode back the way they had come.

Phinehas continued to hold the royal heir close to his side. As his grandfather and great uncle passed, his eyes met the eyes of both men. The eyes of the elders asked a question, but the eyes of the youngster did not have an answer. It was a passing moment, an uncomfortable moment.

Pharaoh called his son to his side.

Both boys responded, hurrying to obey the monarch's directive. Standing close to Pharaoh while watching his family's patriarchs walk away, the Hebrew boy wondered where his allegiance belonged.

Early the next morning, in the predawn torchlight procession, Phinehas walked behind the little prince who walked behind his father. Every morning, the entire palace rose and dressed in darkness. Then they joined Pharaoh to call the sun back to their land. It was always a silent procession. This morning, Phinehas could not even hear the usual tapping of Jambres's scepter on the brick pavement. He remembered that it had been swallowed by the hooded serpent.

Arriving at the pool of the Pharaoh on the banks of the Nile, the royal entourage waited in silence. From a nearby temple, a gong sounded. The torches were extinguished. Then Pharaoh raised his arms and called to the eastern sky, "O mighty sun, return to those who love you."

Phinehas watched the eastern sky. It did seem that the sun responded to the voice of Pharaoh. Immediately, it popped above the horizon filling the sky with fiery gold and red.

With the help of his assistants, Pharaoh then removed all of his garments except his loin covering. He stepped down into the pool. Dramatically, he filled both palms with water from the Nile. He brought the water to his lips and kissed it. "Father of life, your children have come to greet you."

Tap, tap, tap, tap. Phinehas knew that sound—a wooden staff was steadily hitting the brick pavement. Phinehas turned his head in the direction of the sound. This time, he was not surprised to see Grandfather Aaron with Moses. Both men walked to the edge of the pool and looked down at Pharaoh. Their faces were stern and uncompromising.

Phinehas knew that men did not approach Pharaoh with such boldness and live. The slave boy held his breath. He felt fear rising in the pit of his empty stomach. He did not want to see his grandfather killed on the banks of the Nile.

Moses lifted his staff, and then he rapped three times on the pavement, officially proclaiming that he had taken the stage. Moses then nodded to Grandfather Aaron who loudly spoke in the language of the Egyptian court. "Our God has sent us to say, 'Let my people go into the wilderness to meet with me.' If you do not do this, our God will strike the Nile, the lifeline of your nation. The water within its banks will turn to blood. The fish will die and the people of Egypt will thirst."

Phinehas watched as Grandfather Aaron turned and took the staff from Moses's hand. Deliberately, he held it over the water in the pool of the Pharaoh. Then he brought it down, striking the water. Immediately, in that place, dark red blood bubbled to the surface. It filled the pool and flowed out to mix with the current of the river. Pharaoh screamed in horror and quickly splashed out of the blood-filled pool.

His loin cloth dripped dark coagulating blood. Immediately, Pharaoh ripped the disgusting fabric from his body, accepting a clean linen cloak for a covering.

Jambres hurried forward to demonstrate that he could also turn water into blood, but Pharaoh was not attentive to the demonstration. Instead, he was looking beyond his personal pool to where the river was broad and turning blood red. Dead fish were beginning to float to the surface. A stench was enveloping the land.

Phinehas watched the ruler of Egypt. His body had become like the many statues of previous monarchs, rigid and royal. "Dig wells. We need water."

After that order, Pharaoh strode back to the palace.

Phinehas looked around for Grandfather Aaron and Moses. There seemed to be no trace of the Hebrew patriarchs. How could they just come and go at will? Were they the embodiment of Egyptian gods? Phinehas thought about the paintings of the many Egyptian gods. He remembered two Egyptian deities with a large serpent for a staff. They guarded the gates of the underworld. Grandfather Aaron and Moses seemed to have the attributes of those gods.

After a week of confinement in his royal apartments, the crown prince was bored. Phinehas started another game of hide-and-seek. Instead of hiding, the little prince ran to an inset panel in the wall of his bedroom. He pushed with all his strength, and then he called, "Phinehas, come help me."

Obediently, Phinehas pushed with the prince. To his surprise, the wall moved; and suddenly, instead of a wall, there was a passage.

With miniature royal authority, the prince announced, "This is a better place to play hide-and-seek."

"What is this?" Phinehas asked.

"An escape," the prince answered. "If I am in danger, I can go through this tunnel and get to the river. It comes out close to the royal barge."

Suddenly, Phinehas was overcome with curiosity. "Can we explore it?"

"Yes!" The prince pointed to a burning lamp.

Phinehas grabbed it, and both boys entered the dark passage.

Together, they moved in silence, respecting the eerie dancing shadows and holding fear at bay with their boyish desire for adventure. Approaching the river, an unusual sound filled their ears, like the croaking of a frog. Gradually, the sound increased until it seemed that an army of frogs must have invaded the land. When the boys stepped out of the passage, they saw legions of frogs, leaping from the Nile in multiple waves.

For a moment, the crown price and his slave stood, speechless. Then the price turned on Phinehas. "Your people have caused this problem."

"My people?" Phinehas responded with amazed anxiety. "How can people cause frogs to come out of the Nile?"

"Those two old Hebrew men!" the prince angrily answered. "My father told me that they threatened an invasion of frogs."

"Maybe they aren't men," Phinehas replied.

The little prince became silent, considering the response of his slave. Moments later, the prince was climbing a pile of rocks, getting away from the frogs, calling Phinehas to climb with him.

From the height of several boulders, Phinehas observed that nearly every section of level land was covered with moving frogs, and he wondered, what role did Grandfather Aaron have in this plague of amphibians? How could frogs relate to the ancient promises?

A week passed. It was nearly noon when Phinehas led his young charge past the heaps of dying frogs that lined the road from the palace to the temple complex. The stench almost overpowered both boys. Nevertheless, Jambres had demanded that both Pharaoh and his son were to be present today. They were to escort the sacred bull as it paraded along this route to purify the land and the air.

Phinehas could see the sleek animal standing at the top of the first ramp. It shook its magnificent horns as it looked out over the polluted landscape. Jambres stood on one side of the animal. Pharaoh stood on the other side. Phinehas nudged the crown prince to hurry, but before the boys arrived at the base of the final ramp, two old Hebrews seemed to appear out of nowhere. Both boys stopped, afraid to cross paths with the two men.

From the top of the ramp, Jambres called, "The frogs are dying. The land will be clean, again. We do not need your magic."

Pharaoh added, "Return to your people. Help them gather straw and make bricks. They need your magic."

Neither Moses nor Aaron spoke.

Phinehas watched as Grandfather Aaron turned to Moses and took the long wooden staff from his hand. The slave boy felt his insides quiver with fearful anticipation.

Again, Aaron lifted the staff. This time, he struck the ground. A black cloud of gnats rose from the dust.

Immediately, the air was thick with small flying insects. Phinehas could barely see the temple walls. He heard the sacred bull snorting and sensed that the attendants were struggling to return the animal to the inner rooms. He heard both Jambres and Pharaoh shouting to their gods, demanding that the insects vanish.

At first, the boys felt smothered by the cloud of bugs. The tiny insects were in their mouths, their eyes. They were working their way through their hair and crawling along the crisp pleats of their linen clothing.

Phinehas glanced down at the crown prince who was spitting and jumping and crying. The slave boy took the little boy's hand and led him running back to the palace. Phinehas took the prince straight to the bathing chamber where he poured jar after jar of water over the screaming child until the boy felt some reprieve.

The crown prince fell asleep that night behind and beneath layers of linen gauze. Phinehas sat at the foot of the royal bed, swatting and shooing the annoying bugs. Such misery! It came from Grandfather Aaron and his brother.

Resentment smoldered in the heart of the slave boy.

While the plague of gnats lasted, Phinehas heard over and over the whispered refrain, "This is the hand of the God of the Hebrews."

Again, the crown prince was ordered to remain in his royal apartments. No one saw the face of Pharaoh, and the boy who was next in line for the throne became increasingly irritable and pouty. One day, he ordered that Phinehas receive ten lashes from the master of the household because he did not like the way Phinehas played with him.

That was the day the gnats went away, but soon, the flies came to torment the people of Egypt.

After the beating, Phinehas stayed in the slave quarters while his back healed. There, other Hebrews whispered amazing news. The flies were only in the homes of the Egyptians. There were no flies in Goshen where the Hebrews lived. Not one Hebrew had been bitten in all of Egypt!

On the day that Phinehas returned to his duties, he heard the crown prince screaming. The royal child was screaming in pain like the slave boy had screamed with each lash of the whip.

Phinehas opened the door. The little boy sat inside a tent of gauze. Servants stirred the air with palm branches to keep the flies from landing. Still, every once in a while, a fly would slip between the folds of fabric and bite the little boy viciously.

Phinehas wanted to feel sympathy for the child, but he was still hurting from his own torment. The slave boy turned away from the prince. He went out onto the balcony. The flies did not bother him. From there, he looked out over the river. Immediately, his eyes were drawn to two old men standing beside the palace wall—Grandfather Aaron and great Uncle Moses.

Phinehas watched Moses raise his staff. He heard both men pray for Pharaoh and the people of Egypt. They prayed that the plague of flies would cease and the Hebrews would then be allowed to go into the desert to worship their God.

A small skiff came through the reeds in the river. A man jumped out and pulled the shallow boat up onto the riverbank.

Phinehas felt his heart jump. He knew that man. It was his father. Phinehas felt tears of homesickness well up in his eyes.

The slave boy watched as his father spoke to Aaron and Moses. Then all three men turned and looked up at the palace. The younger man waved, and Phinehas waved back. His father had seen him and that was a comfort.

A few weeks later, Phinehas stood in his usual place at the entrance to the sacred rooms in the Temple of the Cult of the Bull. The morning lessons for the little prince had abruptly ended. Up and down the corridors, everyone was running and screaming, "The sacred bull is dead!"

Only Jambres retained his composure. The old priest stood like one of the many columns that supported the temple. For a few uncomfortable moments, he turned his beady eyes on Phinehas.

It seemed to Phinehas that the old master of magic must somehow know he belonged to the family of Moses and Aaron; therefore, he must be responsible for the death of their god. Phinehas swallowed hard and then tried to appear relaxed.

The crown prince came over, and the slave boy was thankful for his presence. Both boys knew this was a time to be silent and respectful. They watched as the magnificent bull that had been the center of worship for this region was hoisted onto a wagon.

A funeral procession quickly formed. Without being told, the little prince stepped into his role as the representative of his father. He walked behind the wagon.

Phinehas followed from the side of the road. He knew they were going to the embalmers. This animal would be buried with all the trappings of a high official.

As the procession made its way past the homes of various palace officials, Phinehas could see that many people were disturbed today. They were in their fields running from animal to animal. And all the animals in the fields were dead!

The slave boy whispered to himself, "Are Grandfather Aaron and Great Uncle Moses somehow responsible?"

Four days later, on a glorious sunny morning, the little prince was very excited. He danced and wiggled, running back and forth through his royal chambers while Phinehas struggled to complete his morning routine. At noon, when the sun was directly overhead, the young prince was going to join his father at the royal foundry to greet a new golden bull.

When the child was finally properly dressed and fed, Phinehas hurried him away from the palace toward a place on the banks of the Nile where black smoke continually rose from the furnaces where gold was smelted and animal-shaped gods seemed to leap from the glowing liquid. Today, it would be a new calf for the Temple of the Cult of the Bull. This new god would live in the most holy chamber. He would protect the new sacred bull and all the priests of the temple.

As the boys approached, it was easy to see that only one furnace was fired up. The others stood like sooty sentinels for the royal gathering. A raised platform had been constructed. Pharaoh was already in the seat of honor, Jambres standing beside him. Quickly, the crown prince ran up the steps and sat at his father's feet, while Phinehas stepped back into the obscurity of the other Hebrew attendants.

Curiously, Phinehas looked around, hoping to recognize someone from his family or their Hebrew community. Near the burning furnace, he saw his two uncles, Nadab and Abihu. They were sweaty and covered with black ash from shoveling fuel into the furnace. For a moment, the boy's eyes locked with theirs, but they did not show any indication that they recognized him. A moment later, the temple musicians took their places. Court attendants began placing garlands of flowers around the podium where the golden calf would be displayed.

From behind one of the furnaces, two old Hebrews joined the ceremony. Phinehas recognized them immediately. He could not believe that Aaron and Moses would come uninvited to such an auspicious event.

Moses rapped his staff on the side of the furnace three times, and every eye focused on the two men. Dramatically, Moses handed his staff to Aaron. Then he reached into the mouth of the cold furnace and filled his hand with soot.

Grandfather Aaron took a step forward. His two sons stopped shoveling fuel and stepped up to stand on either side of their father. Aaron made fearless eye contact with the ruler of Egypt. "You are waiting for a man-made god to come out of this furnace. We are waiting to go worship the God who made all men. He is a powerful God, who demands that you respect his request."

"Never!" Pharaoh responded.

Immediately, Moses tossed the soot into the air, and festering sores erupted on both people and animals. But the Hebrews remained untouched.

Jambres cursed. Pharaoh began calling for the physicians. The crown prince began to wail, and Phinehas hurried to the little boy. He took him by the hand and led him straight back to the palace. For the entire walk, Phinehas could not take his eyes off the boils. One after another, they broke through the little boy's skin. His arms, his shaved head, his bare shoulders, chest, and back were covered with pussy lesions. Every time Phinehas looked, another seemed to have emerged. At the palace, the physicians were waiting to clean and scrape each lesion.

All night, the little prince wailed. Jambres paced the halls of the palace, chanting and cursing. And Pharaoh sat like a statue submitting to the painful remedies of the physicians. In his heart, he cursed the God of the Hebrews.

In response, the Spirit of God abandoned him to the demons of the underworld.

Two weeks passed. The crown prince had skin that was scarred but healed. In the early morning darkness, a gong sounded in the palace. Once again, Pharaoh was going to greet the morning sun and kiss the Nile. Everyone hurried to join the procession.

Silently, Phinehas guided the crown prince to his place behind his father. Then the slave boy stepped to the side, to walk with the other Hebrews who worked in the palace. They watched as Pharaoh and Jambres called to the sun and then smothered their gasps of horror and amazement as the golden rays revealed the ravaged faces and scarred flesh of all the Egyptians.

There was another smothered gasp. It came from the Egyptian attendants. Moses and Aaron stood in the blaze of the rising sun. Like two powerful messengers from a glorious being, they confronted Pharaoh and Jambres.

"This is what the Lord, the God of the Hebrews, says: Let my people go, so that they may worship me, or this time I will send the full force of my plagues against you.[7] At this time tomorrow I will send the worst hailstorm that has ever fallen on Egypt, from the day it was founded till now. Give an order now to bring your livestock and everything you have in the field to a place of shelter, because the hail will fall on every person and animal that has not been brought in and is still out in the field, and they will die."[8]

Phinehas briefly studied Pharaoh. His scarred face was set like the Sphinx. Then Phinehas looked around to judge the reaction of the other Egyptians in the morning procession. He could see that they took the words of his grandfather seriously. They were nervously edging away, ready to run to their homes to provide shelter for their slaves and their animals.

A little skiff slipped through the tall reeds that grew along the riverbank. It pulled up so Moses and Aaron could step in. Once more, Phinehas saw his father. The two looked at each other for a long moment. Phinehas saw his father mouth be safe. Before stepping into the little boat, Moses raised his hand toward heaven, and black clouds appeared on the far horizon. Distant thunder rumbled ominously, and lightning flashed from heaven to earth.

Aaron announced, "This time tomorrow!"

Phinehas watched the reeds close behind the little skiff that held his family. His heart went with them. They were his people headed for his home in Goshen. In his mind, he saw the face of his mother, and the slave boy discretely wiped a tear from his eye.

The early morning gong did not sound, or if it did, it could not be heard above the roaring thunder, the pelting hail, and the crashing lightning. Phinehas sat on the royal bed with the little prince in his arms. From this place, he could see hail as large as his fist bouncing on the balcony. The balls of ice rolled into the room. Tall trees beat against the building. Lightning danced along the ground. Both boys trembled.

In the audience hall of the Pharaoh, a giant palm crashed through the roof. Hail and rain poured into the room while lightning seemed to split the sky above the gaping hole.

In the midst of the chaos, Pharaoh shook his fist at the storm and screamed, "Enough! I command you to stop!"

The elements seemed to jeer at the monarch as they sent a greater downpour into his audience chamber.

Deflated, but still resolute, Pharaoh ordered, "Get me three strong Hebrew slaves. Send them out through this storm and tell them to bring Moses and Aaron back to me. Do not return to me without those two old men!"

It was late afternoon, the storm still raged. Moses and Aaron with their escort of Hebrew slaves strode through the rain and hail, untouched.

Pharaoh met them at the entrance to his ravaged audience hall. Jambres was not with him. "I have sinned, and I have brought the wrath of your God on my people. Pray to your God. The thunder and the hail must cease, or we will all die."

Aaron responded, "Our God has made a demand of you." Lightning struck a nearby tree. Immediately, thunder shook the building.

"You may leave! You may leave!" Pharaoh screamed.

Moses replied through Aaron, "When I am out of the city, I will pray to my God. This storm will stop, and then you will know the power of my God." Moses turned to leave, then he stopped and addressed the Pharaoh once more. "Still, you do not fear the God of the Hebrews."

A short time later, the storm suddenly ended. The black clouds disappeared, and sunshine streamed through the gaping hole in Pharaoh's audience chamber. Then Pharaoh reversed his decision, and with his fist raised toward heaven, he announced, "The Hebrews will never leave this land!"

Together, Phinehas and the crown prince pushed against the recessed panel in the boy's royal sleeping chamber. The hidden door opened and both youngsters, with lamps in hand, escaped the confines of the princely apartments. It was just two days after the violent storm.

Coming out near the place where the royal barge docked, they could see slave crews everywhere, moving debris and repairing structures. The boys climbed a large pile of boulders. From that vantage point, they spotted Pharaoh and Jambres inspecting the destroyed flax and barley fields. They also recognized the silhouettes of two old men, emerging from the reeds near the river and determinedly approaching the flattened fields. Without any pretense or protocol, the men confronted Pharaoh and Jambres.

The boys could not hear their verbal exchange, but the body language of the men told their story—another plague was about to be unleashed.

Phinehas turned completely around to scan the landscape for signs of the next onslaught. He spotted a strange black cloud hovering above the horizon just beyond the river. Tapping the young prince on the shoulder, Phinehas pointed to the approaching mystery.

For a moment, the son of Pharaoh looked puzzled. Then, the boy became angry. "Why is your God doing this to my people?"

"Our God is calling us to meet him in the wilderness. Your father refuses to let us leave Egypt," Phinehas answered.

"Why?" the little boy selfishly ranted. "Why would you want to leave me? We have fun together. It is better to be a slave in Egypt than a freeman in any other part of the world."

The Holy Spirit answered through the grandson of Aaron, "Jambres has told you many times that life is about responsibility. He has told you that first, you must do your duty to the gods. After that, everything will fall into place."

The crown prince scowled. "I don't like that answer!" He stomped his little royal foot.

A big brown locust landed on the rock by the boy's foot. Then a whirring sound suddenly overtook both boys, and immediately after that, the air was filled with flying insects. Everywhere the boys looked, the vegetation along the banks of the Nile was black with creeping, chomping, and buzzing insects.

Both boys were now brushing the bugs out of their hair, shaking them from their clothing and beating them away from their faces. Phinehas was the first to make a protective move. He grabbed the prince by the hand and led him down the boulders. Both boys dove into the secret passage. Raising their handheld lamps, they were amazed to see even the rock walls of the tunnel crawled with moving insects.

Once again, the little prince slept and lived within a tent of gauze. But the royal child could not escape the ravenous onslaught of locusts. They plastered their bodies against his fine linen curtains. They ate through the folds of sheer fabric and found numerous routes to resting places between the boy's bedtime covers.

The other Hebrew slaves in the palace whispered incredible news to Phinehas. There were no locusts in Goshen. There, the spring vegetation was lush and little Hebrew children were already gathering it to supplement their diet. Contemplating this latest news, Phinehas walked out onto the balcony. From that place, overlooking the river and the palace grounds, the slave boy could see. Not one green leaf had survived the invasion of locusts.

Soon, there was more news, passed discreetly from slave to slave throughout the palace complex. Moses and Aaron had been summoned to meet with Pharaoh and Jambres.

The palace slaves had secretly watched the event. Jambres had cursed under his breath and ground his teeth through the entire meeting. They had seen Pharaoh drop to his knees in front of the two Hebrews. They heard him say, "I have insulted and angered your God. Forgive me once more, and beg him to remove this deadly plague from our land."

The slaves reported that Moses then left Pharaoh. Outside the palace walls, both men lifted their hands and their voices, calling to the God whose name is I Am. Suddenly, a mighty wind blew across the land, sweeping the locusts into black buzzing clouds that moved swiftly toward the Red Sea.

The next morning, Phinehas escorted the little prince into Pharaoh's audience chamber. Other slaves were busily sweeping dead locusts out of the corners, pushing them into nasty dark piles. The crown prince looked around the room, obviously still in a state of disarray with repairs in progress. Then he looked at his father. "Why have so many bad things happened? Have we displeased the gods?"

Phinehas watched Pharaoh clinch his fists. Then the monarch replied in a measured, angry tone, "No, those old men have just taken advantage of some unusual natural occurrences. They want to trick me into believing it is the will of their God to allow the slaves to leave. But I am also a god. It is not my will to destroy Egypt. Now, I need those slaves more than ever! I will not release the slaves from their duties, even for one day! I am Pharaoh! I have spoken. My word is law in the land of the living and in the realms of the underworld."

The crown prince looked up at his father with admiration.

Phinehas observed the royal pair, and he instinctively knew. He had just heard the voice of the Evil One speaking through Pharaoh. The slave boy felt a cold shiver of apprehension.

A meal had been prepared. Phinehas led the little prince to his seat. He held the water bowl so the royal child could wash his hands. The boy smiled up at him, and Phinehas naturally smiled back. Then the boy reached across the table and took one of the sweet treats that had been specially prepared for the meal. He placed it in Phinehas's hand, and he grinned at his companion. "This is for you. I'll bring more back to our room."

Phinehas let out a small relieved sigh. The prince was still his friend.

A gong echoed through the dark halls of the palace. Both boys left their beds. Phinehas helped the little prince with clothes and a quick wash. Then he brought him to his place in the predawn procession to welcome the sun and bless the Nile.

Two slaves carrying torches led the way, while other slaves followed with more torches. Phinehas knew the path by heart. He knew the chants. Every morning, it was the same. The slave boy knew the motions so well that he just did them while his mind wandered to his family, to their morning routine.

Phinehas glanced at Pharaoh. By torchlight, he was a frightening and commanding figure.

The torches were extinguished. Then the chants began. Jambres and then Pharaoh said the prescribed words.

Darkness remained.

Phinehas saw the priest and the monarch exchange horrified glances.

The monarchy and the priesthood then called together, "O great sun, ruler of the heavens, return to us. We need your light and warmth. Return to us, your children."

The darkness only seemed to intensify.

First, there was horrifying silence. Then Phinehas heard frightened low murmurs spreading among the Egyptian attendants.

Suddenly, Pharaoh shouted, "I want to know. Does the sun shine in Goshen? Send trusted servants and bring back an answer." Grabbing a torch from a nearby slave, Pharaoh ordered that it quickly be lit. Then he led the procession back to the palace.

That day, the sun remained in the underworld. It remained in the underworld for an extended time. Only the Hebrews in Goshen could affirm that three days of darkness had passed for the citizens of Egypt.

Once again, the crown prince was confined to his royal apartments. Torches and lamps burned constantly, but their light seemed to be continually sucked into the blackness. Phinehas stepped out onto the balcony. In the distance, he could see a faint glow, and he knew that was his home in the land of Goshen. Below, he could see several torches approaching the palace, and he wondered who would be about during such a fearful event.

Hearing footsteps in the hallway, Phinehas went to check. One of the Hebrew slaves was spreading the word. Aaron and Moses were coming to a private audience with Pharaoh. Other slaves were watching from hidden alcoves, and more reports could be expected.

A short time later, Phinehas heard the report.

It was a meeting like no other. Pharaoh had met with those men in private. This time, no Egyptian was allowed to see his humiliation.

Pharaoh had actually dropped to the floor facedown. He then *said, "Go, worship the* LORD. *Even your women and children may go with you; only leave your flocks and herds behind."*

But Aaron, speaking for *Moses said, "You must allow us to have sacrifices and burnt offerings to present to the* LORD *our God. Our livestock too must go with us; not a hoof is to be left behind. We have to use some of them in worshiping the* LORD *our God, and until we get there we will not know what we are to use to worship the* LORD.*"[9]*

At that point, the humiliation of Pharaoh ended and another spirit took over. Pharaoh suddenly clenched his fists and sprang to his feet like a man ready to fight. Enraged, he screamed at Aaron and Moses, "I have made enough concessions! *Get out of my sight! Make sure you do not appear before me again! The day you see my face you will die."*

Then for the first time, Moses spoke directly to Pharaoh. *"Just as you say," Moses replied, "I will never appear before you again."[10]*

Wide-eyed, Phinehas asked, "What will happen next?"

The Hebrew slave replied, "There is going to be a meeting. All the representatives of the twelve tribes will be gathering with

Moses and Aaron. They will tell us what to do. The plan will be passed from home to home."

Phinehas nodded and quietly closed the door to the royal apartment. He checked; the prince was still sleeping.

The daughter of Putiel, who was married to Eleazar, sat quietly in a corner of the room. Her eyes moved from face to face. All the sons and grandsons of Aaron were present except for Phinehas. Her only son remained at Pharaoh's palace. Anxiously, she waited for Moses or Aaron to speak.

Finally, Moses stood. "The Lord has said, 'I will bring a final plague on Egypt. Then Pharaoh will order you to leave his land. Tell the people to go, right now, and ask their slave masters for payment—silver, gold, and other valuables.'"

Around her, there were murmurs of assent, but the daughter of Putiel did not really care about her back wages. She wanted her son, Phinehas, back in her home with the family. Once again, she focused on the instructions from Moses.

"On the tenth day of the month, take a male lamb into your home, a year-old, without blemish. Care for it until the fourteenth day. Then at sundown, all the lambs are to be slaughtered. Take some of the blood; put it on the sides and the tops of the doorways in the houses where you live. Roast the whole animal over a fire and then eat it with bitter herbs and unleavened bread. Stand at your tables, dressed for a journey. Eat quickly. While you are eating the meal, God will pass through the land of Egypt. Where he does not see the blood, he will stop and every firstborn male within that house will die, but where he sees the blood of the lamb on the wood of a doorway, he will pass over that house."

The daughter of Putiel stopped listening to Moses. Her mind flew to her son, her firstborn. Somehow, they must get him out of the palace. Phinehas must be in this house, and the protective blood of the lamb must be on the doorposts, or...

The mother of the slave boy could not let her thoughts go any further. She looked across the room at Eleazar, her husband. Their eyes met, and she knew that he shared her concern.

Phinehas heard a light tapping at the door to the royal apartments. He stepped away from the game he was playing with the prince to see who was at the door. Phinehas opened the door slightly.

One of the Hebrew slaves from the palace staff whispered through the crack, "Ask the little prince for your wages and then meet us by the royal barge. We are all leaving the palace and returning to Goshen."

"What?" Phinehas was shocked. He looked back, over his shoulder, at his playmate. "I can't just leave. I have a responsibility to the prince."

"Be there!" the other slave responded tersely. "If you don't come, we will leave without you, and then you will be the only Hebrew in the palace."

Before Phinehas could glean further details, he felt the prince behind him. Instantly, the Hebrew slave vanished down the long corridor. Phinehas turned to face the son of Pharaoh.

"Are you going to leave me?" the little boy asked.

Phinehas looked into the face of the child who had been his companion for nearly a year. They had bonded. In many ways, they now depended on each other. Phinehas shook his head negatively. Both boys returned to their game.

Eleazar pulled the lamb into the house. The animal did not like being separated from the rest of the flock, and it resisted entering a structure that was for people. Eleazaer forced the animal through the doorway and tied it to a wooden beam in a corner.

His wife was packing all their belongings into tall reed baskets. She looked up. Her eyes asked, "Where is our son?"

Eleazar answered, "Phinehas did not return to Goshen with the rest of the palace slaves."

The Hebrew mother did not say a word she just looked at her husband. It was a look that demanded action.

Eleazar responded, "Phinehas will be here for the meal."

The daughter of Putiel returned to her packing. As she worked, every movement was part of her constant petition to the God of Abraham. "Bring my son home."

The sun was slipping down toward the western horizon. The last fingers of light stretched across the Nile. Phinehas stood in his place for the evening procession to the Pool of the Pharaoh. He looked around. All the other Hebrew slaves were missing. Only Egyptian attendants stood with Pharaoh and Jambres to bless the sun as it dipped into the underworld.

Suddenly, Phinehas felt so alone, so disconnected from his family and his people.

In Goshen, families were gathering. The head of each household had taken the lamb from their home and slit its throat. Now the blood was draining into basins and bowls.

The ceremony at the Nile was ending. Phinehas stepped forward to take the crown prince by the hand and lead him back to his royal apartments. Abruptly, an Egyptian officer stepped in front of him.

"You're a Hebrew, aren't you?"

Phinehas was startled and did not know how to reply.

The officer continued, "What are you doing here? All the other Hebrews have returned to their communities. Here"—the Egyptian took a heavy gold necklace from around his neck and put it over the head of the slave boy—"take this. It is my offering to your god. Leave this place."

Speechless, Phinehas looked around. The crown prince now stood beside him.

The royal child took Phinehas's hand and spoke to the officer. "Phinehas is my friend. That is why he remains in the palace. He is staying with me."

The officer glared down at the child. "If you are his friend, you will send him back to his people. If you want to grow up to be the next ruler of Egypt, you will respect the demands of the god of the Hebrews."

"You cannot speak to the royal child with such directness and disrespect!" Jambres inserted himself into the conversation.

Immediately, Phinehas guided the little prince away from the arguing adults.

The night was quiet, very quiet. Phinehas helped the little prince bathe and find a restful position under the linen covers. Since there were no other slaves in the palace, Phinehas picked up one of the long-handled fans and stirred the air so the little boy would be comfortable as he fell asleep.

Unexpectedly, the boys heard a scraping sound. The prince sat up in his bed. Both boys turned toward the secret panel and watched in amazement as it moved and then opened.

First, the boys saw a hand with a small lamp, and then Eleazar stepped into the room, a Hebrew wearing only the soiled tunic of a slave. He did not acknowledge the little prince. His eyes were fixed on his son, and with one gesture, he called Phinehas to follow him back into the secret tunnel, back to their community.

Phinehas looked at the prince. Then he looked at his father. For a moment, he felt torn. Then within his chest, something stirred, and he had to respond. He ran to Eleazar. Before leaving with his father, Phinehas looked back at his friend, the prince. The boy gave a slight nod, permission was granted.

Father and son stepped into the tunnel. Together, they closed the panel behind them. "How did you know about this tunnel?" Phinehas asked.

His father answered, "Prince Moses lived in these apartments many years ago."

At the river's edge, Eleazar led his son through the tall reeds to the place where he had hidden a small papyrus skiff. Within moments, the little boat was skimming over the smooth waters of the Nile. The full moon made the Nile look like an endless carpet of fine linen.

It was an unusual night. At first, Phinehas could not figure out what was so different. Then he realized that all of the typical night insects were silent. As their boat passed the estates of the wealthy, not even a guard dog barked. All of nature seemed to be holding its breath.

Eleazar paddled steadily, pushing their little craft to move faster than the assisting current. There was an unspoken urgency in each stroke. Phinehas picked up a paddle. He matched his stokes to the strokes of his father. Together, they sped toward Goshen on a night like no other.

"Hurry! Hurry!" Eleazar urged Phinehas to jump out of the little boat and run over the marshy delta toward the mud huts where the descendants of Levi lived.

Phinehas obediently began an energetic sprint, passing his father but stopping short at the doorway to his home. His hand was on the doorpost, and just above his fingertips, the wood was deeply stained with blood. "Father? What is this?"

"Blood," Eleazar answered as he pushed his son through the door. "That blood will keep you alive tonight!"

Before Phinehas could say more, he found himself wrapped in his mother's arms.

Squirming out of his mother's embrace, Phinehas looked around the room. He saw that even though it was very late at night, his uncles and cousins had come for a visit. Everyone was dressed for travel. The men were holding their staffs. The whole family was standing around a table unusually laden with a whole roasted lamb. There were bowls of bitter herbs and piles of new fresh greens. Unleavened bread was stacked on the table, and more of the flat bread had been piled into baskets. Everyone was eating quickly, grabbing chunks of meat, and dipping flat bread into crushed bitter herbs.

Phinehas's mother guided him to the table and placed a piece of unleavened bread in his hands. "Eat as much as you can," she said.

Bewildered, Phinehas turned to his father. "What is happening tonight?"

Between bites, his father answered, "We are leaving Egypt!"

Phinehas looked from person to person. "Did Pharaoh give us permission?"

This time an uncle responded, "No! But after tonight—"

Grandfather Aaron interrupted, "After the Fear of Isaac walks through the land of Egypt, Pharaoh will send us out of this land."

"The Fear of Isaac?" Phinehas repeated.

Grandfather Aaron responded, "I am speaking of our God, the Creator of the Earth. He promised a Deliverer to restore the children of Adam to the pleasures of the garden. He is the God who visited with Abraham, with Isaac, and with Jacob. He made promises to those men—a home for our people. Our God always keeps his promises."

"Why is our God walking through the land of Egypt, tonight?" Phinehas asked.

"He will be looking for the blood," Grandfather answered.

"The blood on the doorframe?"

"The blood of this lamb," Eleazar clarified as he pointed to the meat on the table. "Every firstborn male who is not in a shelter marked with blood will die tonight."

"Does Pharaoh know this is going to happen?" Phinehas asked.

"Why do you care?" an uncle interjected.

"The crown prince, he is my responsibility," Phinehas countered. "He is also my friend."

Eleazar held up a silencing hand so that his brother would not reply. Then Eleazar looked at his son. "Pharaoh is responsible for his own son, just like I am responsible for you."

Grandfather Aaron stopped eating and looked at Phinehas. His eyes were old and soft.

Everyone in the room knew that the head of their family was about to say something important, so they also stopped eating.

"A message has been sent to Pharaoh. It contains the exact words of God. *About midnight I will go throughout Egypt. Every firstborn son in Egypt will die.*"[11] At that moment, a distant moaning broke the stillness of the late night.

"There is no blood on the door of the royal apartments!" Phinehas cried in alarm.

Eleazar responded. "Pharaoh was warned. He could have taken steps to save his son."

Grandfather Aaron spoke again. His voice was gentle but firm. "Tonight, God's Appointed Death walks through the land of Egypt. For the firstborn in every family, there is only one way to live. The blood of the Passover lamb must be on the doorpost and that person must be in the house."

"God's Appointed Death?" Phinehas repeated. "Grandfather, you say it like it is the name of a person?"

Aaron stopped eating. He thoughtfully placed the chunk of meat that was in his hand back into the wooden bowl.

Everyone at the table stopped eating. Without consciously realizing, each person held their breath. Their eyes were on the head of their family, waiting for his answer to a child's question.

For a long moment, Aaron also appeared to be waiting for the answer. Finally, he nodded his gray head in satisfaction.

The family expelled their breath.

Aaron looked directly at Phinehas. "The God of Abraham, Isaac, and Jacob spoke to Moses and said, '*The blood will be a sign for you on the houses where you are; and when I see the blood, I will pass over you.*"[12] Aaron thoughtfully paused. Then he solemnly pronounced, "God's Appointed Death is God, himself, stretching out his powerful arm and acting on his word. He is using blood, wooden beams, and human obedience to bring forth our deliverance."

Chapter 1

At the Feast of Dedication

*Then came the Festival of Dedication at Jerusalem. It was
winter, and Jesus was in the temple courts walking in
Solomon's Colonnade.*

—John 10: 22–23

"Father, my death is approaching. I feel the appointed time
pressing on my soul." Jesus moaned as a wave of sadness
engulfed him. "Every day, my enemy taunts me. His evil angels
accuse me through the unholy caretakers of your Temple.
Demonically inspired hecklers join them to mock me. Their words
rake like claws, gouging my heart." In the comfortable darkness
of the olive-press cave, Jesus leaned into the solid strength of the
limestone walls. Tears ran down his face and wet his beard.

"Yeshua my son, I feel their words too." The voice of God
rolled through the underground chambers. His audible words did
not disturb the sleeping disciples. Only Jesus heard. Only Jesus
was comforted.

God continued, "Our angels in the throne room gasp at
the audacity of that rebellious cherub called Satan. I know he
constantly shoots deceptive thoughts into your mind. I know you
are battling every moment, taking captive every lie and giving it
no place to take root in your mind." God smiled tenderly, and
Jesus felt the warmth of his Father's approval.

For a quiet moment, Jesus held that warmth in his heart. Then he responded, "Truth and security, I know it only exists in your holy kingdom. I cling to every word in the Torah and the prophets. I cherish every directive and every explanation from your Spirit. In every feast and every Temple ritual, I see myself and my mission."

The walls of the cavern vibrated. Jesus felt the movement of sinless feet, and he knew his own angelic army was marching.

God spoke again. "The choice remains with you. At any time, you are free to abandon the humanity you have chosen. Thousands of angels stand ready to battle Satan for you."

"It would be a hollow victory," Jesus answered. "I would annihilate Satan and his kingdom. I would regain unchallenged ownership of Earth, but the law of our kingdom would still defeat me."

"*For the wages of sin is death,*"[1] God quoted the statute Jesus was referring to.

"I am the only one who can pay for all the rebellion. I am the only one who can fulfill the promise I made to Adam and meet the requirements of our kingdom law." Jesus sighed.

God did not disagree. Instead, he informed, "Your army wishes to pay their respects. They are waiting for you on the walls of the city, at the entrance to the Temple."

At the mouth of the cave, Jesus paused to quickly immerse in a small pool of water. Coming up out of the water, the crisp predawn air washed over his wet body. Redressed, he then exited the cave and walked through the enclosed garden, down the lower slopes of the Mount of Olives toward the bridge that crossed the Kidron Valley. Ahead of him, the city glowed. A ring of fire hovered over its walls, and above the entrance to the Temple, warrior angels with outstretched swords formed a glowing tower that disappeared into the predawn clouds.

Jesus stopped. He smiled to himself, and with a remembering tone, he said, "Thank you, Father. You comfort and reassure me like you reassured Jacob in his distress."

Then Jesus heard his Father's reply, an exact phrase that he had spoken to Jacob, "*Earth will be blessed through you.*"[2]

With confidence in his step, Jesus continued toward the city. At first, Jesus heard the music just in his heart. Then it grew louder and louder. His angelic army was singing.

> *Lift up your heads, O you gates;*
> *Be lifted up, you ancient doors,*
> *that the King of glory may come in.*
> *Who is this King of glory?*
> *The LORD strong and mighty, the LORD mighty in battle.*
> *Lift up your heads, O you gates;*
> *Lift them up, you ancient doors,*
> *that the King of glory may come in.*
> *Who is he, this King of glory?*
> *The LORD Almighty—he is the King of glory.*[3]

From the highest point on the angelic stairway, a seraph flew directly toward Jesus, bowing as his feet touched the road.

Jesus beckoned for the messenger to stand and speak.

"Singing has now ceased in heaven. All eyes are on you. Our hearts are with you. You can be certain. We will hold back the forces of the Evil One until God's appointed time. This is the word of God for you, '*It is I who have created the destroyer to work havoc; no weapon forged against you will prevail, and you will refute every tongue that accuses you.*'"[4]

Taking the angel's hand, Jesus spoke. "Your name is Ophaniel, isn't it?"

"Yes." The angel bowed his head, humbled by the personal recognition.

Jesus smiled. "Sometimes, the Spirit opens my heavenly memory." Then Jesus continued, "In this human body, with this human mind, there is always a struggle to be confident in my divinity and my mission. Today, I needed reassurance from heaven. Thank you."

From the pinnacle of the Temple, one trumpet blast welcomed the dawn. Immediately, the heavenly army vanished, and Jesus found himself standing at one of the entrances to the Temple. On the other side of the gate, he heard a team of Levites pulling together to open the massive doors. The first to arrive, he slipped off his sandals, tied them to his sash, and then entered the outer court of the Temple.

The torches of night were slowly dying. Without the normal crowds, Jesus moved easily over the vast paved area reserved for non-Jews, through the entrance to the Court of the Women, past the low wall that indicated the entrance to the Court of the Israelites. Closer and closer, he moved toward the place where all morning and evening worship began, the Altar of Burnt Offerings.

Jesus could see. The morning sacrifice had already begun. The lamb was hanging from rings attached to one wall of the Temple. Blood was spurting from its slashed throat, pouring into a golden basin.

Directed by the Holy Spirit, Jesus watched. Basin after basin filled, and each was quickly carried to the altar. Some blood was sprinkled on the white stone walls on each side of the massive altar. The rest was then dashed into a large opening at the base of the altar. Day after day, morning and evening, blood was thrown against the large white stones that made the lower portion of the altar. The entire lower section of the altar, all four sides, was permanently stained. Jesus knew that blood could never be washed away.

He turned back to the lamb. Its blood was no longer spurting, just slowly oozing. The animal hung like a limp bag of wool.

The Holy Spirit spoke. "Blood is the life-giving part of the sacrifice."

Jesus nodded, acknowledging the instruction.

At that moment, Jesus felt the Holy Spirit, like a warm breeze encircling his chilled body, engulfing his humanity. Unexpectedly, the breeze stopped, and Jesus sensed that the Spirit was all around him like a protective embrace. The Holy Spirit's commentary on the morning service continued, but now, Jesus viewed the activities around the altar through the glowing mist of heaven.

"So much blood," Jesus commented.

"The battle begins with blood," the Holy Spirit replied. "It was the first plague. All of God's people were enslaved, not one was free. Aaron took the wooden rod and touched the water of the Nile. Blood spread to every region where God's people lived in captivity. There must be enough blood for everyone."

Jesus responded to the Holy Spirit, "Every captive touched the blood. Then frogs, the symbols of demons, attacked. Both Egyptians and Israelites were tormented by those creatures from the pit of Satan."

The Holy Spirit then turned Jesus back to the lamb. Its skin had been removed, and it was being cut into six sections.

Obediently, Jesus watched, waiting for further insight. He noted the carefulness of those who used the knives. No bones were broken. Muscle was separated from muscle. Six white-robed priests waited. Each received a portion of the lamb. Solemnly, they processed up the ramp toward the burning fires on the upper surface of the altar. They were joined by two other priests. One carried the wine offering, and the other carried the unleavened bread offering.

The Holy Spirit spoke again. "Do you remember when your cousin John heard my voice? He pointed to you and said, '*Look, the Lamb of God, who takes away the sin of the world.*[5] It will be the time of the morning sacrifice when you, like this lamb, become the sacrifice."

Two priests walked between the fires that burned on top of the altar. Each one added a long beam of wood to the central fire.

Handfuls of salt were then thrown onto each part of the morning sacrifice. The Holy Spirit said, "I will preserve your life."

Then the six priests who carried the sacrifice began tossing the body of the lamb, piece by piece, into the fire. The bread was broken; half of each loaf was added to the flames. The wine was poured, like blood, into the proper place on the altar.

"The end?" Jesus chokingly asked.

"No," the Spirit answered. "Watch!"

While the coals glowed, red and orange, the flames licked the wood and the meat. Then one priest approached with a long poker. Methodically, he began to move the six parts of the lamb within the fire until he had put the pieces back together in the shape of the original animal.

"Surely your life will be separated from your body. Your flesh will be cut. Your blood will be poured out. But I will remain with you. I will restore your body and call it back to life after three days," the Holy Spirit confidently stated.

"What about the bread?" Jesus asked.

The Holy Spirit answered, "Half of the bread is placed on the fire for the morning sacrifice, and the other half is placed on the fire for the evening sacrifice. Then the sacrifice is complete."

"Hear O Israel, the Lord our God is One." The deep male voices of the priests who had completed the morning sacrifice rose like the smoke from the burning meat. Chanting as they moved in single file, the priests walked past Jesus to their next assignment.

Beyond the altar, Jesus saw one priest slowly ascending the stairs to enter the Holy Sanctuary and burn incense on the small altar that stood in front of the great veil.

Immediately, there was activity everywhere in the vicinity of the great altar. Barefooted priests and early worshipers gathered. The Levitical choir lined up. A loud clang reverberated through the Temple courts. Every man prostrated himself on the stone floor. Jesus also stretched himself fully across the flat stones, his arms extended toward the sanctuary. Soon, white smoke billowed out from the open doors of the Holy Place. It floated upward like the pillar of cloud that led Israel out of Egypt.

"The prayers of all mankind and especially your prayers come before God every day," the Holy Spirit whispered. "They rise like this smoke."

"The LORD *bless you and keep you; the* LORD *make his face shine upon you and be gracious to you; the* LORD *turn his face toward you and give you peace."*[6] With outstretched hands, the priests who had served that morning chanted the blessing over the people.

The choir began to sing.

> *The Lord reigns, he is robed in majesty;*
> *the Lord is robed in majesty and is armed with strength.*
> *The world is firmly established; it cannot be moved.*
> *Your throne was established long ago; you are from all eternity.*[7]

"Before we created this planet, before you breathed life into Adam and Eve, we recognized the potential for sin, and we made a plan," the Holy Spirit whispered.

"I remember," Jesus responded. "It is not an easy plan."

The silver trumpets sounded. The choir began the second verse, and the people got up from the floor. Jesus moved to the place where the rabbis sat and taught whoever stopped to listen. He took his usual place.

Nicodemus walked by and greeted him. A few of the early morning worshipers stopped.

"Rabbi?" a man called to Jesus. "I heard that you cast a demon from a man who could not speak. When the demon was gone, he began to speak."

"Is that true?" another asked.

"It is true! I was there," Peter shouted a response as he led the other disciples to join Jesus.

"He does these things by the power of Satan!" the Pharisees muttered as they pressed close, attempting to gather evidence and to counter his influence.

Others in the gathering crowd tested him by demanding for a miraculous sign.

Jesus knew the thoughts of both the skeptical and the Temple elite so he said to them: "A nation divided by disagreements will be ruined, and a building without proper supports will collapse... Now if I heal and drive out demons by the power of the Evil One, by whom do these other teachers in the Temple drive them out?"

Above the melee of opinions, a woman exclaimed, "Your mother is such a fortunate woman!"

Jesus responded, "More fortunate are those who hear the word of God and obey it." These words were directed toward the Pharisees who hung on the periphery of the crowd, conferring after each statement. Peter kept a wary eye on those men. He sent James and John to casually stroll by and listen to what was being said.

James returned, reporting to Peter that those men wanted an opportunity to speak to Jesus privately, away from the crowds.

Jesus was still teaching. "The people of Nineveh will fare better at the judgment than the citizens of this nation. They repented when Jonah brought them a message of salvation. Now one greater than Jonah brings you a message from God, but so many here reject it." He paused and looked at the faces that surrounded him. Many appeared angry.

Jesus stood. He was finished with this unreceptive crowd. But before he could signal his disciples that they were leaving, one of the Pharisees approached and invited him to an afternoon meal.

In his heart, Jesus heard the Spirit's direction. So he, with his disciples, followed the man away from the Temple to the wealthy section of the city. Everyone went in, and without stopping at the water jars, Jesus and his disciples settled themselves around the low table in the dining hall. The Pharisees remained standing by the water jars, dipping and pouring, carefully alternating hands for the prescribed washings.

Peter was the first to notice their condemning glances and pious scowls. He whispered to his brother, Andrew, "I forgot. In a home like this, we are expected to dip and pour water over our hands before sitting at the table."

Andrew glanced at Jesus. Then he responded to his brother. "Jesus didn't wash. I just watched him and did what he did. What do I know about the protocol for homes in the upper city?"

Peter turned his head so he could see Jesus comfortably reclining, leaning on his left elbow. But the atmosphere in the room was not comfortable. Jesus had locked eyes with the condemning eyes of his host. With confident directness, Jesus addressed the standing men and their spirits. "You foolish Pharisees, you carefully clean the outside of the cup, but you leave the inside filthy. You are so concerned with appearances. That is why you make a show of counting each leaf and each seed when you give God a tenth of your harvest. At the same time, you neglect justice and godliness. Oh, and when you go to the market and the synagogue, how you love to be recognized and respectfully greeted." Jesus stood and stepped away from the table. His disciples followed their master's lead, standing and stepping away from the table. They exchanged glances that said, I don't think we will be eating this meal.

Then Jesus led his disciples to exit the room, but he paused in the entryway. There was a pregnant silence as Jesus stood face-to-face with his host and the other important guests. "Unclean—you are unclean, like unidentified graves which people stumble over, unaware.

One well-known teacher responded with alarm, "Rabbi, you insult us!" Jesus faced him. "You are a man with great education, but you do not use your knowledge to help people. Instead, you burden them down by adding convoluted regulations to the laws of Moses. Woe to you on Judgment Day."

Jesus stepped back so he could take in the entire group of men, representative of the Temple leadership. "You revere the men of old who killed the prophets. You build their tombs and pay respect with your words; therefore, you are also responsible for the blood of God's prophets."

Angry voices fueled by evil spirits shouted back.

"How can this man who accepts the title 'Master Rabbi' speak such gross insults?"

"Is this any way for a guest to behave?"

"Truly, this man is from Galilee! Only Galileans would be so rude!"

By the Spirit, Jesus could feel his own disciples pull back in fear. They knew these angry men wielded enough power to have them beaten and imprisoned. These men could expel them from the Temple and from every synagogue in the land.

Over the melee of comments, another expert in the law voiced a final objection and Jesus answered him directly. "You experts in the laws of Moses—I fear for you! You have hidden the true knowledge of God from yourselves and from the people,"

Then Jesus turned and left. His disciples followed silently. The Pharisees and teachers followed him outside, berating and challenging him for every word he spoke.

Leaving most of them behind, Jesus with his disciples returned to the Temple. The day had progressed. The crowds had grown. In the Court of the Gentiles and the Court of the Women, thousands had gathered shoulder-to-shoulder so movement was difficult. Looking over his shoulder, Jesus could see that a few Pharisees were still following, but not as closely because of the pressing people.

Beside one of the columns, Jesus paused and the men who were his close followers gathered around to hear his thoughts.

"As I have said many times before, *'Be on your guard against the yeast of the Pharisees, which is hypocrisy.'*"[8]

Jesus pointed to the table where the poor were paying for the small birds that would be their sacrifices. *"Are not five sparrows sold for two pennies? Yet not one of them is forgotten by God. Indeed, the very hairs of your head are all numbered. Don't be afraid; you are worth more than many sparrows."*[9]

The Pharisees who had been following Jesus were now pressing close, trying to involve themselves in the private moment that Jesus was having with his disciples.

Jesus saw them and addressed his next remark to them. *"And everyone who speaks a word against the Son of Man will be forgiven, but anyone who blasphemes against the Holy Spirit will not be forgiven.*[10] When you throw up a barricade against the quiet urging in your heart that says believe, you are denying the Spirit of God."

Jesus turned back to his disciples. "Do not fear these men. Their authority is limited. *When you are brought before synagogues, rulers and authorities, do not worry about how you will defend yourselves or what you will say, for the Holy Spirit will teach you at that time what you should say."*[11]

Someone walking by recognized Jesus and shouted, "There is the healer!"

"The rabbi from Galilee is here!" another announced.

The crowd surged.

The strong fishermen who were Jesus's disciples made a barricade with their bodies so Jesus would not be physically overwhelmed.

From somewhere in the sea of pressing bodies, a voice called, "Rabbi, tell my brother that he must divide the inheritance evenly with me."

Jesus answered, "Am I an arbiter of estates?"

Immediately, Jesus made eye contact with some of the teachers of the law. "No, I am a teacher who expounds on the word of God. Be careful! Greed is a trap. Once you are ensnared, it is difficult to escape."

One teacher dropped his head as Holy Spirit conviction tried to establish a foothold in his heart.

Jesus then turned back to the crowd and began telling a story. "The fields of a certain rich man produced a larger crop than expected. After pondering the problem of sales and storage, the man decided to tear down his old barns and build larger ones. With satisfaction in his heart, he said to himself, 'Now, I will have more than enough for many years.'"

Jesus paused to let his eyes roam over the faces in the crowd. Most were open to the idea of prosperity. Some were even living in luxury.

The Holy Spirit highlighted one man, and Jesus looked directly at him as he continued the story. "That very night, God spoke to the man, 'You are a fool! Before dawn, your life will be taken from you. Then who will inherit all you have stored?'"

Jesus returned his attention to the whole audience. "Right now, stop worrying about enough food and adequate clothing. Do not lay awake at night considering various ways to protect and grow your wealth. Our Father in heaven knows your needs. Seek him and his kingdom first. Do not be afraid to sell all you own and donate to the poor. That way, you will acquire treasure in heaven. It cannot be stolen or lost. Remember, your heart remains close to your treasure."

A man in the crowd then pushed through and loudly asked, "Rabbi, did you hear about the men who were killed by Pilate's soldiers while they were at the altar offering their sacrifices?"

"It happened yesterday," another shouted.

More voices added information.

"They were Galileans, probably Zealots."

"Did you know them?"

"Were they worse sinners than Jews from Jerusalem?"

Jesus shook his head negatively as he began to respond.

Governor Pilate and Chief Centurion Longinus looked down on the milling masses in the Temple courts.

Pilate commented, "Usually, I only leave my comfortable palace by the Great Sea for the major gatherings in Jerusalem, but now, with so much unrest, I feel obligated to show up for every occasion, even their Feast of Dedication."

Longinus responded, "If we could just get that bandit who calls himself Barabbas then things would settle down. Some say he is another deliverer like Judah Maccabee who will put an end to all foreign occupation."

Pilate looked at the commander of the fortress that was attached to the Jewish Temple in Jerusalem. "At this feast, more than any other, the Jews dream of throwing off the oversight of Rome and living as an independent nation. They believe it will happen when their Messiah emerges from the population." Pilate shook his head at the absurdity of such thinking. Then, he turned back to his military commander. "What do we know about this man Barabbas?"

"Yesterday, we killed some of his followers, but we kept one man for questioning."

Pilate gave a satisfied nod.

Longinus continued, "Barabbas heads up a network of rebels. His men are responsible for most of the highway robbery in Judea. They are also attacking the estates of the wealthy. His men used to work mostly in Galilee, but now, they have extended into our jurisdiction."

"Old Antipas can't take care of the problems in his own territory. He lets them grow until they spill over into my region," Pilate complained.

Pragmatically, Pilate then returned to dealing effectively with this threat to Rome's authority. "Did you find out where this bandit messiah is hiding?"

Longinus answered. "We believe he is somewhere beneath the northern area of this city."

Pilate raised a questioning brow.

"From the Temple Mount, extending beyond the northern walls of the city, there is a maze of underground caverns and winding passages. Some are man-made. Some are natural. We have good access through the stone quarry. I have sent men in there. A few never returned," Longinus reported.

"Smoke him out," Pilate tersely directed.

"I'll meet with my officers tomorrow. We will devise a plan," Longinus replied.

Pilate gave another satisfied nod, then he changed the subject. "I brought twelve gold shields with me from Caesarea. I had them specially made to honor our emperor and to commemorate the new territories that have been added to the empire. I want the shields hung in the banquet hall in Herod's old palace. They are to be in place within two days. On the first day of next week, the military officers who defeated the Nabataeans are gathering here, in Jerusalem, to toast Rome and to celebrate their victory. We are hosting the occasion. Everyone will be housed in the old palace. Food and drink will be plentiful."

"Since King Antipas caused the problem that forced Rome to attack the Nabataeans, is he paying for some of this?" Longinus asked.

"I'll send him a bill," Pilate smugly replied. "But I am not sending him an invitation."

Longinus chuckled. "May the gods of Rome always smile on you and frown on all your enemies, both political and military."

Pilate nodded again. Then he became very serious. "I received a letter from my cousin in Rome. By order of the emperor, there has been a major bloodbath. Nearly everyone who was appointed to a position of importance by Sejanus has been executed. Their immediate and sometimes their extended families have been killed: wives, children, servants—everyone! The violence associated with this retribution is horrible: pillage, rape, even desecration of the bodies. Barbarians behave with more decency than those who acted on behalf of Rome in this instance."

Longinus's face mirrored the seriousness of his superior. "I know you received the appointment to govern this province from Sejanus. I want to assure you, I have had no communication from Rome calling for your detainment."

Pilate gave another affirmative nod. At the same time, an unintended sigh of relief slipped out.

Both men then turned their attention back to the masses of people filling each section of the Temple.

Jesus pulled on the sleeve of Peter's robe. Peter made eye contact with him, and Jesus indicated that it was time to break free from the crowd that had gathered around them.

Peter signaled the others and together the men made a human wedge, forcing an opening in the crowd so Jesus could walk toward an exit.

Escaping most of the people, Jesus, with his friends, strolled through Solomon's Colonnade. Suddenly, he was noticed again. A crowd gathered around him. "How long will you allow us to wonder? Are you the Messiah? If so, announce it."

Jesus stopped walking. "I have told you and shown you, but you do not believe. I speak and I heal in my Father's name. Isn't that the answer to your question? Some recognize my authority like sheep recognize their shepherd. They follow me, and I have promised them eternal life."

Then the crowd became angry. They picked up stones and raised their hands to throw them.

But Jesus responded to their anger with a question. "I have healed and fed many. Which specific good deed offends you?"

"Your good deeds do not offend us. It is the way you speak, like you are equal to God. That is blasphemy!"

Jesus answered, "I have not spoken an unlawful word. I have only done the works of my Father. He is in me, and I am in him."

Angry hands reached for his robe. Stones flew through the air. After a few moments, confusion reigned because Jesus and those with him had slipped away, escaping their grasp.

Then Jesus took the twelve who were his closest disciples across the Jordan to the place where they had begun their ministry with John the Baptist.

Chapter 2

Lazarus Dies and Lives Again

Now a man named Lazarus was sick.
He was from Bethany, the village of Mary and her sister
Martha.

—John 11:1

In the dark room behind the perfumer's shop, Mary the sister of Lazarus turned over in her sleep. Her hand brushed the sleeping face of her husband, Jonathan. She roused just enough to feel his scratchy beard and to appreciate the sweet fragrances from their business. Then she drifted back into comfortable slumber.

"Open up!" A sudden banging at the front door of the perfume shop brought both Mary and Jonathan into complete wakefulness.

"That is not a Jewish voice!" Mary commented in alarm while Jonathan lit a small lamp and threw a robe over his tunic.

Quickly, Jonathan made his way to the front of his shop. Mary followed, crouching and peeking from behind the counter.

Jonathan opened the door just a crack.

Three soldiers from the fort were impatiently waiting in their own torchlight. One of them thrust an empty alabaster container into the face of the perfumer. "The governor's wife needs more of the same ointment that you made for her previously."

Jonathan nodded and hurried back into his shop to quickly gather the ingredients to soothe skin irritations.

Mary breathed a sigh of relief and returned to her bed. She knew when her husband lifted the covers and slipped in, pressing his body against hers so they fit together like one unit. Mary whispered, "I can't believe soldiers came to our door in the middle of the night for ointment!"

Jonathan answered, "When the itch is bad enough and you have the authority to do something about it."

Mary chuckled lightly, "Even the most powerful couple in this land must deal with ordinary problems."

Sleep quickly overtook Mary and Jonathan again. It was peaceful and sweet until another knock. This time, at the side door to their shop. It was a soft knock. Mary heard it first, and then she shook her husband.

Again, Jonathan went to the door. Mary followed, peering over her husband's shoulder. This type of predawn knock always meant someone had passed away during the night. Embalming spices were needed immediately because the burial would take place in the morning. While Jonathan packed their little wagon with myrrh and aloe, Mary always found out who had died and who left behind. She offered her sympathy and often her tears mingled with theirs.

Closing the door behind their sad customers, Mary and Jonathan simultaneously turned toward their living quarters behind the shop. They each took two steps toward their bed. Then from the Temple the morning trumpet sounded and all of Jerusalem knew sunrise was upon them. Jonathan looked at his wife. "I guess we will not be going back to sleep."

Mary nodded and moved on toward their backroom abode to roll up their mats.

Another knock, an urgent knock, stopped the perfumer and his wife in their tracks. Both exchanged glances that said, Certainly, this has been an unusual night! What can be next?

Jonathan opened the door, and immediately, he recognized a servant from the estate of Lazarus, his brother-in-law. "Come in. Come in."

"What is your news?" Mary anxiously hurried forward.

"Your brother," the servant addressed Mary. "He is very ill. His body is hot, and he is drifting in and out of consciousness."

"Jesus?" Mary said the name of the one man who had never failed their family.

"I will find him," the servant responded. "Your sister said he must be summoned without delay."

"Take the road toward the Salt Sea," Jonathan advised. "Go to the river crossing. I believe you will find him on the other side, about a day's journey from the city."

"A day to reach him, a day to travel back to Bethany," Mary calculated aloud while she threw necessities into a large basket.

"For whatever you need," Jonathan said as he pressed a bag of coins into the servant's hands and walked him to the door.

At the door, the servant bent his head and quietly spoke to Jonathan, "Bring enough burial spices. Martha said to prepare for both the best and the worst."

Jonathan glanced back at his wife.

Obviously, she had heard, and she responded. "Just find Jesus, and do it quickly!"

It was late afternoon. Standing on top of a small hill, Jesus looked out over the people. They were milling about in conversational groups or seated with their families. From the base of the hill to the brush covered banks of the Jordan, the people just lingered. Jesus understood. They were held in this place by the Spirit of God. He could see the Holy Spirit moving over the crowd, ministering to each person.

Jesus was also held in place by his attentiveness to the Spirit. Carefully, he watched, looking to see if the Holy Spirit was going to highlight someone.

On his right side, John tapped him on the shoulder. James tugged at the other corner of his robe. Behind him, Jesus sensed that one of his disciples had spread a cloak on the ground.

"Master, be seated," Thomas urged. "You have been standing since dawn."

James added, "No one else is coming forward. In all these people, there is not one sick or demon possessed person. So take a few moments for yourself."

Judas stepped up with a handful of dates, and Andrew offered some water, fresh from the spring.

"And we have bread," Thaddaeus announced. "It was baked this morning." He pressed a loaf into Jesus's hand.

With a nod of appreciation, Jesus sat down, accepting the food, setting the water close by.

At that moment, five women gathered at the base of the hill. Their youngest offspring clung to their robes while around them their older children laughed and chased, pushed and screamed. Stumbling and tripping over each other, the group began their chaotic ascent.

James looked down the hill and glared at the approaching commotion. His brother John also sent an unheeded, nonverbal warning. Andrew moved to intercept the women with their unruly offspring, but he was not as fast as the six-year-old who dashed up the hill and ran across the cloak where Jesus was resting. Laughing joyfully, the boy darted between James and Judas, knocking over the water jug that sat beside Jesus. Two other youngsters chased the boy, over and around the recent mishap.

The cloak was wet. Jesus was wet. The playing children did not even pause to recognize their rude and inappropriate behavior.

At first, the disciples were stunned. Then Peter moved to impose himself between the children and Jesus. At the same time, he roared at their mothers, "Women, supervise your children! Take them and their games down by the fording place. Can't you see that the rabbi is resting?"

Momentarily, the women were speechless. Then one woman began to apologize. "We are sorry. We only approached so this man from God could touch and bless our children."

"Take them away! Take them away!" Peter emphatically responded while the rest of the disciples backed him up with stern glares.

When Jesus saw this, he was indignant. Standing, he gestured inclusively for all the children to run to him. And he laughed as each child ran full force into his sturdy body. Grabbing the smallest, he swung him into the air above his head. Another he picked up, tucking the child under his arm like a sack of barley while he pretended to carry him away.

All the children were soon laughing and climbing on the man who seemed to have endless energy and child-like playfulness.

They chased. They climbed. They tickled. They teased until all the children collapsed on the ground around the famous rabbi from Nazareth. Then Jesus sat down with the children and he looked up at his disciples. *He said to them, "Let the little children come to me, and do not hinder them, for the kingdom of God belongs to such as these. Truly I tell you, anyone who will not receive the kingdom of God like a little child will never enter it." And he took the children* one by one *in his arms, placed his hands on them and blessed them.*[1]

After he had blessed the children, Jesus motioned for their mothers to come forward and be seated.

The women sat on the grass behind their children. Two of the mothers discreetly positioned their youngest ones so they could quietly nurse.

Then, Jesus began a story just for the disciples and these women. "There once was a local judge who feared neither God nor man. In his town, there was a widow who expected a just verdict for her case. She would accept nothing less.

"For some time, he refused to rule on her case, but finally, her persistence forced him to act in her favor. He knew it was the only way he could continue his life in peace."

Jesus paused to look at each person sitting close to him. To the women, he gave a nod of approval, affirmation for their persistence in bringing their children to him.

Then he continued the story, "Please believe me. My Father will hear those who cry out to him day and night. He will see that they receive the justice they deserve. God is looking for faith that refuses to give up. He is looking for faith that holds on and expects a response from heaven. *Without faith it is impossible to please God, because anyone who comes to him must believe that he exists and that he rewards those who earnestly seek him.*"[2]

Jesus then stood. Once more, he blessed the little group sitting around him. Then he led his disciples to the cave where they had been sleeping each night.

Dawn arrived quietly. Jesus moved out of the bushy hollow close to the river where he had been praying. Picking up dead sticks as he walked, he was soon at the mouth of their cave ready to build a fire and bake some flat bread.

Peter was the first to smell the smoke of a fresh fire. He hurried out of the cave to take over the breakfast duties. He just knew it was wrong for Jesus to serve them. He felt that he, above all, should be serving Jesus.

In the vicinity of their cave, other fires were popping up where people had spent the night, anticipating another day of miracles and teaching. In the distance, Jesus saw a man walking swiftly toward the river crossing. The Holy Spirit highlighted the man; so for Jesus, he was a person of interest.

Turning to Peter, Jesus said, "Set the cooking aside. Go to the river crossing and meet that man. See what news he has for us."

By the time Peter brought the man to Jesus, others had also made their way up the hill to ask for healing or to challenge the controversial rabbi with theological questions.

Peter pushed roughly past a pretentious trio of Pharisees, but then, he waited for Jesus to finish with a young child who was covered with a skin irritation.

The child left with clear, fresh skin. Then Peter hurried forward. "This man is from the household of Lazarus, your dear friend."

The servant stepped up. "Rabbi, your dear friend is sick."

Peter immediately responded, "Master, I will tell the others to prepare to leave."

Jesus held up his hand and then he repeated what the Holy Spirit had told him. "My Father has allowed this illness. It will not end tragically. This is the beginning of an event that will glorify both God and his son." Then Jesus turned to Peter. "Feed this man and see that he gets some rest before he returns to the home of Lazarus."

"Burn the bedding. Wash his body completely." Martha was in charge, and servants moved quickly under her direction. "Jonathan, bring the spices, and Mary, there is a large white shroud in the storage room at the back of the house."

Choking on silent sobs, Mary left the room to find the seamless sheet of linen that would encase her deceased brother.

Then fueled by heartbreak, Martha channeled her own sorrow into the practical aspects of a burial that must take place before sunset. Like the commander of a legion, she directed her campaign. "I need runners."

Howling and sorrowful shrieks suddenly filled the courtyard. Martha knew the mourners had arrived. Shortly after that, four young men stood in the doorway of the room where Jonathan was applying a sweet-smelling ointment to the cold skin of his brother-in-law.

Martha instructed the men, "Run to the estates of our neighbors. Tell them Lazarus, son of Bohan, has died. As the sun sets this evening, he will be placed in the family tomb." She turned to the smallest of the young men. "You, run to the Temple." She handed him a small scroll. "Give this to the keeper of the records. He will announce the death in the Sanhedrin." To herself, she added, "My brother has many friends in that great assembly." With a simple wave of her hand, Martha sent the men on their way. The elder sister of Lazarus then turned to another servant who had just stepped into the room. "Bring the bier to the front of the house. Send someone to sweep out the front room of the burial cave. Remove the stone so fresh air can enter the lower chambers of the tomb. Also, take additional spices to the tomb so they will be ready for a second application before we leave Lazarus." Martha's voice broke. The woman who was the backbone of her brother's estate dropped to the floor and sobbed.

Mary returned to the room, carrying the folded linen. She was shocked to find her stalwart sister collapsed and overcome with sorrow. Immediately, Mary dropped to her knees and took her sister in her arms.

Together, the sisters rocked and moaned their loss. "My brother… my brother."

"He was in the prime of his life."

"He should not have died. If only Jesus had been here."

Jesus glanced at the three Pharisees who were pressing themselves closer and closer, trying to push past the group that had been brought forward for healing. Turning his complete attention back to the afflicted, he healed and blessed each person before lifting his head to make eye contact with the impatient men from the Temple in Jerusalem.

Casually, Jesus gave Peter a slight nod.

Immediately, his disciples moved like a trained unit, surrounding the Pharisees, cutting them off from the other people, and making them the center of attention.

Jesus then stepped up, facing the representatives from the Temple "Yesterday, you must have started walking before dawn. How else could you have arrived so early this morning? What is your pressing question?"

The eldest of the three stepped forward. He cleared his throat and then asked, "Can a man divorce his wife and remain in good standing in the community of Israel?"

"Seriously?" Jesus responded. "You came all the way from Jerusalem to this desert place to ask that question? In the Temple library, there are numerous copies of the books of Moses. I'm sure you have read them. What do they say?"

One of the other Pharisees replied, "Moses allowed a dissatisfied man to sign a certificate of divorce and then to send his wife away."

Jesus looked at the Pharisee who had not spoken. He was a man, much younger than the other two. Above his head, the Holy Spirit opened a scroll, and Jesus saw this man looking lustfully at his neighbor's daughter. Jesus took several steps until he was face-to-face with this young man. "Do you have a wife?"

The man seemed so shaken by the question that he did not respond.

Another answered for him, "Of course he has a wife! A man with his position in the community and who sits in the Sanhedrin must have a wife."

"Is she a faithful woman?" Jesus asked.

The man nodded affirmatively.

Jesus then looked the young man squarely in the eyes. He ignored the other Pharisees. He knew they were just using this situation to hopefully trap him into contradicting the laws God had spoken to Moses. *"It was because your hearts were hard that Moses wrote you this law,"* Jesus replied. *"But at the beginning of creation God, 'made them male and female. For this reason a man will leave his father and mother and be united to his wife, and the two will become one flesh.' So they are no longer two, but one. Therefore what God has joined together, let man not separate."*[3]

In stunned silence, the three Pharisees stepped back. The disciples moved aside so the dissatisfied men could slip back into the hillside population.

Noon came and went. The crowd kept growing. The disciples held their places, protecting Jesus from the press of people. From dawn until dusk, they funneled the sick to him in an orderly manner. As the crowd finally thinned, Jesus turned and led his men back to the cave where they spent each night.

On the packed earth at the mouth of the cave, the disciples built a fire. In its dancing light, they relaxed and recovered from their busy day.

Peter asked, "Master, what will you do for your friend, Lazarus?"

Jesus shook his head negatively as he answered, "At this time, there is nothing to do."

Peter gave a little relieved sigh.

The other disciples who were listening nodded and flashed satisfied smiles.

John commented, "It's good to know that Lazarus no longer needs your help."

Jesus responded, "Every situation that is placed in my Father's hands and not tampered with will end gloriously." Then Jesus began telling a story that had happened nearly twenty years before. "A man had two sons." Jesus paused thoughtfully, remembering Bohan and his two sons, Lazarus and Nodab. "Nodab, the younger son, coaxed his father into giving him his share of the estate. The property was divided between Nodab and Lazarus. Soon after that, the younger son took his wealth and left for a distant land. There, he foolishly wasted his inheritance, living without restraint. Soon, he had spent everything.

"Then a severe famine ravaged the country where he was living, and he had no way to provide for himself. Starving, he found a job feeding pigs. He was so hungry that the pig slop looked like a banquet spread before him.

"In his hopeless situation, Nodab remembered his father. He said to himself, 'My father's servants fare far better than I. I will swallow my pride and return to my father's estate. I will admit my sin, hiding nothing, and then I will beg for a servant's position in the home where I was once a master.' So he left that place on foot.

"As Nodab made the journey home, he joined a caravan, taking care of the camels so he could have food and the protection of traveling with others. Not far from Jerusalem, he left the caravan and continued alone to his father's estate.

"Before he reached the estate, his father saw him coming down the road. Filled with love for this wandering son, Bohan ran to Nodab, threw his arms around him, and kissed him.

"Then Nodab said, 'Father, I am so ashamed. Half of your estate is gone, wasted. Let me be a servant.'

"Bohan ignored his son's request. Loudly, he called the servants. 'Bring the best robe. Put a family ring on his finger and new sandals on his feet. Kill the fatted calf and prepare a feast. Tonight, we will celebrate. This son of mine was lost, like a child gone to the grave. But now he has returned to me.'

"While Bohan was welcoming Nodab, Lazarus—the elder son—was out working on the estate. In the evening, when he returned to the manor house, he heard music and dancing. The house was full of guests. After hearing that this celebration was for his wayward brother, Lazarus became angry and refused to join the guests.

Bohan tried to reason with his oldest son, but Lazarus was enraged and full of resentment.

John spoke first. "Nodab? Is he the man who works with your kinsman, Toma, on the caravan routes?"

"Yes," Jesus answered. "Nodab is the younger brother of Lazarus. Toma met Nodab when he joined the caravan on the journey back to his father."

James then spoke up. "So Lazarus of Bethany is the elder brother in your story?"

"Yes. For several years, there was tremendous animosity between the brothers." Jesus looked at the faces of his disciples. He could see that they wanted to hear the rest of the story. "When I was a young man, still apprenticed to my father, we were at the estate of Bohan. There had been a terrible accident. Lazarus was seriously injured. Bohan was dead. Toma brought me in to see Lazarus. His healing manifested when he forgave his younger brother. That is when Lazarus and I became friends. That is when I first met Mary and Martha."

Small flames licked the glowing coals of the campfire. Peter picked up a large piece of broken pottery. He pushed all the coals into a heap so it would be easy to start a fire in the morning. Then the men spread their cloaks on the ground. Each man found his own comfortable position, and soon, they were all sleeping.

Jesus remained beside the pile of glowing coals, waiting to hear God speak his eternal name.

"Yeshua?"

"Yes, Father." Jesus lifted his face and looked up into the starry sky. With his mortal eyes, he could see no farther than other men, but through the Holy Spirit, he envisioned the throne room of heaven.

"Your friend Lazarus has been carried through the Gates of Sheol. At this moment, he is sleeping in the maze of tunnels on the pleasant side where all the faithful wait to hear the voice of their Messiah."

"What about my enemy, Satan?" Jesus asked. "What role did he play in this?"

"Satan introduced the illness that destroyed the life of your dear friend. It was his evil hope that you would rush to Lazarus only to be trapped and killed by those important Jews who have been incited against you."

"And now?" Jesus raised the question.

God answered, "Death and Satan are guarding the Gates of Sheol. They are gloating over their victory, and they are planning for the day when those gates close behind you."

"My visit to that place will be surprisingly short," Jesus responded.

"Three days," God confirmed.

"My enemy knows I have a close friendship with Lazarus and with his family. It has been almost a lifelong relationship." Jesus felt righteous anger boiling within. "My friends, my close friends that I love like family, should not suffer loss at the hands of Satan!"

"Wait one more day," God instructed. "Then go to Bethany. Go to the tomb. Have them remove the stone. When the stone has been pulled away from the grave, the Holy Spirit will give you the words to say."

One day later, before Earth had rotated into dawn, Jesus stirred the coals and added twigs to make the morning fire. As usual, Peter was the first to wake up. He grabbed the water jug and started toward the spring, but Jesus called after him. "Wake the others. Today, we need to leave before the people who are camped here realize we have gone to another place."

Quickly, Peter roused the other disciples, gathering them around the fire.

Then Jesus announced, "We are going to Judea."

James and John were the first to respond. "Judea? The Jews tried to stone you there! It's not safe."

Jesus answered, "I walk in the daylight of my Father's directions. I will not stumble and fall, like one who walks in darkness. My Father has shown me that our friend Lazarus is sleeping. I'm going there to wake him up."

Peter and Andrew exchanged confused glances. Andrew said, "Master, sleep is good for anyone recovering from an illness."

Other disciples offered their thoughts. "If Lazarus sleeps, his body will heal quickly."

Immediately, Jesus understood. His disciples were confused. So he spoke clearly. "Our friend Lazarus is dead."

Jesus heard the shocked and sad reactions of his friends. So he offered assurance. "This is good. It is for the glory of God and the strengthening of your faith. So let us go to him at this time."

Judas quickly cautioned, "The family of Lazarus lives less than half a day's walk from the Temple. If certain men know you are within reach, they will find a reason to stone you."

Then Thomas stepped forward and faced Judas. He said, "We are not afraid to go where our master goes. Then turning, he said to the rest of the disciples. "Our devotion requires that we die for him if necessary." Like a military unit, the men from Galilee closed ranks, rashly proclaiming their ability to defend and protect their master.

Only Judas stood apart. With arms folded across his chest, he sent his own condescending message through his body language. As he sneered at his fellow disciples, a question suddenly popped into his mind. Does Jesus need the crude protection these Galileans offer or the sophisticated plans of a man who understands how to manipulate Temple politics?

Judas looked around. Who had asked that question? He could see no one so he accepted it as his own brilliant thought.

Unseen, Satan and Raziel snickered. How easy it was to place their own thoughts into the mind of Judas.

"His pride has opened the door for us," Raziel commented.

Satan responded by quoting from the writings of King Solomon. *"Pride goes before destruction, a haughty spirit before a fall."*[4]

Among the other disciples, analysis of the dangers continued. But Peter remained quiet. With his eyes, he suspiciously scrutinized Judas like a fisherman studying an ominous horizon. Peter then leaned over and spoke to his brother. "Through his family, that man has many connections at the Temple. I think he knows more about the plans of the enemies of Jesus than he has been telling us."

"Possibly," Andrew replied. "James and John have business connections with the home of the high priest. Maybe they can find out if this animosity toward Jesus is official or just some ruffled feathers."

Peter nodded. "The house of Zebedee supplies the table of the high priest with the best fish from Galilee. I'll speak to James and John on the way."

Martha lifted her mourner's robes as she carefully climbed the staircase that led to the solitude of the flat roof on the manor house of her brother's estate. On the main floor, sitting or standing, every cushion and every bit of floor space was occupied. Numerous friends, relatives, even curious acquaintances felt obligated to stay with the family for seven sad days. They all had to be fed. Most were spending the nights.

Martha sighed as she settled herself to watch the sunset. She wanted to just think about her brother, to forget about directing the servants and feeding their guests. In the courtyard below, the hired mourners continued to wail. Martha pressed her teeth together. Their screeching set her nerves on edge. But what would people say if she paid those irritating women and then ordered them out of the courtyard?

Determinedly, Martha ignored the wailing and focused on the road. Coming over the horizon, a group of men was steadily walking toward the estate. Martha stood to get a better look. Then she lifted her robes and hurried down the staircase. Forgetting decorum, she pushed past the hired mourners and ran out the gate, down the road, and away from the estate.

Of all the men who had come to show their respects to the family, the man walking down the road with his closest friends was the most important. This was the man who always brought amazing peace into every situation. Without a thought for her own dignity or the way others might talk, Martha lifted her mourning robes higher so she could run faster. She ran past the village where the servants lived without glancing to either side. Her eyes were on the one man that her heart had been longing to see.

Then in the dust of the road, she dropped to her knees. "Jesus, if only you had come sooner, my brother would not have died. Yet even now, I feel certain that God will give you whatever you ask."

Jesus bent over and took Martha's hand. He helped her to her feet. His disciples waited with quiet respect for the family of their deceased friend.

Still holding Martha's hand, Jesus said, "Have faith. Your brother will live again."

Martha responded, "At the Temple men argue over the resurrection of the dead. Some believe all the descendants of Abraham will come out of their graves when the promised Messiah comes to us. Others say there is nothing after the grave. I am only a woman, unqualified to participate in that debate. But when I think about my brother"—Martha covered her mouth with both hands, choking back her sobs as she murmured—"he was such a good man." Regaining her composure, she emphatically added, "I believe he will come out of the tomb in the resurrection at the last day."

Jesus paused. He heard the Holy Spirit's instructions. Then he locked Martha's eyes with his own eyes. Confidence and conviction flowed into the moment.

Jesus said, "I am the one who opens the tombs and calls the righteous to life. Do you believe my words?"

Martha hesitated.

Jesus could see her sensible mind warring with her broken heart. She wanted to believe that somehow Jesus could change the fact that her brother was gone. But could she risk having her heart broken again? Finally, she stepped out in faith and gave an answer she could not explain. "Yes, Lord," she replied, "I believe you are the One we have waited for, the Messiah, and the fulfillment of all things." Then Martha quickly moved the conversation into a more comfortable direction. "Mary will want to speak with you."

After Martha said this, she hurried back and entered the house. She was not unaware that some of the very men who had come to their home to properly show their respect and sympathy were men who would stone Jesus to death if they got an opportunity. Over the past four days, she had overheard many of their conversations.

Standing in the doorway, Martha anxiously looked around the room. Then with a wave of her hand, she called her sister, Mary, aside. "The teacher is here," she said in a confidential tone."

When Mary heard this, she moved quickly. Not speaking to anyone or even making eye contact, she just walked purposefully out the door, away from the manor house. But she could not make such a hasty exit unnoticed. Her husband Jonathan followed. The men who were conversing with him also followed. The mourners began a series of louder wails than before as they jumped to their feet.

Now, everyone on the estate was aware that the sisters of Lazarus were headed down the road toward the family tomb. It was their duty to stay with the bereaved for a full seven days so every person present joined the procession of mourners.

Jesus had not entered the village. He was still at the place where Martha had met him. With his disciples, he was sitting on a low stone wall, shaded by ancient trees.

Peter was the first to jump to his feet. "Master!"

Jesus glanced down the road that led to the estate of his friend. "My friends and my enemies are approaching," he casually commented.

Thomas stepped up, and the other disciples took equally aggressive stances.

Jesus calmly shook his head and gestured for his protective friends to be at ease.

Martha led the small crowd. She hurried forward and immediately began to apologize. "I did not mean to bring everyone here."

"Martha, Martha, do not fret. Everything that happens is for the glory of God." Jesus then stepped aside, lifting his arms to welcome Mary.

She fell at his feet. Her mantel dropped into the dust of the road, and her body trembled with grief. Between heartbroken sobs, she said, "Master, my brother should not have died. If only you had been here."

In response, a wave of sincere wailing rose from those who had followed Mary. "Lazarus, Lazarus, you were a good man, our friend. It was not your time to leave us."

When Jesus saw Mary weeping and heard the sorrow of the Jews who had come with her, his own eyes filled with tears. He was deeply moved in spirit and, at the same time, troubled. The Spirit had revealed to him an overwhelming presence of gloating demons.

"My brother, Lazarus," Jesus sobbed as he dropped to his knees. "You have experienced an evil you did not deserve." With both hands, Jesus scooped dust from the road and poured it over his head. On his cheeks, the dust became streaks of mud. Beside Mary, Jesus put his face to the ground. He groaned loudly and his body shook. It shook with shared sorrow and righteous rage. The kingdom of Satan had attacked his friend!

"See how our master loved Lazarus, like his own family," Thomas commented.

And the other disciples murmured in soft agreement, some of them dropping into the dust of the road and following Jesus in the Middle Eastern demonstration of grief.

Gradually, the renewed wailing died away. Jesus slowly stood. He helped Mary to her feet. Briefly, he looked beyond the crowd into the smug face of Death. Then he turned back to the sisters. "Where is the tomb" he asked.

"Come, we will show you," they replied.

Walking toward the family tomb, the professional mourners renewed their high-pitched wailing. Jesus also wept with an intensity that was startling. They were his tears for every deceased son or daughter of Adam—past, present, and future.

Then the Jews spoke softly to each other, "See, he loved Lazarus!"

But influenced by the demons who followed and took pleasure in mocking their Creator, some of them said, "Rabbi Jesus is called the Healer. Why didn't he save his friend from the grave?"

At the tomb, Jesus obviously trembled with emotion. With angry strides, he led as many as could fit down a few steps into the weeping chamber at the entrance to the family graves. Mary and Martha with their husbands stood on either side of Jesus. Some of his disciples were able to crowd in behind, but most of the people remained outside.

At first, Jesus and the sisters of Lazarus just stood quietly in the outer room feeling the relief of being separated from the clamor of too many guests and hired mourners. A thin shaft of light entered the room through a small window in the wall. By that light, they could just make out their surroundings. It was a man-made cave, hewn from the natural rock of a hillside. Within that first room, a large stone had been laid across the entrance to steps that led further down into the deeper chamber where Lazarus was now decomposing.

Peter looked around the room. Then he whispered to John who stood beside him. "I never like going into these places. It reminds me of the time I had to help my father move the bones of my grandfather into an ossuary box."

John pointed to the stone that lay almost flat on the floor, plugging the entrance. "There are probably a lot of those boxes in little niches down there. I'm sure the parents of Lazarus are in this tomb and maybe his grandparents too."

"I know where the body of Lazarus is, but what about the soul of Lazarus?" Peter asked. "Where is the life that God gave him?"

"The sages teach that it lingers close to the body for three days," John answered. "Then, when it sees that the face is changing, it seeks the One who gives life to each man. An angel is then assigned to escort the deceased to Sheol." As he spoke, John pointed toward the small window. "Yesterday, the spirit of Lazarus left through that opening."

Abruptly, Jesus turned to Peter and John, interrupting their quiet exchange and startling them with the intensity of his facial expression. "Remove the stone," he said.

For a shocked moment, Peter and John remained frozen in place.

From the family, there were several horrified gasps.

Martha immediately stepped between Jesus and his disciples. "No, Lord," Martha protested, "by this time, the odor is overwhelming. He has been there four days."

Then Jesus replied, "Didn't I tell you if you would believe, you would see the glory of God?" He spoke firmly with an authority that moved both Peter and John into immediate action.

They hauled away the stone. Then Jesus looked up, into the light that was streaming through the window. Within that opening, he could see the spirit of Death, trembling and clutching the keys to the Place of the Dead. Beyond the evil that was so close, he knew his Father held all authority in the universe. Faith bubbled up from a lifetime of experience. In a clear unwavering voice, he said, *"Father, I thank you that you have heard me. I know that you always hear me, but I said this for the benefit of the people standing here, that they may believe that you sent me."*

When he had said this, Jesus called in a loud voice, "Lazarus, come out!" [5]

Momentarily, Death lost its grip on the keys. They dropped from his evil hand. He quickly retrieved them, but it was too late.

Within the blackness of the lower chamber, there was a shuffling and a scuffling.

In the weeping chamber, each person held their breath while chills ran up and down the spines of all but Jesus. With his spiritual eyes, Jesus could the Holy Spirit infusing Lazarus with life. He could see the assisting angels sent from his Father's throne.

"Yeshua!" God spoke into the heart of his son. "I want you to be certain. I want you to see this. I have the power to release you from the grave! Death must obey. Our enemy will not be able to hold you in the grave!"

The Holy Spirit continued to reveal to Jesus the glorious scene unfolding in the depths of the tomb. Angels dressed in brilliant white were lifting his friend, propelling him up the steps.

Up, up, out of the black hole, the dead man came out, encased in a seamless shroud, his hands and feet wrapped with strips of linen, and with a cloth still around his face.

At first, everyone gasped and fearfully stepped back, but Jesus said to them, "Take off the grave clothes. Release him."

Immediately, John hurried forward, pulling the cloth away from his face.

Peter shouted, "It is Lazarus!"

"In the flesh!" John joyfully responded as he lightly slapped Lazarus on the cheek and tugged at his beard.

At first, Lazarus appeared a little dumbfounded, but after a moment, he found his voice. "Why have all of you come to the family tomb, and how did I get to be in this place?" He looked down at the shroud that still covered most of his body. Then he looked back into the faces of his friends and family. "I died?"

"Four days ago," Martha excitedly announced as she and Mary rushed forward. Many hands now reached out to touch Lazarus to free his arms and his legs.

Jonathan pulled the burial shroud away, exposing his brother-in-law to all who were in the cave. "This is not a spirit or a trick!" he announced.

For one unashamed moment, every eye examined the body of the man who had been decomposing for four days. Peter then stepped forward, offering his own robe. "You need some clothing before you walk out of this cave."

Martha and Mary then properly looked away while the men covered the nakedness of their brother.

Judas was the first man to exit. He immediately went to some of the men from the Sanhedrin who were standing nearby. Excitedly, he described the event that had just taken place, finishing the details as Lazarus stepped out of the cave.

Shouts of wonder and joy mingled with gasps of horror. How could this be explained?

Some said, "Jesus of Nazareth is the Messiah we have waited for."

Those who stood with Judas declared that Rabbi Jesus was nothing more than a dangerous trickster. Somehow, he had made it appear that Lazarus had died and then returned to life. What other explanation could there be?

Gradually, the excited crowd at the tomb drifted apart. Most returned to the estate to fill the tables with food to laugh and celebrate. Others began their homeward journeys with a story to tell. Judas walked with his friends from the Sanhedrin. Every step of the way back to Jerusalem, he listened to their angry version of the event. Nothing he said could convince them of the genuineness of the miracle.

What would it take for these important men of the nation to recognize everything Jesus offered?

Sitting on the wide step next to the Beautiful Gate, Ichabod positioned his beggar's bowl so it could easily be seen. Then he looked across the bridge that led to the Mount of Olives, and he thought about the news he had recently heard. A well-known gentleman, Lazarus of Bethany, had died. Since he had no children, the estate would go to his younger brother. He knew that a delegation of men from the Temple had gone to the village of Bethany to sit with the family. They had gathered on this very step and then walked together.

A few coins fell into his bowl, and the beggar looked up in appreciation. When he looked back at the pedestrians on the bridge, he was shocked. The very men who had gathered on this step four days earlier preparing to mourn with the family of Lazarus for a full week were returning. Their stride, their hand gestures, and their facial expressions all indicated extreme agitation.

Ichabod sat up, alert to the approaching conversations.

"Lazarus came out of his tomb!"

"Was he ever in the tomb? Was he really dead?"

"Of course he was dead!"

"How do we know for sure? We arrived after the burial."

"That healer! He is full of tricks!"

"The next thing you know, he will proclaim himself the Messiah and gather an army."

"Everyone will join him! No one will fear fighting the Romans because they will believe if a soldier gets killed, the healer will just bring him back to life. This story will make most people think there is no limit to his power."

"When the people hear about this, there will be no holding them back. They will declare that the healer is the Messiah they have been waiting for."

"From all over the nation, the Jews will rise up and place him on the throne. There will not be an authority on earth powerful enough to restrain them."

Ichabod turned his whole body around, trying to hear as much as possible before the men passed through the gate and disappeared within the Temple complex.

In the high court, Caiaphas presided over an emergency meeting. "We are here to consider recent rumors regarding the so-called healer and teacher, Jesus from Galilee."

For a moment, there was silence. Then Nicodemus stood and briefly looked around at the other sixty-nine members of the Sanhedrin.

Most looked away, but a few made eye contact and nodded their heads indicating their support for Nicodemus and the rabbi he frequently championed.

"Rumors?" Nicodemus protested. "This body deals in facts that are supported by at least two credible witnesses. Do not waste our time with rumors."

"He raised a man from the dead!" Caiaphas exploded. "A number of men in this room saw Lazarus of Bethany walk out of his family tomb."

Nicodemus smirked and then lightly chuckled. "That is a problem for you. You do not believe there will ever be a resurrection from the grave. It is not a problem for most of us. We believe when the Messiah comes, he will call the dead back to life. Are we all present to hear that you now believe this, also?"

"No! No!" Caiaphas stood. His face turned red as he shouted, "Jesus of Nazareth is not the Messiah! This is a hoax by a very clever and dangerous man. He is deceiving the entire nation! He is leading the people down a road that leads to destruction!"

From the assembly, someone proclaimed, "The Messiah cannot come from Galilee. Only traitors and troublemakers come from that region!"

"If the people rally to a messiah, Roman soldiers will begin nailing every Jew they can catch to a cross. It has happened before," Annas added heatedly.

The oldest members of the assembly nodded their heads in sad agreement. They remembered the slaughter that had taken place soon after the death of King Herod. Thousands of crosses had lined the main roads.

Nicodemus responded, "Has the rabbi from Galilee announced to the people that he is the Messiah? Has he called for an army to fight the Romans?"

"He doesn't need to say, 'I am the Messiah.' When he brings a dead man back to life, all the people naturally conclude that he is the Messiah!" Caiaphas shouted.

"Death penalty! Treason! Blasphemy!" Inflammatory words exploded throughout the room.

In scattered pockets, anxious men whispered, "Lazarus is his coconspirator, and for that, he must die."

"This event cannot have any credibility."

"Murder?"

"We can pay someone."

Joseph of Arimathea then rose from his seat near the wall. He called over the shouting, "Let's hear some reliable witnesses. Was Lazarus really dead? Who saw the grave clothes removed?"

A murmuring wave of curiosity rolled through the room. Then there was silence. Was anyone going to come forward as an official witness?

Finally, several Pharisees made their way to the front, each repeating what they had seen and heard. Before the last man completed his account, the room erupted again. "Why are we just talking?" Something must be done! "Here is this man performing Messianic signs. The people believe he can heal them, feed them, and now, bring them back to life! If we let him go on like this, everyone will follow him! Then the Romans will come and take away our authority in this Temple, and the people of our nation will be slaughtered."

Joseph of Arimathea pushed his way to the front of the room. He turned and faced the members. "Listen to the things you are saying," he pleaded. "You want to kill this man because he blesses the people! He has not committed any crime. The Romans are not disturbed by his presence."

Then...Caiaphas, who was high priest that year, spoke up, "You know nothing at all! You do not realize that it is better for you that one man die for the people than that the whole nation perish."[6]

The power of that one statement struck silence throughout the Sanhedrin and brought each man to his feet. Within that assembly, there was now an unspoken understanding that a prophetic declaration had been made.

Simon son of Hillel called for a vote. "A resolution is now placed before you. Do we seek to remove Rabbi Jesus by any lawful method, or do we confirm his teachings and miraculous activities?"

"Remove him! Remove him!" The shouts were overwhelming.

The few men who raised their voices in support of Rabbi Jesus felt heartbroken as a sense of the inevitable washed over them. Without help from God, the rabbi from Nazareth was destined to be a dead man.

The captain of the Temple guard stood in the doorway and Judas stood with him. The captain turned to Judas. "Do you hear what they are saying about your master? It is only a matter of time. A large reward is being offered. Someone will come forward with information that this court can use for a conviction."

Judas did not reply. He just turned and walked back to the home of Lazarus in Bethany, considering with every step the events of the last two days. Jesus had called Lazarus back from the Place of the Dead. Judas had seen that miracle with his own eyes. He had touched the grave clothes and even the living body of the man who had been dead for four days.

A thought suddenly popped into Judas's mind, Surely, the Messiah cannot die. No man can take his life. Another thought quickly followed, There is a reward for the person who helps the Temple guards arrest Jesus.

More thoughts—Judas's mind suddenly filled with ideas. "It is time to be proactive," he muttered. "If Jesus finds himself about to be arrested or about to be stoned, he will have to use his power to defend himself. The high priest and the members of the Sanhedrin will be forced to recognize that Jesus has authority that no man has ever had before. They will place him on the throne of David."

In his imagination, Judas saw the coronation. He pictured himself at the head of the procession while the rest of those Galilean fishermen who called themselves disciples were relegated to the rear.

When Judas arrived at the home of Lazarus, he found the house full of guests. From everywhere, people had come to see the man who had been dead for four days. Unnoticed, Judas strolled into the manor house. He passed Peter and John. Neither man looked up. Judas observed Lazarus and Jesus reclining, each with a cup of wine. Pausing in mid-conversation, Jesus looked directly at Judas. The master's eyes held an unspoken question.

Since the question was not spoken, Judas did not offer any information. He passed into the next room. There he found an unoccupied corner. Remaining solitary, Judas reclined on some cushions and continued to spin his demonically inspired fantasy.

Chapter 3

Away From the Crowds

So from that day on they plotted to take his life. Therefore Jesus no longer moved about publicly among the people of Judea. Instead he withdrew to a region near the wilderness, to a village called Ephraim, where he stayed with his disciples.

—John 11:53–54

Manaen with Cuza pulled aside the heavy drapes and waited for King Herod Antipas to call them into his audience chamber. The king appeared to be taking a little nap so both men wrapped themselves in patience, remaining in place, attentive and ready to deliver their report. Those were the expectations for their positions as advisors to the tetrarch.

It had been at least six weeks since they had last reported the financial matters of Galilee and Perea to King Antipas. His finances were no longer uppermost in their minds. With seventy others, they had been commissioned by Jesus to spread the good news of the Kingdom of God. Now as they traveled from town to town, auditing tax records, they told everyone who would listen that God loved them. Cuza often told the story of how Jesus had healed his little boy, and Manaen laid hands on the sick, proclaiming new life in the name of Jesus. There had been wonderful manifestations of the power that was within that name.

Antipas stirred. Then he sneezed.

Manaen cleared his throat.

The king glanced toward the door, then he straightened himself in his royal chair. "Come in." Antipas sneezed again and then blew his nose on a large piece of linen. "Is the news good?"

Cuza answered, "You have taken in more revenue than you have spent. That is always good news."

Manaen added, "We are still making payments to the commander of the Imperial Forces stationed in Syria because of his involvement in the war with the Nabataeans."

Cuza interrupted, "Relating to that, we received an invoice from Pontius Pilate."

Antipas coughed and turned a little red in the face, spluttering as he spoke, "What right does the governor of Judea have to send me a bill?" He reached for the scroll in Cuza's hand.

Coughing and muttering, Antipas read. "So, Pilate held a victory celebration in my father's old palace, and he expects me to pay for it!" Antipas looked up at Manaen. "Did I receive an invitation?"

"No," Manaen replied. "I believe this was a military event."

"I am the head of an army," Antipas countered. "My soldiers fought the Nabataeans."

Carefully, Cuza pointed out, "Sir, our forces were defeated. That is the reason reinforcements from Syria took over the campaign."

"That does not make me responsible for their victory celebration!" Antipas threw the scroll on the floor. "I will not pay this bill unless I receive a directive from Tiberius!"

The drapes at the entrance were pulled aside again.

All three men looked up.

A servant announced, "A delegation of Pharisees has arrived. They represent the Assembly of the Sanhedrin and wish to meet with you on an important matter."

"Send them in," Antipas directed as he blew his nose again.

Manaen recognized each man. He introduced them as they entered. "Gamaliel, grandson of the great Hillel; Nicodemus, a senior leader of the party of the Pharisees; Joseph of Arimathea, a merchant and member of the assembly; also Yonatan who represents the interests of Galilee in the high court."

Gamaliel was the first to speak. "Your Majesty, we are sending a complaint to Emperor Tiberius, and we want you to add your name as well as your influence."

Yonaton smoothly added, "You are not a foreigner sent to rule our land. You understand the requirements of the laws that Moses gave us. Governor Pilate has no regard for our customs. He does not understand the heart of a Jew."

"Neither does he feel constrained by the directives of the emperor," Joseph asserted.

"How has my friend, the governor, insulted you?" Antipas asked. As he spoke, Antipas held his linen handkerchief over his nose and mouth to conceal the grin he could hardly contain.

"He held a military event in Herod's palace."

Antipas nodded. "Technically, the palace belongs to the Roman government. The governor can use it for any event without consulting me. But usually, he defers to the protocol of reserving it for my visits to Jerusalem."

Gamaliel continued, "To honor the emperor and his victory over the Nabataeans, Pilate had twelve gold shields placed in the great hall. To commemorate this event, the shields are to remain in the palace indefinitely!"

"Are they just plain gold?" Cuza asked.

Nicodemus responded, "The name of the emperor is boldly engraved on each shield. It is not just the name of a man. It is the name of a self-proclaimed god!"

"*You shall have no other gods before me.*" Manaen quoted from the law.

Yonaton completed the quotation. "*You shall not make for yourself an image in the form of anything in heaven above or on the earth beneath or in the waters below. You shall not bow down to them or worship them; for I, the LORD your God, am a jealous God, punishing the children for the sin of the parents to the third and fourth generation of those who hate me, but showing love to a thousand generations of those who love me and keep my commandments.*[1]

Gamaliel stepped forward. "Those shields are idolatrous. They endanger our nation, and they must be taken out of our city!"

Nicodemus added, "We have appealed to the governor, but he will not listen. This is just like the incident several years ago. You remember. He brought the Roman standards into the city. Only fear of retribution from Rome moved him to reverse that action."

Manaen commented in a confidential tone, "Your governor has much to fear at this time. He was given this post by Sejanus, and Sejanus has fallen into disfavor with the emperor."

Antipas added. "Sejanus has been killed. His wife, his children, and his servants have been executed. Death squads have been sent to the homes of most of his appointees and their associates." Very purposefully Antipas stepped on the invoice he had thrown onto the floor. With his sandaled foot, he ground it into the mosaic tiles. "Do you have a written complaint that I can sign?" He turned to Cuza. "Bring my royal seal. Manaen, arrange for a carrier."

Immediately, there was a scurry of activity. A table was brought in. Scrolls were signed and sealed. When all was completed, wine was served. As the men were drinking, Antipas asked, "Is there any other news from Jerusalem?"

Casually, Nicodemus said, "A friend of ours had been dead for four days, and then he walked out of his tomb."

"Really? How?" Antipas leaned forward to catch the response.

"Jesus, the healer from Galilee!" Yonaton said the name like a curse.

"Details! Details! Tell the story," Antipas demanded.

"It's a very simple story," Joseph responded. "I have spoken to Lazarus of Bethany, myself. He was very ill, and then he died. The family prepared his body with spices, wrapped him in a shroud, and placed him in the family tomb. Four days after the burial, Jesus came with his disciples."

"Don't believe a word this man is about to say!" Yonaton interrupted.

Stepping between Joseph and Yonaton, Gamaliel signaled for calmness. "This story has caused considerable debate." Then he nodded for Joseph to finish.

"Jesus went into the outer room of the tomb with some family and friends. He had them remove the stone that covered the entrance to the burial chambers. Then he called, 'Lazarus, come out of there!'

Nicodemus jumped into the story. "Lazarus came out. He was still completely wrapped in his burial shroud. He could not move until they untied him. He is alive! I have also visited with him."

"Where is this Rabbi Jesus?" Antipas asked. "I would like to speak with him."

"We don't know," Nicodemus replied. "He left the city."

Antipas turned to Manaen and Cuza. "Can you find him for me?"

Tactfully, Manaen replied. "We can send out inquiries. But he may be in another jurisdiction, and we do not have authority to search there."

"But I must speak with him," Antipas insisted.

Cuza cautioned, "A man who can bring the dead to life can also resurrect secrets and people from the past."

Antipas shivered as he remembered the long-haired prophet of the desert. He turned to Manaen. "What did you do with the body of the prophet called John the Baptist?

"His disciples took it away and buried it," Manaen answered.

"What about his head?"

Cuza responded, "We gave that to you on a silver platter."

"Can this healer bring a man back to life after his head has been separated from his body?" Antipas looked worried.

"Sir," Manaen answered. "Some things are better left alone. I don't think you want to experiment with that question."

"You believe Rabbi Jesus can bring the dead to life, don't you?" Antipas trembled as he waited for his advisors to speak.

Both men nodded and said yes with conviction.

As the delegation from Jerusalem left the room, Nicodemus paused and spoke confidentially to Cuza and Manaen. "I know in my heart that Rabbi Jesus has been sent from God. I can see that you two know that also."

"We are his followers," Cuza unashamedly confirmed.

"Use your positions to protect him," Nicodemus advised. "He has powerful enemies."

In the village of Ephraim, the late winter rains were falling. Through the window of the house that Judas had rented, Jesus could see the stone sheep pens filled with animals, heavy with the expectation of birthing. Beyond the sheep enclosure, he observed the barley fields, green and growing. He estimated Passover was about six weeks away. The Holy Spirit had spoken to him, and he knew this Passover would be the time of his death and resurrection.

Jesus then glanced around the room at his disciples, sturdy fishermen restlessly held in one room by the whims of weather. Today, they were quiet, not competing for his approval or putting each other down. As his eyes moved from face to face, the Holy Spirit whispered, "James and John the sons of Zebedee. They are your cousins. They have been close to you since childhood. James will be the first to give his life for your kingdom. John will be the witness who lives 120 years to keep your story alive. Peter will have a long life and continue his leadership until both he and his wife are bound and taken to the cross. Andrew, Bartholomew, James, Matthew, Philip, Simon, Thaddaeus, and Thomas will all travel the world with the good news of salvation. Satan will incite mobs, and at some point in their ministries, they will each be killed by deceived men."

"And Judas?" Jesus silently asked. Jesus focused on the disciple who sat apart from the other men. He was not like the others, rooted in the business and politics of Galilee. Judas had family ties to the Temple. Matthew, who also had a background in money, seemed to be the only disciple with whom he had any relationship.

Moving over Judas and highlighting him, the Holy Spirit responded, "He is the one who will try to promote himself by joining your enemies."

"How will his life end?" Jesus asked the Holy Spirit.

"At this time, the answer to that question rests on the choices he will make. If he will choose to listen to me, he has hope and a future. If he listens to the deceiver, he may throw his future away."

To himself, Jesus remarked, "This man has been with me for three years, and he has so many fine qualities." Then Jesus walked over and sat beside Judas, opening a conversation. "Were you able to visit with your family while we were in Judea? How is your father? Did your sister get married?"

Judas's answers were short. He did not pick up the conversation.

Jesus did not press Judas. Instead, he moved to where his other disciples were sitting.

They stopped talking and looked up at Jesus expectantly.

Jesus began teaching. "Each man is responsible for the knowledge he has received from the scriptures, from my teaching, and from the Spirit of God whispering into his heart. It is like riches that have been entrusted to each one."

"I have always wanted to be a wealthy man," Peter quipped.

The others laughed, and Jesus responded, "Peter you have great wealth. The real question is, How will you use your wealth?"

"Once, a man prepared for an extended journey. Before the day of his departure, he gathered his servants. To his most able servant, he entrusted five bags of gold. He then handed two bags of gold to another trusted servant and one bag to a servant he considered reliable. 'Look out for the interests of my estate,' he directed. Then he went on his journey.

"The first two servants immediately began investing according to the needs of their master's estate. The third servant, the one with only one bag of gold, dug a hole and buried the wealth, checking frequently to see that none was lost."

"Poor business move," Matthew commented. "That man needs to buy something inexpensive and then sell it for a higher price."

"Or he could purchase a position as a tax collector," Thomas sarcastically remarked.

With a slightly raised voice, Matthew rejoined, "Every tax collector I know has more than enough money!"

Jesus raised his hands for silence, and then he continued his story. "Years passed. Finally, the master of the estate returned to audit the holdings of his estate. The servant who had invested five bags of gold proudly produced another five bags of gold. The servant who worked with only two bags of gold also doubled his investment."

The disciples nodded showing their interest. Even Judas seemed to be drawn into the story.

Jesus gave a little satisfied smile and continued. "Smiling broadly, the master of the estate responded, 'Well done! I will give you more gold and greater responsibilities.'"

"Those two men knew how to invest," Judas announced.

"Fishermen know how to invest," Andrew added in a slightly challenging tone.

"We would have taken the two talents and purchased a boat. Then after fishing for a season, selling all of our catch at market price, we would have enough money to purchase a second boat, doubling our catch."

"That's the way fishermen do it!" Peter announced.

"Merchants do it the same way," Judas countered. "We just don't deal with smelly fish and leaky boats."

Peter, Andrew, and Judas were glaring at each other. Philip brought everyone back to the story. "What happened to the man who buried his bag of gold?"

Jesus replied, "Then the servant who had received only one bag of gold came forward. He said, 'Master, here is the wealth you placed in my hands. Nothing has been lost.'

"Angrily, the master of the estate responded, 'And nothing has been gained? You are a lazy servant! At the very least, you could have placed this gold with the bankers and received a little interest for me.'"

"He just gave back the gold!" Judas restated.

"Remember," Jesus cautioned. "This story is not just about gold. It is also about the treasure of spiritual understanding that I have been pouring into you for about three years. I am the Master Rabbi. Everything I have spoken and done is the wealth, like bags of gold. Some have understood more, some less, but each of you has received a good amount."

Then Jesus went back to the story. "The master turned to his assistant and said to him, 'Take the bag of gold from this worthless servant. Give it to the servant who now has ten bags of gold. Then remove this man from my estate. He shall no longer be associated with my name.'"

Seriousness washed over the disciples. Jesus took that moment to look at each face. His gaze finally rested on Judas. "My Father in heaven knows exactly how much understanding each man has received. He is watching to see how you will use it to make choices and how you will deposit it in other people. I have told you before, and I now, tell you again. 'The time is approaching. I will die. I will live again after three days, and soon after that, I will leave you.' Time will pass. Then I will return and ask to see how you have invested your treasure of knowledge and experience."

The men remained quiet. No one knew how to respond. Jesus looked out the window. The rain had stopped. Jesus spoke to the men in the room. "It is time to return to Capernaum. You need to see your families. I'm sure your homes need some spring-time repair. Let's go in the morning. We will stay there until it is time to return to Jerusalem for Passover."

In the cool of the evening, Jesus slipped away from the house. He climbed the highest hill and looked out over the flat land below. Settling on a rock, he opened himself to heaven, waiting to hear God call his name.

There was a longer silence than usual. Then from behind, he heard, "Yeshua? Is that your name, or are you just Jesus, an ordinary and very confused man?"

Jesus knew that voice. He easily recognized the evil that emanated from the massive spiritual being who lurked in the damp brush close to his back. Without turning, Jesus replied, "You may pretend you are not certain of my identity, but I am certain of your identity." Recalling his earthly lifetime of Holy Spirit revelation, Jesus confidently stated, "Before I spoke this world into existence, before I knelt in the dirt and formed Adam and Eve, you were the most perfect of all the angels, full of wisdom and beauty. When you saw the love that I lavished on my son Adam and my daughter Eve, when you realized that I shared with them the qualities of the Godhead, you became jealous."

Jesus turned around and spoke directly into the bush that partially concealed Satan. "My Father, the Holy Spirit and I watched you leave your assignment in heaven. You went to Eden, the garden of God."

The Holy Spirit opened his eternal memory. In his mind, Jesus clearly saw Lucifer, formerly the covering cherub.

"Every precious stone adorned you…Your settings and mountings were made of gold; on the day you were created they were prepared. You were anointed as a guardian cherub…On the holy mount of God; you walked among the fiery stones…blameless in your ways until…. you sinned. So I drove you in disgrace from the mount of God, and I expelled you…I threw you to the Earth!"[2]

"Threw me to Earth?" Satan mocked.

Behind him, a chorus of jeering laughs filled the spiritual space.

"Earth is mine because Adam ate the fruit, giving his allegiance to me," Satan countered.

"Within the plans for the creation of Earth with men and women made in the image of God, we made preparations for such an event," Jesus replied.

"I remember," Satan sneered. "Yeshua the Creator would become a man. He would do what Adam and Eve could not do, keep the law of God faultlessly."

"I have," Jesus stated.

"So far," Satan countered with a wait-and-see inflection. "You have not completed your life as a man. *Who can live and not see death, or…escape the power of the grave?*[3] It will be a painful death. You will curse God. You will curse all mankind—then it will be over. You will be mine!"

In his heart, Jesus could hear the response of the Holy Spirit, the words of the prophet Isaiah. "Yeshua, *You who bring good news to Zion…and to Jerusalem, lift up your voice with a shout, lift it up, do not be afraid; say…"Here is your God! See, the Sovereign LORD comes…and he rules with a mighty arm."*[4]

The Evil One could also hear the words of the Holy Spirit, and he scoffed, "Your arm rules? That arm is going to be nailed to a cross! How is that ruling?" Then he sadistically added, "None of your disciples will stand beside you. In one way or another, each man has opened himself to my influence. Each man will fail."

Jesus shook his head, resisting the idea.

"Let me show you," Satan pushed. "Peter, your most loyal and outspoken follower, I can turn him against you. I can turn all of his passionate beliefs into condemning lies. When I am finished, he won't recognize the man he has become."

"No!" Jesus stood. "Do not think I am like you, playing games with the lives of men. Do not think you are like me—as Yeshua equal to both God and the Holy Spirit and as Jesus equal to Adam. *Do you not know? Have you not heard? The LORD is the everlasting God, the Creator of the ends of the earth. He will not grow tired or weary, and his understanding no one can fathom.*[5] Peter is not a perfect man. All of my followers are flawed. But my Father and the Holy Spirit are working to give *strength to the weary and* increase *the power of the weak. Even youths grow tired and weary, and young men stumble and fall; but those who hope in the* LORD *will renew their strength.*[6] All of my disciples may fail in a moment of crisis, but heaven always provides a path to redemption."

Jesus then stepped aggressively toward his enemy. "Leave me, Satan. I am your Creator, and I have spoken!"

Sometime later, when Jesus returned to the house, he found most of his disciples sleeping. Only Andrew and Thomas were in quiet conversation. Jesus heard Andrew say, "When Jesus sets up his kingdom, I believe Peter will be the ruler on his right."

Thomas agreed. Then he added, "Judas thinks that he will be the minister of finance."

Andrew scoffed, "Anyone but Judas."

Jesus walked past the talking men without comment. The anticipation of an earthly kingship and the positions that would be available in that kingdom was a frequent topic of both agreement and disagreement. In the morning as they began their journey, Jesus would tell everyone again. "Do not expect me to lead an army or take up residence in Herod's palace. Expect me to die and then come back from the dead in three days."

Chapter 4

Leaving Capernaum

*When it was almost time for the Jewish Passover, many
went up from the country to Jerusalem for their ceremonial
cleansing before the Passover. They kept looking for Jesus,
and as they stood in the temple courts they asked one another,
"What do you think? Isn't he coming to the festival at all?"
But the chief priests and the Pharisees had given orders that
anyone who found out where Jesus was should report it so
that they might arrest him.*

—John 11:55–57

Centurion Longinus strode into the barracks in the Antonio Fortress. He paused at the entrance to the common room and looked around. Most of the men were whiling their time with wine and games. This laziness was about to end.

With an official clattering of metal on leather and hobnail sandals on stone, the commander of the Antonio Fortress stepped into the room. The duty man announced his presence, and all the men quickly stood, ready for orders.

"The spring feast of Passover will commence in four weeks. Pilate has sent orders from Caesarea. This city and all the roads leading into the city are to be cleared of bandits. We have information that the most active bandits are living in the tunnels and caverns beneath the northern section of the city. These can be accessed from the stone quarry."

Longinus paused. Then he began pointing to various men. "I want three squads to go into those tunnels. Map them. Look for evidence of habitation. If you find anything, we will return with larger forces."

The duty man efficiently arranged those Longinus had pointed out into squads of eight, each with an accompanying officer. "The rest of you are to patrol the streets of the city."

Longinus turned to his duty man. "Do we have civilian clothing?"

The junior officer answered, "Ten or twelve outfits."

"Use them," Longinus directed. "Blend into the population and listen. Be especially aware of those who speak with a Galilean dialect. Most insurrectionists come from that region. Bring all suspects in for questioning."

The commander turned cleanly on his heel, ready to exit the room, and then he paused to issue one more order. "Bring my horse to the gate. I will be following the squads into the stone quarry."

The commander of the Antonio Fortress had been waiting at his base camp since morning. Now, the sky above the stone quarry had clouded over and a soft drizzle was falling. Longinus looked up at the overcast sky. Then he picked up the reins to his horse, all the while thinking about his men searching within the bowels of the earth. He led his horse into the shelter of the open cavern.

Slowly walking the perimeter of the massive entrance to the deep labyrinth, he could see that several passages extended from this sheltered entrance into underground blackness. They were huge passages, big enough to pull giant blocks of stone from the foundations of the earth.

The wait continued to be tedious. Impatiently, the centurion examined the entrance to each passage, peering into the endless blackness, listening for his men. In the largest passage, he thought he saw a glimmer of torchlight.

Just to break the monotony, Longinus mounted and nudged his horse through the passage entrance, toward the flickering light. Slowly but persistently, he urged his animal deeper and deeper into the large tunnel. Sudden screams echoed along the limestone walls. Then the screams turned into deafening silence. The distant light disappeared. Longinus felt his horse rear and violently spin around. In the blackness, the commander lost all sense of orientation. He only knew that he had sailed through the damp air, hitting the wall of the passage and then falling to the floor. He heard his horse galloping and whinnying, the sounds diminishing as his animal raced toward open space. Cursing and muttering, Longinus groped his way back. Crawling through the black passage, he followed the sound of his fleeing horse.

The entrance was not far away, and Longinus soon found himself in the comfort of waning daylight. The screams concerned him, so he grabbed a torch from the pile of supplies, lit it, and reentered the cavern on foot.

A short distance beneath the surface of the earth, Longinus found that the passage split. He turned to his right and continued, careful to maintain silence. A little further and the passage split again. Looking around for a landmark, Longinus noticed a winged seraph carved into the stone wall. He remembered it and turned right again.

His torch flickered, and the Roman commander began to doubt the wisdom of this venture. The passage split again, and as Longinus peered into the blackness of a new tunnel, he distinctly saw another flickering light.

He breathed a sigh of relief. One of his squads must be in that passage. With a more confident step, Longinus turned to the right again and proceeded toward the light. Suddenly, the commander stopped short. There were bodies on the floor of the cave, eight of his men. By his own torchlight, he examined each man and found no evidence of violence. Their torches had burned out, but the walls of the cave still glowed with a fearful iridescence.

Unexplained terror washed over the commander. Moving with a swiftness that belonged to a much younger man, he made his way back to the fresh air of the entrance where his other two squads waited with their maps and reports.

Longinus gathered his men and grimly announced. "Eight men have died, and one, the commander of the squad, is unaccounted for."

The soldiers looked at each other, shocked and concerned. A simple search had turned deadly.

"The bandits?" one squad leader asked.

"Unknown," Longinus replied. "But we must recover the bodies and, if possible, find the missing soldier. We go in armed, prepared to either attack or defend."

A scuffling sound within the open cavern brought all the men to alert. Each man grabbed his sword and small shield, quickly taking shelter beside the boulders on either side of the cavern.

Longinus signaled three men to move forward.

The men silently followed the wall of the quarry, slipping into the cavern on one side of its entrance. A moment later, someone shouted. "We found him! It's the commander of the lost squad."

Two men half-carried, half-dragged their comrade into the damp twilight. The rest of the men gathered around.

At first, the man seemed disoriented, babbling about a strange light, a giant glowing man, and a blast of fire.

Longinus gave the man some wine, and then he got in his face. "What happened?"

"We came to the end of the passage. It was blocked by a pile of rocks from the floor to the ceiling of the cavern. We could see light between some of the rocks so we assumed the bandits were on the other side. I told my men to carefully move a few rocks so we could peek through to the other side. They moved two or three rocks. Suddenly, fire shot out. It knocked me into the wall. When I woke up, I knew my men were dead. I saw a large glowing man standing in front of the pile of rocks. He looked at me and silently pointed toward the exit. On the way out, I got confused. I have been wandering in the tunnels for a while." The soldier looked up at Longinus. "Do you believe me?"

The commander of the Antonio Fortress nodded. "I saw the bodies." He pulled a rolled parchment from the soldier's belt. "Is this your map?"

The soldier nodded.

Longinus studied both the map and the surrounding terrain, straining to see in the remaining daylight. "I think you were under the place of crucifixion near the rock that looks like a skull." Longinus looked around again, and then he ordered. "Make camp here. In the morning, we will remove the bodies. Do not speak about this incident." Under his breath, he added, "I'm sure there is a rational explanation."

The fishing boats were securely moored and the citizens of Capernaum were gathering at the city gate. Jesus waited with the growing crowd, expecting his twelve to meet him, ready to begin the walk to Jerusalem. Peter was the first to arrive with his wife and two daughters. Peter's father, his brothers, and the other men from their family followed.

Jairus, president of the synagogue in Capernaum, stepped over to speak to Jesus. "I want to personally invite you to a betrothal celebration. My daughter, Shira, has become of age. I have found the perfect man for her, and this event would not take place if you had not come to my home when my little girl was so sick."

Jesus glanced over at the giggling maidens. His quick eyes spotted Shira, laughing with her friends.

"Your daughter's laughter brings joy to my heart," Jesus replied. "I'm sure your celebration will be after the Days of Unleavened Bread. I do not expect to be in town. But your daughter and her bridegroom have my blessing."

Jairus moved on to speak with others. Andrew dropped his bundle on the road near Jesus. Peter gave last-minute instructions to his wife before he said good-bye, leaving that part of his family in town. James and John stepped away from their parents to stand with Jesus. Matthew, along with his father and brothers, hurried toward the gate. From every direction, the men of Capernaum gathered to walk together. A smaller group of women and children clustered in excited preparation.

Jesus looked around. All his disciples were with him. Jesus was about to raise his hand and get his own little group moving. Then he paused.

"Jesus! Jesus!"

Jesus smiled and bent down to catch Casper. The little boy ran ahead of his mother, full force into the solid body of his friend.

Before Joanna could get to Jesus and her son, Casper began, "Jesus, we are having Passover dinner in Herod's palace. This year, I do not have to stay with the little children. I have learned the four questions, and I will say them for everyone. Would you like to come to our Passover dinner?"

"Thank you, Casper. It is kind of you to ask, but I have my own plans for Passover."

Just then, Casper's mother stepped up. "Forgive my son. He has a lot to learn about palace protocol. The Passover meal with Antipas is by invitation only."

Jesus chuckled. "I am not disappointed."

Joanna pressed a large bag of coins into Jesus's hands. "Cuza and I want to pay for all your Passover expenses, the lamb, food preparation, a room, even servants. We want you to have a wonderful feast."

Jesus responded, "My Father always provides, and often, he has chosen to provide through you and your husband. Tell Cuza to remember that his position as finance minister for Herod Antipas cannot alter my destiny. Alarming and amazing events will take place during this Passover. Tell him not to intervene in any way. You and your family must trust that my Father, God, is controlling every moment of my life. Nothing can happen to me that has not already been planned in the throne room of heaven. And no man can do anything to change the plans of God."

Joanna looked concerned.

Jesus laid his hand on her head. "What I have told you will make sense as events unfold." Then he obviously felt the weight of the bag filled with coins. "The meal you have paid for will be the most memorable feast in the history of the world. It will be studied, talked about, even detailed in writing. My Father thanks you. This gift has been recorded in heaven."

Casually, Jesus passed the bag of coins over to Matthew, who carried them to Judas. For a moment, Jesus watched as Joanna caught her son and both of them climbed into the sedan chair that would carry them to the Passover celebration in Herod's Jerusalem palace.

Then Jesus raised his right arm and signaled his disciples. "On to Jerusalem!" But before he could take the first step, a well-dressed young man fell on his knees in front of him.

"Teacher of righteousness, tell me. What are the things I must do to merit eternal life?"

"Teacher of righteousness? Is that my new title?" Jesus shook his head. "Righteousness belongs to God alone. Still, you have asked a good question, and I will answer."

The disciples who were ready to travel with Jesus gathered around to hear what their master would say.

"Keep the commandments that Moses received on the mountain. Do not murder or steal. Do not commit adultery or become a false witness, honor your mother and father—"

The young man interrupted, "I have been faithful to the law since childhood."

The Holy Spirit hovered over the moment and confirmed what the young man had said. Jesus looked into his face. The sincerity of this young man was obvious.

Within the heart of Jesus, love prompted an invitation. "Come, follow me. Sell everything you own. Give your wealth to the poor. Then you will have treasure in heaven." Again, Jesus repeated the invitation, "Become one of my disciples."

Joy left the young man's face. "You don't understand," he stammered. "I have responsibilities—property, servants, and businesses." Then he stood and walked away.

Sadly, Jesus turned to those who were with him. "It is very difficult for the wealthy to respond to the call of the Kingdom of God."

In silent astonishment, his disciples waited for Jesus to offer further commentary.

Jesus then said, "I tell you, it is more likely that a camel will pass through the eye of a needle than a wealthy man will obtain entrance to the Kingdom of God."

Amazed commentary passed from man to man "We have always understood that God blesses those who keep his laws most perfectly."

"If those blessings prevent one from entering God's eternal kingdom, then who will enter?"

Jesus looked at his followers. "God is making a way, equal access for all who believe."

Peter then said, "Master, I hope you recognize we all have left everything to follow you! We had good businesses. We were at home with our wives and children. Now, we travel with you from place to place, even into danger."

The other disciples who had gathered around nodded their heads in agreement. A few commented about the threats from the Temple elite, and the arrest warrant that had been issued by the high court.

Without responding to the comments about his own peril, Jesus began walking toward Jerusalem, teaching the twelve who walked with him. "I want to assure you. Everyone who has left home, family, farms, or businesses for me will receive from the hand of my Father at least a hundred fold, in this life, and in the life to come."

Then Jesus added, "Do not be impressed by wealth. Importance in this world does not translate into importance in the kingdom of heaven. What I say may surprise you. Many who now seem to be greatest in wealth and position will be least in my kingdom."

Behind them, Jairus raised his arm and signaled the people of Capernaum. "On to Jerusalem!"

The women picked up their food baskets. Some linked arms with close friends. They stepped onto the road, singing as they began the trek to the city that was central to the plans of God.

> *"May God be gracious to us and bless us*
> *and make his face shine upon us*
> *so that your ways may be known on earth,*
> *your salvation among all nations."*

The men responded. With staffs in hand and solid strides, they rolled out their hardy baritone melody.

> *"May the peoples praise you, God;*
> *may all the peoples praise you."*[1]

Under the cover of songs and chatter, Judas spoke confidentially to Matthew. "The Temple police are looking for Jesus. I know the captain of the Temple guard. He will place his men at every city gate."

Matthew responded, "The captain of the Temple guard has been trying to arrest Jesus for nearly a year. We always slip by his men."

Judas countered, "This time, there is a substantial reward!"

Matthew replied, "Several times, guards have been sent to arrest Jesus while he was in the Temple. They confronted him, but they did not arrest him. It seems just the look in his eyes prevents them from following the dictates of their superiors. He stares at them, and they become almost immobile."

Judas thought for a moment. Then he said, "Yes, you're right. They have had many opportunities to arrest Jesus, and they have never been able to accomplish it."

Matthew shrugged. "Jesus is the Messiah. His destiny is in the hands of God. It is only a matter of timing. Soon, he will step up and declare himself King of the Jews." Having made this statement, Matthew moved up to walk with Philip.

As the sun touched the western horizon, the travelers from Capernaum felt cheered by the golden rays that illuminated the clouds. After a day of steady walking, the thought of setting up camp for the first night invigorated everyone. Jairus pointed to a large clearing close to the road and the families from Capernaum moved to establish their campsites. Jesus stepped off the road. He led his twelve away from the traffic, away from the clustered campsites of family and friends. Deliberately, Jesus put a little space between himself and the rest of the town's people.

From Capernaum to this first campsite, Jesus had only offered a few brief teachings. Most of the day, he had been listening to snatches of conversations. From those conversations, Jesus knew each man who called himself a disciple expected that Jesus would soon announce the overthrow of the Roman government and the establishment of a true Jewish nation. The Holy Spirit had revealed to him that the entire nation had been struck with Messianic fever, and that his name was on all lips.

Sitting with his back to a tree, Jesus waited while Thomas quickly built a fire. The rest of the men threw their staffs in a pile and spread their cloaks on the ground, ready to hear any word their master might speak.

When all were seated, Jesus told them, "We are on our way to Jerusalem. There, everything that is written by the prophets concerning the Son of Man will be fulfilled."

Jesus watched the men smile and share congratulatory nods. With a sigh, Jesus continued. "When most men read the scriptures, they hold on to the words that offer blessings and make them feel good. It is easy to ignore the difficult passages. At this Passover Feast, we will all deal with the difficult prophecies concerning the Messiah. He will become a prisoner of Rome, mocked and spit upon. He will be whipped and crucified, but on the third day, he will return to life."

Jesus waited for a response, but none came. He looked at the faces of the men who had been with him for about three years. He could tell. They could not accept his words.

"Jesus?"

The moment to press his point was now lost.

"I have food for your men." Aunt Salome stepped into the firelight, offering a covered basket. "I made this bread, and I also have a bag of salted sardines from Zebedee's last catch. Allow me to serve you and your men."

Jesus nodded and sincerely expressed his appreciation as she gave him a portion. She then passed the food to her sons, James and John. Next, she moved on to Peter and Andrew.

Jesus watched. All the men watched because there seemed to be a message attached to how and when she served each man. The last man to be served was Judas, the only disciple who was not from the region of Galilee.

Zebedee came into their campsite. He left a jug of water, and his wife made sure each man received a drink. By the time Salome had cleaned up from the meal, darkness had completely overtaken daylight. The clouds concealed the moon so the fire became their primary source of illumination. By its flickering glow, Jesus watched as Salome discreetly pulled James and John aside. She spoke with both sons, quietly and insistently.

Then the mother of Zebedee's sons walked past the fire and came to Jesus. James and John were with her. Quickly, the brothers glanced around to assure themselves that the other disciples were engaged in their own conversations. Very humbly, Salome knelt down in front of Jesus.

Responding, Jesus said, "There is no need to be so formal. You are family, my mother's sister. What can I do for you?"

Aunt Salome then said, "I have one request. Grant that these two sons of mine may sit, one on your right and one on your left when you take the throne of David." She gestured toward James and John who were standing close by.

Both men shifted uncomfortably. They noticed Peter's curious eyes focusing on the scene, and they felt a rush of heat that did not come from the fire.

"That is a bold request," Jesus answered. "I do not think you understand what you are asking." He looked at James and John. "Do you think you can drink the cup I am going to drink?"

"Oh, yes," they answered in a confident tone.

For a long moment, Jesus did not respond. He stared into the fire, seeing within the flames the persecution that each of his close followers would endure. At last, Jesus said, "I certainly will share my cup with you, but I cannot designate those places of honor. My Father will choose who he wishes to honor." With a sad wave of his hand, Jesus dismissed the family of Zebedee.

The incident had not gone unnoticed. Peter had been within earshot. He told Andrew. Andrew told Philip. Philip told Matthew and Thomas. The story flew from disciple to disciple with embellishments and comments.

When all ten had heard about this, they became indignant with the family of Zebedee.

Jesus heard the grumbling so in the morning, he called them together.[2] "My kingdom is not like the kingdoms of this world. *Instead, whoever wants to become great among you must be your servant, and whoever wants to be first must be your slave— just as the Son of Man did not come to be served, but to serve, and to give his life as a ransom for many."*[3]

A few dark and suspicious looks were thrown in the direction of the sons of Zebedee, but conversations on the topic ceased. Once more, Jesus and his men merged into the pedestrian traffic on the road from Galilee to Jerusalem. They expected traffic to become heavier as the road split and headed toward Jericho. Most travelers would veer east toward the Jordan River just to avoid camping in Samaria. Jesus and his men would travel with them, skirting the border of Samaria on the way to Jerusalem.

Chapter 5

On the Road to Jerusalem

As Jesus approached Jericho, a blind man was sitting by the roadside begging. When he heard the crowd going by, he asked what was happening. They told him, "Jesus of Nazareth is passing by.

—Luke 18:35–37

The road forked. Jesus with his disciples took the road to Jericho traveling southeast along the border. This road was packed with Jews from every town north of Samaria. Up and down the road, the word passed from traveler to traveler. "Rabbi Jesus is on this road. He's traveling to Jerusalem with the people of Capernaum."

Excitement crackled like sparks of static electricity. Speculation passed freely from person to person. "Is Jesus going to Jerusalem to become king? He could raise an army overnight!"

"He healed my son. Will he heal every diseased person in the nation?"

"I was in a crowd of more than five thousand, and he fed all of us! No one needs to be hungry when Jesus is present!"

"He is the Messiah! I know he is!"

A few cautionary voices shared their inside information, "I have heard that he has angered the Temple authorities, and he is wanted by the Temple guard."

"That shifty high priest, Caiaphas! He's so involved with the Romans that he might as well be one of them!"

A stranger from Chorazin approached Peter. "Did your master really call a dead man back to life?"

"He did," Peter emphatically replied. "I was there. I saw it with my own eyes."

"Then he must be the Messiah!" the man exclaimed as he turned away to share the thrilling news with those walking nearby.

Andrew tapped his brother on the shoulder. Then he pointed to a group of men standing a respectable distance from the road. "Those poor men are the living dead," he remarked.

Peter looked at the men who were obviously diseased. "Leprosy—I have seen total restoration with just a word from Jesus. Still, every time I get close to that disease, a jolt of fear rolls through my body."

"What must a man do for the hand of God to turn so violently against him?" Andrew mused. He counted ten men, all disfigured and in advanced stages of the disease.

As he passed, Peter kept a cautious eye on the pitiful men, thankful that they stood at a distance.

Suddenly, the lepers became excited and called out, "Jesus, Master Rabbi, look at us!"

Jesus heard them, and he stopped, turning in the direction of their desperate voices.

Everyone around him also stopped. Then a collective gasp went up from the travelers on the road, "Lepers!"

When he saw the men, Jesus stepped to the edge of the road. Undisturbed by their flesh-eating illness, he began a conversation with them. It was a shouted dialog because the men kept the required distance between themselves and others.

Jesus asked, "Why have you called me?"

One man responded, "We have heard that you are a man from God. You speak and every curse is broken; every illness is cured."

"This is true," Jesus replied. Then he said, "Go, report to the local priest so he can administer the rites of cleansing."

Immediately, the men turned back to the town. Without any physical evidence to support their Spirit-inspired conviction, the lepers hurried to find the priest, the only man who could officially readmit them into Jewish society.

As each man took that first step in faith, Jesus spoke to his Father, "These ten have moved on just my word. Honor their faith in me."

And as they went, they were healed. Raw flesh turned into new skin. Rotted toes and fingers became whole and healthy.

The men began to leap and whoop with excitement. They started to run toward the town.

Their exuberance was catching. Andrew slapped Peter on the back. Peter loudly announced, "Those men are healed!"

But one leper stopped. He turned, and instead of hurrying to the priest, he ran back to the road, praising God in a loud voice. Overwhelmed with emotion, he threw himself at Jesus's feet, thanking him through laughter and tears. He was a Samaritan.

Firmly grasping the man's hand and helping him to his feet, Jesus asked, "Didn't healing go forth for ten men? Where are the other nine? No one has returned to praise God except this foreigner!" Then he said to him, "Return to your family. Have a good life. The faith you acted upon has made you well."

Every person who saw this event was amazed and the story was quickly passed. Up and down the road, it moved faster than any man could walk.

For Jesus, this was a contemplative journey. Instead of teaching his twelve as they walked, Jesus thoughtfully listened, and he was disturbed. As much as he had taught about the Kingdom of God, his disciples were still expecting him to take up residence in Herod's old palace. They argued over who would oversee the treasury and who would direct the military. Those who considered themselves more than capable were ready with advice on dealing with Rome and reconstructing government in Jerusalem. On one point, there was unity; their time with Jesus qualified each for a greater role in his kingdom than anyone else who had ever proclaimed allegiance.

After another day of walking, evening overtook the Passover pilgrims. With the palms of Jericho in sight, Jesus helped his men set up a campsite for the night.

Settling around the fire, Jesus looked each man in the eye. Then he began, "The kingdom of heaven is like the grape harvest. The owner of a large vineyard went out early and hired workers to harvest his grapes, promising each a denarius for a day's labor.

"He needed to bring the harvest in quickly so about nine in the morning, he brought in additional workers. At noon, he found more workers. At three, he hired an additional crew; and, finally, at five in the evening, when only a few hours of daylight remained, he found more men to work in his vineyard.

"As the sun was setting, the men lined up to receive their wages, beginning with those who were hired last. Each man received the same pay, one denarius. Those who had worked the entire day were dissatisfied with their pay and voiced their complaint.

"But the owner of the vineyard had a good response. 'You received exactly the wage I promised. You were not cheated. If God puts it in my heart to be generous, I can do that. After all, it is my money.'

"The kingdom of my Father is totally inclusive—men, women, children, Jews, and non-Jews. Citizenship is given, not earned. Those who think they deserve a position of importance in this kingdom will most likely be disappointed. Remember, I have said to you, 'The meek will inherit. The last will be first, and the first will be last.'"

The fire burned down to coals. Each man quietly spread his cloak on the ground. Wrapped in individual thoughts, they all slept. But Jesus remained by the smoldering coals, praying for his closest friends, praying that the Holy Spirit would build them up and equip them for the days ahead.

The date palms of Jericho gently swayed in the morning breeze, and the fresh scent of balsam filled the air. Blind Bartimaeus kept a firm hand on his nephew's shoulder as they walked to his usual spot, close to road that passed Herod's old winter palace. This wide road ran through Jericho and on to Jerusalem. Before each major feast, it filled with generous pilgrims.

Bartimaeus loved the seasons of the Lord when Jews from every corner of the world found their way to Jerusalem, often through Jericho. Then, through his ears, his world grew bigger than his own darkness. Sitting by the road, he heard stories from all over the nation, even from distant lands. This year, he heard the name of a rabbi, Jesus from Nazareth. Everyone had a story to tell about this amazing teacher. He was called the Healer! The blind, the lame, even lepers regained their health when he spoke. Rabbi Jesus had called a dead man back to life! It was so amazing! With each story and each passing conversation, hope began to grow in the beggar's heart. This rabbi could be none other than the legendary righteous descendant of David. He would reestablish both the people and the nation of Israel.

Relying heavily on his unimpaired senses, Bartimaeus studied the rhythm of the road. The crowds flowed in eager waves. When their singing and shouting along with the shuffle of feet died down, the beggar knew there was now a little space between groups of travelers. Then the beggar would relax and dream about meeting the healer. When the chatter picked up and the dusty ground vibrated with the footfalls of the crowd, blind Bartimataeus would extend his bowl and lean forward to hear snatches of conversations as the people passed.

"Rabbi Jesus is traveling with his men from Capernaum."

"He has healed every person on this route, even lepers!"

"This Passover, the people are going to make him king! I'm sure of it."

Bartimaeus began to stop people and ask, "Is this the group from Capernaum? Are you from Capernaum?"

Finally, after asking again and again, a young boy replied, "I'm from Capernaum. Yes, Jesus is walking with us."

Bartimaeus then called out, "Rabbi Jesus, Son of David, have mercy on me!" He called desperately, loudly, repeatedly.

Those who were walking in front of the people from Capernaum rudely answered him. "Be quiet, old man."

But Bartimaeus shouted all the more, "Promised One, Seed of David, have mercy on me!"

Jesus heard the insistent calling of his name. Over the heads of his disciples and the other people who pressed to be close to him, he could not see Bartimaeus, squatted, extending his beggar's bowl.

Above the edge of the road, the Holy Spirit hovered, illuminating the desperate man.

Responding to the heavenly sign, Jesus stopped and, directing his disciples, requested that the man be brought to him. When he came near, clutching Philip's robe so he would know the way, Jesus asked him, "What do you want me to do for you?"

"I want to see," he replied.

Jesus then said to him, "Your faith is great. Receive your healing." Immediately, Bartimaeus could see, and he followed Jesus, loudly praising God. When all the people saw it, another miraculous story traveled in both directions along the road to Jerusalem. Messianic excitement flowed the length of the highway.

In a government building near the old palace complex, Zacchaeus, the chief tax collector for the city of Jericho, focused on the document before him. Abruptly, a minor tax official hurried into his office.

Zacchaeus looked up, acknowledging his subordinate as the man placed a bag of coins on the table.

"I know I have arrived late," the man apologized. "The road is unbelievably crowded. I could only move at the speed of those around me. Somehow, I got caught among the citizens of Capernaum. The famous Rabbi Jesus is with them. On this trip to Jerusalem, he has healed lepers. He just healed the blind beggar named Bartimaeus!"

"Jesus!" Zacchaeus exclaimed as he dropped the report he had been working on.

"Yes," the subordinate replied, pushing the bag of coins closer to his superior. "That is the reason that I could not get this to you before you began this report."

"Jesus!" Zacchaeus exclaimed again. The senior tax collector for Jericho did not even glance at the money. He just left it on the table. Moving quickly as he spoke, Zacchaeus headed for the door. "I have heard so much about the man. I met him once, several years ago, when Matthew of Capernaum held a banquet." Running out of his office, Zacchaeus finished by saying to himself, "How I have longed to hear him again."

Arriving at the road that went through the city, Zacchaeus realized his subordinate had not exaggerated the size and the excitement of the crowd. "Where are you from?" Zacchaeus tried to get the attention of anyone passing by the side of the road.

For the most part, he was ignored, actually overlooked for he was as short as a child.

Zacchaeus tried again, this time stepping onto the road, forcing a man to stop and respond.

"Yes, we are from Capernaum."

"Jesus? Where is Jesus?" Zacchaeus demanded.

"Ahead," the man answered.

"How far? Zacchaeus demanded.

The man shrugged. "He's probably close to the spring in the center of town."

Zacchaeus did not wait to hear more. He stepped off the road and broke into a run. Sprinting along side streets and cutting through gardens, the little man arrived at the spring ahead of the pack that surrounded Jesus. Looking at that crowd of full-sized men and women, he knew he needed to get above them. So he climbed a sycamore tree. Its sturdy branches hung over the road, allowing the short man an unobstructed view in every direction.

He could see the next wave of Passover pilgrims approaching, children chasing each other, women bunched together and carrying baskets of food, and strong broad-shouldered men walking purposefully in the center of the road.

Zacchaeus silently congratulated himself. "Clever and shrewd, that is how I go through life. That is the reason I am the chief tax collector for the city of Jericho, and that is the reason I am now sitting above the crowd, waiting to see Jesus pass by."

When Jesus walked under the tree, he stopped.

The men around him also stopped. They looked at each other, asking with their eyes, What is happening? Why aren't we walking?

Jesus looked up into the overhanging branches. Everyone around Jesus also looked up.

Matthew exclaimed, "Zacchaeus, my friend, what are you doing in that tree?"

The rest of the disciples laughed. There was a comical quality to the moment. Each one remembered the pompous little man who had come to the banquet Matthew had held for Jesus a few years earlier. Now, to see him in a tree!

Jesus held up a restraining hand.

Obediently, his disciples stowed their laughter and waited to see what would happen next.

Jesus extended his hand. "Zacchaeus, come down so I can talk with you. Really, I have much to say. May I stay at your house today?"

So the little man came down at once. On the ground, he straightened his robe and adjusted his turban. Then Zacchaeus bowed and offered him the hospitality of his home.

From the onlookers, there was a sudden swell of chatter. All the people began to comment, "Jesus is going to be the guest of a sinner."

Instinctively, the disciples tightened their circle, separating Jesus and Zachaeus from the people. Within that circle, Zacchaeus stood up. At first, he puffed up, ready to use his authority to demand respect. Then his eyes locked with the sinless eyes of Jesus, and, at that moment, the Holy Spirit revealed to the chief tax collector his own sinfulness.

For a moment, Zacchaeus felt like he could not breathe. In his mind, he saw face after face, distressed over the amount of money he had demanded. He felt such compassion for those people, such remorse over the wrongs he had done to them. Tears formed in his eyes, and he said, "Rabbi Jesus, I must make right many wrongs! I will give half of my possessions to the poor, and those I have cheated, I will pay back four times the amount."

Jesus said to him and to those standing nearby who were so ready to call Zacchaeus a traitor, "This day, salvation has come to the household of Zacchaeus. He is a true son of Abraham. So end your criticisms, for the Son of Man came to seek and to save even tax collectors."

"Dates?" Zacchaeus offered Jesus a plate of the famous Jericho dates. "Cuza, the finance minister for your king, was recently at the market. He was negotiating for these very dates, but I slipped in over his bid. So for this Passover, old Antipas will have to make due with fruit of slightly lesser quality."

Jesus took a date and commented, "I'm sure my friend Cuza holds no hard feelings." Then Jesus leaned back into the cushions, and he began to teach. "When I was a young boy, Herod the Great died. His sons hurried to Rome because kingship could not just be inherited. It had to be bestowed by the emperor. With my kingdom, it is similar. Another is claiming my throne; therefore, I must return to my Father, the ruler of the universe, with evidence that I should become the ruler of Earth."

Around the table, the disciples and other guests nodded their heads, indicating understanding. Everyone had heard how the sons of Herod had each presented their case to the emperor. They knew that the kingdom had been divided and a section given to each.

Jesus then said, "This is also the pattern of my kingdom. I must return to my Father in heaven to receive my crown. Unlike recent history in our nation, my kingdom will not be divided. I will receive all or nothing. Like the sons of Herod, I am leaving my servants with valuable assignments, and when I return, there will be rewards for those who have been faithful and punishments for those who have been disloyal."

"Rabbi?" Zacchaeus asked. "Will you go to Rome to receive your crown?"

"My crown can only be given by God. I must go to him. Please realize I am speaking of my kingdom in terms that you understand. I am not setting up a kingdom like the Empire of Rome. My kingdom begins in the heart and mind of each person. I am presenting a new way to govern. Mine is a government without physical boundaries. In my kingdom, gold and silver are so commonplace that locked storehouses are unnecessary. My greatest treasure is the allegiance of my citizens. I know you expect the Messiah to form an army. So be assured, I am building my army each day. This army conquers by serving each other from the heart. This army fights by surrendering." Jesus paused. He thoughtfully looked past all the confused and attentive faces.

Then he quietly added, "I know I will need to show you how to participate in this kingdom." There was another long pause. "I will show you."

Jesus dropped his head and said no more. Around him, the conversations began with cautious whispers and gradually grew into loud speculative buzzing. Each mind ignored the phrases it did not understand. Each heart embellished its Messianic dreams. Finally, finally, the words of the prophets would be fulfilled.

Comfortably resting on a deep cushion, Judas pondered each word Jesus had spoken and every miracle he had seen. In his mind, the words of Jesus had to mean that he would soon remove the Romans and take over the government of Israel. He would put the Temple establishment in its place.

Judas chuckled to himself as he imagined the Temple guard approaching Jesus to arrest him. In his mind, he saw the guard fall back, turn, and flee. Those men would be unable to touch Jesus. His power was far greater than theirs. Judas nodded his head. Now, he understood why Jesus said that his army would not fight. They would not need to fight. Every force would just surrender to Jesus.

For Judas, this vivid fantasy was more delicious than any food the chief tax collector of Jericho could offer.

Chapter 6

At Bethany before Passover

Six days before the Passover, Jesus came to Bethany, where Lazarus lived, whom Jesus had raised from the dead. Here a dinner was given in Jesus' honor. Martha served, while Lazarus was among those reclining at the table with him.

—John 12:1–2

Mary sat with her eyes properly downcast as Simon, her brother-in-law, began his usual lecture. She was required to be present, and she knew that nothing other than her silence could help her husband through this ordeal.

Simon cleared his throat. He looked up from studying the accounting from the perfume shop. Then, in a serious tone, he said, "Jonathan, you and Mary have much to learn about business." He glanced again at the bottom line. "You did make a small profit, and you did manage to repay the money I lent so you could own your own business, but your profit should have been much larger." Simon studied the ledger again. "Burial spices—your markup should be greater."

Jonathan protested, "People need burial spices at the worst moment of their lives. Many of those people are not wealthy. The wealthy seem to live forever while the poor die young. I will not overcharge grieving people."

"You're too soft," Simon gruffly muttered. Simon looked again at the ledger. "I see you get a good price for healing balm."

Jonathan chuckled. "Pilate and his wife buy most of my balm, and I charge them top price. Every time they are in the city, soldiers from the fort come to make their purchase."

Simon added his own chuckle to Jonathan's. "Yes, always charge the Romans more than we charge our own people. That is good business in Jerusalem."

Simon moved to another section of the ledger, household expenses. "You and Mary spend a lot on food," Jonathan's older brother observed. Slowly shaking his head, he cautioned, "A few coins saved is like money earned."

"There are some needy families. They have a lot of children and not enough food," Jonathan explained. "Also when Jesus and his men are in the city, Mary likes to serve them."

"Will you allow your wife to feed so many irresponsible people that she puts you in a debtor's prison?"

Jonathan hotly responded, "Simon, you know that is an exaggeration. I owe nothing."

"And you have practically nothing!" Simon exclaimed. "You should be lending money. At the very least, you should be leaving some silver with the bankers so they can invest it."

"My inventory has value." Jonathan shoved his inventory under his brother's nose. "Look at this list—frankincense, myrrh, balsam, spikenard, aloe, rue, rosemary, cinnamon, and much more. I have rare fragrances that come from all over the world. My shelves are filled with beautiful alabaster containers. They are all imported."

Simon looked his younger brother in the eye. "Are you getting much business from the Upper City where the wealthy live?"

"My shop is in the shadow of the Temple," Jonathan answered, "maybe a little too close to the Roman fortress. I don't think the wealthy have found my shop."

"Then we need to get the word out. I have friends who have friends. I will tell them there are bargains to be found at your shop. But don't give anyone a real bargain. Just make each man feel good about his purchase."

Simon thought a moment. Then he said, "Jesus and his men have come for Passover. They are staying with your brother, Lazarus." He nodded toward Mary as he spoke. "I have already sent the first invitations. Everyone knows I am making a banquet to honor Lazarus who was dead and now lives and also to honor Jesus who called him back from the Place of the Dead. My friends from Jerusalem want to question Jesus about the event." Turning back to Jonathan, he offered, "I will be sure to mention your perfume shop in casual conversation. It will be a good afternoon." Then returning to Mary, Simon said, "Your sister Martha is taking charge of this meal. There isn't a better hostess in all of Bethany." Pointedly, he added, "I know your sister is glad you are here at this time. Your assistance will be invaluable to her."

Mary found her voice and replied sharply, "My sister does well with or without me."

Simon seemed irritated by the tone of Mary's voice so he shot back, "It is best for the women of this family to keep busy. Problems develop when women have time on their hands. Since you and Jonathan are staying in my home for the next eight days, I expect to see you helping with the banquet. My wife will also be assisting with the cooking and purchasing."

Mary lifted her eyes, boldly challenging the head of her husband's family with her direct gaze. "The only thing that interests me about your banquet is the fact that Jesus will be present. He left quickly after calling my brother back to life. In all the excitement, I did not get to properly thank him."

Mary rose from her cushion, straight and defiant. "Have you properly thanked him for healing your skin condition? Leprosy?"

"Don't say that word!" Simon jumped to his feet. "Outside of this family, no one must know!"

"This banquet, it isn't much of a thank-you. It won't cost much. But I guess it will make Jesus feel good." Mary felt courage rising so she continued in a taunting tone. "Let me see. Your advice was to never really give anything of value. Don't dip into the profits. Just offer some phony recognition."

Jonathan could see the tension escalating between his wife and his brother. Quickly, he scooped up his financial records. He grabbed Mary by the elbow, effectively steering her out of the room.

Simon called after them, "You need to be a more submissive wife, interested in your husband's success! You know, women can be divorced for not bridling their tongues."

Longinus heard angry voices in the corridor outside his office.

An agitated Jewish voice demanded, "What are you going to do about the bandits operating at the city gates?"

Another gruff voice exploded, "We were at the Fish Gate transacting business when we were attacked! At the gate, we were attacked! There wasn't a Jewish guard or a Roman soldier in sight!"

Longinus pushed through the heavy curtains that covered his doorway. He took two decisive steps and then confronted the complaining men. One man he recognized immediately, Joseph of Arimathea. His purple cloak was torn. Dirt and blood splattered his clothing. The other man was older. He wore the turban of a trader, and a long sword hung from his belt. There was strength in that man, like the strength of a steady pack animal.

Joseph addressed the commander of the Antonio Fortress first. "You know me. We have had several occasions to share a meal."

Longinus nodded. "I remember you."

"This is Toma of Bethlehem, a master merchant and caravanner. Early this morning, we were at the Fish Gate. I was negotiating a purchase when suddenly we were attacked. Bandits! Their leader got in my face. With his short sword, he cut the bag of coins off of my belt."

"You saw his face?" Longinus eagerly asked.

"I know his name," Toma broke in. "I used to pay him protection money, but he no longer honors those agreements. It was Barabbas with his band of cutthroats."

Joseph forced himself back into the conversation. "Two of my servants were wounded. One may not live."

"My drovers are armed, and they put up a good fight," Toma added information. "I lost a strong camel. They took mostly wineskins and other food products." Toma stepped back, shaking his gray head as he muttered, "I cannot believe that Jewish men would rob their own, and then I would have to go to the Romans for help. At the gates of Jerusalem! At the gates of Jerusalem!"

"Then what happened?" Longinus pressed for more information.

Joseph replied, "Toma's men chased the bandits. But at the stone quarry, they seemed to melt into the rocks."

Thoughtfully, Longinus nodded his head. "I will find that man, Barabbas, along with his followers. I expect to have him in my prison before your sacred feast begins. Leave information with my assistant. I will summon you to verify that I have apprehended the right man."

As Joseph and Toma exited the fortress, Toma was worriedly muttering again, "Should one more Jewish man die on a Roman cross because I am a witness against him?" The thought clearly concerned him.

It was late afternoon on the sixth day of the week. Sabbath was fast approaching. Mary stood with her sister, Martha, surveying the preparations they had made for the banquet that would take place tomorrow afternoon.

"The tables are set, the cushions laid." Martha turned toward the entrance. "We have water for hand washing."

"What about perfumed oil?" Mary asked. "Is Simon offering that courtesy to his guests, especially his honored guests?"

Martha pursed her lips together before responding, "Simon is a cheap host!"

Mary's eyes opened wide. She had never heard her older sister speak so critically of an important man in the community.

Martha continued, "He did not want to spend more than a day's wages on this event. I had to shame the man into giving me more than one goat from his flock. If he had not had his own wine, we could not have purchased any."

"You have plenty of fresh bread and sweet honey cakes," Mary consoled.

"Since all the grains and all the yeast must be removed from the house this week, his wife and I emptied his storage bins," Martha announced. With a little satisfaction, she added, "I cooked every lentil, every dried bean and seasoned them well. His storage area for dried foods is now so clean that it is ready for the traditional search on the eve of Passover."

Mary smiled a little as she responded, "I know you did a thorough job. The meal will be wonderful. Jesus and his men will appreciate all you have done."

Martha let out a small weary sigh. "We are finished until tomorrow afternoon. All we have to do then is place the food on the tables and then leave the men to help themselves. I have arranged for two servants to come after sundown to clean up."

Mary gave an appreciative nod. Her sister always thought of everything.

As the sisters left the banquet area, Mary lingered in the entrance. It bothered her that Simon was not offering anything of real value to Jesus, his honored guest. In this meal, there was no element of sacrifice. There was no recognition that Jesus was obviously the Messiah, the future King of the Jews. She thought about the gift she had brought from the storeroom of their perfume shop, an alabaster box containing all the nard they owned. She had planned to give it to Jesus, to kneel at his feet, and place it in his hands. She knew he would thank her, but then he would just pass it over to Judas. That disciple would sell it, adding the money to their treasury—it seemed too much like a business transaction.

Mary's heart longed for more. She wanted to publically honor Jesus. She wanted to do something personal, something that would be so over the top that everyone would recognize it as an act of devotion usually reserved for the coronation of ancient kings.

It was late afternoon. Simon stood at the door of his banquet room, greeting each guest, overseeing the hand washing. He quickly swept the room with his eyes. All were present, each man reclining in his place at the low tables. Jesus rested in the most honored position, to the right of the host's seat. Lazarus was stretched out on the left side of the host. Simon gave a satisfied nod. Dramatically, he turned and shut the door to the room. It was the signal for the banquet to begin.

Immediately, Martha rushed forward and placed a large loaf of bread in Simon's hands. Mary brought the wine jug to the table. She began with Jesus, filling his stone cup until it flowed over onto the table covering. Their eyes met, and Mary thought her heart would explode with adoration and thankfulness.

Jesus nodded and smiled at her. He knew what she was feeling. He understood the symbolism of the overflowing cup.

Mary then moved quickly from man to man, filling each cup with watered wine.

As soon as the last cup was filled, Simon lifted the loaf of bread. He broke it into two equal pieces, and then began chanting the traditional blessing, "Blessed are you, O Lord our God, Ruler of the Universe, who gives us bread from the earth."

Simon broke off a small piece of bread. He tasted it. Then he gave the half in his right hand to Jesus and the half in his left hand to Lazarus. Each man broke off a bite-sized piece, eating it appreciatively. Then each man passed his half to the person reclining beside them. So the first bite of bread circulated in both directions from the host to the honorees, to the other guests.

Simon then raised his cup, a goblet carved from translucent alabaster. The honorees responded by raising their stone goblets. The other men then lifted their goblets as Simon chanted the traditional prayer, "Blessed are you, O Lord our God, Ruler of the Universe, who brings forth grapes from the vine."

Simon sipped from his cup. Jesus and Lazarus sipped from their cups. The other guests then drank from their cups.

As soon as the cups were placed on the table again, Martha and Mary swooped into the room, arms laden with food—platters, bowls, baskets, the products of Martha's culinary skills.

Most of the men ignored the women. This service was expected. Cooking, serving, and childbearing, those were the duties of women. But each time either Mary or Martha set a dish close to Jesus, he remarked, "This looks wonderful! I can't wait to taste it! Martha, you are an amazing cook! Thank you, Mary." Every comment was personal, every word genuine.

When the banquet had been spread, Mary and Martha withdrew, their tasks complete. Martha wearily walked to the back of the cooking area to soak her feet in a basin of cool water. Mary hurried to her room to fetch the gift she had brought for Jesus.

In the banquet hall, thirty men ate with their fingers, dipping their bread into spiced beans and savory stew. Lazarus shared his disappointingly limited memories of death. Simon promoted Jonathan's perfume shop. One of Simon's friends smugly commented to Matthew, "You don't get a feast like this one very often."

And Matthew replied, "Zacchaeus, the tax collector at Jericho, laid a magnificent banquet for us just a few days ago. The wine was rich. The dates and figs were plump and delicious." Matthew quickly glanced at the food that had been laid out for the men. "No Jericho dates today!"

"You ate in the home of a tax collector!" the man exclaimed.

Before Matthew could inform Simon's friend that he was a former tax collector, Jesus began a story. "*Two men went up to the temple to pray, one a Pharisee and the other a tax collector. The Pharisee stood up and prayed about himself: 'God, I thank you that I am not like other people—robbers, evildoers, adulterers—or even like this tax collector. I fast twice a week and give a tenth of all I get.'*

"*But the tax collector stood at a distance. He would not even look up to heaven, but beat his breast and said, 'God, have mercy on me, a sinner.'*

"*I tell you that this man, rather than the other, went home justified before God. For everyone who exalts themselves will be humbled, and those who humble themselves will be exalted.*"[1]

The curtain that separated the banquet room from the cooking area moved a little. No one noticed.

Mary slipped into the room, moving quietly along the wall, behind the reclining men. She did not glance around. Her eyes were on the guest of honor. Arriving at the feet of Jesus, she dropped to her knees. With one quick movement, she broke the thin stem of alabaster that sealed the pint-sized container.

Heavy and sweet, the aroma slowly drifted through the banquet hall.

One-by-one, the men looked up. Nostrils flared. Eyes widened.

Jonathan softly gasped, "Mary? Not now!"

Lazarus and Simon echoed, "Mary! What are you doing?"

Simon sat up and leaned over to sternly direct his sister-in-law. "Mary! Go back to your room."

Her brother, Lazarus, sat up and added his whispered directive, "You are out of place. Leave quickly!"

But Mary ignored them.

Shocked silence gave way to audible gasps. Her name was whispered throughout the room, "Mary, the sister of Lazarus."

"Mary, the wife of Jonathan the perfumer." Every eye was on this unbelievably brash woman.

They watched as tears fell from Mary's downcast eyes. They dripped onto the cushion where Jesus reclined. Then with a trembling hand, Mary poured the expensive perfume on Jesus's feet. Her modest mantel slipped from her head and dropped to the floor, allowing Mary's long dark hair to cascade freely around the feet of Jesus. Grabbing a handful of that hair, she liberally smeared the heavy oil into his skin with her hair. And the house was filled with fragrance.

Jonathan stood to remove his wife from the banquet hall, but Jesus caught his eye and mouthed, "No."

Jonathan returned to his place beside Lazarus.

Then Mary stood and moved closer to the table. She tilted the alabaster box again, pouring the remainder of the oil onto Jesus's hair. She used her free hand to cover his forehead and channel the oil away from his eyes. It ran along his beard and dripped onto his white robe. When the container was empty, she placed it on the floor and used both hands to massage the oil into Jesus's hair and beard. The linen fibers of his robe and even his undergarments absorbed the escaping droplets.

"A year's wages," Matthew whispered to Judas.

And Judas responded by protesting loudly. "This perfume is worth a year's wages. It should have been sold and the proceeds given to the poor!"

Peter quickly exchanged glances with his brother, Andrew. Both men knew that Judas cared little about the plight of the poor. His interest was in the contents of their community money bag because he was a thief.

More men found their voices.

"This is inappropriate!"

"So extravagant!"

"So wasteful!" Simon muttered.

Mary had dropped to her knees again, and she remained there, trembling and overcome with emotion.

"Leave her alone," Jesus replied to the critical men in the room. Then Jesus stood. Oil was still dripping from the ends of his hair and his beard. His fierce eyes swept the room, stopping at Judas who had made the loudest objection. Jesus countered his objection by saying, "It was the plan of my Father that this perfume would be applied at my burial. That time is quickly approaching."

Jesus then moved his gaze to Simon and then back to Judas. *"You will always have the poor among you, but you will not always have me."*[2]

Then he placed both hands on Mary's perfume-drenched hair. He bent over and kissed the top of her head. Coming back to his full height, Jesus swept the room with determined eyes. *"Truly I tell you, wherever this gospel is preached throughout the world, what she has done will also be told, in memory of her."*[3]

Judas felt the sting of public rebuke. In his mind, resentment exploded. This woman was now receiving public praise because she had moved forward with an act of anointing that was so extravagant that the wealthiest men in the nation would consider it an excess.

Quietly, Judas slipped out of the room, out of the house. On the road just beyond the gate, a crowd was gathering. All around, he heard, "Rabbi Jesus."

"Messiah!"

"Crown him king!"

Vexed by the recent outlandish scene, Judas pushed through the excited people. Alone on the road to Jerusalem, he calmed down and considered recent events. Jesus had accepted this royal anointing. It would only take a small incident to push him into accepting the mandate of the people.

A voice in his head suggested, Betray Jesus to the chief priests.

Judas looked around for the voice that had spoken, but he seemed to be alone.

Again, he heard, Betray your master to the chief priests. The people will rise up with a crown. Jesus will then accept the crown. And, you, like Mary, will be praised for taking such a bold step.

Judas continued to consider the idea. He remembered the times when men had tried to stone Jesus. He remembered when the Temple guards could not arrest him. No one can harm Jesus. That voice in his head was very insistent.

By the side of the road, shadowing every step that Judas took, Satan continued to persuade. "You can demand money for information. You can have silver in your hand while you watch Jesus escape. You will become the driving force behind his kingship. For that, Jesus will publically praise you. He should give you a very important position in his kingdom."

It was night, the beginning of the first day of the week, when Judas entered the city. First, he went to see the captain of the Temple guard. Together, they went to a magnificent home in the Upper City.

Judas waited in a hallway. He heard other important men arrive. Quiet conferring voices leaked through the heavy draperies.

After awhile, the captain of the Temple guard returned. He swept aside the curtains, ushering Judas into a spacious meeting room. All conversations stopped. The most influential men in the nation paused to see the man who would come through the entry.

Sensing that he was the focus of attention, Judas hesitated in the doorway. Initially, his instincts shouted, "Flee!"

But before his legs could move, another voice filled his head. "Go on," Satan whispered. "Do what needs to be done. Without your assistance, Jesus will never step into his Messianic role. Create the situation that will create the King of the Jews, the new ruler of Israel. Create the scenario that will make you more important than the men you are now meeting with."

Then Judas found his voice and asked, "How much will you give me if I lead your men to Jesus? I know where he stays at night, and I can take you to him when the crowds are asleep in their homes."

"Where is he staying now?" the captain of the Temple guard asked.

Judas replied. "For now, he is spending each night in the home of Lazarus in Bethany."

Caiaphas cautioned, "We cannot invade that man's home and take Jesus quietly. Lazarus has servants. He has important friends."

Judas quickly offered, "I do not expect Jesus to stay there for many days. He prefers lonely places where he can pray for most of the night, undisturbed."

Caiaphas asked, "Can you send a message to us when he moves to a secluded place?"

"Well…," Judas deliberately hesitated.

The captain of the Temple guard spoke up. "If I were in your position, I would want to see the silver."

"Yes, I understand your hesitation," Annas agreed as he walked over to a large wooden chest. The former high priest opened it.

Judas nearly choked when he saw the stacks of silver coins within that chest.

Caiaphas quietly asked again, "Can you send us a message when he moves to spend the night in a secluded place?"

Annas quickly inserted, "After the days of Passover and Unleavened Bread."

Caiaphas agreed, "Yes, when many have left this city and returned to their own homes, it will be a better time."

Judas was listening, but he could hardly pull his eyes away from the stacks of coins in the open chest. When the men stopped talking, Judas took a deep breath and looked back into the eyes of Caiaphas, the high priest. "What do you want with Rabbi Jesus?"

Caiaphas answered, "We want to question him privately."

Annas stepped up. "The crowds make it impossible for us to have a meaningful conversation."

Judas glanced at the silver again. "You would pay this much for a conversation?"

Caiaphas rejoined, "Do you believe your master is the Messiah?"

"Yes," Judas answered with conviction.

"Before we can make such a statement, we must be sure," Annas stated.

Another priest moved into the conversation. "We must ask him questions. We must hear from witnesses, and he must show us how he does the amazing things we have heard about."

"You can't hurt him!" It was both a request and a statement of faith from Judas.

"Hurt him?" Caiaphas shook his head negatively.

Once more, Judas felt pulled to look inside the open chest—so much silver! Slowly, Judas nodded in the affirmative. He took the money bag from his belt and held it open.

So they counted out thirty silver coins. Five coins they dropped in his bag. The rest, they set aside, payment for completion of the job.

With a satisfied nod, Judas closed his moneybag and reattached it to his belt. The captain of the Temple guard escorted him to the street.

Night had fallen. He walked to the home of his parents in the city.

Chapter 7

A Royal Entrance

The next day the great crowd that had come for the festival heard that Jesus was on his way to Jerusalem. They took palm branches and went out to meet him, shouting, "Hosanna!"

—John 12:12–13

Martha was serving Jesus. Moving from man to man, she passed out freshly baked cakes, urging each to eat more so there would be no waste when she had to remove all the leaven and flour products from her storage area later that week.

As the meal was ending, Judas casually strode through the gate, onto the estate that belonged to Lazarus of Bethany. He sat down next to Matthew, accepting food from Martha. Offering an answer to the question in Matthew's eyes, he said, "I went to visit my parents."

Jesus glanced up over his cup of water. His eyes met with the eyes of his wandering disciple. Judas's pupils were pools of blackness, and from their dark depths, demons named Greed and Self-promotion glared back at their Creator. Immediately, Jesus knew. Judas had had an encounter on the road and was now as demonized as many he had delivered.

For a moment, Jesus studied the situation. He knew that Judas was not totally under the control of Satan. Greed and Self-promotion had built fortified strongholds in his mind, but he could still break free. It was a matter of choice.

Jesus then pushed the remainder of his food away. He stood up and began teaching. "This morning, I want to consider a portion from the story of Job." From memory, Jesus quoted, *"My troubled thoughts prompt me to answer because I am greatly disturbed."*[1]

As he spoke, Jesus fixed his eyes on Judas.

The demons within trembled. Judas responded to their discomfort by looking away from Jesus and shifting his position frequently.

"The joy of the godless lasts but a moment."[2] Gathered around their master, the other eleven hung on every word and nodded in eager agreement. Lazarus stood and moved so he sat behind his attentive companions. Martha placed her bread basket on a bench and then sat a little removed from the men so she could hear this teaching. To hear the scriptures quoted so beautifully and flawlessly moved each heart, except the heart of Judas.

Judas got up again and walked farther behind the group, away from the direct gaze of Jesus. There, he paced through the remainder of the teaching.

Though evil is sweet in his mouth and he hides it under his tongue, though he cannot bear to let it go and lets it linger in his mouth, yet his food will turn sour in his stomach; it will become the venom of serpents within him. He will spit out the riches he swallowed; God will make his stomach vomit them up.[3] *What he toiled for he must give back uneaten; he will not enjoy the profit from his trading.*[4]

Jesus paused and then added his own words. "For, he has betrayed a friend. Yes, he has sold his loyalty."[5]

The bag with five pieces of silver weighed heavily on the mind of Judas. It tugged at the belt around his waist. A voice in his mind said, Jesus knows, but it is all right. If he didn't want you to continue with your plan, he would openly rebuke you. This is just a general teaching. It is not directed toward you.

"*The heavens will expose his guilt; the earth will rise up against him…Such is the fate God allots the wicked.*"[5] As he concluded his teaching, Jesus brushed several tears from his eyes.

Lazarus came forward to thank Jesus for beginning the day on his estate with scripture. Before offering a manly embrace, he paused and commented, "My sister was a little extravagant when she anointed you. The fragrance is as strong today as it was yesterday."

Jesus responded, "Her actions were completely in line with the will of my Father. Do not chide her and do not allow Simon to berate her." Jesus then smiled. "Every breath I take reminds me of Mary's selfless devotion. For me, it will be a source of personal comfort during this Passover season."

As Lazarus threw his arms around Jesus's shoulders, he asked, "What are your plans for the day?"

"We are leaving for the Temple shortly," Jesus answered. "But we will return to your gracious home before sunset."

"I will go with you, and Martha will have a meal waiting when we return," Lazarus replied.

In the Antonio Fortress, Pilate joined Longinus in his quarters. "What is your assessment of the city on this occasion?"

Longinus signaled that drink should be offered to the governor. Then he answered, "The Jews are only in the preliminary phase of this celebration. The city seems filled to capacity, but more are coming. Every road that leads into the city is clogged with pilgrims. Every house has taken in guests. Every square cubit of land sports a campsite."

"Water?" Pilate asked.

"The new aqueduct from Bethlehem to this city is flowing unobstructed. There seems to be adequate water for all," Longinus replied.

"Is anyone from the Temple complaining?" Pilate asked with an undertone of contempt.

"Not a word," Longinus answered as both men silently acknowledged the ironic fact that the Jewish leaders, who had lodged a serious complaint with the emperor when Pilate had confiscated Temple funds to build this aqueduct, now enjoyed the benefits.

"To this day, that black mark remains beside my name in the ledgers of Rome," Pilate growled.

Longinus passed a small scroll with a broken seal over to Pilate. "This communication from the emperor will not make you happy."

Pilate read it twice before he exploded. "Antipas, along with the Jewish leadership complained to the emperor about the gold shields in a Roman palace!" Pilate threw the scroll onto the table. "Antipas is just trying to get the emperor to extend his domain to include Judea. He doesn't care about those gold shields."

Flatly, Longinus stated, "The emperor demands that you remove the shields before this feast begins. I can move them to the temple of Roma and Augustus in Caesarea. They will be out of the city by morning."

"Do it," Pilate growled. "This is not a battle I am willing to engage." Then he added, "Speaking of battles, how goes the search for the bandits and their leader?"

"I have men hiding in wait, day and night. It is just a matter of time. Those bandits will return to the quarry," Longinus answered.

Pilate nodded. He turned to leave, speaking as he exited. "I want a quiet feast—no disturbances and no reports to Rome."

In the Upper City of Jerusalem, Caiaphas smoothed the many layers of his finely woven robes. At the entrance to his home he joined his father-in-law, Annas. Together, with many attendees, they began a slow pompous parade through the city toward the Sheep Gate. There, they would meet with the shepherds of Bethlehem to select the high priest's lamb from thousands of lambs that had been led to the market at the base of the Mount of Olives.

Leaving Bethany, Jesus with Lazarus and his twelve close disciples merged into the eager masses moving along the lower slope of the Mount of Olives toward Jerusalem. For Jesus, it was a surreal journey. Within that city, the high priest and his associates had already declared that he must be arrested on sight. The Holy Spirit had revealed that one of his twelve had accepted payment to facilitate his capture. Now, on this beautiful spring day, so aware of his Father's plans, he casually walked toward his death.

Excited chatter and Messianic speculation swirled around Jesus. The scent of Mary's anointing infused every breath, reminding him of her self-sacrificing love. As he strolled with his disciples, the words of the Psalmist rolled through his mind. *Many bulls surround me; strong bulls of Bashan encircle me.*[6] In his memory, he recalled the winter feast of Hanukkah. He could see the stern faces of the Temple guards who had tried to arrest him for healing on the Sabbath. He could see the demonically inspired hostility of the crowd that had tried to stone him for speaking truth. Surely, King David had written prophetically about the fate of the Messiah. *"Roaring lions that tear their prey open their mouths wide against me. I am poured out like water, and all my bones are out of joint. My heart has turned to wax; it has melted within me. My strength is dried up like a potsherd, and my tongue sticks to the roof of my mouth; you lay me in the dust of death."*[7] Feeling the heaviness of the things that lay ahead, Jesus walked a little slower than usual.

Coming over the crest of a hill near the village of Bethphage, the distant walls of Jerusalem popped into view. The city with its magnificent Temple was always a breathtaking and encouraging sight.

Jesus paused with his companions. He could see that the road below and beyond was filled with Passover pilgrims, excited and joyful. Beyond what most eyes saw, the Holy Spirit revealed to Jesus his angelic army. They lined the road, evenly spaced, standing in solemn attention. Michael, their commanding cherub, flew to hover over the center of the road. He raised his sword in silent salute. The rest of the angels followed the example of their commander, lifting their swords and leaving them high in the air.

Ophaniel flew to Jesus's side, bowing and saying, "We salute you and we remain ready for your command."

Responding to heaven's recognition, Jesus turned to James and Thomas. "Go quickly to the village down the road. As you enter, you will find a colt tied beside its mother. It will be a young animal, not yet trained to accept a rider. Untie it and bring it to me. If the owner questions you, tell him that Jesus the Master Rabbi needs it for this afternoon."

Judas quickly stepped forward. Reaching for his money bag, he asked, "Do you need money, a rental fee?"

Jesus waved him off.

Without hesitation, Thomas and James hurried into the village. They found the donkey exactly as Jesus had told them.

Straightway they untied the colt, coaxing the animal away from its mother.

"Wait! What are you doing?" The owner blocked their path.

James answered, "Our master, Rabbi Jesus of Nazareth is entering the city!"

Thomas added, "He is coming in through the Sheep Gate!"

Excitedly James announced, "Every king of Israel enters Jerusalem through the Sheep Gate, and when they come to take the throne peacefully, they come riding on a donkey! Jesus has requested the use of this animal."

The owner looked at both men, and then he looked at his untried donkey. "You might want another donkey, maybe the mother of this colt. This animal has never felt the weight of a man. It could be a very undignified entrance."

"No," James replied. "Our master wants this donkey. We will return it to you this evening."

Filled with anticipation, Thomas and James brought the young donkey to Jesus, meeting up with their traveling companions where the roads intersected.

Eagerly, Lazarus and the disciples gathered around. They threw their cloaks on the colt and helped Jesus mount.

Ophaniel, the angel that had been by Jesus since birth, kept a calming hand on the untried animal as Jesus settled in place. Then Lazarus picked up the reins and began the procession, guiding the donkey down the center of the road. The people cheered!

Lazarus shouted, "Make way for the One we have waited for. I was dead, and now, I am alive! Rabbi Jesus called my name, and I came out of my tomb."

Up and down the road, the words of Lazarus were passed from person to person.

The people responded by shouting, "Messiah, Son of David! Enter your city!"

Amazingly, the young donkey remained calm, steadily lifting her hooves like a well-trained animal. As Jesus rode along, people tossed their cloaks onto the road so the donkey's hooves would never touch the dirt.

This was a royal procession! This was how King David and his son Solomon had come into the city! The people picked up branches from the roadside and waved them. They danced and sang, "Look, he is the Anointed One. The favor of God is on his face."

Then, when Jesus and his disciples came near the place where the road goes down the Mount of Olives, they threw off their restraint and joined the people, praising God for all the miracles they had seen. Peter was the first to shout, *"Blessed is the king who comes in the name of the Lord!"*

John could be heard above everyone. *"Peace in heaven and glory in the highest!"*[8]

Around them, the people chanted, "He heals the sick! The lame walk and the blind see. Even the dead are brought back to life!"

"He enters the city in peace. Every knee will have to bow. No weapon can be raised against him," Judas confidently proclaimed a bloodless victory.

Messianic excitement moved from man to man up and down the road. This could be nothing but a royal procession. The people were stirred up to proclaim him king, but for all the wrong reasons. Only the angelic host knew the cost of his kingship, and they stood at attention along both sides of the road, numb with respect and horror.

A few Pharisees in the crowd pushed forward. Reaching the disciples, they shouted, "Teacher, stop your disciples! Silence these people. No man can receive such honors!"

"You cannot enter the city like this!"

"What about Rome?"

"The Messiah will not come from Nazareth!"

"This is blasphemy! It must cease immediately!"

Briefly, Jesus stopped his donkey. With astounding authority, he addressed his opposition. *"I tell you…if these people keep quiet, the stones will cry out."*[9] He looked down at the men who were so concerned about what the authorities might say. "Haven't you heard the words of Zechariah read in the synagogue? *'Say to the Daughter of Zion, "See, your king comes to you, gentle and riding on a donkey, on a colt, the foal of a donkey."'*"[11]

With his heels, Jesus then nudged his young donkey forward. The protesting Pharisees were quickly engulfed by the surging crowd.

More cloaks were thrown in the path of the donkey. Palm branches waved in Jesus's face. Everyone was shouting and reaching out to touch. Progress slowed. The crowd kept growing and pressing in.

Andrew, Philip, and Thaddaeus pushed ahead of Lazarus who was leading the donkey. They made a muscular wedge, breaking a path with their own bodies. The rest of the disciples flanked Jesus. Thomas and Judas became his rear guard.

Ahead, the chaos of the Passover sheep market spilled onto the road. At the same time, the excited crowd surged around Jesus, so as he approached Jerusalem, the road was blocked. He had to stop and wait. The Sheep Gate and the walls of city stood directly in front of him. When he saw the gate and the city walls rising majestically in front of him, he became overwhelmed with emotion. Choking back his tears, he loudly moaned, *"If you, even you, had only known on this day what would bring you peace—but now it is hidden from your eyes."*[11]

At that moment, the Holy Spirit opened the sky above the city, and Jesus saw the future—Roman troops, leaping flames, slaughtered people. Beautiful Jerusalem was being ravaged, leveled so not one stone remained on top of another. Every tree in the land was being cut down. Across the centuries, battles raged. Corpses stacked up like firewood. Future crusades and mechanized wars destroyed both the land and the descendants of Abraham.

Jesus moaned. The scenes broke his heart for his people. He had to warn them. Above the haggling of the vendors, above the voices of the Passover pilgrims, Jesus shouted, *"The days will come upon you when your enemies will build an embankment against you and encircle you and hem you in on every side. They will dash you to the ground, you and the children within your walls. They will not leave one stone on another, because you did not recognize the time of God's coming to you.*"[12]

No one stopped to listen. No one seemed to notice that a warning had been given.

Jesus then saw Michael fly down and use his sword to draw a line along the center of the road. People and animals moved quickly to the sides of the road, and Lazarus led the little donkey forward, toward the Sheep Market.

Approaching the gate, Jesus saw that another cheering procession was coming out of the city. The high priest with his important dignitaries led a joyful crowd of celebrating citizens out of the city, toward the Sheep Market.

For a moment, both processions stopped and stared at each other. Caiaphas and Annas could not believe their eyes. The very man they wanted to confront now confronted them! He was sitting on a donkey, the very picture of King David entering the city.

The people surged ahead of him and those that followed exclaimed, "Hosanna! This is the Son of David, the one we have waited for!"

"Blessed is the One who comes in the power of God!"

"Hosanna in the highest!"

"No! No!" Caiaphas protested.

Behind the high priest, his own procession became excited. They asked, "Who is this entering the city like a new king?"

The people from the countryside loudly replied, "This is Jesus, the rabbi from Nazareth in Galilee. Leading his donkey is Lazarus of Bethany, the man who was dead but now lives!"

Turning to look at those who were in his own procession, Annas could not believe his eyes. Both processions were merging. "No! No!" he shouted, "This is no king! This rabbi from Nazareth is not a descendant of David! You are being fooled. The dead do not live again!"

Once more, Michael swept his sword through the excited crowd that filled and blocked the entrance to the city.

The sea of humanity suddenly parted. Annas and Caiaphas fell back against the stone wall beside the gate, their eyes fixed on Jesus as he rode, erect and regal, through the Sheep Gate and into the city. Masses of energized people followed him. Within the city, the crowd fanned out into the narrow streets. They parted ways, hurrying to find places to sleep, food to eat, friends, and relatives. Each person had stories to tell, and every story was about Rabbi Jesus of Nazareth.

Huddled beside the great arched entrance to the city, the priests and Pharisees said to one another, "Something must be done. The whole city is clamoring to make him king."

Through clinched teeth, Caiaphas growled "Can we afford to wait until after the feast?"

Annas answered, "Look at the people. If we tried to take him now, those crowds would stone us." Annas then turned to the captain of the Temple guard who was with them. "Find your friend, that man who is one of his close followers. We must speak with him again."

After Jesus and his disciples had entered the city, they continued on to the Temple. Cheering crowds moved with them. The whole city was stirred.

Pilate glanced out the window, and then he turned to the centurion who commanded his garrison in Jerusalem. "There is a lot of commotion around the Temple this afternoon."

Longinus picked up a scroll and studied it briefly. "I requested a schedule of events for this feast." His finger ran across the lines of print and stopped. "The high priest is bringing his sacrificial lamb into the Temple this afternoon. It involves a procession with cheering and waving branches." He looked up at the governor of Judea, noting from the expression on his face that his answer had been satisfactory.

Chapter 8

Chaos in the Temple

*Jesus entered Jerusalem and went into the temple courts. He
looked around at everything, but since it was already late, he
went out to Bethany with the Twelve.*

—Mark 11:11

Just after sunrise Jesus, with his twelve, was on the road again, walking, listening to one excited disciple after another. Each man had his own view of yesterday's thrilling entrance. On one point, they all agreed. The ordinary people were ready to rise up and follow Jesus all the way to the throne of David. After that, each man had his own fantasy regarding his personal involvement and the role he would play in the new messianic government of Israel.

For each man, Jesus had the same reminder. "There are many prophecies regarding the Messiah. All must be fulfilled. I have told you before, I will die, and after three days, I will live again. We cannot just ignore the prophetic words that do not please us. The Messiah is first a suffering servant, and then he becomes a reigning king."

Peter was the first of the twelve to change the subject. "I'm hungry!"

Thomas commented, "If we hadn't left so early, I'm sure Martha would have at least offered us some bread."

James quickly defended Martha. "Martha is very busy today. She is cooking all the grains and dried foods in her food storage area so all can be eaten before the first day of Passover."

Ahead, Jesus spotted a fig tree. He pointed and all the disciples felt their hopes rise—figs for breakfast. Jesus quickened his pace and was the first to arrive at the tree.

Its leaves were full and green, a sign that the tree should have already produced fruit. Eagerly, Jesus began spreading the leaves apart, looking for fresh figs. But there were none. This tree had no fruit. Then he said to the tree, "You are so like the nation of Israel, lovely to look at, but producing no food for your own starving people as well as the starving throughout the world. At the touch of your Creator, fruit should have appeared, even fruit that was not yet in season."

Righteous indignation rushed through Jesus. For him, that tree became the leaders of his nation, the ones who were responsible for the spiritual nourishment of the people. He gave the tree a rough shake and pronounced, "No one will ever gather and eat from your branches again!"

His disciples heard this pronouncement, and they were surprised to hear that their master had such passion over a few figs.

Jesus then turned his back on the tree and continued down the road. His disciples followed. Their discussions had turned to food and convenient places to purchase a meal within the city.

Food! Mary, the mother of Jesus, made a mental list of the things she would need to purchase at the market. Four sons were with her, James, Jose, Jude, and Simon. Each man had a wife and children. Her family's campsite on the Jerusalem side of the Mount of Olives was now much larger than during her first years of marriage to Joseph.

"James?" Mary called her second son. "I want the oven set up, with a fire burning in it. Tell my daughters-in-law to be ready to bake bread when I return."

"Enos?" Mary called her eldest grandson. "Come with me to the market. I need a strong young man to carry our food supplies."

"Passover!" Peter's sister, Miriam, and her guest, Mary of Magdela, both said the word together with the same frantically overwhelmed tone. "We've only got three days to get every crumb out of the house, to purchase, and prepare food!" Like mirrored twins, both women quickly tied their loose hair with light scarves. Belting their robes, they grabbed cleaning rags and hand brushes. Together, they attacked the food storage bins, working while chanting the regulation that their mothers had taught them. *"Celebrate the Feast of Unleavened Bread, because it was on this very day that I brought your divisions out of Egypt. Celebrate this day as a lasting ordinance for the generations to come.[1] For seven days no yeast is to be found in your houses. And anyone…who eats anything with yeast in it must be cut off from the community of Israel. Wherever you live, you must eat unleavened bread."[2]*

About mid-morning, both women straightened up and surveyed their task. The food storage area was completely empty, swept, and washed. In another room, there was a small pile of dried beans and grains to be cooked and eaten before the day the lambs were to be slaughtered. Both women let out a satisfied sigh. Then Mary made a slightly sarcastic observation. "Today, every woman in Jerusalem is cleaning and cooking, but where are the men?"

"At the Temple, casually strolling through the courts," Miriam replied. "My husband and my son got out of here as quickly as possible this morning."

"Before you could ask them to help," Mary huffed.

"Cleaning and cooking is usually women's work," Miriam replied with resignation.

With a little fire in her eyes, Mary rejoined, "The command of the Lord is to clean out the yeast. It does not specify who does the cleaning. Maybe next year, I'll hire a couple of men."

Miriam laughed. "You can say that because you own a business. Men work for you and you pay them wages." Miriam sighed. "It's hard for me to imagine that kind of life."

Mary dropped her gaze and paused before admitting, "It can be a lonely life. Most women don't want to be my friend, and men don't like me either, except Jesus. If he had been with us today, he would have moved all the heavy bins before we could get our hands on them. That's just the way he is."

"I've heard so many stories." Miriam picked up a mixing bowl, poured in flour, oil, and water. Then she sat on the floor and began kneading the dough. Mary brought over a bag of dried beans and began sorting through them pulling out small stones and twigs. Miriam commented, "Jesus has visited in our home."

"Have you seen him with the crowds?" Mary asked. "Have you seen the miracles?"

"No," Miriam answered.

"I was a miracle," Mary quietly offered. "My face and my hand were scarred. I was an abused and divorced woman, so angry— Jesus changed all of that. Now, sometimes, I travel with him. I hear him teach. I bring sick women and children to him, and he heals them."

"Oh, I want to hear him! I want to see a miracle!" Miriam exclaimed.

There was a little challenge in Mary's tone as she suggested, "We could leave that dough to rise and put these beans in a bowl to soak. Probably, we could find Jesus teaching in the Temple. He comes for every feast."

"Could we? Should we?" Miriam gasped.

"Let's do it!" Mary answered decisively.

Approaching the beautiful double gated entrance to the Temple, the people on the road pressed together, a solid mass of humanity. Shoulder to shoulder, body against body, they funneled through the ornate arches. Jesus and his disciples moved with the current of the crowd.

Beside one gate, Ichabod awkwardly curled in his worn leather chair, holding his beggar's bowl. He listened to snatches of conversations and pleaded with his eyes.

Many dropped coins, silently thanking God that they had not been born so impaired. Following Jesus's directions, Matthew and Judas forced their way across the current of people to greet the beggar.

Judas dropped several coins into the beggar's bowl while Matthew spoke. "Our master says, 'God has not forgotten you. His deliverance is closer than you think.'" The two disciples then slipped back into the ever-moving crowd, all drawn to the center of life for every Jewish person, the Temple.

Entering the Temple area, Jesus turned immediately to the place of teaching, Solomon's Porch. It was here that the rabbis sat, daily expounding on the mysteries of the word of God. Eager students gathered, often questioning each Master of the Torah. But on this day, Solomon's Porch had been completely transformed, overflowing with bartering and business transactions.

At the columned entrance, Jesus stopped. The pressure of the crowd behind him could not propel him forward so the moving mass of humanity split and flowed around him, each man intent on procuring Temple shekels or Passover sacrifices.

Standing beside Jesus, surveying the scene, Peter casually commented, "It seems that the Passover market of the high priest has overtaken the area of Torah instruction."

Like a man shocked by a sudden outrage, Jesus took a moment to respond. His Father's house had been turned into an Eastern market, every man haggling and bargaining at the top of his lungs!

With an angry snort, Jesus sniffed the air, nostrils flaring. Turning his head from side to side, he pointedly observed the miserably corralled animals and imprisoned birds. Wetting his lips with his tongue, Jesus tasted the spiritual atmosphere.

"Dung! Everything is covered with flies, like miniature demons from hell!" Jesus hotly pronounced his words with obvious disgust. Then he pulled a small cloth from his belt and spit into it like he was removing something very nasty from his mouth.

There was a fire in his heart, and it could be seen in his eyes. With a little trepidation, the disciples watched their master. No one had the courage at that moment to ask a question so they silently waited to see what Jesus would do next.

"Oh, that one of you would shut the temple doors, so that you would not light useless fires on my altar!" Jesus announced. He looked up toward the golden crown on the sanctuary building. There, in the spirit realm above the melee of money-making, he could see. Satan had set up a throne. From that elevated position, the Evil One was directing all the transactions in Solomon's porch.

Looking up into the eyes of his enemy, Jesus boldly proclaimed, *"I am not pleased with you...and* my Father *will accept no offering from your hands.* From every corner of the world, true believers have come to honor God. In this place, his *name will be great among the nations, from where the sun rises to where it sets."*[3]

Immediately, a gust of wind blew through the columned corridor. Jesus felt his angelic army take their protective positions.

The disciples sensed the spiritual tension in the air, but they did not understand that good and evil were about to confront each other, in both the heavenly and the earthly realms.

Their eyes remained on Jesus as he deliberately walked over to the place where he usually sat and taught. Two money changers occupied the spot. Standing in front of their table, men from Rome and Crete were negotiating the exchange of their coins for Temple shekels. The disciples could almost see the spirits of

Greed and Dishonesty that swirled around the transactions. Jesus did see them.

Casually, like the man next in line, Jesus stepped up to the table. With brooding sharpness, he followed both transactions closely. Varying rates of exchange, deliberate confusion, slight-of-hand, nothing escaped his observation. As the transactions concluded in favor of the Temple, the slightly bewildered men turned to leave.

Jesus stopped them. Quickly, Jesus picked up several shekels from the table. Giving each man the appropriate amount, he said, "Never let it be said that thieves are allowed to operate unchecked in my Father's house."

Immediately, the men behind the money table exploded. "You cannot take our money!"

"Guard! Guard! Where are the Temple guards?"

The heavenly sentries quickly propelled more people into the market area so the guards could not push through to arrest Jesus.

Above the den of bartering and the bleating of terrified animals, Jesus shouted, "God says, '*I am a great king…and my name is to be feared among the nations.*'[4]" Jesus then violently *overturned the tables of the money changers and the benches of those selling doves. "It is written," he said to them, "My house will be called a house of prayer,' but you are making it a 'den of robbers.'*"[5]

Coins flew and then clattered to the pavement. Men of wealth dropped to their knees, scrambling to retrieve their rolling coins.

A riotous cheer rose from the people as coins scattered under their feet. The eager masses surged forward again, diving for coins and further impeding the advance of the Temple guards.

Feathers fell from the sky as gray and white doves frantically beat their wings, rising as one flock toward the open horizons. Jesus continued to shout as he moved from vendor to vendor, tossing tables and freeing animals.

In the midst of the melee, he came across a priest, wide-eyed and open-mouthed. Jesus got in his face. "*And now, you priests, this warning is for you. If you do not...resolve to honor my name,"* says the LORD *Almighty, "I will send a curse on you, and I will curse your blessings. Yes, I have already cursed them, because you have not resolved to honor me.*[6] Go now! Give this message to your fellow priests!"

Then Jesus began wildly shoving the overturned tables into a broken heap. Fear filled the hearts of many, and they stepped back until a clearing had been made and the place of instruction had been reestablished in Solomon's Porch.

Jesus shoved a final table away from the area. Bags of fine flour for grain offerings fell from the table and burst open on the paving stones of the floor. Then Jesus strode over to the place where he usually taught and he began to sing.

> *One thing I ask of the Lord, this only do I seek:*
> *that I may dwell in the house of the LORD*
> *all the days of my life,*
> *to gaze upon the beauty of the LORD*
> *and to seek him in his temple.*[7]

Another unexpected breeze blew through the columned corridor. It briefly lifted the fine flour and stray feathers as the evil spirits fled from the sinless descendant of Adam.

The people gathered round. The disciples pushed their way forward to stand beside their master. Now that he had taken authority over the corruption in the Temple, each man knew Jesus must be the Messiah. Who else could do such a thing and remain untouched!

Judas, especially, looked around, amazed that the Temple guards had yet to approach. He spoke to Matthew. "Surely, no man can touch our master."

Somehow, the blind and the deaf found their way into this outer area of the Temple. Jesus healed them.

Mary of Magdela with Miriam, the sister of Peter, had followed the exciting word-of-mouth. "Jesus of Nazareth has trashed the Temple market."

"The bankers have lost most of their profits."

"There are no animals for sale in the Temple."

Breathless from the exciting news and their struggle to get through the crowd, the women forced their way to the place where they saw the disciples standing behind Jesus. There were no guards in sight, but the Temple officials had just pushed through, and they were now confronting Jesus.

"Why have you moved the Temple market? Who gave you the authority to clear away the merchants and designate this area for teaching?"

"This area was set aside for the instruction of the people when construction on this part of the Temple was completed," Jesus answered. "But as to your question about authority, by what authority did John baptize and declare the age of the Messiah? If you will answer my question about authority, then I will answer yours."

The Pharisees and chief priests huddled together. Briefly, they debated an appropriate response, but they could not settle on an answer without attached repercussions. So they lamely replied, "We don't know."

The people who were standing close enough to hear laughed.

Then Jesus said, "So I will not respond to your question regarding my authority."

And the people laughed again.

Then Jesus turned to the crowd, and he began a story. He looked at the people. He spoke to the people. But everyone knew that his words were for the Temple elite who were still hovering nearby.

"A man had two sons. To the first son, he said, 'Go and work in my vineyard today.' The son replied rudely. 'I have my own plans for the day. I will not go to the vineyard.' But later, he did go to the vineyard and work.

"Then the father went to his second son. 'Go and work in my vineyard today.' The second son nodded agreeably and promised to get right to work. But throughout the day, he found many other distractions, and he never went to the vineyard.

"Now let me ask. Which son honored his father?"

"The first," they loudly answered.

Jesus turned and made eye contact with those Temple authorities who were standing nearby. He said, "You have told everyone that you always keep the law; and therefore, they should look to you as an example of a righteous child of God. But I tell you, the tax collectors and the prostitutes show more honor to God than you do. They are entering the Kingdom of God ahead of you. John brought a message from heaven. You rejected his message, but the tax collectors and prostitutes opened their hearts to righteousness. So, who is the true child of God?"

Jesus then turned back to the people who were hanging on every word. "I will tell another story. A landowner planted a fine vineyard. It had a wall, a winepress, and a watchtower. He leased it to local farmers and then moved out of the country. When the grape harvest approached, the landowner sent servants to collect his share of the fruit. But the tenant farmers treated his servants badly, even killing some.

"Then the landowner sent other servants who were treated in the same way. Finally, he sent his own son, expecting that he would be treated differently. But when the tenant farmers saw that the son of the landowner had come for his share of the crop, they plotted, and then they killed the son.

"When this landowner returns to his vineyard, what will he do to those tenant farmers?"

"He will punish those men severely. Surely, he will put them to death!" the crowd replied. "Then, he will find other tenant farmers who will give him both profits and respect."

Andrew quietly commented to his brother, "The servants in this story are the prophets. Over the centuries, every true prophet with a message from God has been mistreated and often killed."

Peter agreed. Then he asked, "But who is the son?"

Andrew did not answer and Peter said no more. Each man had a thought, a memory of the many times that Jesus had spoken of his death, but neither man could bear to even consider the reality of those statements. They chose to think of Jesus calling Lazarus back to life, entering Jerusalem on a donkey, and taking authority over the corrupt money-making schemes of the high priest. Peter and Andrew turned their attention back to their master. The crowd was calm and hanging onto every word.

Jesus said to them, "Have you never read in the Scriptures: 'The stone the builders rejected has become the cornerstone'?[8] Have you heard our sages tell the story of the Temple capstone?"

Jesus looked around at the expectant faces, and then he began another story. "When Solomon commenced construction of the Temple, he ordered that the stones be measured and cut at the quarry. The plans were carefully drawn with exact measurements and placement for each stone. There would be no hammering and chiseling on the Temple mount.

"The first stone the workmen cut was the capstone, the last to be used. It was hauled to the construction site and set aside while the rest of the building slowly rose, stone by stone.

"It took many years to complete Solomon's Temple. All that time, the capstone rested in the dirt. Weeds and grass grew over it. From time to time, the builders glanced at the extra stone, but they quickly concluded it was not the right fit, worthless. Many years passed. The stone was nearly hidden and definitely forgotten.

"Then the day came when the foreman of the building project called for the final stone, the capstone. The foreman at the quarry emphatically informed him that the capstone had been delivered. The builders searched the Temple mount for the missing capstone.

Someone stumbled over the old stone, buried in overgrowth, and often rejected.

"Then there was a flurry of activity. The stone was cleaned and hauled to the center of the Court of the Israelites. It was not long before the trumpets sounded and the choir sang while the capstone was raised to complete Solomon's magnificent Temple. So we have the saying, '*The stone the builders rejected has become the capstone; the Lord has done this, and it is marvelous in our eyes*'."[9]

The hovering Pharisees heatedly whispered to each other.

"Do you know what this man is saying?"

"He is comparing himself to the capstone."

"So, he is unrecognized now, but he will be elevated later?"

"To the sound of the trumpet? Like a king?"

"Humph! And we are the ignorant laborers, stumbling through the weeds, looking for a chiseled stone that is right under our noses? He insults us!"

Jesus looked directly at the agitated men. "How humiliating it would be to stumble and trip over such a stone because you were not looking as you walked, but far worse, for such a stone to fall upon you. Surely, you would be crushed to death."

In each parable that Jesus told, the Pharisees and chief priests understood by the Spirit that Jesus had a warning for them.

Insulted and angry, those men withdrew from the place where Jesus was teaching to one of the private rooms attached to the Temple. There, the men discussed everything they had seen and heard regarding what Jesus had done and said that day. Passionately, they argued for a way to arrest Jesus, but because they feared the great crowds that filled the Temple courts and hung onto every word he spoke, they accomplished nothing.

Miriam followed the retreat of the Temple authorities with her eyes. Then she turned to Peter. "Those men are very angry and very powerful."

Peter answered, "They do not have greater power than the Messiah. Look!"

Miriam followed her brother's line of vision to see Mary from Magdela helping an old hunched woman, bringing her to Jesus.

"What's going to happen?" Miriam asked.

"Watch!" Peter stated with confidence.

Miriam watched Jesus take the woman's hand and speak very quietly to her. Then he touched her back, and the woman suddenly straightened up. She began turning and twisting, moving her body like a young woman. Jesus laughed. Mary jumped up and down and hugged the woman.

"Well?" Peter asked.

"He is the Messiah!" Miriam exclaimed.

After that healing, the people surged forward, all trying to get a word or a touch. Peter moved away from his sister to take a protective position. All the disciples had to work at holding back the crowd and maintaining order.

"Help me!" Mary grabbed Miriam's hand. "Go into the crowd. Find those women and children who are weak and sickly. Bring them to one of the disciples, and he will let you through so they can get to Jesus."

Thrilled to be part of the Jesus experience, Miriam dove into the pressing crowd, searching for the weakest and the overlooked, those who needed a little help to make their way forward.

Within the crowd, there were some non-Jews from Greece. They came to Philip requesting a few moments with Jesus. Philip brought their request to Andrew, and together, the men approached Jesus.

Jesus responded, "These men have traveled to Jerusalem for the most significant Passover since the first Passover when blood was applied to the doorframes. This is the time when the Son of Man will be glorified. They will see it happen. Right now, if I speak to them, they will not understand." He sighed. "Even you do not understand. Now, go tell them to ponder this saying. 'Any man who holds on to his life will lose it, but the one who gives up his life will be given eternal life.'"

Before Philip and Andrew could carry the message back to those men, Jesus wondered aloud, "Will these men satisfy their curiosity and then go their way, or will they become my devoted servants? During these spring feasts, each man will have to make that choice."

Then Jesus looked searchingly into the eyes of Andrew and Philip. "My Father will honor those who go where I go." A shadow of sadness then passed over Jesus's face. Sadly, he shook his head. "The words I have spoken are difficult, but should I flee from the hour that is upon me?

No, this is the reason for my life."

Glancing again toward the golden spikes that crowned the sanctuary, he could see that the throne of the Evil One had been removed. His own heavenly army now occupied that space. Jesus shouted, *"Father, glorify your name!"*

Then a voice came from heaven, "I have glorified it, and will glorify it again."

The men from Greece exclaimed, "He speaks and the angels answer!"

The crowd that was there and heard it said it had thundered, but many *others said an angel had spoken to him.*

Jesus then turned to the men from Greece and he *said, "This voice was for your benefit, not mine. Now is the time for judgment on this world; now the* evil *prince of this world will be driven out. And I, when I am lifted up from the earth, will draw all people to myself."*[10]

"Lifted up?"

Refuting objections rose from the people nearby. "What? The Messiah rules forever."

"The throne of David has no end. Why is he talking about a Roman cross?"

"Who is this Son of Man who will be lifted up?"

Then Jesus told them, "I am the seed of the woman, a son of humanity and a son of heaven. I will only be here to instruct you for a little while. Then I must leave.

In the governor's apartments in the Antonio Fortress, Pilate looked out the window, and then he turned to his wife who had joined him to look at the sky. "Did you hear thunder?"

For a long moment, Procila silently studied the cloudless afternoon sky. Then she spoke very seriously to her husband. "That was not the sound of ordinary thunder. The god of this nation was speaking. Armies are moving. Preparations are being made for battle. A cosmic war is imminent."

Pilate studied his wife like she had studied the sky. He respected her intuition; so far, her advice had saved him from the wrath of Rome. He knew her to be a woman with extraordinary spiritual insight so he asked, "Are these people about to revolt?"

"No," she answered. "I sense a spiritual battle over this land, this city, this Temple. We can only hope that the victor will be gracious to those living in the land."

Procila then gasped. "Do you see it?"

"What?" Pilate gruffly responded.

"A shimmering cloud, rising from the Temple."

Pilate stared but saw nothing.

Then the cherubim, with the wheels beside them, spread their wings, and the glory of the God of Israel was above them. The glory of the Lord went up from within the city and stopped above the mountain east of it.[11]

"It is moving!" Procila exclaimed. "Crossing the valley and descending on the Mount of Olives. It is at the place where they burn the red heifer."

Pilate looked at his wife, confusion written on his face. "I know how to prepare for battle and how to wage war, but I cannot deal with battles between gods that I cannot see."

Procila responded, "It's not about seeing with our eyes. It's about feeling with our hearts and then responding to those feelings with the correct action. It is all about choices. Often, human choices turn the battle."

Unable to formulate an intelligent response, the governor of Judea turned away from the window. He went to the wash basin and began cleaning up for his evening meal.

"I will seek further understanding." Procila had the last word on the subject.

Chapter 9

A Criminal Named Barabbas

A man called Barabbas was in prison with the
insurrectionists who had committed murder in the uprising.

—Mark 15:7

From a rocky outcropping that overlooked the stone quarry north of the city, Barabbas judged the distance from the sun to the horizon. "Let's go." He called to his men as he slipped his short sword back into the sheath that hung from his belt.

Silently, his men followed him. At the road, they separated, blending into the late afternoon arrivals, listening to snatches of conversations. A famous teacher, a rabbi from Galilee, had demolished the Temple market that morning. Barabbas considered the story but did not call his mission off. He knew that was only a temporary disruption. The commerce of the Temple would be reestablished quickly, and when the high priest sent his servant to collect his share of the day's revenue, Barabbas and his men would lift it from him. Their mission would continue as planned.

At the entrance to Solomon's porch, Barabbas and his men casually gathered. The notorious rebel noted that the evening market was smaller than he had expected. Some animals were wandering without a tether. Animal pens had been tipped over. There were no doves in the cages. And many broken tables were piled to the side. But at the far end of the vast area, bartering had resumed. Sales were being made, and coins were being exchanged so there was still a profit to be made.

"That man, his name is Malchus. He is the personal servant to the high priest."

Barabbas turned to see the man that his follower was pointing out. The man was moving from vendor to vendor, collecting that portion of the daily profits that belonged to the high priest. One of the Temple guards accompanied him.

Barabbas kept his eyes on Malchus while sending each of his own men to take positions around the market.

As Malchus made his final collection, one of Barabbas's followers bumped roughly into the guard. Barabbas then quickly pulled his own sword and pushed the point threateningly against the stomach of the man whose arms were occupied with a large chest filled with gold and silver coins. "I'll take that money box. Tell your master every family will eat the Passover meal, even the families of those men who have been forced into fighting and hiding."

Malchus had no choice, hand it over or die. He dropped the box and ran.

Immediately, Barabbas scooped it up. The men who were with Barabbas quickly set up a commotion, calling, "Thief! Thief!" They pointed at various men. They began running and shoving people out of their way.

One of the Temple guards was not distracted by the confusion. His eye was on Barabbas who dashed for an exit, money box in hand. The guard took up the pursuit, catching the bold criminal on the threshold of the Beautiful Gate.

Abruptly, Barabbas turned on the man, ruthlessly sticking his short sword deep into the guard's abdomen. Without pausing to assess the outcome, Barabbas continued his flight.

The Temple guard collapsed and died. Ichabod the crippled beggar saw everything.

"Can I expect some protection from Rome?" Caiaphas glared at the commander of the Antonio Fortress. "Your men stand on the northern wall of the Temple complex. Their uncircumcised eyes observe every sacrifice and every movement on the Temple mount. But they are good for nothing! Yesterday, the Temple market was demolished and robbed. Not once, but twice! One of the Temple guards was killed!"

Longinus nodded thoughtfully. Then he asked, "Can you identify the robber?"

"It was the highwayman called Barabbas. He took the money box from my servant."

Longinus nodded again. "How do you know this?"

"We apprehended one of his men, and he talked with the help of the whip."

Maintaining an expressionless face, Longinus restated, "You said there were two incidents?"

Caiaphas huffed. "That arrogant rabbi from Nazareth destroyed the market on Solomon's porch."

"Did he take anything?" Longinus asked.

"No." Caiaphas huffed again. "He cleared the area that was usually reserved for the rabbis to teach."

"Then what did he do?" The commander calmly asked. In his heart, Longinus was enjoying this prolonged questioning and the obvious frustration of the high priest.

"He went to his usual place, and he taught the people."

"So this rabbi did not steal anything," Longinus stated. "He just reclaimed the area for its intended purpose."

The high priest turned red in the face. He huffed. He spluttered. "Is this all I am going to get from you, question after question? I want some action! I want to see Barabbas behind bars, and I want to see this rabbi—"

Caiaphas stopped short. He knew he could not say that he wanted to kill Jesus. So he lamely completed his thought by saying, "I never want to see the rabbi from Nazareth again."

Longinus allowed a calculated uncomfortable silence. Finally, he responded, "We have already laid a trap for the man who stole your money. We expect to arrest him soon. As for the other man, Rome has no laws regarding arrogance or teaching in your Temple. Rome is not concerned with your religious squabbles."

"I'm going to speak to Herod Antipas about this," Caiaphas blustered. "We'll compose another letter and send it to the emperor."

Longinus then took an intimidating step toward the high priest. He looked the man hard in the eyes, tough soldier to cagey politician. "Give Emperor Tiberius my regards. Tell him we are doing as he requested. We are allowing you to govern your own people. We are allowing you to police your Temple and your city. My soldiers will help you catch this wide-ranging notorious thief, but keeping order in your Temple is your problem. The emperor has given you that right, and I am here to protect your rights." Longinus paused then he added, "Just remember, you do not have the right to kill a man. Keep those stones on the ground and out of angry hands."

The moon was nearly full. Its white light bathed the campers on the Jerusalem side of the Mount of Olives. Without his disciples, Jesus made his way between the family campsites to the place where his family always set up their tents. James was the first to notice that Jesus had stepped into their firelight.

"Well, brother, you are the talk of the city!" He shook his head from side to side. "Remember when I told you that you could not be a famous prophet if you stayed in Nazareth? I don't have to worry about that any more. Your name is on every pair of lips."

Jesus just smiled and shrugged. "Where's mother?"

"Here I am!" Mary came running from behind a tent. "It's so good to see you." She reached up and threw her arms around his neck, pulling him down so she could kiss him on each check. "Come sit by the fire. Have you eaten?" Mary began putting a small meal together.

Other members of the family gathered around. Mostly, they stared. They had heard so much about Jesus, and now, he was in the camp. Enos stepped up and gave his uncle a manly hug. Joses's little daughter came forward, offering a cup of water.

Jesus noticed that her hand was wrapped in strips of linen, so as he took the cup, he bent. "What happened to your hand?"

Her mother, Deborah, answered, "She fell against the oven."

"It hurts," the girl said in a tiny voice.

"May I look at it?" Jesus asked as he squatted so he would be at eye level with his young niece.

The girl nodded, and Jesus carefully unwrapped her little hand. In the moonlight, it was easy to see the raised blisters and the red skin. Jesus bent his head and kissed the little hand.

A gasp went up from the gathered family. Everyone could see. The blisters were suddenly gone. The skin had become pink and healthy.

James took a closer look, and then he straightened up and looked at Jesus. "I do not understand, but I have no more criticisms. Over the years, I have challenged everything you have done and said. I was wrong. You really are a man, unlike any other man."

Jesus gave his brother a strong hug. "All is forgiven."

Mary hurried back to Jesus with a plate of food. He took the dish from her and then steered her away from the rest of the family. For most of the evening, he sat alone with his mother, eating the meal she had prepared and speaking of the reason he had been born.

It was very late when Mary crawled into her shelter, and later still when Jesus returned to the olive-press cave where his disciples were sleeping. He stepped carefully around their sprawled and snoring bodies. Close to the stacked baskets, he wrapped his cloak tightly around his body and lay down to sleep.

Through his dreams, the Holy Spirit took him back to the first Passover, back to the little huts in the delta land of the Nile. He saw Moses confronting Pharaoh, face-to-face. Then Jesus heard the Spirit say, "Pharaoh, Pharaoh, in the flesh you were just a man, but your spirit was the spirit of Satan."

As the dream progressed, Jesus focused on Moses and Aaron. He saw Aaron take the wooden staff from Moses. He saw Aaron's arm extended, the wooden rod touching the water. God spoke. *"Now you will see what I will do to Pharaoh: Because of your mighty hand he will let them go; because of your mighty hand he will drive them out of his country."*[1] As Jesus watched, the water that flowed in the Nile became blood, and that blood seemed to come from the hand that held the wooden staff.

Jesus slept. In his dream, he watched the plagues unfold— frogs, lice, flies, cattle disease, infectious boils, hail, locust, and darkness. God continued to speak in the dream. "Your sinless blood confronts all the agents of evil. Like the frogs driven from their river habitat, it brings them out of hiding so they can die in the light."

As the dream continued, the agents of evil melted away. The voice of God became silent. Suddenly, the face of Satan, first like a fierce lion, then like a screaming eagle, filled the dream. In an instant, that evil face became a snorting bull, and finally, it became a man in the likeness of Pharaoh. Pharaoh confidently announced, "I will kill all the sons and daughters of Adam. The seed of every woman shall die! All humanity belongs to me."

Jesus then heard himself in the dream. It was his heavenly voice, the voice of Yeshua. "My blood will stop you!"

Then a cross was raised up high above the earth. Jesus looked down from that vantage point and saw multitudes from the past and far into the future. In his dream, Jesus spoke again. It was part of a verse often recited during the Passover meal. *"I will redeem you with an outstretched arm and with mighty acts of judgment. I will take you as my own people, and I will be your God. Then you will know that I am the* LORD *your God."*[2]

In a whirlwind of gray and white clouds, the dream suddenly ended, and Jesus woke up. He made his way to the garden just outside the cave. At the well, he lowered a jar and got a drink of water. Then he moved into a secluded grove of trees. He dropped to his knees. Leaning over an immovable boulder, he prayed.

Heavenly visitors came and went. Moses assured him that resurrection was reality. Elijah spoke of courageously confronting evil. Angels recalled the creation and the fall of Adam. They repeated the promises that Yeshua had made to his friends on Earth through the prophets.

At dawn, Jesus stirred the coals from last night's fire. He added some twigs and sticks. It wasn't long before his disciples were up and ready to walk back into Jerusalem, back to his Father's house.

Chapter 10

Should We Resist Rome?

While all the people were listening, Jesus said to his disciples,
"Beware of the teachers of the law."

—Luke 20:45–46

A basket of fresh bread and another basket of dried fish waited beside the morning fire. With grunts and a few grumbles, the disciples responded to the early morning sunshine. They stumbled to the fire. Jesus sat there, offering each man the food his mother had provided as he had left the family camp.

Soon after that simple meal, the men were on the road again, headed for the Temple. As they approached the city, they saw the fig tree. It had withered from its roots. Peter remembered this was the very tree that Jesus had hoped to eat from. Surprised, he said, "Rabbi, look! The fig tree! Yesterday, it was strong and healthy. Today, it is completely dead!"

"Have faith in God," Jesus answered. *"*This withered tree is a small thing." Jesus then pointed to the Temple Mount. He said, *"Truly I tell you, if anyone says to this mountain, 'Go, throw yourself into the sea,' and does not doubt in their heart but believes that what they say will happen, it will be done for them. Therefore I tell you, whatever you ask for in prayer, believe that you have received it, and it will be yours."*[1]

For a moment, he stopped walking, and he turned to face his followers. "It is time to stop competing with each other. It is time

179

to let old grudges and resentments die. Forgive all insults so your Father in heaven can forgive you."

Once again, Jesus led his disciples into Solomon's porch. The area for teaching remained open to all the rabbis, with the market operating at the far end. Jesus took his usual place and people gathered around him immediately. Jesus did not disappoint them. He posed a question. "How is one admitted to the Kingdom of God?"

Then he answered. "It is like receiving an invitation from a king. Once, there was a king who prepared a wedding banquet for his son. His servants ran throughout the country to deliver invitations to a select group of dignitaries, but those important men snubbed the king. They refused to come.

"The king sent a second invitation, describing the wonderful meal and the fantastic entertainment that was waiting. Again, those who were invited snubbed the king. They ignored the second request and returned to their businesses. A few mistreated the king's messengers.

"The king was furious. He sent his army to destroy those he had invited. Then he said to his servants, 'This banquet I have prepared will be enjoyed. Go out into the streets. Give an invitation to every person you see. Tell them to come, and a wedding garment will be provided for each one.'

"So the servants gathered the people, all they could find—the good, the bad, the beautiful, and the ugly. The banquet hall was filled. Then the king spotted one man, totally out of place. That man was not wearing a wedding garment.

"The king hurried over to the man. 'How did you gain admittance without the beautiful garment I provided?'

The man did not answer, but a servant stepped up to say, 'I saw this man discard your beautiful garment and straighten his own clothes as if that would be good enough.'

"Once again, the king was both insulted and enraged. "'Remove this man from my banquet and from my kingdom,' the king shouted."

As Jesus finished the story, he saw a group of Pharisees along with some of the associates of Herod Antipas approaching. When they had worked their way through the crowd, he looked each man directly in the eye and said, *"For many are invited, but few are chosen."*[2]

Jesus knew that the high priest and his associates were watching closely. Through the Spirit, he also knew that these men were spies, sent with questions meant to trap him into speaking a traitorous word.

One of the spies stepped up. "Good Rabbi, we know you are a master of the Torah. Please answer a question for us. Should we, who have pledged our lives to God, pay taxes to Caesar or only to the Temple?"

Jesus heard murmured interest in the crowd. Everyone knew that over the years, a number of men had proclaimed themselves to be the Messiah. Each had gathered followers as well as bands of armed men. All of the self-proclaimed messiahs had insisted that Rome had no right to tax the Jews. Only God, through the Temple system, could demand revenue from the people of God.

A hush fell over the crowd. Everyone waited to hear what the rabbi from Nazareth would say.

Extending his hand, Jesus said, "Someone? Please place a denarius in my hand."

Jesus then took the coin and held it up for all to see. "Look at the imprint on this coin. Who do you see?"

"Caesar!" The response was overwhelming.

Jesus said. "Then, the coins of the Roman Empire must belong to Rome. So *give back to Caesar what is Caesar's, and to God what is God's."*[3]

The men who had been sent by the high priest and the people who crowded close fell silent. The wisdom of the rabbi astonished them.

It was not long before the high priest sent other men. *Some of the Sadducees, who say there is no resurrection, came to Jesus with a question. "Teacher," they said, "Moses wrote for us that if a man's brother dies and leaves a wife but no children, the man must marry the widow and raise up offspring for his brother. Now there were seven brothers. The first one married a woman and died childless. The second and then the third married her, and in the same way the seven died, leaving no children. Finally, the woman died too. Now then, at the resurrection whose wife will she be, since the seven were married to her?"*[4]

"Such an unfortunate woman!" Jesus casually commented. "I find it hard to believe that such a story actually happened."

The people laughed.

As the laughter died away, Jesus replied, "Nevertheless, I will respond to your hypothetical situation. You do not know the scriptures or the power of God. When the dead leave their graves, they will be like the angels, not married.

Now about the resurrection of the dead—I know you will not accept the writings of the prophets, only the books of Moses. So please, recall the story of Moses at the burning bush. This occurred well after the death of Abraham, Isaac, and Jacob. Still God said, *'I am the God of Abraham, the God of Isaac, and the God of Jacob'? He is not the God of the dead, but of the living. You are badly mistaken!*[5] There is life after death. Men and women will leave their graves and worship their Maker."

A well-known rabbi stepped up to listen to the discussion. Appreciating the answers Jesus had given, he posed a question. "Which commandment is the most important?"

Jesus answered, "First, *love the Lord your God with all your heart and with all your soul and with all your mind and with all your* strength. *The second is this: Love your neighbor as yourself. There is no commandment greater than these."*[6]

"Good answer!" the rabbi exclaimed.

Standing nearby, the men, who had been sent to spy, muttered and scowled.

Jesus then said to the rabbi, "I can see your mind and your heart are close to the heart of God."

In the market place in the Upper City, Kheti carefully displayed fine wine cups and ornate Seder plates beside an arrangement of gold and silver platters. The old Egyptian merchant had given up the caravan routes to sit in a little booth and make fine imports available to the wealthy families of Jerusalem.

Leading just one camel laden with merchandise, Toma moved from booth to booth offering wares to various merchants. Kheti's booth was his real destination. When he arrived, the lifelong friends greeted each other with a warm hug and kisses on both cheeks.

"Is the Passover market good this year?" Toma asked as he began unpacking beautiful handblown glass goblets.

Kheti chuckled. "Herod Antipas is having a large Passover Seder. He wants to impress someone, maybe the governor. Herod's finance minister purchased twenty silver wine goblets."

"Royalty is good for something," Toma quipped.

Kheti stepped a little closer to Toma and spoke confidentially. "Caiaphas, your high priest, was looking at items in my shop. He had a friend with him. They were talking about a man from Nazareth, Rabbi Jesus. Isn't that Joseph's boy?"

"Yes." Toma stopped unpacking merchandise and focused on his old friend.

"Two days ago, Joseph's boy totally disrupted the Passover Market in the Temple. The high priest receives the revenue from that market. Caiaphas is very angry. He wants to kill Jesus."

"Did you hear anything else?" Toma asked. "They called him 'a dangerous messiah.'"

For a long moment, both men were silent, remembering the little boy on Joseph's lap, the journeys to Egypt, and back to Israel. Both men recalled the amazing story that Joseph had told them. Finally, Kheti broke the silence, "Since his father is dead and you are an elder kinsman, I thought you should warn him."

Toma agreed, "I will speak to him after the Passover meal. There will be time for a quiet talk then."

The sun was dropping toward the western horizon. The Levitical choir was singing. Above their rich baritones, Jesus could hear his own heavenly choir. Abruptly, he stood and excused himself from those who were waiting for the next parable. His disciples followed him. He entered the Court of the Gentiles, walking briskly on to the Court of the Women. At the base of the semicircular steps that led into the Court of the Israelites, he stopped to personally receive this gift of praise from his own angelic choir.

> *The Lord is exalted over all the nations,*
> *His glory above the heavens.*
> *Who is like the Lord our God,*
> *the One who sits enthroned on high,*
> *Who stoops down to look on the heavens and the earth.*[7]

The angels saw their Creator had come to receive their praise. Above the beautiful earthly melody they sang,

> "Yeshua, we *have seen you,*
> *high and exalted, seated on a throne;*
> *And the train of your robe filled the temple.*"[8]

The angels bowed, covering their faces with their wings. Continuing with the same melody, this time in hushed tones they sang, "Oh, the love you have shown! You left your Father and your home to walk with men."

Once again, the angels joined the Levitical choir, singing with them, several octaves higher.

> *He raises the poor from the dust*
> *And lifts the needy from the ash heap;*
> *He seats them with princes, with the princes of his people.*
> *He settles the childless woman in her home*
> *As a happy mother of children.*[9]

In the Court of the Women, no one moved until the song ended, and even then people seemed reluctant to continue their ordinary lives. The Spirit of God hovered in that place, touching each heart. Jesus felt the presence of his Father, the warm embrace of the Spirit. For a few moments, his disciples were speechless, unable to think of a question or a criticism. The Holy Spirit then highlighted a woman who was standing nearby. Jesus turned to her and said, "May your womb be full."

Initially, the woman was stunned. Then she burst into hysterical laughter and went away, unable to control her joy. A trumpet sounded from the highest point of the Temple complex. It broke the holy atmosphere. The people responded to its silver tones by moving toward the exits.

Jesus and his disciples moved with them, exiting through the Sheep Gate onto the road. As the men filed past the Pool of Israel, Jesus said to Peter, "Return to the olive-press cave and wait for me there." Then he stepped away, swallowed up by the moving mass of people that filled the road.

Peter turned to tell the others. He got the word to every man except Judas. Judas seemed to have been separated from the group.

Past the Antonio Fortress, Jesus followed the road that the locals called "The Way of the Cross." It ran north of the city, past the outer wall, through the old stone quarry. It passed the place where Romans executed those who were unfortunate enough to be condemned by Roman law. It was the road for every traveler destined for Caesarea and for every criminal destined for the cross.

As sunset approached, very few were leaving the city. Soon, Jesus found himself alone, walking by white moonlight, guided by the Holy Spirit.

At the quarry, Jesus stopped. He sat on a chiseled boulder, waiting to hear his heavenly name, satisfied to spend whatever time was required. It wasn't long before he heard, "Yeshua?"

He turned to find Moses standing beside him.

"We brought you to this place to show you things that will strength your resolve."

Jesus nodded. He knew this evening was important.

Moses pointed to the place of execution. At the moment, there were no crosses, just holes in the ground with sturdy beams stacked nearby, waiting for a crossbeam and a victim. Moses waved his arm and the Holy Spirit swooped in, visually removing layers of rock and stone, exposing an underground cavern below the crucifixion site.

In the sky, the scroll of history opened up for Jesus. He saw the city of Jerusalem, besieged by Assyrian troops, and he watched as Jeremiah, a prophetic priest, led his fellow priests out of Solomon's Temple. It was a dark night. They carried the Ark of the Covenant and all the holy furniture with proper respect, down into a cavern. Reverently, they placed each item. Then they filled the entrance with stones. As they left, one man chiseled a seraph on the wall of an underground passage, but he was quickly forbidden to leave any other clues.

The scroll of history closed, and Jesus looked in the present, past centuries of debris and tons of rock. The Holy Spirit illuminated the underground cavern. Within that space, angels continued the ministry of the Temple—maintaining the light of the menorah, replenishing the loaves of bread, guarding the Mercy Seat that had been placed, like a lid, over the gold-plated box that held the stone tablets of the law.

Moses said, "They are waiting for the blood of the Lamb of God to fall on the Mercy Seat. When your blood touches the golden cover that rests between the Ten Commandments and the eyes of your Father, you will have taken the punishment for everyone who has broken the laws of God. An angel will fly immediately to the throne room in heaven bringing your blood to God!" Then the system of killing animals and sprinkling their blood will be finished."

Moses sat down beside Jesus. He put his arm around the sinless descendant of Adam. "When I chiseled the law into those stones, when I used to stand before the Mercy Seat and talk to you, I did not understand about the blood and the Mercy Seat. And even now, after living in heaven for so long, I wonder how the Creator could die for the created. All of heaven is both horrified and amazed."

Jesus responded honestly, "In my humanity, I am terrified. Death on a cross is more than death. It is torture. My enemy will make sure that this body experiences all the pain it can bear before it gives out. He wants me to curse my Father. He wants me to die with my heart full of anger and unforgiveness for the men who are doing this to me. If that happens, I will have failed. I will belong to Satan. Adam and his descendants will be locked in death."

"You will not fail," Moses declared.

After their conversation, Moses sat with Jesus the man for a long time. As the night deepened, Jesus drew strength from his companionship.

Slowly, the moon and the constellations moved across the sky. Further down in the quarry, desperate men sat around a small campfire. From within the nighttime shadows, Jesus and Moses watched as soldiers silently approached then moved stealthily from boulder to boulder, suddenly attacking the men at the campfire. There was a brief fight. Short swords were no match for broad Roman blades. The local terrorists were quickly subdued, bound, and marched toward the fortress.

Moses said to Jesus, "I will leave you now."

The men embraced quickly and then Moses was gone.

Jesus continued to watch.

The Roman commander lingered at the scene. Obviously, he was a careful man, doing a final check of the area. Jesus noticed that he paused to tighten bloody strips of linen wrapped around his forearm. Then he mounted up. Once more, the senior centurion warily circled the area on horseback, looking to see if anyone had gotten away. It was then that he noticed Jesus.

Riding directly toward Jesus, he drew his sword and challenged, "What is your name, and what is your business in this place?"

Without standing, Jesus answered, "I am called the Rabbi from Nazareth."

Longinus lowered his sword and reined in his horse. He looked down at Jesus. "I know about the Rabbi from Nazareth. Why are you here without your disciples, without the crowds that follow you everywhere?"

Jesus answered, "I came to this place to speak privately with my Father."

"Your father?" Longinus repeated as he glanced around. "Does your father belong to the men who follow Barabbas?"

"No," Jesus answered. "My Father is the God who is worshiped in the Temple." Jesus pointed toward the starry sky. "He created this world, and he lives beyond all those stars."

"I have been told that madmen often live in these caves," Longinus replied. "You are speaking nonsense."

Jesus responded with his own challenge. "Look into my eyes. You will see there are no demons clouding my sanity, and you will see no Dishonesty."

Longinus did look into the eyes of the famous rabbi. The goodness and the kindness took his breath away. It touched his heart in a way that it had never been touched before.

In a soft voice, Jesus then said, "I know you. You are loyal to your superiors and careful to support the empire of Rome. You have taken the oath of your office seriously. This is good." Jesus paused, and then he said, "Continue to do your duty with diligence, even those things that may disturb your sense of right and wrong."

Jesus stood and slowly approached the commander of the Antonio Fortress. As an experienced soldier, Longinus should have readied his sword, but Jesus had so unnerved him that he just sat on his horse with his sword resting loosely in a hand covered with dried blood.

"You were injured?" Jesus pointed to the hand and arm.

Longinus shrugged. "I can still hold my sword. That is what counts."

"May I see the injury?" Jesus asked.

"It may bleed again," Longinus stated as he put his sword away and began to unwrap the blood soaked strips of linen that bound his forearm. He extended his arm for Jesus to see.

There was a deep gash from elbow to wrist. Jesus leaned forward and blew on it. Instantly, the arm was totally healed.

Dumbfounded, Longinus looked down at his forearm. Had it really been injured? He looked at the bloody strips of linen in his lap, then back at his arm.

"Rabbi?" The commander had questions, but the man he had been speaking to seemed to have disappeared.

Longinus then made another wary circuit of the area. The hooves of his horse echoed eerily throughout the quarry. With chills running the length of his spine, the commander halted his animal and silently surveyed the moonlit quarry. Obviously, he was alone in that place without any reasonable explanations. With a bewildered shake of his head, the commander dug his heels into the flanks of his horse. He urged his animal to move quickly back to the fortress. The bloody strips of linen remained tucked in his belt, tangible proof of his injury and his unusual encounter.

Chapter 11

What Will Be the Signs?

When Jesus had finished saying all these things, he said to his disciples, "As you know, the Passover is two days away—and the Son of Man will be handed over to be crucified."

—Matthew 26:1–2

Instead of going to his usual place in Solomon's porch, Jesus led his disciples into the Court of the Women to the place where the collection boxes were lined up. Mary of Magdela and Miriam, the sister of Peter, with her teenage son, John Marc, found the men in that place. Joining the disciples, they settled in to enjoy the spectacle of giving.

From Jerusalem, from every corner of Judea and beyond its borders, Passover pilgrims lined up to present their offerings. The very wealthy brought their servants, and the servants carried large boxes filled with coins that had been saved for a year or more.

Each extremely large offering was recognized with a shout from those standing nearby, sometimes with a blast on a shofar.

Jesus sat down in that place. He directed his disciples to observe the parade of offerings.

Judas stepped up to Jesus and asked, "Master, should I deposit an offering for you?"

Jesus answered, "No, we have come to recognize the largest offering ever given."

Jesus watched Judas's eyes widen as he anticipated the sight of so much wealth in one place at one time.

Morning moved toward noon. Jesus sat quietly, observing the people, waiting for the Holy Spirit to highlight the one he had come to recognize.

The well-to-do came and went. Their gold and silver coins clinked and clattered as they cascaded into the large offering bins. Each donation to the Temple seemed larger than the previous one. The crowds cheered. The disciples cheered. The women commented on the clothing, and the various cultures represented. The outpouring of such wealth was truly amazing.

Ignoring the ostentatious giving, Jesus remained silent. Directed by the Holy Spirit, he focused on one woman at the edge of the crowd. Dressed in tattered gray, illuminated by the Holy Spirit, she glowed with goodness. For Jesus, a scroll opened above her head. It told the story of a true Naomi—widowed, childless, forced to live so meagerly that daily food was a luxury.

Jesus nudged Peter. Pointing, he said, "There, that woman is bringing the gift that has touched the heart of God."

"Where?" Peter looked for a well-dressed woman with an escort.

"There," Jesus repeated as he pointed to the little lady in shabby gray. She was shyly skirting the crowd. Unobtrusively slipping from column to column, she headed for an offering box with quiet determination.

Peter passed the word to Andrew. Then Andrew told his nephew, John Marc, what Jesus had said.

Andrew repeated the information for James and Thaddaeus. Soon, all the disciples were ignoring the parade of prosperity and watching the poor woman. Several times, the servants of the wealthy pushed her aside so their masters could bring their gifts unimpeded. But she stood by and waited until there was a slight lull in the onslaught of giving. Then she hurried forward and dropped one, two copper coins into the box.

In the silence of that moment, everyone heard their tiny clinks. Many turned to see who had been so insolent as to give such a meager offering.

Reacting to their shocked stares, the woman hid her face. Then she quickly pushed her way back into the anonymity of the crowd.

Jesus began speaking to his disciples. *"Truly I tell you,"* he said, *"this poor widow has put in more than all the others. All these people gave their gifts out of their wealth; but she out of her poverty put in all she had to live on."*[1] My Father has seen this. In heaven, the trumpets are sounding. The angels are shouting the praises of this woman who has given everything. Right now, she is returning to the hovel where she lives. She has no provision for the Passover meal. She has no food in her dwelling."

Jesus stood. "Now I am ready to give my Passover offering." He pointed to Judas and Matthew. "Find this woman. Give her twice the amount of money needed to purchase a lamb and everything else for the Passover meal. Tell her, 'God, who sees what is done in secret, knows her need. This reward is from him.'"

"But, Master," Judas started to object. "How will we find her in such a massive crowd?"

Jesus looked at Matthew and said, "The Holy Spirit will lead you to her. He will see that you are successful."

Then Jesus led the women and the rest of his disciples to Solomon's porch. There, he began to teach. With his hands, he gestured toward the other teachers. "You must listen to their instruction," he said. "These teachers are the representatives of Moses so listen well. But I caution you, do not follow their example for they do not practice what they preach. Their main function is to add regulation upon regulation to the established laws. They just make lives burdensome, not righteous."

Jesus noticed that some of his challengers had worked their way to the front of his audience, so he addressed them. *"Woe to you, teachers of the law and Pharisees, you hypocrites! You shut the door of the kingdom of heaven in people's faces."*[2]

The watching crowd laughed, and the Pharisees turned red. One of them responded angrily, "Explain yourself, Rabbi! You cannot just make unfounded accusations!"

"God in heaven sees all. Woe to you, when you travel the empire to make disciples. You produce men who mindlessly imitate but do not love either God or man. You are blind guides, following the glint of gold while not seeing the one who owns all the riches in the world."

Jesus then made a sweeping gesture with his arm. "You are so careful about cleanliness. On the outside, you are beautiful, but inside, there is dung and death. Clean the inside first."

Jesus turned back to his audience. "Did you see the whitewashed tombs beside the roads to the city?"

"Yes!" they answered.

"The Pharisees tell you to imitate their lives, which are devoted to complicating and confusing the laws of Moses. Their lives are like those whitewashed tombs. They have an appearance of purity. Yet inside, there is only death and decay."

Jesus stood. His disciples sensed that he was ready to exit so they moved to open a path through the people. The Pharisees moved into a pious little group. They stood in arrogant unity, sneering at the Rabbi from Nazareth.

Suddenly, Jesus turned on the Pharisees. "You slithering snakes! How do you plan to escape hell?"

Jesus then looked around at the people he had been teaching and the crowds beyond. He shook his head sadly as he said, *"Jerusalem, Jerusalem, you who kill the prophets and stone those sent to you, how often I have longed to gather your children together, as a hen gathers her chicks under her wings, and you were not willing."*

Jesus then pointed toward the sanctuary. *"Look, your house is left to you desolate...* The Ark of the Covenant is missing. The Shekinah glory has left this place. And now, I am leaving. *I tell you, you will not see me again* in this place *until you* welcome me with respect and *say, 'Blessed is he who comes in the name of the Lord.'*[3]

Without another word, Jesus walked away. His disciples followed, considering all they had heard that morning and wondering about the comments Jesus had made.

Finally, Thomas walked up close to Jesus and said, "Surely some glory remains in this place. It is the pride and the focus of every Jew in the empire."

Philip agreed. "Look at the way the afternoon sun shines on the stones. These walls and all the buildings sparkle like the throne room of God."

Andrew added, "In all the world there is no structure as grand as this Temple. It honors God."

Jesus stopped walking. He looked up at the Temple structures. With his right arm, he pointed to the magnificent edifice of white stone, crested with pure gold. "Do you see this grand complex of buildings and courts? A day is coming when not one stone will be left on top of another."

The disciples gasped. The women exchanged horrified glances. Everyone looked up at the massive stones. Each block of limestone was larger than a poor man's home. They were immovably wedged into retaining walls, buildings, and large areas of pavement.

Jesus began walking again. His friends silently followed him. As they left the Temple Mount, Matthew and Judas rejoined them. Then, as a group, they made their way through the narrow streets, stopping to purchase a little food. All around, people surged and pressed against one another. That was the way it was in the streets and markets of Jerusalem at Passover time.

Near the Sheep Gate, Judas felt a hand on his arm. It pulled him into a market stall while the rest of the disciples continued toward the road. He heard a familiar voice.

The captain of the Temple guard whispered, "Caiaphas wants to speak to you."

Judas waited a moment. Then he stepped out of the stall and turned back toward the Temple, away from Jesus and the other disciples.

As Jesus was sitting in the enclosed garden on the Mount of Olives, his disciples came to him. They took in the view of the city and the Temple. Then they said, "You have spoken about the destruction of the Temple and this city. When will it happen? How will we know when all things are coming to an end?"

Jesus answered, "Watch. Do not be misled by another who claims to be the Messiah. Many will make that claim. There is only one true Messiah. He is the Word who spoke Earth into existence. He is the one who was a friend to Abraham. He spoke to Moses through the fire of the burning bush, and he became the seed that was planted in the womb of a woman. The angel came to that woman and said, 'Name your son Jesus.' Test every Messianic claim by these criteria.

"Before I come into full rulership, time will pass. Throughout the world, there will be wars and ideological conflicts. Do not be overwhelmed with fear. These things must happen before the end comes. It is just the beginning of labor—birth will come much later."

Peter commented, "My wife has given birth two times, and from the beginning of her pains until the actual birth, time passed slowly. It seemed like an eternity. Each time we feared that she would not live to produce a live child."

Jesus responded, "Yes, expect to endure troubles of increasing severity." Jesus looked at the two women who were sitting behind the men, Mary of Magdela and Miriam the sister of Peter. "Women understand what I am saying. They have experienced wave after wave of pain, each pain harder to endure. But they also know each pain is a promise. Joy awaits them. I declare, you will see me returning to this place. It will be a bright and glorious event, like lightening flashing from east to west. The dead will rise from their graves to meet me, and every living person will drop to their knees, unable to produce any response other than submission to the authority of the king."

Jesus looked at the attentive faces of his disciples. "During the time of the birth pains, you will travel throughout the world, teaching the things I have taught you. When the truth of my Father's kingdom has been carried to every corner of the world, then the great and terrible Day of the Lord will come and his Messianic Kingdom will be a reality."

John Marc left his mother's side and moved to sit between Peter and Andrew, intent on every word that Jesus spoke. Those words seemed to be for him as much as for his uncles.

"As you travel and preach, you will meet opposition—hatred, lies, hardships, the whip, jail, even death. Some will follow my teaching, but not all will remain faithful to it. Beware of false prophets who say they speak my words, but who really speak the lies of my enemy. I am telling you what to expect so you will not be misled."

Jesus then stood and pointed toward the city. "In heaven, a decree has been signed. This city will soon be destroyed. Watch for the sign from the scroll of Daniel, an abomination in the holy place of the Temple.

"When you see that event, leave the city immediately. Tell all of my followers to flee like Lot leaving Sodom, and do not hesitate. Pray to my Father for mercy because unbelievable disaster is about to fall."

"But, Master," Matthew asked, "hasn't the prophecy of Daniel already happened? We celebrate the Feast of Dedication every year because we overcame the invaders. We tore down the image that had been set up in the Temple. We purified the Holy Place and relit the altar and the lamps."

Andrew countered, "But our Holy Place was desecrated again. The Roman general, Pompey, walked into the Most Holy Place, and he erected a statue to Zeus."

Simon the Zealot was quick to point out, "That statue has been removed, but Rome still rules our nation and oversees every rite and ritual in the Temple."

Like a watchman, keen to spot an attack, Jesus scanned the distant hilltops. Then he responded, "My enemy is always looking for an opportunity to establish a false god in a true house of worship. Plans are now being made in the council of the Evil One. He will attack this Temple. He will end the sacrificial system, and he will cause the people of this nation to be removed to distant lands. This city will become desolate. But my followers will hear the warnings of the Holy Spirit. They will listen to his directions and be saved."

"Will there be a sign?" Andrew asked.

Jesus answered, "When you look out and see armies entrenched around the city, flee to the mountains. Do not delay."

For awhile, the disciples were silent. The destruction of beautiful Jerusalem was difficult to imagine.

Jesus broke into their silence. "You must be aware that Satan repeats patterns of behavior. Over the centuries there have been several successful attacks on Jerusalem and the Temple. It will happen again, and if this Temple is rebuilt, you can expect the pattern to be repeated.

"Now I say to you, do not bow your heads in discouragement. Immediately after those terrible days, look up. The sky will announce my return: *'the sun will be darkened, and the moon will not give its light; the stars will fall from the sky, and the heavenly bodies will be shaken.'*[4]

"From the prophet, Joel?" Peter asked.

Jesus nodded. "Watch the sky, day and night. God communicates with the wise men of the Earth through signs in the heavens. My enemy has no authority over the heavenly bodies, so he cannot use them to deceive."

From behind the men, Mary from Magdela spoke up. "Your mother told me there was a special star that announced your birth. Wise men from the court of an Eastern king followed that star to Bethlehem."

"That is true," Jesus confirmed. "Soon after you see these signs in the sun, the moon, and the stars, *then will appear the sign of the Son of Man in heaven. And then all the peoples of the earth will mourn when they see the Son of Man coming on the clouds of heaven, with power and great glory. And he will send his angels with a loud trumpet call, and they will gather his elect from the four winds, from one end of the heavens to the other.*"⁵

"When will this happen?" Andrew asked.

Jesus answered, "You are men who have raised crops to feed your families. You do not ask for a specific day and month for the harvest. Instead, you look for signs that your plants are growing and developing. So when you see all these things I have mentioned, you know that my return is near. I tell you, the generation that sees the signs in the heavens will not pass away before the end comes. Remember, heaven and earth will disappear, but my words will remain solid."

"Tell us," Peter pressed. "Be more precise. What other indicators can we look for?"

Jesus answered, "*But about that day or hour no one knows, not even the angels in heaven, nor the Son, but only the Father.* Yet, because Satan repeats his deceptions with predictability, I can tell you, *as it was in the days of Noah, so it will be at the coming of the Son of Man. For in the days before the flood, people were eating and drinking, marrying and giving in marriage, up to the day Noah entered the ark; and they knew nothing about what would happen until the flood came and took them all away. That is how it will be at the coming of the Son of Man.*" "Until that time, the seasons of life will continue. Then suddenly, the trumpet will sound and the heavens will roll back. Two men will be working side by side in a field. One will be lifted up into the clouds the other left. Two women will converse while grinding their flour. One will be taken up to live eternally, and the other left to the fate of those whose names are not written in the Book of Life.

"*Therefore keep watch, because you do not know on what day your Lord will come.*[7]"

Jesus paused and looked into the eyes of his friends. "Each man here believes that I am the Messiah and that I will be the supreme ruler of a kingdom. Before I take the throne, I must return to my Father to receive the kingdom from him. You will be left to carry out my instructions, to oversee the kingdom until I return. Will you be faithful servants?"

Then Jesus began a story. "The master of a great estate left his servants to care for his property. He went on a long journey. He did not return for a long time. His servants became slothful about maintaining the estate. They wasted their wages on excessive food and strong wine. But one day, their master returned. He caught them in irresponsible behavior. Immediately, the unfaithful servants were removed from the estate, never to return. Do not be caught unprepared."

Jesus looked at the serious faces of his followers. He said, "I can explain this best with another story. It happened at the wedding of Mary, the sister of Lazarus. The Holy Spirit has brought it to my memory for this moment, for your understanding."

Jesus picked up the water jug and refreshed himself before he began.

"My servants will be expecting me like a bridal party expects the bridegroom and his friends. At the home of Lazarus, everyone was waiting. In the courtyard, ten maidens had gathered in happy anticipation. Each girl had a burning lamp. Five girls had prepared with extra oil for their lamps, and five had not. The bridegroom was expected at any moment, but time passed. Twilight became darkness. Excitement waned and sleepiness prevailed."

Jesus turned his attention to Mary and Miriam. "You both know Mary the sister of Lazarus who is married to Jonathan the perfumer?"

Both women nodded.

"I was with her family, waiting for the bridegroom to arrive. By midnight, nearly everyone had fallen asleep, except Mary. She was sobbing at the gate, sure that her bridegroom was not coming. But in the darkest part of the night, we heard the cry, 'Your bridegroom is coming! Hurry to the gate and meet him.'

"Then all the maidens who had fallen asleep in the courtyard woke up. They prepared their lamps. Five of the young ladies were terribly dismayed. Their oil had burned away, and without a light for the road, they could not join the procession.

"'Help us!' they begged the other girls for more oil. But the girls who were prepared had only enough oil for themselves. They could not share."

Jesus shook his head as he recalled the scene. "There was a lot of hysteria in the courtyard, weeping and drama. But finally, the five unprepared girls ran down the road to wake the local oil merchant so each could purchase an adequate amount.

Meanwhile, the bridegroom and his friends arrived at the gate. They brought the sedan chair into the courtyard. Mary climbed into the chair. It was lifted onto the shoulders of Jonathan's friends. The five maidens who were prepared began to dance and the procession began. We carried Mary all the way to Jonathan's home in Jerusalem. The girls who were ready went into the wedding celebration. And the door was closed. Jonathan's brother, Simon, stood at the door.

Later, the five foolish maidens arrived. They knocked on the door, but Simon refused to open it."

Thomas then said, "Master, speak on this subject directly, without a story."

Jesus responded, "My coronation is only for those friends who are watching for my return and prepared to join me. Everyone else will be left outside. So remain watchful. No man knows the day or the hour of my coronation."

The sun had set. Only the white light of a full moon illuminated the enclosed garden where Jesus sat with his disciples. Mary and Miriam moved back to the hard packed area in front of the olive-press cave. They began stirring the coals and adding twigs so they could cook a small meal for the men before they returned to Miriam's home in the city.

Both women worked quietly so they could hear the things Jesus had to say to the men.

When the meal was ready, they caught Jesus's eye and he quickly finished his teaching.

The meal had ended. The men were sitting around the glowing coals of the cooking fire, considering all that Jesus had said to them that day. John moved to sit next to Jesus. He said, "Master, tell us more about the great and terrible Day of the Lord."

Jesus responded. "On that day, I will return to you from my Father's throne room. I will return in my own divine authority, but I will still be a descendant of Adam, the son of man that you know.

"*When the Son of Man comes in his glory,* the sky will glow like a golden fire with many embers. *And all the angels with him,* a mighty army, will be his honor guard. *He will sit on his glorious* white *throne. All the nations will be gathered before him, and he will separate the people one from another as a shepherd separates the sheep from the goats. He will put the sheep on his right and the goats on his left.*

"*Then the King will say to those on his right, 'Come, you who are blessed by my Father; take your inheritance, the kingdom prepared for you since the creation of the world. For I was hungry and you gave me something to eat, I was thirsty and you gave me something to drink, I was a stranger and you invited me in, I needed clothes and you clothed me, I was sick and you looked after me, I was in prison and you came to visit me.* [8]

"In amazement, the righteous will respond, 'When did we do these things?'

"*The king will reply, 'Truly I tell you, whatever you did for one of the least of these brothers and sisters of mine, you did for me.'*" [9]

John commented, "Many times you have said that God has mercy on those who are merciful. Is this part of his mercy?"

Jesus nodded. "Oh yes," he thoughtfully replied. "This is one of the great mercies of God."

"Then the king will turn to those on his left. He will command that they be thrown into the pit of fire prepared for the devil and his angels because they did not have compassion for their brothers and sisters."

Jesus stood, indicating that his time of teaching had ended. But as he stepped away, he said, "Passover is just two days away. That is when I will be placed in the hands of the Romans and crucified."

Then he moved to the dying fire and began banking the coals so a fire could be started in the morning. Peter quickly moved to complete the chore. The other disciples retreated to their favorite sleeping spots inside the cave. Jesus watched until each man was asleep.

Then he stepped into a secluded grove of olive trees and prayed, "Father God, increase their rest tonight. Strengthen their bodies, their minds, their spiritual understanding. Prepare them for the sacrifice of the Passover Lamb."

Jesus paused. He sensed a darkness that was deeper than the darkness of night.

His prayer continued, "Satan is lurking near this place. I feel his presence at the mouth of the cave. He is studying each of my disciples, looking for their weaknesses, planning to tear each man down to his own evil level. Father, your entire kingdom on Earth sleeps in this cave.

"Your Holy Spirit has explained the message of the prophet Zechariah. Satan will *strike the shepherd, and the sheep will be scattered.*[10] Each man will flee in fear. Don't let anyone go too far. Keep them from the cliffs and the evil agents who are waiting to destroy them. Each man must be protected from his own failures."

Suddenly, the sky seemed to open, and Jesus saw heaven. His enemy, once the beautiful archangel Lucifer, now the evil deceiver, Satan, stood at one of the pearl gates, demanding an audience with God.

Michael with his angelic army refused to let Satan in so the enemy of God shouted his demands. "The Creator and all his disciples must be placed on the altar. All must go through the fire. Each man must be tried. Are they men who have passed the test? Should they be admitted into the Kingdom of God?"

From the throne room of heaven, God answered. "The sacrifice of my son is sufficient for all humanity. Nevertheless, I have confidence in the men my son has chosen. You may strike each one with fear. You may try to deceive and discourage, but you may not physically harm them."

Like an enraged lion, Satan snarled his response. "Are you placing any limitations on the test I have planned for Yeshua, the one called Rabbi Jesus of Nazareth?"

For a moment, all of heaven held its breath. Then God answered, "No restrictions. You may do everything you have planned."

The vision faded. The night stars reappeared in their correct positions. Jesus stood and moved away from the seclusion of the trees. Continuing in prayer, he approached his sleeping disciples, stopping first where Judas lay, covered and curled in a fetal position. "Father, my disciple Judas has already been approached. The love of money and the flattery of men have temporarily blocked his ability to hear your Spirit. Forgive him for being complicit in the plans of my enemy. He has been deceived."

Jesus moved to where Peter was sleeping. "Father, you know this man considers himself to be my protector, my most loyal supporter. Do not allow despair to overtake him, when he fails to meet his own expectations."

John was changing position without waking. Jesus stepped over to his cloak-covered body. "Father, this man's love is strong. Protect his heart. Give him your responses."

Jesus then turned to James, then to Andrew and Philip. He walked over to where Matthew was snoring. Then he went to Simon the Zealot, to Thomas, and Thaddaeus. He touched each man. All twelve were presented to his Father for a blessing that preserves like salt sprinkled on the meat before it is thrown into the fire on the altar. For surely, these men would be part of his sacrifice.

Chapter 12

The Passover Meal

Get rid of the old yeast, so that you may be a new unleavened batch—as you really are. For Christ, our Passover lamb, has been sacrificed.

—1 Corinthians 5:7

Toma walked with the commander of the Antonio Fortress through the dark corridors, past cells filled with incarcerated Jewish men. He looked into their eyes and saw hopelessness. Rome had beaten the life out of them. It seemed God had also failed them. Toma looked into his own heart. He remembered what Herod's soldiers had done to his family. What was he doing in this place?

The commander stopped at a cell that contained only one man. Longinus beat on the door with the hilt of his short sword. Roughly, he ordered the man inside to come forward and press his face against the small barred window. Then Longinus turned to Toma. "Is this the man who took your money? Is this the highwayman called Barabbas?"

Toma looked at the man who snarled through the bars like a caged beast. A flash of recognition passed between the two men. Toma hesitated. Then he looked back at the Roman commander. "I cannot be certain that this is the man."

Longinus shrugged as he led Toma out of the prison in the lower level of the Antonio Fortress. "We already have enough evidence for Pilate to send that man to the cross. He and his men stole a money box from the high priest's servant. He killed a Temple guard. We have heard the witnesses. Pilate will sign the decree as soon as all the statements have been recorded."

The two men stepped out of the tunnel into the paved courtyard of the fortress. All around, Syrians wearing Roman uniforms lounged in groups, sharing wine and bread, playing various games of chance.

Longinus strode over to one rowdy group. He barked orders in Greek. The raucous huddle quickly dispersed into a crisp military line, except for one naked and bloodied soldier sprawled on the paving stones. A centurion's red cloak and a crown made from twisted thorns lay nearby.

Angrily, the commander of the fortress paced in front of the line of men. He said nothing. The rhythmic click of the hobnails on his military sandals sent chills up and down Toma's spine.

As Toma watched, he saw the injured soldier covered by the red cloak and then carried away.

Finally, Longinus stopped pacing. He walked over to a very solidly built soldier. The Roman commander pulled the short-handled three-stranded whip from his belt. He gave it to the muscular soldier. "The emperor has forbidden this game, except with a prisoner who has been sentenced to die. We cannot loose good soldiers in a game of chance." He turned to the man who held his whip. "Twelve lashes each."

Longinus turned back to Toma and then silently led him out of the Roman fortress.

Jesus and his disciples sat quietly around their morning fire. It was the fourteenth day of the month, the first day of unleavened bread and the day when all the Passover lambs had to be slaughtered at the Temple. Looking at Peter and John, Jesus said, "Go and prepare the Passover meal so we can eat together."

"Is there a room for us, or should we prepare to eat here, at our campsite?" John asked.

Among the disciples, a few commented, "On the day before Passover, it will be impossible to find a room."

Jesus ignored their negative comments. Calmly, he directed Peter and John, "Go to the gate in the lower city. Near the well, you will see a man carrying a jar of water. Peter, you will recognize the man. Follow him. When he enters a house, go to the owner and request his largest room. He will show you a room on the rooftop. It will be furnished and available for us."

Without questioning further, Peter and John got up and walked into the lower city where working class people lived. They knew it was well past time for the women to draw water for their homes. Men might be getting water for livestock or business purposes.

Both men found a place not far from the well and sat to watch the people come and go. Suddenly, Peter jumped up. "I know that man!"

John followed Peter's pointed finger with his eyes.

"That man works for my brother-in-law. He's drawing water. We'll follow him."

Peter and John quickly moved to walk behind the servant who was carrying a large jar of water on his shoulder.

"My sister's home!" Peter exclaimed as they followed the man through the gate. Peter hurried past the servant to the shop in the back of the house where his brother-in-law busily filled sacks with dried herbs and his nephew, John Marc, sewed them shut.

"Yes, yes, Jesus can use the upper room. My family will have our Passover downstairs. Go speak to Miriam. She can prepare all that you need." Impatiently, Peter's brother-in-law returned to the tasks he needed to finish before the evening sacrifice ended and the killing of the Passover lambs began.

Without announcing himself, Peter burst into the cooking area of his sister's home. The only person he saw was Mary of Magdela. She looked up from the sweet raisin and fig mixture that she was mashing. "Why are you in this home?" she abruptly asked.

Peter bristled a bit. He quickly retorted. "And why are you in this home?"

"Your sister had a room available for a Passover guest," Mary flatly answered.

Peter grunted. What could he say? During Passover and for all the major feasts, the people of Jerusalem always opened their homes, welcoming guests to their city.

But this woman annoyed him. Every time he had to sail to Magdela to purchase sails for his fishing boat, he went to her sailmaking establishment. She was always there, in his face and uncompromising until the transaction was completed. And on the occasions that she was with Jesus, it seemed she did not show any of the disciples the respect that a man should get from a woman. So, instead of speaking politely, Peter just grunted again.

John intervened. He picked up the conversation and said, "We need to speak to Miriam. Jesus needs the upper room in this house for his Passover meal. Miriam's husband said to make all the arrangements for the meal with her."

Very matter-of-factly, Mary responded. "Miriam went to the market. You will have to find her there so she will purchase enough food." Mary then turned her back on the men and continued mashing the dark, sticky fruit.

Peter and John hurried off to the closest food market.

In Herod's Jerusalem palace, Cuza and Manaen surveyed the tables that had been set up in the banquet hall, checking and rechecking the arrangement of the cushions. Pilate would be to the right of Antipas. Longinus would be next to Pilate. Manaen had placed himself on the left side of Antipas.

Cuza set the scroll containing the order of the readings and blessings at Manaen's place. "I expect you will move through the rituals quickly," he commented. "Last year, Antipas rambled on and was totally lost before the second cup."

"I remember," Manaen wryly replied. "I could skip half of the typical blessings and only you and I would know."

Cuza concurred. "Pilate and his commander should not even be at this meal. Neither of them have been circumcised. I'm sure."

Manaen shrugged. "It's a political gesture. Since Pilate has not been recalled to Rome, Antipas thinks it would be advantageous to make an alliance with him."

Cuza nodded. He had been the financial officer for Herod Antipas for many years. He knew the ways of this king. "What about servants for the meal?" Cuza asked.

"No Jewish man or woman will be working tonight," Manaen answered. "I've recruited several Syrian soldiers. They will perform the usual pouring of the water and washing of the feet for the male guests. They will offer perfumed oil and show each man to his place. During the meal, they will present the Seder plate to each guest and serve the food." Manaen gestured toward another table at the far end of the room. "The women's table will already have all the elements of the Passover meal and other foods in place. They will serve themselves. I'm sure your wife can direct the ladies so they are following the order of the meal with the men."

Cuza nodded. For formal occasions, this separation of men and women was expected.

A distant trumpet sounded. Both men paused. They knew the evening sacrifice had begun, earlier than usual on this special day. "Let's get our lamb and take it to the Temple," Manaen suggested. "We want to be in the first group."

Both men hurried to the courtyard where a large year-old lamb had been penned and cared for since the first day of the week.

At the market near the Sheep Gate, Peter and John completed the purchase of their Passover lamb. They tied a rough rope around its neck so it could not escape as they worked their way through the crowded streets to the broad steps of the Temple.

When they arrived, many men were already waiting in that place, holding their lambs and carrying stout sticks of pomegranate wood. Peter and John worked their way forward, getting as close to the Temple gates as possible. They wanted to be in the first group that was admitted into the area close to the altar where the lambs would be killed and prepared.

While they waited, Peter looked around. Through the crowd, he saw Toma with his son, Seth. Both men waved and nodded their recognition. John became engaged in a conversation with a man who had traveled from Cyrene with his two boys, Rufus and Alexander. For them, this was the event of a lifetime. The man had worked and saved for this Passover experience since the birth of his youngest boy, and they would not be returning to Cyrene until after the next feast.

During the conversation, Peter glanced at the boys' feet. He then nudged John, "Tell them to take off their sandals and tie them to their belt. No one can wear shoes in this part of the Temple."

John nodded and passed the message to Simon, the boys' father.

The trumpets sounded. The gates opened. Rows and rows of white robed priests stood ready with golden basins and sharp knives. The Levitical choir began chanting the beautiful psalms for this season as a wave of men and animals poured into the Court of Israelites. Each pair of men with their lamb found a place in front of one of the priests.

Once they had settled into their place, Peter recognized the man to his left, Cuza from Capernaum. The men briefly greeted each other, and Peter commented on the size of the lamb the men had chosen for their Passover meal.

Manaen responded before Cuza could answer. "There will be many guests for the Passover meal in Herod's palace tonight."

As a single person, all the men positioned their lambs. Each pair of men laid their hands on their lamb, confessing their sinfulness, accepting the blood that was about to spill as the blood that preserved their lives.

A gong sounded, and one man in each pair took the knife from within the basin that the priest held.

John held their lamb while Peter took the knife and quickly slit its throat. The priest placed a golden basin on the pavement, while John lifted their animal so the blood would drain quickly into the basin.

Peter tied its hind legs to the pomegranate pole. Then he and John placed the pole across their shoulders, holding the dead animal in an upside-down position until the blood had completely drained.

Several times, the priest checked. When the blood no longer flowed, he took the basin and passed it down the line of priests. When the basin reached the altar of burnt offering, some of its blood was sprinkled on the lower stones of the altar. The larger part of the blood was thrown into an opening at the base of the altar. Later, it would be washed through a drainage system that emptied into the valley below the Temple.

Without conversation, the men broke into groups of four. They worked together to untie their dead lambs and then pass the stick of wood through each lamb's mouth and out its rear. Two men then supported two lambs by laying the sticks across their shoulders, while the other two men worked on the lambs. All the time, the animals were treated with respect. No bones were broken. The kidneys were cut out. With some of the fat, the kidneys were put aside to be placed on the altar later. Then the skin was completely removed in one piece.

Gradually, the white paving stones on the Temple floor became dark and sticky with blood. The white robes of the priest were splattered. Not a man in the place escaped being touched by the blood. Throughout, the choir sang.

When every lamb and been prepared and was once again wrapped in its own skin, the trumpet sounded. The exit gates were opened and all the men, with their Passover lambs, walked out of the Temple. This ritual was then repeated two more times before the sun set and Passover began.

Throughout the city, large ovens burned in courtyards and portable ovens burned at campsites. Every Passover lamb must be roasted over burning coals. Peter and John hurried back to the home where they would eat. They found the oven, hot and ready. Soon, their lamb was roasting.

In the cooking area, Miriam chopped bitter herbs. Mary was wrapping stacks of unleavened bread. She looked up. "Peter, we need the wine and the water carried to the upper room."

Peter started to object, but before he could speak, John was lifting the heavy water jar. Peter hurried over to help. And so, throughout the early evening, one lamb roasted, and later, a second lamb was placed in the oven. Peter and John made trip after trip, from the cooking area to the upper room—basins, towels, plates, cups, wine, unleavened bread, chopped bitter herbs, sweet fruit dip, boiled eggs, fresh spring greens, and finally, the roasted lamb carefully carved and laid on a platter.

Just as the sun was setting, Miriam lit the Sabbath lamps. John hurried to the upper room to light the lamps on the table and in the niches around the room. He could hear voices below and knew that Jesus had arrived with the rest of the disciples. John took a quick glance around the room. All was ready.

Energetically, John Marc ran up the steps and stopped beside John. "My mother said I could eat the Passover meal with Jesus and his men. Do you think it will be all right?"

Lightly, John stroked the boy's cheek. "No whiskers yet. But I'm sure Jesus will be glad to have you."

"I'm the youngest. I can chant the four questions," John Marc offered.

Modestly gathering her robes, Procila stepped into the wide sedan chair with her husband. Longinus, on horseback, gave the signal. Their military bearers lifted the chair smoothly, and with an armed escort, they began the short trip to Herod's palace.

Pilate sniffed the air. "I'm starved. Tonight, the entire city smells delicious. Roasted lamb—I'm looking forward to the meal."

Procila replied, "This is more than just a meal. There will be a lot of preliminary ritual before the main course."

"More Jewish nonsense," Pilate complained. "I just want a good meal."

"Until you understand their feasts and their Temple rituals, you will never know the heart of the people," Procila advised.

"And what do I want with the hearts of these people?" Pilate countered.

"You want to be a successful ruler." Procila counseled. "You want that Roman peace."

"The emperor's fantasy," Pilate quipped. "Rome rules through its military. That is reality."

"Dreams foreshadow reality," Procila whispered.

Pilate sat up and leaned close to his wife. "Have you heard from the gods?"

Procila quietly answered, "There is betrayal in the air. I do not know if gods will betray gods or mortals will betray mortals, but I have seen the symbols of deception at the hand of a friend and death that is unjust."

Pilate responded with an involuntary shiver. Through a small slit in the curtains, he could see his commander. Would Longinus betray him? Was this invitation from Herod Antipas the prequel to his own demise? In the distant city of Rome, had his name come before the emperor attached to some trumped up accusation?

Silently swallowing his fears, Pilate responded pragmatically to his wife. "Death and deception constantly float on the winds of this empire. We cannot live in fear of what might be."

On the Mount of Olives, beneath a canopy of live olive branches, Mary the mother of Jesus spread the Passover meal on a low table that her capable sons had easily constructed. James pulled the lamb from their portable oven. Her sons, daughters-in-law, and grandchildren all stood around, waiting for the final preparations.

For a moment, Mary stepped back, allowing her daughters in-law to complete the meal. She moved away from everyone to a spot beneath an old tree. The fact that Jesus was not with them tugged at her heart this evening.

Looking up through the budding branches, she said, "God, you gave me a son. You sent an angel who said, '*You are to call him Jesus. He will be great and will be called the Son of the Most High. The Lord God will give him the throne of his father David, and he will reign over Jacob's descendants forever; his kingdom will never end.*'[1] I did not understand at the time. I still do not understand, but tonight, I fear for my son. Fear is holding my heart. God, I'm begging you. Take care of our son, Jesus."

Mary glanced at the table. James was holding the first cup of wine, ready to lead the blessing and pass the cup. Quickly, Mary moved to join her family.

"Blessed are you, O Lord most high, who creates the fruit of the vine and who has brought us to this Passover season." James chanted the blessing. He took a sip and passed the cup.

As the family members each took a sip, James explained. "This is the cup of sanctification. When you drink this cup, you identify yourself as a descendant of Abraham submitting only to the laws of God."

In the upper room, Jesus reclined in the place of honor. John filled the cup at his place, and Jesus lifted it. *And he said to them, "I have eagerly desired to eat this Passover with you before I suffer. For I tell you, I will not eat it again until it finds fulfillment in the Kingdom of God."*

After taking the cup, he gave thanks and then *said,* "This cup is for you. It is the work of the Spirit to free you from all the entanglements of Satan. The enemy of God has not ensnared me so I will not drink, but you must drink. *Take this and divide it among you. For I tell you I will not drink again from the fruit of the vine until the Kingdom of God comes."*[2] Jesus handed the cup first to John, who reclined on his right. Then he took the cup from John and passed it to the left, to Judas who drank. Then Judas passed it on to the rest of the disciples. Peter's nephew was the last to drink.

As the men completed the first of four shared cups of wine, Jesus *got up from the meal, took off his outer clothing, and wrapped a towel around his waist. After that, he poured water into a basin.*

Immediately, John Marc jumped up from his place at the end of the table. "Rabbi Jesus, mother said that I should be the servant tonight."

"No," Jesus gently responded. "It is my desire to be both the servant and the master of this meal. Go, recline on your cushion. Allow me the joy of washing your feet."

Jesus set the basin so it would catch the water as he dipped and poured water over first one foot and then the other. He spoke quietly to the boy as he dried each foot. "I want to thank you for going out into the desert with me to watch the sacrifice of the scapegoat. That was a special time for me."

And then Jesus moved the basin. He *began to wash his disciples' feet, drying them with the towel that was wrapped around him.*[3] First, his cousin John. "We have been together since childhood, playing on your father's boats, walking to Jerusalem three times each year. Every moment has been precious to me." Jesus kissed John's feet.

Then Jesus moved the basin next to the cushion where Judas lay. His dusty feet hung over the water. At first, Jesus was silent as he dipped and then poured water over each foot. But as he dried Judas's feet, Jesus said, "We have walked many roads together. You have seen the power of God. With Matthew, you went out and spoke the word that heals and brings new life, but you have yet to learn to distinguish between the directives of the Holy Spirit and the deceptions of the devil. That saddens me." With his hands, Jesus caressed the feet of Judas. A tear fell. Then Jesus moved on.

He emptied the dirty water from his basin and then returned to where Simon the Zealot reclined. Jesus dipped and poured a fresh stream over each foot. His thoughts went back to Nazareth. "Can any good thing come out of Nazareth?" Jesus repeated the saying. "You and I both came out of that place. We grew up running in and out of our father's shops. You were my first friend."

"No," Simon protested. "You were the true friend. When the Romans put my father on a cross, you and your father stayed at the cross with me. You were the true friend."

Quickly, Jesus kissed Simon's feet, and then he moved on to Matthew.

"Am I doing a good job, Matthew? You're used to trained servants who know how to wash feet properly."

Matthew chuckled. "I haven't dealt with a trained servant for several years now. And I don't miss that dull, pampered life. The excitement of the kingdom of heaven: authority over sickness, death, and demons—I want nothing more."

"The kingdom is yours," Jesus announced as he gave each foot a playful squeeze.

Jesus moved over to James, the brother of John and a son of Zebedee. "*You love righteousness and hate wickedness; therefore God, your God, has set you above your companions by anointing you with the oil of joy.*[4] Of these twelve, you will be the first to complete your kingdom assignment. I will come to you at that time." Jesus kissed his wet feet and then dried them with a towel.

Jesus emptied his basin again and then returned to the table with fresh water. For each disciple, he had a personal word, a gentle touch, and a gesture of affection. Then he came to Peter, who sat up. Planting both feet on the floor, Peter raised protesting hands and firmly said, "Do you plan to wash my feet?"

Jesus answered, "I know you do not recognize the importance of what I am doing. In the future, you will understand."

"No," Peter protested, "You are the Messiah, not a common servant."

Jesus answered, "Unless I wash you, you will not be part of my kingdom."

"Then wash me Lord," Peter replied. "Pour water over my head and my hands. I must be part of your kingdom!"

Jesus responded, "In the Temple, the priests completely wash their bodies every morning, but throughout the day, they just wash their feet as needed. You were baptized by John, and you have spent the last three years with me. Once you have been completely immersed, you only need to wash your feet to be clean." From his kneeling position behind the table, Jesus looked up. His eyes rested briefly on Judas. Then he quietly finished by adding, "You are clean, all but one."

When he had finished washing their feet, he put on his clothes and returned to his place as master of the Passover meal. *"Do you understand what I have done for you?" he asked them. "You call me 'Teacher' and 'Lord,' and rightly so, for that is what I am. Now that I, your Lord and Teacher, have washed your feet, you also should wash one another's feet.* No one is a master over another. All are servants. *I have set you an example that you should do as I have done for you.*[5] *Now that you know these things, you will be blessed if you do them."*[6]

Jesus caught John Marc's eye and nodded toward the small table where the food was waiting. The lad jumped up from his place next to Peter, and he lifted the heavy tray containing bowls of spring greens, finely chopped bitter herbs, and sweet mashed fruit dip.

In Herod's banquet hall, Joanna listened as Manaen guided the men through the order of the meal. She passed the spring greens to Procila, softly directing each woman to take a few, dip them in salt water, and only eat after the chanted blessing. After swallowing the greens dipped in saltwater, Joanna held up her hand so the women would listen.

Casper stood beside his father. "On this night, why is our bread without yeast? And on this night, why do we eat bitter herbs with our meal? Tonight, why will we dip in both the bitter herbs and the fruity sauce? And tonight, why are we reclining on cushions and not sitting upright on the hard floor?"

Joanna felt a rush of pride for her son, so poised and intelligent. Briefly, she remembered the night when he had struggled for every breath, and then suddenly, he was totally healthy. In the little town of Cana, Rabbi Jesus had spoken the healing word to her husband, and at that moment, her son had returned to her from the brink of death.

Under her breath, Joanna whispered, "Thank you, God."

At Mary's campsite on the Mount of Olives, Joel's little daughter had asked the four questions, and now, James was expecting answers. He took the middle piece out of a stack of three pieces of unleavened bread.

"Enos?" He turned to his own son. "Why is this the season of only eating unleavened bread?"

Confidently, Enos answered, "It was the command of God so that our ancestors could leave Egypt quickly."

Mary added, "This flat bread is the food of the poor, and as slaves, they ate it often."

Jude then spoke up. "I heard a teaching from our brother, Jesus. He compared yeast to sin. So this bread represents nourishment without the contamination of sin."

"Interesting thought," James commented. He held up the piece of unleavened bread, studying the stripes and piercings that had been made during the baking process. "Without sin, untouched by evil." He broke the bread and began the blessing. The whole family joined in.

In the upper room, Jesus took the middle piece from three large pieces of unleavened bread. He held it up, thoughtfully running his fingertip along one of the lightly browned stripes that Miriam had pressed into the dough.

Then John commented, "I can see the lamplight through the little holes in the bread."

Jesus thoughtfully nodded. *He* then *took bread, gave thanks and broke it, and gave it to them, saying, "This is my body given for you; do this in remembrance of me."* He gave the first piece to John saying, *"Take it; this is my body."*[8]

The meal continued, bitter herbs on unleavened bread, and then bitter herbs and sweet fruit on unleavened bread. Lamb was served, carefully sliced and separated from the bones. The men ate with their usual competitive banter, but Jesus was mostly quiet.

At one point, Jesus spoke over their conversations, *"Very truly I tell you, one of you is going to betray me."*

His disciples stared at one another, at a loss to know which of them he meant. One of them, the disciple whom Jesus loved, was reclining next to him. Simon Peter motioned to this disciple and said, "Ask him which one he means."

Leaning back against Jesus, he asked him, "Lord, who is it?"

Jesus answered, "It is the one to whom I will give this piece of bread when I have dipped it in the dish." Then, dipping the piece of bread into the bowl of bitter herbs, *he gave it to Judas, the son of Simon Iscariot. As soon as Judas took the bread, Satan entered into him* and took control of his thought processes.

While Judas was still chewing the bread covered with bitter herbs, Jesus beckoned for Judas to come close. *So Jesus told him, "What you are about to do, do quickly."*

But no one at the meal understood why Jesus said this to him. The disciples watched Judas leave his place at the table, put on his cloak, and walk out of the room. *Since Judas had charge of the money, some thought Jesus was telling him to buy what was needed for the festival, or to give something to the poor.* [9]

Chapter 13

Bread and Wine

Even my close friend, someone I trusted, one who shared my
bread, has turned against me.

—Psalms 41:9

"Blood! Frogs! Lice! Flies!" Procila tried to keep up with the ladies at the table, placing a small drop of wine on each of their silver plates. But as the name of each plague was spoken, she saw the plague mirrored in her plate, and a demonic face appeared. Both the face and the plague disappeared when the next drop of wine touched the plate.

"Cattle disease! Boils! Hail!" Procila turned pale. The cup of wine in her left hand trembled.

"Locusts! Darkness! Death of the Firstborn!" Procila forced herself to get the final drop of wine on her plate.

Concerned, Joanna reached over and placed her own hand on the shoulder of Pilate's wife.

Herodias, Herod's wife, asked, "Are you feeling ill?"

Procila replied, "This ceremony is very disturbing to me."

The rest of the women looked puzzled. Herodias casually responded, "It's just an old tradition. It's practically meaningless."

"But I looked in my plate, and I saw—" Procila stopped. She knew these women would not understand that there were portals through which a few privileged humans could see how the spiritual realm influences the natural world.

At the men's table, Longinus asked, "Do the Jews really believe their god brought the Egyptian Empire to its knees through these plagues?"

"Yes!" Cuza and Manaen answered almost simultaneously.

Antipas then added, "The problem is, they think he will do it again."

"To the Roman Empire?" Pilate retorted.

Antipas replied, "Hence, they are looking for another deliverer like Moses."

"A man of miracles?" Longinus asked.

Antipas answered, "Our historians tell us that Moses as a young man was a very successful military leader for Pharaoh. Our people keep looking for a military leader who will defeat the armies of Rome."

"Foolish," Pilate spoke softly. "They should look for the man who has received power from the gods."

Antipas then said, "I've heard of a man, a rabbi from Nazareth. He does miracles. I'd like to have an audience with him."

Cuza and Manaen exchanged cautious glances.

Pilate answered, "He is probably in the city tonight."

Longinus casually inserted, "Every Jewish male is in the city tonight!"

The soldiers began serving platters of roasted lamb with savory side dishes. Conversation turned to other topics.

In the upper room, the platter of sliced lamb was empty. Across the table, there were scattered crumbs of unleavened bread and empty side dishes. Beside Jesus, there was a vacant cushion. Conversations ranged along the U-shaped table, most of them focused on the hope of a new Messianic government.

Jesus lifted the final piece of unleavened bread, *gave thanks and broke it, and gave it to them, saying, "This is my body given for you; do this in remembrance of me."*[1]

Very quietly, each disciple broke off a piece. Each disciple ate, wondering about the phrase, "This is my body, broken for you." Casual dinner conversations ceased. All eleven men now focused on Jesus.

In the same way as it is done at every Passover meal, *after the supper,* Jesus *took* the third cup of wine. "You have all been taught that this cup symbolizes the blood of the lambs. When we drink from this cup, we remember Egypt, the lamb that was killed before sunset, and the blood that was painted on each doorpost with hyssop. This is the cup that turned the Death Angel away from each home. Now, I am *saying, "This cup is the new covenant in my blood, which is poured out for you.*[2] On this Passover, my blood will stain the wood and fall on the Mercy Seat for all humanity."

Jesus gave the cup to John who took a sip. Then he handed it across the empty cushion, which was Judas's place, to Simon the Zealot who drank, and that disciple passed it on to the rest of the disciples.

As the men finished the third cup, Jesus continued to teach. "Our time together grows short. I will soon leave you. You will search for me, but where I am going, you cannot come."

Along the table, puzzled glances flew from disciple to disciple. Peter started to question that statement, but Jesus cut him off. "Tonight, I announce an additional commandment: Love each other in the same way that I have loved you. This is how you will demonstrate that you are my disciples."

Concerned, Peter asked, "Master, where are you going?"

"Do not worry over this," Jesus answered. "You cannot go to this place now, but you will go later."

"Why? Is it too dangerous?" Peter asked. "Master, don't you know? I am not afraid to die for you!"

"Really?" Jesus spoke softly. Only a few heard. "This very night, before the rooster crows, you will deny having any relationship with me. Three times you will deny me."

Jesus took a moment to look at each of his disciples. "You must be aware my enemy is on the prowl tonight." Jesus looked straight at Peter. "Don't you know? Satan has asked to shred your soul. Peter, I have prayed for you that you may come through this test. I have faith that you will not fall so far from me that you cannot forgive yourself and return. Then when you return, help your brothers. Each of you will be recovering from an evil assault."

Jesus could see the concern in each man's eyes. So he offered reassurance. "In the past, I sent you out to heal the sick, to cast out demons, and to tell the people that the kingdom of heaven is beginning on Earth. I was not with you. You were without purse, bag, or sandals, but did you need anything?"

"Nothing," they answered.

"When I return to heaven, it will be the same. You will preach, baptize, heal, and deliver. I will see you from my Father's throne room, and I will make sure you have all the help you need."

An audible sigh of relief went up from the men.

Jesus did not let them rest with his comforting words. "Tonight, the prophecy of Isaiah is about to be fulfilled. I will be *led like a lamb to the slaughter*,[3] and I will *be numbered with the transgressors*."[4]

"Master, how can you be called a violator of the law, a criminal?" the Zealot asked.

Jesus countered, "Do you have a sword with you tonight?"

"I always carry a sword," the Zealot answered. "And Peter has one also!"

"It is a common belief, especially in Jerusalem, that only criminals carry concealed weapons," Jesus replied.

"Master!" Peter protested. "You know that some of us have always carried swords."

"Yes," Jesus casually answered. "I will be found in the company of two Galileans carrying swords. That will be enough to fulfill the prophecy and to bring about my conviction."

Jesus shrugged again, like he was throwing off the weight of the last verbal exchange. "Now, let's bring this disturbing conversation to an end. We have one more cup to drink, the Cup of Praise. You will drink this cup now, but I am waiting to drink it with you when we all gather in my Father's home." Jesus passed the cup.

As each man drank, Jesus said, *"Do not let your hearts be troubled. You believe in God; believe also in me. My Father's house has many rooms; if that were not so, would I have told you that I am going there to prepare a place for you? And if I go and prepare a place for you, I will come back and take you to be with me that you also may be where I am. You know the way to the place where I am going."*[5]

"What?" Thomas protested. "Master, how can we find the way?"

Jesus replied, "When you were boys in the synagogue schools, you were taught about the veil that separates the Holy from the Most Holy Place in the Temple. It is not one piece of fabric. Rather, it is many layers of heavy linen, adorned with gold and hung in a maze-like pattern that has an arm-length of thickness. On the Day of Atonement when the high priest goes into the place where God dwells on Earth, he must navigate through the layers of fabric, finding each opening so he can move closer and closer to God. I am like that maze of curtains, the path you must navigate. There is only one way to the heart of the Father. You come to him through me.

"For three years, you have been with me. We are now close friends. Every word I have said, every action you have seen was from the heart of my Father. So I can say you now know the Father."

"Master," Philip said, "Your words are very confusing. Please, speak to us plainly."

"Very well," Jesus said. *"Whoever believes in me will do the works I have been doing, and they will do even greater things than these, because I am going to the Father. And* then *I will do whatever you ask in my name, so that the Father may be glorified in the Son. You may ask me for anything in my name, and I will do it.*[6]

"Again, I must tell you that love is of supreme importance in my kingdom. You must stop your competitive exchanges. You must care for each other and work for the success of your brother. You all say that you love me. If this is so, do the things I have instructed you to do.

"When I speak of leaving you, do not be alarmed. I am not deserting you. *And I will ask the Father, and he will give you another advocate to help you and be with you forever—the Spirit of truth.*[7] This is the same Spirit that has connected me with my Father in heaven. Soon it will be yours like it has been mine."

Jesus stood, and he raised both hands in blessing. His disciples got up from their places and moved close so that he could easily touch each one.

"Shalom." Jesus moved his hand from disciple to disciple, touching each man on top of his head. "I give you peace." He kissed James and John on the top of their heads. Jesus moved over to Peter and Andrew. He held both men firmly, a hand on each man's shoulder as he admonished, "Do not allow your hearts to become troubled or afraid."

The disciples then sat on the floor, crowding close to Jesus's feet. Like children, they looked up at their teacher.

Empowered by the Holy Spirit, Jesus looked into their eyes. He saw their concern, mixed with confused messianic-hope. With an encompassing gesture, Jesus squatted down at their eye level. *"You heard me say, 'I am going away and I am coming back to you'…I have told you now before it happens, so that when it does happen you will believe."*[8]

Jesus paused and he looked around the room. He glared into each dark corner, and then he looked hard through the only window in the room. Turning back to his disciples, he said, *"I will not say much more to you, for the prince of this world is coming. He has no hold over me, but he comes so that the world may learn that I love the Father and do exactly what my Father has commanded me.*

"*Come now; let us leave.*⁹ We will sing the traditional hymns as we walk back to our camp beside the cave."

Jesus stood and began the song.

> *Not to us, Lord, not to us,*
> *but to your name be the glory,*
> *because of your love and faithfulness.*¹⁰

One by one, the men stood, each man joining in, some with lusty voices, some with broken baritones. Jesus led his disciples out of the room, down the stairs, out into the moonlit streets of Jerusalem. John Marc stayed with the men, walking between his uncles, Andrew and Peter.

Throughout the city, Passover meals were coming to an end. From open windows, snatches of the Passover psalms drifted across the path of Jesus and his little band of kingdom men. Above the melee of melodies, Jesus could be heard singing from his heart.

> *What shall I return to the Lord for all his goodness to me?*
> *I will lift up the cup of salvation*
> *and call on the name of the Lord.*
> *I will fulfill my vows to the Lord*
> *in the presence of all his people.*
> *Precious in the sight of the Lord*
> *is the death of his faithful servants.*
> *Truly I am your servant, Lord;*
> *I serve you just as my mother did;*
> *you have freed me from my chains.*
> *I will sacrifice a thank offering to you*
> *and call on the name of the Lord.*
> *I will fulfill my vows to the Lord*
> *in the presence of all his people,*

*in the courts of the house of the Lord—in your midst, Jerusalem.
Praise the Lord.*[11]

Procila pulled her robes together and climbed into the sedan chair. Before she was settled, Pilate joined her. Their military bearers lifted the chair smoothly. Procila heard the palace gates open. Pilate stuck his head out from the curtains to acknowledge a farewell salute. Then they were moving again, led by Longinus, through the streets of Jerusalem, back to the Antonio Fortress.

Procila ran her hand over a large wine stain on the front of her robe. "I cannot believe that I spilled the entire cup of wine!"

Pilate glanced over at his wife's ruined robe. "So that was the fuss at the women's table."

Procila sighed. "After the meal, Joanna passed a full cup of wine over to me. She said, 'This represents the blood of the lambs. Take a swallow and pass it on.' I put the cup to my lips, but then, in the cup, I saw a lamb with a slit throat. That lamb then turned into a man, raw from the whip and hanging on a cross. I was so shocked, so horrified that I dropped the cup."

"Do you have an interpretation?" Pilate asked.

"It is the death of someone or something totally innocent, and many in the spirit world are horrified," Procila answered.

"The death of innocence," Pilate repeated. "I don't think I know anyone who is truly innocent." Then he changed the subject. "Do you hear the songs these people are singing. From every house, I hear the same theme."

> *All the nations surrounded me,*
> *but in the name of the Lord I cut them down.*
> *They surrounded me on every side,*
> *but in the name of the Lord I cut them down.*[12]

Pilate listened again, and then he commented to his wife, "My command of their language has improved over the years. They used to call me names, and they thought I did not understand until the day I had the name-caller whipped. Do you understand this part of their Passover song?"

> *Shouts of joy and victory resound in the tents of the righteous:*
> *"The Lord's right hand has done mighty things!*
> *The Lord's right hand is lifted high;*
> *the Lord's right hand has done mighty things!"*[13]

Procila replied, "These people really do believe their god is going to send a deliverer who will decimate Rome and establish a new Jewish nation."

"If that day ever comes," Pilate predicted, "it will not just be soldiers who spill their blood. Women and babes will die in the streets. Consider that as an interpretation for your vision."

The governor and his wife heard the gates of the fortress opening. Their conversation ended.

Judas sat in the dark corridor outside the banquet hall in the residence of the high priest. The captain of the Temple guard had ordered him to wait. Caiaphas did want to speak with him, but his Passover meal could not be interrupted so Judas waited.

Suddenly, the door to the banquet hall opened. Light from multiple oil lamps spilled across the mosaic floor. A child ran from the room, hurrying for a door that opened onto the street. "Elijah? Elijah, prophet of old, have you come to our house tonight?"

At that moment, the Holy Spirit tried to break through the deception Satan had placed on this disciple. "Jesus told you John the Baptist came with the Elijah message that ushers in the Messiah."

Satan swooped in with a twisted response. "Yes, and because Jesus is the Messiah, no one can harm him. You will bring these men to him. They will question him. Jesus will give answers and demonstrate the miraculous. Then the Temple leadership will fall on their faces before him. They will officially proclaim that he is their Messiah-king—it is inevitable. Your job is to make it happen."

Spirits named Pride and Self-exaltation then moved in, filling Judas with fantasies of appreciation. Caiaphas would give him a position of honor in the Temple. Jesus would elevate him above the other disciples, those ignorant fishermen from Galilee. Peter would have to show him some respect. Silver and gold, no more sneaking from the treasury; he would have an abundant supply.

Judas did not even notice that the child quickly returned to the banquet with the disappointing news that Elijah had not come on this Passover night. The door to the banquet hall closed again, leaving Judas in the dark.

But the wait was not long.

The captain of the Temple guard stepped out of the banquet hall. He motioned for Judas to follow him into another room. Moments later, Caiaphas, the high priest, stepped into the room. "You have actionable information?" Caiaphas asked.

Judas nodded affirmatively. "Tonight, Jesus and his men will be sleeping in the garden that surrounds the oil-press cave on the lower slopes of the Mount of Olives."

Caiaphas looked at the captain of the Temple guard for input.

"I know the place," the captain answered.

Caiaphas stroked his beard thoughtfully. "It was our plan to wait until after the eight days of Passover."

Judas spoke up, "Tonight is the night. Everyone in the city of Jerusalem has eaten a large meal. They are now sleeping. Jesus will never be more alone than he is tonight."

The captain of the Temple guard added, "If we delay, the people may rise up and proclaim him to be their king before this holiday season ends. His name is on every lip."

"Yes," Caiaphas muttered, "I saw the way he entered the city."

Annas stepped into the room.

Caiaphas looked up to greet his father-in-law, a former high priest. With a few words, he updated his political and spiritual mentor.

"Let me make a suggestion," Annas offered. "Send the Temple guards with some of your trusted servants and a few soldiers from the fortress to apprehend Rabbi Jesus. This man"—he pointed to Judas—"is right. There will never be a better time to do this. Bring him to this house. We can gather witnesses and convene a small court, not all seventy. Ten will be sufficient, and we will question this man to see if he is a threat to us or to this nation. After we have established our case against this so-called rabbi, we will call the entire assembly into session."

Caiaphas nodded in agreement. Turning to Judas, the high priest said, "Go with the captain. Lead him to the place where your master and fellow disciples are sleeping tonight. I want no confusion. You are to positively identify Rabbi Jesus before we take him. Now, go."

The captain of the Temple guard stepped toward the door. Caiaphas and Annas began to confer quietly. But Judas did not move.

At the door, the captain looked back at Judas quizzically. Caiaphas and Annas noticed that their informant was not leaving. Their conversation ended. All eyes were on Judas. There was a long moment of strained silence. Finally, Annas said, "Ahh, the man wants his silver."

Caiaphas nodded his head in agreement while directing the captain. "It's in my treasury, already counted out." He turned back to Judas. "I believe we agreed on a total of thirty pieces of silver, and you have already received a deposit on that amount."

"Yes," Judas answered.

Caiaphas then added, "I want you to know, if you do not deliver Rabbi Jesus tonight, you will return every coin, and you will pay with your skin."

"Thirty-nine lashes," Annas emphatically stated.

Judas replied, "I will not disappoint you."

Hovering over the transaction, Satan rubbed his hands together in satisfaction. His plan was coming together. Cautiously, he looked around. As far as his eyes could see in the spiritual realm, there was no sign of the Holy Spirit, the archangel Michael, or the angelic armies of God. Finally, he had total access to Yeshua-in-the-body-of-a-man.

Satan turned to Raziel, his second-in-command. "To save his skin, a man will say or do anything and Yeshua has determined to live as a man."

Raziel answered, "He may go all the way and die, but if he embraces even one thought that is not in line with the character and law of God, then he becomes our captive."

"Just a thought or an unchecked emotion that he does not cast out of his mind," Satan repeated. "Anger. Bitterness. Unforgiveness will then take residence in his mind."

Raziel added, "Revenge. Self-pity. Self-preservation, those demons are also waiting for an opportunity to move into his thoughts."

"No human can suffer the way this man is going to suffer without holding an ungodly thought or unchecked emotion," Satan stated with satisfaction.

"And if he discards his humanity, picking up his divinity...," Raziel proposed.

"We still win. This whole experiment, Yeshua living as a man and dying in place of Adam and all of his descendants, it will have failed. The Earth and its inhabitants will be our kingdom forever. God will have to deal with me as an equal."

"I feel confident," Raziel stated. Both rulers of evil then left the room. They rose high above the city, taking a vantage point where they could observe and direct every player in their Passover pageant. Evil agents were given assignments. Lookouts were posted. The only human who could not be manipulated was Yeshua-Jesus.

Chapter 14

In the Garden

Then Jesus told them, "This very night you will all fall away
on account of me, for it is written: 'I will strike the shepherd,
and the sheep of the flock will be scattered.'"

—Matthew 26:31

Casually clustered, singing verse after verse of the Passover psalms, Jesus and his disciples slowly made their way toward one of the city gates. Opting for the longer route, they took the path that wound down through the Kidron Valley and then back up the Mount of Olives. It was a bright night, cool but filled with the promise of spring. Crisp green scents filled the air, and around Jesus, the heavy fragrance of Mary's anointing still clung to the fibers of his clothing.

They walked through a small vineyard. The leaves were just buds emerging from pruned branches. But each bud held the hope of a good late summer harvest. Jesus began to teach. *"I am the true vine, and my Father is the gardener.*[1] He is a faithful gardener, not neglecting what is necessary for the future crop."

Jesus stopped and examined one of the vines, running his finger over the flat ends where branches had been removed. "My Father *cuts off every branch in me that bears no fruit, while every branch that does bear fruit he prunes so that it will be even more fruitful.*[2] Each of you is like one of these branches. See how each branch is connected to the main stem? When I return to my Father, you will not see me like you do now. Still, you must remain attached to me. *If you remain in me and I in you, you will bear much fruit; apart from me you can do nothing.*"³

Jesus began walking again, across the valley toward the rising slope. He continued to teach, and his disciples pressed in so they would not miss a word.

*"If you remain in me and my words remain in you, ask whatever you wish, and it will be done for you.*⁴ Never forget," Jesus added, "*as the Father has loved me, so have I loved you. Now remain in my love. If you keep my commands, you will remain in my love.*"⁵

A cloud passed over the full moon, and for a few minutes, Jesus and his disciples found themselves in darkness. Jesus stopped walking. He sensed evil all around. Slowly, he turned back and looked at the city. "Father, show me."

The Holy Spirit immediately swooped in and opened the doorway to the realms of good and evil.

Jesus saw Satan on his throne, issuing orders from high above the city. A cold wind blew from that open door, causing each disciple to grab the edges of his cloak and wrap himself.

"Master, let's move on," Peter urged.

Jesus nodded and walked on. The moon lighted the path again. Scattered olive trees threw eerie shadows across the mountainside. Jesus spoke to his men in a somber tone.

"The ruler of the Kingdom of this World is set on our destruction tonight. He has turned all the world against us. *If the world hates you, keep in mind that it hated me first. If you belonged to the world, it would love you as its own. As it is, you do not belong to the world, but I have chosen you out of the world. That is why the world hates you. Remember what I told you: 'A servant is not greater than his master.' If they persecuted me, they will persecute you also.*⁶ But take heart. You will teach the same good news I have taught. Some will be captivated by the message of the kingdom of heaven. Others will only seek to do you harm. They will hate my name because my enemy, Satan, has deceived them. They do not know the love my Father has for them."

There were many camps on the mountainside. As Jesus and his men came up out of the narrow valley, they saw the glowing coals of dying campfires dotting the gently rolling slopes. "Ah," Jesus said, "I have spoken to so many, in the Temple and on hillsides like this one. How will each person choose? It is an eternal question for each one."

Now the path wound among the campsites. Jesus spoke softly so that his voice would not disturb those who were sleeping on the full stomach of their Passover meals. He went on to say, "We only have a little time to be together."

Hearing this, some of the disciples responded, "What is he talking about?"

Jesus heard their question, and he answered. "Soon, you will weep and mourn while our enemies celebrate. But take heart. Your sadness will turn into joy when I live again—just three days of sorrow."

Again, Jesus stopped walking. He stood, surrounded by his friends. Moonlight highlighted their concerned faces.

"Let me encourage you." He smiled reassuringly at each man. "After the events of this Passover, you will be able to ask for anything in my name, and you will receive it. Your joy on Earth will be like the joy of heaven."

Jesus looked back at the city again. The throne of Satan was still visible to him, and there was much activity around it. "This is the season of your deliverance, and for this Passover season, I came into the world."

"Yes! Now you are saying things we understand," Philip announced.

Thomas added, "We know you are the Deliverer of Israel."

"The Messiah we have waited for," Peter announced. "Our loyalty is unshakable!"

"Do you really understand?" Jesus shook his head sadly. *"A time is coming and in fact has come when you will be scattered, each to your own home. You will leave me all alone."* Jesus sighed. Then he added, *"Yet I am not alone, for my Father is with me. I have told you these things, so that in me you may have peace* when everything seems to be falling apart. Remember *in this world you will have trouble. But take heart! I have overcome the world s*o trouble can never really overcome you."*⁷*

It was midnight, the changing of the guard in the Antonio Fortress. Longinus stiffly returned the salutes of his men. Then he remained in command position as the first watch returned to their barracks. For a few moments, the ranking centurion under Governor Pontus Pilate stood in the courtyard taking in the sounds of the fort and the city. Responsibility weighed heavily on his shoulders. Most of his men were sleeping, but there was something stirring tonight. Longinus sensed it.

Hobnails clicking on the stone steps, the commander of the fortress climbed the stairs to the walkway that topped the walls of the Roman fort. From there, he could see most of the fortress and much of the city. He glanced toward Pilate's quarters and saw that his lamps had been extinguished. Making a mental note not to disturb the governor, he continued his final surveillance.

Dancing torchlight drew his attention. Glancing down into the courts of the Temple, he was surprised to see the Temple guard gathering, about twenty men, armed. Before he could send a messenger to investigate, one of his own sentries approached.

"The captain of the Temple guard has received credible information that there may be an uprising during this Passover holiday. He is going to apprehend the leader, and he requests a squad of Roman soldiers for additional authority."

Longinus briefly considered the request. Then he responded, sharing his rational with the guard. "There is a spirit of rebellion in the city tonight. We cannot ignore it. Send a squad of six to escort and assist if necessary."

After a quick salute, the sentry turned on his heel, efficiently carrying out his orders.

For a while longer, Longinus observed the activity below. There was something ominous about this night—like the last watch before a planned attack. He remembered the story he had heard at Herod's palace: plagues, a Death Angel, the destruction of the Egyptian empire.

The Temple guard left through a small gate, and Longinus turned back to his own responsibilities. He completed his circuit of the fortress, pausing just one more time when he heard a slight disturbance. Was a woman crying, in the governor's quarters? Pilate's wife? The strange sounds ended quickly so he shrugged it off and proceeded to his own bed.

On this night, there was no joy in heaven. The musical vibrations of this glorious realm had become still, silent. Every angel and God, himself, now focused on twelve men, walking along a dirt path toward an olive grove called Gethsemane. Every sinless heart in the Kingdom of God was drawn to Yeshua-Jesus, the Creator who had voluntarily left his eternal home to rescue the descendants of Adam. For centuries, all of heaven had been watching the animal sacrifices, understanding that one day, their own Yeshua would die.

Now from the path on the Mount of Olives, Yeshua's voice rang through the portals of heaven, *"Father, the hour has come."*

Every angel responded, dropping to their knees, faces covered. They knew it would soon be the time of sacrifice. Overcome with emotion, they listened to Yeshua-Jesus.

"Father, glorify me in your presence with the glory I had with you before the world began."[8]

The Holy Spirit suddenly flared as he sent heavenly affirmation down to Jesus.

Then. the Archangel Michael flew into the throne room. "Satan has placed all his forces above Jerusalem. They stand in battle formation."

"The attack we have been expecting," God stated. He gave Michael a directive nod.

The angel who commanded the holy armies, put a golden shofar to his lips and blew the call to gather the hosts of heaven.

Gabriel pointed to Ophaniel, a seraph who often directed the angel choir above the throne.

Immediately, Ophaniel led his band of angels from the throne room in heaven down to Earth. They gathered in the garden near the olive-press cave. It was their assignment to be with their Creator, to support his petitions with their own intercession.

The angels, who had been sent to minister, watched Jesus as he stopped by a low stone wall. For a moment, he rested, like a man carrying a great weight. Then he got renewed strength from their heavenly presence and began another prayer.

Around him, his disciples knelt, struggling to connect with heaven. But the men were physically weary and emotionally confused, unable to recognize their heavenly support.

Jesus stretched out his arms, grabbing James and John by the shoulders and pulling them toward him. His rested his head on John's shoulder as he prayed, "Father, *I have revealed you to those whom you gave me out of the world…For I gave them the words you gave me and they accepted them…I pray for them. I am not praying for the world, but for those you have given me…I will remain in the world no longer, but they are still in the world, and I am coming to you. Holy Father, protect them by the power of your name… so that they may be one as we are one. While I was with them, I protected them and kept them safe by that name you gave me. None has been lost except the one doomed to destruction so that Scripture would be fulfilled.*"[9]

Kneeling angels, unseen by the disciples, added their petitions, naming each disciple, declaring character beyond what each man naturally possessed.

Pushing hard on John's shoulder, Jesus tried to stand, but his hands were shaking, and his knees were weak.

Peter saw his master's struggle so he stood and pulled Jesus to his feet. James and John also stood, supporting Jesus.

Above their own intercession, the angels heard Jesus instruct his remaining disciples, "Stay here and pray for protection from the evil that surrounds us." Leaning heavily on Peter, James, and John, Jesus moved toward a dark cluster of olive trees. When he arrived at that place, he stepped away from his three companions saying, "My soul is burdened to the point of death. Sit here, pray in unity for me and for yourselves. I will go a little farther and speak to my Father." Then *he withdrew about a stone's throw beyond them, knelt down and prayed, "Father, if you are willing, take this cup of suffering from me; yet not my will, but yours be done."*[10]

In heaven, Michael blew his shofar again as he led thousands upon thousands of warrior angels to the mountain where Jesus prayed alone, facedown in the dirt. Rank after rank, they covered the Mount of Olives, facing the army of Satan.

Above the city, every fallen angel hovered around the Prince of Wickedness while his demons propelled a mob of men through the city gate.

For a moment, time seemed to stop. Satan stood and Michael stepped forward. The reigning evil angel locked eyes with his counterpart. Boldly, Satan shouted, "Finally, we face each other!"

Michael replied, "Last time we battled, you were thrown out of heaven. Now we have come to see you dethroned from Earth."

"Dethroned?" the Evil One taunted. "The sons of Adam are with me. Judas, one of the twelve, leads them. They have chosen to totally free themselves from the Creator's rulership."

"You are still the deceiver!" the Holy Spirit announced as he flared across the mountaintop.

Haughtily, Satan countered. "I have just offered men alternatives, and each man at one time or another has accepted, bowing their knee in allegiance to me."

"Not Yeshua-Jesus!" Michael shouted.

Satan laughed. "I am offering him an alternative now, and he is considering it. The cross is not a choice that any sane man would take."

"He will resist you," the Holy Spirit declared. "He will weigh every suggestion that enters his mind against the written word of God, and ultimately, he will subject himself to the plan he made with his Father."

"We will see," Satan retorted. "Remember the last time we battled on the walls of the heavenly city. Yeshua was the divine Creator. Now he is a man with two thousand years of flawed ancestry. I will destroy him. You can only watch."

Ophaniel saw Jesus collapse, sobbing into the dirt. He left the other angels and hurried to assist his Creator. The other angels quickly followed, hovering brokenheartedly, continuing their intercession.

"Father, I know we made this plan together, but my flesh recoils from the pain of the cross. My heart breaks for my followers. I have told them, but they do not understand. And Judas, I loved him. His betrayal breaks my heart. This is too much to ask of any man. Must I become the blood of the lambs, the third Passover cup? Is there no other way?"

Jesus tasted the salt of his own tears mixed with dirt from the garden, and he remembered, through the Holy Spirit, the day he had knelt in the dirt of his own perfect garden, forming Adam from the elements of earth. "Adam, Adam, how I loved you. I loved more than you, my first son of Earth. I loved the genetic seeds of the human race within your body." Jesus sighed. He scooped up a fistful of dark earth, crumbling it between his fingers. "My body must return to the elements of earth before it is glorified so the generations of Adam can regain Earth as it was meant to be."

Slowly, Jesus pulled himself to his feet. Stumbling across the uneven ground, he made his way to his disciples and found them sleeping. He touched Peter's shoulder.

Peter shook himself awake and then quickly nudged James and John into alertness.

Jesus looked down at his friends. He could not hide the disappointment in his voice. "You believe that I am the Messiah, and you support my kingship, but you could not just remain prayerful for one hour. Tonight, we need to watch for the moves of the Evil One and pray for heavenly support." Jesus sighed. "I know your hearts are willing, but your physical bodies are in need of rest." Then as an aside, Jesus added, "That saying is true of my own body. How can I expect more from you?"

Jesus went away a second time, returning to his place of prayer. "My Father, I hear the voice of my enemy. He says I do not need to suffer and die. He offers kingship with a simple acknowledgement of his authority. But I only act according to your directives so I will drink this cup of suffering according to your will. Enable me to endure the physical pain, the emotional heartache. Ooh... my mother. In her heart, she will die with me. My disciples will be terrified for their own lives, chased by demons. Set a guard around each man and woman who is associated with me. Do not allow me to fail by accepting even one thought from the Prince of Evil."

When Jesus came back to Peter, James, and John, he found all three had fallen asleep again. So, sadly shaking his head, he left them and returned to his place of prayer. *"Father, if you are willing, take this cup from me; yet not my will, but yours be done..."*[11]

Ophaniel knelt beside Jesus, shielding him with his glowing wings and placing a hand on his shoulder while Jesus continued in prayer. Anguished, Jesus prayed earnestly, throwing off waves of intimidation and suggestion from the evil one. Sweat drenched his body and fell from his forehead. It was red with the blood of his torment.

At last his struggle subsided. A decision had been solidified. Jesus stood and announced, "There is no other way. A sinless descendant from Adam must pay the price. I will die. I will accept all the pain and all the cruelty. I trust my Father who has said I will rise victorious on the third day."

Then he returned to his sleeping disciples. Through the trees, Jesus could see the dancing flames of approaching torches. Above the trees, he saw the legions of darkness. Quickly, he bent to shake each man. "Get up and pray!"

While Jesus was still shaking his followers into wakefulness, the crowd broke through the trees and entered the enclosed garden. Judas, one of the twelve, was leading them.

All the disciples jumped to their feet, adrenalin surging, anticipating confrontation. Confidently, Jesus stepped away from his men. Facing the Temple guards and Roman soldiers, he recognized priests and Levites from the Temple.

"Who are you looking for?" he asked.

The captain of the Temple guard replied, "Rabbi Jesus of Nazareth."

Taking another step forward, Jesus answered, "I Am he!" As the ancient name of God left his lips, a bright light flashed, and Holy Spirit power went out from him knocking every man in the approaching mob to the ground and sending their demons into temporary retreat.

Emboldened by that display of power, Peter and Simon the Zealot pulled their swords. Several others picked up sticks and stones. Ready for a fight, the disciples watched as the armed mob awkwardly regained their footing. Then accompanied by an entourage of demons, Judas approached Jesus with open arms. But Jesus stopped him and asked, "Do you intend to betray me with a kiss?"

Judas answered, "You will thank me." And he proceeded to pull Jesus into an embrace and to kiss him on both cheeks.

Immediately, the captain of the Temple guard signaled his men to move forward and surround Jesus.

"Lord, should we strike?"

Peter and Simon raised their swords. The other disciples prepared to defend their master.

With an angry roar, the crowd rushed forward.

A burly man who worked for Caiaphas pushed past Peter. Immediately, Peter slashed with his weapon, intending a death blow.

His thrust fell short, only removing the man's right ear.

"Stop! Jesus commanded his men. "There will be no violence on our part. Don't you think I could summon the defenses of heaven, twelve legions of angels? This is not a time to fight, and these men are not our enemies." Dropping to one knee beside the bleeding man, Jesus touched the man's ear, and a new ear instantly replaced the one that had been mangled by Peter's sword.

Once again, the demons lost their hold on the minds of the men. Every guard and soldier, every Temple official stood amazed at the creative miracle that had taken place. With his hand still on the shoulder of the high priest's servant, Jesus looked into the faces of the men who had come to arrest him. Then Jesus said to the officials in the mob, "Am I leading an insurrection against either Rome or the Temple? Did you need to come under cover of darkness with clubs and swords? Every day, I have been in your Temple. You did not approach me there."

Jesus watched as fallen angels swooped in to take offensive positions throughout the mob. Demons then returned, entering the minds of many.

The captain of the Temple guard stepped forward, facing Jesus. "Are you Rabbi Jesus of Nazareth?"

Jesus answered, "I already said I am he. If you came for me, then let these other men go."

Once again, the captain signaled his men. They rushed forward, throwing Jesus to the ground, restraining him while they tied his hands. Those who could not get close enough to lay hands on Jesus grabbed for his fleeing followers.

Young John Marc had watched the arrest in shocked disbelief. Stunned at the sudden violence, he did not respond as quickly as his uncles. A Roman soldier grabbed his tunic, dragging him back toward the frenzied mob. Reacting, John Marc wiggled out of his one-piece garment, running naked up the mountainside, going from campsite to campsite until someone gave him some clothing so he could return to the city.

Chapter 15

Tried by the Jewish Authorities

Then the detachment of soldiers with its commander and the Jewish officials arrested Jesus. They bound him and brought him first to Annas, who was the father-in-law of Caiaphas, the high priest that year. Caiaphas was the one who had advised the Jewish leaders that it would be good if one man died for the people.

—John 18:12–14

Concealed by the brush in the Kidron Valley, Peter, James, and John followed the torchlight as the mob propelled Jesus across the bridge that spanned the valley from the mountainside to one of the western city gates. James said, "We need some help, people with influence."

"Cuza from Capernaum is probably at Herod's palace," John suggested.

Peter added, "My brother-in-law knows some of the important men in the city."

James quickly suggested, "Mary of Magdela is at his house. She has financial resources, and sometimes, a bribe is needed."

John looked at his brother. "Go gather as much support as you can. We will follow to see where they take Jesus."

James started to leave, but Peter called after him, "Get word to Jesus's brothers and his mother. They camp on the mountainside each year."

Without answering, James slipped out of the bushes, through the tall grass toward another entrance to the city. Peter hid his sword under a fallen tree, and then the two disciples stealthily made their way to the path that intersected with the road that crossed the bridge.

After the final uphill push to gain the road, Peter and John found themselves behind the mob, following their heavy footsteps and flickering torchlight. Skirting the Temple, they climbed several steep flights of steps. Then they crossed another foot bridge leading into the Upper City. John whispered to Peter, "They are turning into the residence of the ex-high priest, Annas. He shares this estate with Caiaphas, his son-in-law."

"It's a den of wolves," Peter responded as he glanced over the low wall into the courtyard beside the steps. It was a larger than usual courtyard, shared by two grand houses. Light streamed from all the windows in both homes. A few servants along with some stragglers from the mob lingered by a small fire. At the gate, a woman controlled every man's entrance.

Peter and John stepped back into the shadows. Watching as recognizable members of the Sanhedrin, along with influential Sadducees were admitted, John whispered, "We have to get in and see what is happening."

With Peter close by his side, John approached the gate.

The woman who controlled the entrance glared at him, but John forced himself to smile and speak pleasantly. "I'm from the fishing establishment of Zebedee. I wish to speak to the master of procurement."

The woman responded, "It's awfully late to do business."

"Not for fishermen," John replied. Then he added, "He knows me. My family has an exclusive arrangement to supply fish for this household."

The woman nodded, opening the gate.

John hurried through, but when Peter tried to follow close on John's heels, the woman shut the gate in his face. "Tonight, each person who enters must be somehow connected with this household or the Temple."

Peter nodded and stepped back into the street to wait. Within moments, John returned with the procurement master who admitted Peter to the courtyard. As he passed the woman at the gate, she looked hard into his face. "Are you one of the disciples of Rabbi Jesus, the one they have arrested?"

Adjusting the hood of his cloak so most of his face was concealed, Peter replied, "I am not." Then he quickly followed John, mingling with those who were milling about in the courtyard.

At first, Peter and John strolled around the paved area picking up snatches of conversations. They watched as more dignitaries arrived and entered the house. John signaled to Peter that he was going to follow the next arrivals. Peter nodded and moved closer to the fire where some of the Temple guards warmed themselves.

Time passed. Peter remained by the fire, conspicuous in his silence. Curious eyes studied him from head to toe. Demons assigned to sift him slung accusations into the minds of those who curiously lingered by the warmth. Finally, a passing servant girl paused and looked closely at Peter. Her voice was loud and shrill as she announced, "You were with Rabbi Jesus of Nazareth. I have seen you helping him with the crowds."

But Peter answered. "You have confused me with someone else. Don't speak unless you know what you are talking about!" Then abruptly, he moved to the shelter of the entryway.

Later, that same servant girl spotted Peter huddled by the wall. She said to those around her, "See that fellow? He is a Galilean, a follower of the rabbi who has been arrested."

Peter heard what had been said, and he responded. "Woman, I already told you. I do not know the man."

The servant then turned away, distracted by the demonically inspired laughter of those close to the fire and the first cockcrow of the morning.

Once inside, John found an isolated bench in a corner. From there, he could see Jesus, scuffed up and bruised from the way he had been apprehended. He stood calmly before the former high priest, erect with the bearing of a king.

Annas addressed him, "So I finally meet the infamous rabbi from Nazareth."

Jesus courteously nodded in response, never breaking eye contact.

For a moment, his steady gaze seemed to unnerve Annas. The former high priest looked away and then nervously repositioned himself.

John took that moment to survey the room. He recognized Nicodemus. Judas was there, conversing with the captain of the Temple guard. A few other guardsmen from the Temple and several Roman soldiers held positions around the room. He could feel an evil presence. It swirled throughout the room.

"What is your message?" Annas finally managed to ask a question. "How would you summarize your mission?"

"Summarize my mission?" Jesus repeated. "I have always taught openly—on hillsides, in synagogues, and in the Temple. Thousands have heard me speak. Ask the people. I'm sure someone can tell you what I said."

In response to that statement, one of the Temple officials stepped up to Jesus and slapped him across the face. "Show more respect when you answer the high priest," he demanded.

Stunned silence hit the room. John glanced at Judas and noticed that he appeared shocked by such as unexpected act of violence in this formal setting. John then turned his attention back to Jesus, hoping for a blistering retort.

Instead, Jesus responded like a patient teacher. "If there was something incorrect about my statement, please explain that to me. But if I laid out the facts correctly, why did you strike me?"

Avoiding the real question, Annas picked up on a minor part of his statement. "You said, 'Ask those who heard you.' We will do just that." The former high priest looked around the room, signaling the Temple guards with a curt nod of his head. "Check the ropes that bind his hands then lead him over to face those who are prepared to testify against him."

Nicodemus quickly stepped up to caution, "All witnesses must be certified according to the law. They cannot be paid for their testimony and two must agree."

Annas sneered, "I'm sure I can count on you to object to anything that is irregular."

"Questioning a man in the dark of night is irregular," Nicodemus countered.

"This is just a preliminary enquiry," Annas responded. "Dawn is coming and all official decisions will be made by the light of day, presided over by the current high priest." Then Annas sent Jesus, bound and escorted, across the walkway above the courtyard to the home of Caiaphas the high priest.

John followed, stunned by the events, but still expecting Jesus to suddenly vanish, leaving his captors confused. It had happened before. John ran the memories through his mind, a comfort to cling to.

Judas stepped up, attempting to pull John into a conversation so he could offer an explanation.

A surge of anger washed over John. He clinched his fist, wanting to punch the man who had led a lynch mob to apprehend Jesus. But following the example of his master, he turned his back and refused to acknowledge his fellow disciple. John moved on, keeping Jesus in sight.

Demonically, excited men pushed by. Judas was left to follow the unreasonably enraged mob down the steps that skirted the shared courtyard and across to the home of the current high priest.

In the courtyard, Peter hugged the shadows close to the gate. Others were standing there because the wall served as a windbreak. One of the high priest's servants walked by. He was a relative of the man whose ear Peter had cut off. Slowly, he approached, looking closely at the man who stood by the wall. "Weren't you in the garden with the rabbi we arrested?" The man stepped closer, looking hard at Peter's face. "You are the Galilean who raised a sword and sliced an ear from Malchus!"

Fear swooped in, grabbing Peter, choking him with visions of his own death.

Angrily, Peter replied, "What are you talking about?" And he began to curse.

Just as he was cursing, the rooster crowed a second time. And Jesus, hands bound and flanked by guards, passed by the courtyard. At that moment, Jesus turned and looked straight at Peter.

Then Peter remembered. Before dawn the rooster will crow, and you will have denied me three times.

Brokenhearted, Peter went outside into the night. He returned to the garden where Jesus had been arrested. There, he wept bitterly.

There was insistent knocking on the side door of the perfumer's shop.

Jonathan, expecting to find the relative of someone newly deceased, hurried to answer. He was shocked to see his brother, Simon.

Simon pushed his way into the business. "I don't want anyone to see me," he stated.

Mary came from the back room. She waited to hear the reason for this unusual visit.

"I have only come out of respect for your brother." Simon spoke to Mary. "You must send a messenger to him immediately. He needs to go into hiding."

"Why?" Mary stepped forward.

"Rabbi Jesus has been arrested. Annas and Caiaphas have been plotting this ever since your brother was raised from the dead. Lazarus is next." Simon took a deep shuddering breath. "I have been called to sit with the Sanhedrin at his trial. The court is convening just before dawn. I have already been told how I must vote."

"What will the verdict be?" Mary angrily asked.

"Death," Simon answered.

Mary quickly retorted, "He healed you of leprosy."

Simon responded, "Any man who votes to acquit Jesus will be the next accused."

"But Roman law…," Jonathan objected.

Simon scoffed, "They have brought men to Pilate before. He crucifies each one without asking questions. This Roman governor doesn't care how many Jews die. He doesn't care whether they are innocent or guilty."

"They've got something on Pilate," Jonathan suggested. "He wouldn't do anything for them if he didn't have to."

Simon shrugged, "Probably, but it doesn't change the facts. Lazarus is in danger. Warn him." Without another word, Simon turned and left the house.

In the banquet hall in the residence of the high priest, rows of benches had replaced the tables and cushions used for the Passover meal. The judgment seat had been established on a raised podium at one end of the room, and there Caiaphas presided over the gathering authorities with Annas and other chief priests at his elbow. Judas stayed close to the captain of the Temple guard.

John slipped in, finding a place next to the heavy draperies on the side of the room. Jesus was already standing in the place of the accused while witnesses were lining up in the hallway. John looked at his teacher, his cousin, his best friend. He remembered all that Jesus had told them, and he just could not believe Jesus would not speak an authoritative word that would calm this unbelievable political storm.

Jesus turned and looked at John. For a moment, it was the old Jesus with a look of compassion so deep that it brought tears to John's eyes.

It was only a brief non-verbal exchange. The first witness was being questioned. "How has Rabbi Jesus been undermining the authority of the Temple?"

"He finds the Temple a useless place," the man answered. "He brags that he can destroy it and rebuild it in three days."

"Have any other witnesses heard this?"

Others came forward, some with similar accounts and still others with confusing stories.

Ophaniel lined his angels along the back wall of the judgment hall. With breaking hearts, they continued their intercession on behalf of their Creator.

Behind the judgment seat, Satan had placed his own throne. He had always wanted to pass judgment on Yeshua. And now, working through Caiaphas, he could have that satisfaction.

Leaning forward, Satan urged Caiaphas, "Ask this man, Jesus, if he is the Messiah. Rome crucifies every man who claims to be the Jewish Messiah."

With a hateful smirk on his face, Caiaphas directly asked, "Well, Rabbi Jesus, *are you not going to answer? What is this testimony that these men are bringing against you?*"

But Jesus remained silent and gave no answer.

Again the high priest asked him, "Are you the Messiah, the Son of the Blessed One?"

"I am," said Jesus. "You have read that Enoch saw a vision of the Holy One coming to Earth seated on a throne and surrounded by angels, coming to judge, to punish and to reward. The Holy One that he saw is the seed of a woman and the Son of God. I am that Messiah."

Caiaphas jumped to his feet and screamed, "Blasphemy! Say no more!"

But Jesus continued. With an unflinching glare, he temporarily silenced the high priest. "*And you will see me, the Son of Man, sitting at the right hand of the Mighty One and coming on the clouds of heaven.* I will be the judge, and you will stand before me, accused."

For a moment, Caiaphas trembled. Satan trembled. Then both recovered. With an enraged shriek, *the high priest tore his clothes. "Why do we need any more witnesses?" he asked. "You have heard the blasphemy. What do you think?"*

"Guilty! Death! Blasphemy!" the agents of Satan shot their responses like arrows into the minds of usually dignified men. The members of the highest court in the land shouted like street rabble. "Kill him! Jesus must die!"

A few voices called for calm, for reconsideration, but they were overpowered by the agitated mob.

At daybreak, Annas called for a vote. Except for a few abstaining members, *they all condemned him as worthy of death.*

Demons, evil angels, even Satan, the greatest of all the fallen angels, reveled in the power that was now theirs. Yeshua-Jesus had been rejected and condemned by humanity.

Then, prompted by the forces of evil, *some* of the Temple guards *began to spit at him; they blindfolded him, struck him with their fists, and said, "Prophesy!" And the guards took him and beat him.*[1] Roman soldiers watched, giving their permission by not interfering. This was a Jewish matter. The soldiers from the Roman fortress were merely entertained by the violence.

Above the melee, louder than his own gasps of horror, John heard Judas hysterically shouting, "Stop! Stop! This is wrong! He is innocent! Listen to me! The witnesses lied!"

John saw a couple of the Temple guards turn and lay their fists on Judas, knocking him to the floor. Then totally controlled by Satanic powers, the men pushed Jesus out of the banquet hall, beating him every step of the way until he found solace in a locked cell in the basement of the home of the high priest.

It was a brief rest. By the growing light of dawn, a decision had to be made and acted upon before the supporters of Jesus could rally and bring forth substantial opposition. So, even though it was *very early in the morning, the chief priests, with the elders, the teachers of the law and the whole Sanhedrin, made their plans. So they bound Jesus, led him away and handed him over to Pilate.*[2]

Chapter 16

Tried by Rome

*Pilate called together the chief priests, the rulers and the
people, and said to them, "You brought me this man as one
who was inciting the people to rebellion. I have examined
him in your presence and have found no basis for your charges
against him. Neither has Herod, for he sent him back to us; as
you can see, he has done nothing to deserve death."*

—Luke 23:13–15

The first rays of dawn woke the governor of Judea. It was his
habit to rise early, to set a good example of military discipline
for the men under him. He moved around his sleeping chamber
quietly, slipping into a fresh toga, belting it at the waist, careful
not to disturb his wife. He knew her sleep had been quite fretful.

In the next room, his personal attendant stood ready with
razor and basin. Stiffly, Pilate submitted himself to the morning
routine. A knock signaled the morning report.

Longinus entered. "A delegation from the high priest is
waiting at the entrance to the fort," he announced.

"So early? On the morning after their big religious holiday?"
Pilate looked a little put out. "Bring them into the courtyard. Tell
them to wait."

"They prefer to remain outside," Longinus replied. "Evidently
entering a gentile establishment will make them unclean for
tonight's sacred feast."

"Yes, I remember." Pilate sighed. "My wife told me there are two feasts, one after the other."

Longinus nodded.

Pilate asked, "Do you know the reason for their visit?"

Longinus answered, "They have a prisoner, the famous rabbi who heals the sick and often teaches in their Temple."

"The one who healed the servant of the centurion stationed at Capernaum?" Pilate asked.

"Yes." Longinus nodded. "I had a similar encounter with the man."

Pilate focused on his commander, obviously interested.

"When we apprehended the traitor and thief named Barabbas, his men put up a fight. One of his followers sliced my arm deeply. I had to place a tourniquet around it or bleed to death on the spot." Then Longinus held out his hand to show Pilate that there was not even a scar. "For some unknown reason, this rabbi was sitting nearby. I challenged him. But he did not respond like most men. He should have been intimidated by my position, but he spoke to me as an equal. Then he blew on my arm, and suddenly, it was completely healed."

Pilate looked closely, trying to see any sign of an injury.

"Are you sure they have the same man?" Pilate asked.

Longinus answered, "I have seen his face. I will never forget his eyes. It seems that he fears no man, but at the same time, he understands each man's fear."

"Those rascals who run the Temple and run to the emperor with every complaint!" Pilate exclaimed. "What is their accusation?"

"They say Rabbi Jesus is a traitor, a man who is trying to overthrow the government." Longinus took a deep breath. "They want him crucified."

"I smell a rotten fish here," Pilate responded.

Longinus agreed. "I questioned the men I sent with the Temple guard to make the arrest. They were present at his interrogation, and each man has stated that this is about the laws of the Jews, not the laws of Rome, something they call blasphemy. It is local politics and nothing more."

"Temple nonsense,"Pilate grunted while he waited impatiently for his assistant to drape and pin his toga so it hung correctly from one shoulder. Then he followed his commanding officer to the entrance of the fortress. His judgment seat was already in place on the paving stones near the gate. With a scowl that signaled his displeasure, the governor of Judea took his seat.

The crowd was tired of waiting. Annas shouted, "Jesus of Nazareth is a traitor!" All around him responded by shouting," Death to the traitor!"

Pilate held up his hand for silence. Then he motioned for Annas to come forward with the charge.

Piously, the former high priest announced, *"We have found this man subverting our nation. He opposes payment of taxes to Caesar and claims to be Messiah, a king."* Now, do what Roman law requires!"

So Pilate asked Jesus, "Are you the king of the Jews? Do you hear their accusations? How do you answer?"

Jesus said nothing so Pilate turned back to Annas, "Bring your witnesses."

Annas hesitated as if groping for a response. Finally, he replied, "They got lost in the crowd."

"Well *then," Pilate announced to the chief priests and the crowd,* "You have no witnesses and your prisoner isn't speaking so *I find no basis for a charge against this man."*

But they insisted, "He stirs up the people all over Judea by his teaching. He started in Galilee and has come all the way here."[1]

"Galilee?" Pilate repeated.

"Nazareth is an insignificant town in the region of Galilee." Longinus clarified.

"Under the jurisdiction of Herod Antipas," Pilate stated with satisfaction. "Send this man to Antipas for judgment. He is staying in his father's old palace. It's nearby." Pilate seemed especially pleased with himself as he added, "Wake the Old Fox up. Don't let him lay in bed all day like royalty!"

It was early, but Cuza was taking inventory in the treasury room of Herod's palace. The valuables that had belonged to Herod the Great had to be periodically accounted for. Manaen was delivering the morning report to Antipas as he prepared for the day—an elaborate sacrifice at the Temple followed by another banquet, this one for Jewish dignitaries.

The draperies stirred. A sentry from the gate hurried into the room, offering Manaen a small rolled parchment. Manaen broke the seal and then read aloud.

> To Your Majesty, Antipas son of the Great King Herod,
>
> This morning, I remembered that you wished to have an audience with the newest worker of miracles, Rabbi Jesus of Nazareth. He has dangerously aroused the ire of the Temple authorities. They want me to crucify him.
>
> Since Rabbi Jesus is from Galilee and this is really a matter of Jewish law, I am placing the man in your capable hands. Apprise me of your decision.
>
> Sincerely,
Pontus Pilate
Governor over Jerusalem and Judea

"Rabbi Jesus! In my palace!" Antipas exclaimed. Turning to Manaen he asked, "Should I hear the charges against him or should I just see what the man has to say for himself."

Manaen who had been the king's advisor for many years suggested, "Let the rabbi speak for himself."

Antipas nodded in eager agreement. "Bring him in."

Filled with unease, Manaen hurried to the palace gate. He was surprised to see that an agitated mob had accompanied the soldiers who escorted Jesus.

He heard their shouts. "Death to the traitor!"

"False Messiah!"

"Crucify him!"

Manaen was shocked. How could so many turn on such a kind and Torah observant man?

Deftly wielding his authority, Manaen admitted the soldiers with their prisoner, leaving the others clamoring behind closed gates. His eyes caught the eyes of Jesus, and he felt his own heart break. How he wanted to drop to his knees and cry, "Forgive me! I am nothing more than a puppet for King Herod Antipas. I have no power to change your situation."

It seemed that Jesus knew his heart and instantly understood. With his head, he slightly nodded, giving this man, one of his seventy disciples, the same silent directive he had given to the armies of heaven. Observe, but do not interfere.

Hearing the clamor of the military escort, Cuza came out to see what was happening. He felt stunned. Jesus, the man who had saved his son from certain death, was bound and surrounded by a guard from the Roman fortress.

"What is the meaning of this?" Cuza rushed to confront the soldier in command.

Manaen held up a cautioning hand, but Cuza ignored it, getting into the face of the lead Roman soldier.

The soldiers stopped marching, the highest ranking soldier holding his ground while Cuza stood firm for a response.

"This man is a political prisoner. The governor has sent him to be tried by Herod Antipas."

"Why?" Cuza demanded.

"The Sanhedrin has determined that he should die. Only a governing Roman official can pass that sentence."

After the soldier's response, Cuza continued to block his path. Manaen ran forward. Placing a hand on his friend's shoulder he said, "Jesus must stand before Antipas. Maybe it will turn out well."

Cuza stepped aside, shoulders dropping and tears pooling in his eyes. "We were not able to save the prophet. I fear. I fear that we cannot help this good man either."

There was another shout from the gate. Manaen hurried over to see what was happening. Annas, the former high priest and several important Sadducees had arrived. He let them in.

Like an eager child welcoming his entertainment, Antipas clapped as Jesus was escorted into his throne room. Brushing the Temple dignitaries aside, he immediately tossed a crust of bread toward the prisoner who stood before him. "I have heard of your many miracles. I saved this little piece of bread from my morning meal so you could expand it into a whole loaf."

Jesus glanced down at the bread and then up at the ruler of Galilee. He looked past the son of the man who had killed the babies of Bethlehem, into the challenging eyes of Satan.

Satan sneered, "Herod Antipas can free you. You do not need to endure the pain of the cross. He will give you a position in his government, and I can then arrange an even higher position. You do want to be a ruler? The Roman Empire, even the world can be yours."

"Untie his hands," Manaen suggested.

But Annas and the priests objected loudly. "Do not free him! This man deserves to die! He is a criminal!"

Herod paid no attention to the men from the Temple. He took that moment to unlace his sandal. "Come closer," he beckoned to Jesus. "Look at my big toe. It is red, sore, infected. Touch it and make it like new! I have heard that you do those things." Herod Antipas lifted his foot toward Jesus. "I heard a story that you spit in the eyes of a blind man, and then he could see. Spit on my toe! Go ahead!"

Except for a glance at the toe, Jesus remained erect and unresponsive.

Suddenly, turning red in the face, Antipas brought his foot to the floor and jumped from his royal chair, stomping his good foot. "I am a king! I am to be answered! You cannot just ignore me and stand there like you are my superior!"

Manaen took a step to placate Antipas, but Jesus caught his eye, communicating with a slight negative shake of his head that Manaen was not to interfere.

"He claims to be the new king of the Jews," Annas shouted. "But you are the only king in this room."

"I want some entertainment, and I will have some entertainment from this so-called king," Antipas responded. Then Antipas grabbed his royal robe and tossed it into the arms of the closest soldier. "Make this man look like a king!"

Herod Antipas supervised the dressing of the prisoner. "Now spin him around." Antipas stepped up and suddenly spit on Jesus. "Who spit on you, King Jesus?"

A soldier punched him in the back. "Who delivered that blow?" Antipas tauntingly asked. "A king cannot be too careful. He has enemies all around, and he must know who he can and cannot trust," Antipas mockingly advised.

Annas reached out and yanked Jesus's beard. Another soldier yanked on the other side of his beard, coming away with a fistful of whiskers.

Antipas then smacked Jesus with his scepter, and blood flowed from the wound he inflicted.

At the sight of blood, the powers of darkness shrieked and urged the men into a frenzy of body blows.

Antipas fell back into his chair laughing. Annas and his fellow priests chortled while Manaen and Cuza cried, "Enough! Enough! This behavior is not lawful!"

Finally, the soldiers tired of their sport. One soldier who had been holding Jesus released his grip, and Jesus crumpled to the floor.

Both Manaen and Cuza rushed to Jesus, wiping the blood from his eyes. Manaen looked boldly up into the face of King Antipas. "Are you satisfied? Do you have a verdict?"

Annas and the priests responded before Antipas could stop laughing. "Guilty! Guilty of treason! Kill him!"

Cuza then challenged Herod Antipas. "Are you going to let those men from the Temple tell you what to do?"

Manaen then added, "A few years ago, you beheaded a man of God and had his head brought to you on a platter. Now, in the dark of night, you fear his spirit may be stalking you."

Suddenly, the room became silent. Herod Antipas looked at Jesus, struggling to his feet, holding his battered ribs. A whiff of Mary's perfume, like the fragrance of purity, filled his nostrils. Then Herod Antipas began to shake. "Send him back to Pilate. Get him out of my palace! I will not pass judgment on this man."

One of the soldiers began to remove the royal robe, but Antipas protested, "Leave it on him. He may be a king."

"Joanna! Joanna!" Cuza rushed into his wife's room.

She looked up from the garment she was sewing.

"Jesus has been arrested! He has been taken to Pilate! The high priest and the Sanhedrin are asking for the death penalty."

Joanna jumped to her feet. "I must find Salome and the people of Capernaum."

"His mother and his brothers need to be told," Cuza added.

"Can you stop this injustice?" Joanna asked.

"I don't know." Cuza replied. "I'm going over to the fortress to speak with the commander. He may have some influence."

Judas lingered on the edges of the demonically frenzied mob at the gates of Herod's palace. Over their bobbing heads, he saw the massive gates open. The clamoring crowd then fell back, and Judas caught a glimpse of brass helmets moving as the soldiers from the fortress marched out. Was Jesus with the soldiers, or did he remain behind in the palace?

Judas shoved and pushed, but he could not penetrate the crowd. So he skirted around, scrambling until he found a place at the edge of the road, just ahead of the soldiers. From there, he could see the Roman detail approaching. The soldiers surrounded his master, spears ready for any man who might attempt a rescue or an attack. Judas could not believe what he saw—Jesus, bloodied and bound. What had gone wrong?

Frantically, Judas called, "Jesus? Jesus? Don't allow this!"

And Jesus responded, turning his head, looking directly at him so sadly, so silently.

The crowd was now upon Judas, surging along both sides of the road. The press of moving bodies knocked him down. Then Judas was on his hands and knees, trying to stay abreast of Jesus, trying to avoid being trampled. "Jesus, I didn't mean for this to happen! Do a miracle! Disappear!"

Suddenly, Judas felt a hand on his shoulder. He looked up to see John who was also trying to keep pace with Jesus and the soldiers. "Are you satisfied?" John yelled into his face. "You brought the soldiers to the garden. You are the one who always had grand ideas and schemes to bring Jesus to his Messianic throne. See what you have done!"

"I'll fix it! I'll fix it!" Judas cried and he jumped to his feet and began running toward the Temple.

Longinus heard the crowd approaching. Then from the tower window, he saw them, like a pack of wild dogs nipping at the heels of an isolated lamb. As his men approached the gate, Longinus observed the prisoner, obviously unprofessionally beaten. The sight made him feel disgusted. There was proper military punishment and then there was mob behavior. He knew all those men, soldiers and civilians, had tasted blood. Now they wanted more.

Hurrying down the stairs, he met Pilate at the gate. "The prisoner has been returned to us," he dutifully informed.

"I can hear that!" Pilate groused. "Herod couldn't stand up to Annas and his friends from the Temple."

While two soldiers returned the judgment seat to its place on the pavement near the entrance to the fortress, Longinus conferred with his military escort.

When Pilate sternly strode out to take his seat, Longinus followed. "Now *what charges are you bringing against this man?*" the governor tersely asked.

Annas and the captain of the Temple guard exchanged angry glances. Then they stepped up to speak. "Why are you making this case so difficult? In the past, you have accepted the decisions of our court so you must know *if he were not a criminal…we would not have handed him over to you.*"

Pilate said, "My soldiers have given their report. I have determined that this is not a matter of Roman law. The ruler of Galilee has refused to pass a death sentence on this man. There is nothing more I can do for you. *Take him yourselves and judge him by your own law.*"

"*But we have no right to execute anyone,*" they objected.[4]

Pilate and Longinus exchanged cautious glances. Then Pilate said, "I will speak privately with your prisoner and examine him. *Pilate then went back inside the palace, summoned Jesus and asked* him, *"Are you the king of the Jews?*[5] Are you one of those Messiahs, making plans to set up a government and rule these people?"

"Is that your own idea," Jesus asked, *"or did others talk to you about me,*[6] filling your mind with unfounded suggestions?"

"Am I a Jew? Do I read your scriptures or understand all this Messianic nonsense?" *Pilate replied.* "I deal with those who raise a sword to challenge my authority. But you have not challenged me. Yet *your own people and chief priests handed you over to me. What is it you have done?*[7] How have you offended them?"

Jesus said, "I offend them most because they cannot control or intimidate me. I am a ruler, but *my kingdom is not of this world. If it were, my servants would fight to prevent my arrest by the Jewish leaders. But now my kingdom is from another place,*[8] beyond the stars."

"You are a king, then!" said Pilate.

"One of the gods," Longinus softly exclaimed.

Pilate heard his commander's comment, and a little chill ran the length of his spine.

Jesus never broke eye contact with the governor. He *answered, "You say that I am a king. In fact, the reason I was born and came into the world is to testify to the truth* of my right to rule the kingdom of my Father. My kingdom is a kingdom of the heart. I rule over attitudes and ideas. *Everyone on the side of truth listens to me."*[9]

"What is truth?" retorted Pilate sarcastically. "A man may die for criminal activity, but no one dies for truth." *With this he went out again to the Jews gathered there* on the stone pavement. He took his seat *and said, "I find no basis for a charge against him.* He is not grappling for a throne. He has no armed followers. He has broken no Roman laws. *But* since *it is your custom for me to release to you one prisoner at the time of the Passover, do you want me to release 'the king of the Jews'* or Barabbas who stole money from the Temple and killed a Temple guard?"

They shouted back, "No, not him! Give us Barabbas!"[10]

Barabbas? He was a notorious thief, a murderer, and a leader of ruthless men. Longinus could not believe his ears. The high priest had insisted that Barabbas be apprehended and receive the worst penalty possible. Now he was to be freed so an innocent man could be killed?

Standing among those who had gathered in front of the fortress, John shouted for Jesus to be released, but his voice was quickly overpowered. John looked around, stunned. Who was shouting "Give us Barabbas"? He saw the men of the arresting mob, the household servants from the estates of Annas and Caiaphas, a few Levites, and the captain of the Temple guard. Really, it was not a large number of people, but the volume of their shouts seemed amazingly loud.

While Pilate was sitting on the judge's seat, his wife sent him this message: "Don't have anything to do with that innocent man, for I have suffered a great deal today in a dream because of him.[11] This man is one of the gods, the son of the most powerful god. In the night, I saw the clouds separate and in the gateway to heaven I saw a man on a white horse. It was the rabbi from Nazareth. He had crowns on his head, fire in his eyes, and a sword in his hand.

As Pilate read the message, he paled and his hands shook. Had the gods come to test him? Pilate returned to the scroll in his hands.

"My husband, to you, at this moment, Rabbi Jesus may look like an ordinary man, but in my dream I saw him in the splendor and authority of the gods. Be cautious in your dealings with this god-man. He loves truth and hates lies.

"Then the future was revealed. I saw you, my husband, rise from your grave, gaunt and worm-eaten. You looked into the face of this king on his horse, and it was the face of Rabbi Jesus of Nazareth. A sword, like a beam of fire flew from his mouth, striking you down. Vultures dove for your body, plucking the flesh from your bones. "You must not condemn this man. To condemn him is to condemn yourself."

Pilate's hands shook and the scroll fell to the floor.

Longinus retrieved it, offering it back to the governor.

Pilate waved it away, and Longinus placed the rolled document in his own belt, planning to read it later.

Pilate stood. Mustering all his military dignity, he asked again, *"Do you want me to release to you the king of the Jews?"*[12] *But the chief priests stirred up the crowd to have Pilate release Barabbas instead.*

"What shall I do, then, with the one you call the king of the Jews?" Pilate asked them.

"Crucify him!" they shouted.

"Why? What crime has he committed?" asked Pilate for the third time.

But they shouted all the louder, "Crucify him!"[13]

Pilate turned to his military commander, the expression on his face begging for a suggestion.

"This crowd wants blood," Longinus stated.

"All right," Pilate responded. "I'll give them blood. Bring the prisoner into the courtyard, tie him to the post and whip him!"

"Whip the prisoner," Longinus repeated the order, but the words made him sick to his stomach. He couldn't watch. So hiding his weakness, he sent a subordinate to oversee the punishment. Still, his ears heard the thud of lead tipped whips hitting muscle, tearing flesh down to the bone. He heard the breath expelled from a strong man in a shocked gasp of unbelievable pain, again and again.

Longinus couldn't help himself. He counted, and when the punishment was complete, he rushed into the courtyard to make sure there were no additional blows. What he saw seemed far worse than anything he had seen during his military career. There wasn't a patch of solid skin anywhere on the man's torso.

"Cover him!" Longinus ordered. Then he left to bring his report to Pilate.

One of the soldiers picked up the purple robe that Herod Antipas had used to mock the kingship of Rabbi Jesus. Another grabbed a crown made of intertwined thorns, a sign that a cruel game was about to begin.

The soldiers gathered round. Demons cheered them on while unseen angels wept. One man jammed the crown on Jesus's head so the thorns tore into his scalp. "Tell us, who made you king?"

"What is your ancestry? Do you come from a long line of crazy men?"

"Hey? Where did that blow come from?"

"Is your army coming to save you? Ha! Got you again!"

"You're alone! No one will rescue you!"

Above the human mocking, Satan shouted. "You bleed like a man. You feel pain like a man. There is no divinity in you. All of this suffering because of your twisted interpretation of prophetic scriptures?"

Soundlessly, Jesus's lips moved. "Father God, I am your son… *you brought me out of the womb; you made me trust in you, even at my mother's breast. From birth I was cast on you; from my mother's womb you have been my God. Do not be far from me, for trouble is near and there is no one to help.*[14] But your Spirit remains with me. It whispers, 'Trust, believe every word your Father has spoken to you.'"

"Hey, hey, Your Majesty, you're drooling like a crazy man!" one soldier announced as he pulled the hair from Jesus's beard.

Another soldier smacked the crown of thorns with the butt of his whip so that more blood streamed down Jesus's face. "Hail, King of the Jews!"

Longinus returned at that moment. With a stream of oaths, he ended their game.

Once more, Pilate walked out of his audience chamber. Behind him, two soldiers roughly propelled Jesus from the courtyard to stand behind Pilate's judgment chair.

Since his arrest, Jesus's face had aged. Large chunks of his beard had been ripped away. Dried blood had formed clotted rivers from his hairline to his knees, and from his lacerated back, fresh blood slowly seeped through the fabric of his tunic, onto the purple robe that hung from his slumped shoulders.

John, standing in the crowd, dropped to his knees and wept. How could this happen?

As soon as Annas and his supporters saw Jesus, they shouted, "Crucify him! Crucify Rabbi Jesus!"

Sternly, Pilate approached Annas and the other Jews who supported his petition. "Look at your rabbi." Pilate turned and pointed to the badly beaten man. I have honored your high court by inflicting a brutal punishment, but as far as the laws of Rome go, he has not committed a traitorous act. This man has been sufficiently punished."

More shouts of "Crucify him!" drowned out the rest of Pilate's proclamation.

Other disciples had infiltrated the crowd, and now they stood, shocked and distraught. The memory of Jesus riding into Jerusalem like a king seemed like an impossible moment in time. Yet it had been less than a week. Where were those cheering people? Where was an authoritative voice that would stop this madness?

The forces of Satan had spread out over the city, preventing supporters from coming to raise a countercry. So when Pilate saw that a riot could easily start, he threatened the representatives from the Sanhedrin, "I am going to free this man. Then, you can take him and nail him to a cross. After that rebellious act I will gladly bring the full weight of Roman law upon your Jewish leadership!"

"Our law must be respected," the Jewish leaders angrily responded. "This man has been tried according to Jewish law by our high court. He must die because he claims to be the Son of God."

"The Son of God! Which god? Your Jewish God? My Roman gods?" When Pilate heard their argument, he remembered his wife's warning. Then with fear rising like bile in his throat, he turned his back on the Jews and went back inside.

Alone with Longinus, Pilate asked, "Have you read the message?"

Longinus nodded affirmatively.

"What do you think?" Pilate waited for advice.

Longinus looked down at his arm. "Rabbi Jesus may be the son of the Great God.

"I have to know! Bring him in to me again," Pilate demanded.

Two soldiers escorted Jesus into Pilate's office.

Both Pilate and Longinus were amazed that Rabbi Jesus was able to walk unsupported, with calmness and dignity. They were equally amazed that this mutilated man was not begging for his life.

Pilate stepped up, silently studying Jesus's face. "You are not like any man I have ever tried. *Where do you come from?" he asked Jesus, but Jesus gave him no answer. "Do you refuse to speak to me?" Pilate said,* raising his voice in an attempt to intimidate. *"Don't you realize I have power either to free you or to crucify you?"*[15]

Jesus calmly *answered, "You would have no power over me if it were not given to you from* my Father *above.* You do not know my Father who rules the universe, but the Jewish leaders know all about him. *Therefore,* their leader, *the one who handed me over to you, is guilty of a greater sin."*[16]

From then on, Pilate tried to set Jesus free. He went out to them again and again, *but the Jewish leaders kept shouting, "If you let this man go, you are no friend of Caesar. Anyone who claims to be a king opposes Caesar."*[17]

Once more, Pilate conferred with Longinus. "If these men bring another complaint about me to the emperor, linked with an accusation of treason, I may be the next dead man."

Longinus sadly shook his head. "It is true. Almost every man who was given a position of authority by Sejanus has now been executed for traitorous activity. You are one of the few who lives and retains your position."

"What about crucifying the son of the Great God?" Pilate asked.

Longinus replied. "You must choose between the wrath of the emperor that you know and the wrath of the gods, which is an unknown."

Pilate paced a little, and then he replied, "The emperor is ruthless. The gods may understand mercy. I'm not sure." He sighed. "I have to base my decision on what I know. In the Roman Empire, self-preservation comes first."

Longinus bowed his head. Then he said, "Do what you must to ensure a long governorship and a long life."

When Pilate heard this, he brought Jesus out and sat down on the judge's seat at a place known as the Stone Pavement... It was about noon.

"Here is your king," Pilate said to the Jews.

But they shouted, "Take him away! Take him away! Crucify him!"

"Shall I crucify your king?" Pilate asked.

"We have no king but Caesar," the chief priests answered.[18]

Pilate turned to Longinus. "Bring me a basin of water."

"Crucify him! Crucify him!" In the basement of the fortress, all the prisoners could hear the frenzied mob. "Barabbas!" Over and over, they heard the name of one of the isolated prisoners.

A guard strolled down to his cell and banged roughly on the heavy wooden door. "There's an angry crowd out there this morning, and they are calling your name. Your crossbeam is ready! Ha! I'll just throw it into your cell so you can practice carrying it." With the assistance of another guard, he opened the door and tossed a solid plank of cedar into the cubical where Barabbas crouched on a pile of dirty straw. "You'll be nailed to this piece of wood before this day ends."

Barabbas, the hardened criminal who had killed more than one man with his bare hands, shook. "If he could get his hands on a weapon, he would use it to kill himself. It would be easier than death on a cross.

Outside his cell there was more noise, hobnails hitting the paving stones. A squad of three stopped at the locked door of Barabbas's cell. The criminal heard the lock and then the raising of the sturdy plank that barred the door. "Pick up your cross and come with us."

With a soldier on each side, Barabbas carried the heavy beam from the jailer's dungeon to the seat of judgment just outside the courtyard. When he arrived, the soldiers took the beam and then securely bound his hands behind his back. Roughly, they shoved him forward to stand beside another man, a shadow of humanity so bloodied by the whip that Barabbas wondered what terrible crime warranted such torturous punishment.

Like a wild man, Judas pushed and shoved his way through one of the crowded entrances to the Temple. Frantically, he wove in and out, through the masses of Passover worshipers who filled the Court of the Gentiles, then the Court of the Women. Finally, he made his way to the steps that led to the Court of the Israelites. From there, he ran into the Court of the Priests. At the base of the altar, he found Caiaphas receiving elaborate offerings from the wealthy.

Before anyone could interfere, Judas ran up to him screaming, "Rabbi Jesus is innocent! Do not kill him! I misinformed you! He is innocent!"

Judas then ripped the money bag from his belt and held it out to the high priest. "Take your silver back."

A little smirk formed on the lips of the high priest. "I don't want those coins. I have what I want. Rabbi Jesus will die."

"No! No! You said that you would not harm him!" Judas screamed.

The Temple guards moved in to apprehend Judas. As they grabbed him, Judas threw his thirty pieces of silver at the feet of Caiaphas. "Is that enough to buy a man's life?"

The high priest refused to answer. With his hand, he signaled for the guards to remove Judas from the Temple grounds.

The silver remained on the floor close to the altar. Priests, who had been carrying sacrifices from the preparation tables up the ramp to the fires, stopped. They stood, staring at the coins, unsure how to walk around or deal with the scattered silver.

One of the executive priests who had been part of the interrogation of Jesus stepped up to advise Caiaphas. "We need to get these coins out of here."

"They cannot be returned to the treasury," Caiaphas warned. "We both know this is blood money."

The executive priest turned to an apprentice priest. He said to the young man, "Gather these coins. They are an offering for the poor."

Caiaphas then stepped into the conversation. "Buy a field outside the city walls, a place suitable to bury those who may die and not have a place for burial."

Chapter 17

Prepare for Crucifixion

*But he was pierced for our transgressions, he was crushed for
our iniquities; the punishment that brought us peace was on
him, and by his wounds we are healed.*

—Isaiah 53:5

"Where are the families from Nazareth camping?" Mary
from Magdela, Salome the wife of Zebedee, and Mary
the wife of Clopas walked up and down the lower slopes of the
Mount of Olives, going from camp to camp until they found
Jude, one of Jesus's younger brothers.

"Take me to your mother!" Mary of Magdela directed.

"Gather your brothers, their wives, and children, now,"
Salome added.

There was urgency in the demeanor of these women. Jude
moved quickly, pulling his extended family together. As soon
as Mary the mother of Jesus arrived, Salome rushed forward,
wrapping her arms around her sister.

Mary from Magdela took the lead. "Jesus has been arrested.
He has been condemned to die by the Sanhedrin. They have
taken him to the Roman governor. Annas and Caiaphas are
requesting crucifixion.

"No!" James caught his mother as she fell out of Salome's
embrace, face in the dirt, screaming her denial.

Mary, the businesswoman from Magedla, glanced down at Jesus's mother, and then she turned her attention back to the rest of the family. "Roman policy is to crucify all the brothers and close associates with a convicted traitor." She looked at the family and said, "Pack up and get out of Jerusalem until this calms down."

At that moment, Toma, a relative, burst into the group. "Pilate has given in to the demands of the Sanhedrin. Jesus is going to be crucified."

Mary, the mother of Jesus, began wailing again and her daughters-in-law joined her. The men just stood there, shocked, angry, impotent.

Finally, Toma broke the silence. "Most of the family should leave. The children do not need to see this. Come to my home in Bethlehem. It's a short walk."

James, the second son of Mary, agreed. "I'll take the family to Bethlehem. Then I'll return to see what can be done.

Mary the mother of Jesus pulled herself up from the dirt. She looked at James and then at her other sons. "I'm not going." She turned to Mary of Magdela. "Take me to Jesus. Wherever he is. Whatever happens, I must be with him."

"Mother," James protested.

Salome intervened. "James, you don't understand the heart of a mother."

The wife of Clopas agreed.

Then Mary of Magdela added, "We are just women. The soldiers will ignore us. The men, his disciples, and his close kinsmen need to stay out of sight for now."

Just then, James and John, the sons of Zebedee and Salome, came running up the hillside. Winded from their quick climb, they gasped for breath before blurting out their anguished news, "Pilate has turned Jesus over to the soldiers. They are preparing for a crucifixion now."

"Now!" Toma exclaimed. "I thought there would be time to appeal, at least a day or so."

"Take me to my son," Mary demanded, looking directly at John.

Immediately, John led the way with the four women following.

Satisfied that the death sentence was about to be carried out, Satan elevated his throne once more, above the city. From there, he scanned every street, his evil eyes searching for the followers of Jesus. Peter was in the garden where Jesus had been arrested, sobbing, begging God for forgiveness.

Satan cynically laughed, saying to himself, "God wouldn't forgive me for speaking against his son. Why should he forgive you?" Still, the Evil One found it a little disturbing that God had sent an angel to stand guard over Peter so that evil angels dared not move in to finish him off.

Andrew, Thomas, and Philip had found Jon Marc and returned him to the home of his parents. Now they and many others were gathering in the upper room where the men had shared their last Passover supper. Andrew was leading the prayers. And around that home, many angels stood with drawn swords, ready to engage the forces of darkness.

The Prince of Darkness found Cuza at the entrance to the Roman fortress, trying to get an audience with either Longinus or Pilate. Satan saw that his agents were effectively blocking that meeting.

Then his evil eye focused on Judas. There were no angels of light around that man. Over the past year, choice by choice, he had dismissed all heavenly assistance. Now, Judas only had demons and dark angels by his side. They whispered death. With one black thought, Satan freed his demonic forces to take Judas over the edge.

Satan watched the once-cocky disciple pick up a rope as he hurried out the city gate, toward the place of crucifixion. On the way, there was an old, dead olive tree. Judas stopped there to rest, to lean his back against its thick trunk while he sobbed.

In his head, the evil voices were unrelenting. "Death! Death! There is nothing left! You failed. Now die." In his mind, he saw the bloodied face of Jesus, the sorrowful eyes that used to sparkle with happiness.

Satan sent his own twisted thoughts to Judas. "You are solely responsible for the crucifixion of Jesus. He is the son of God, and God will never forgive you. Your life is over. There is no reason to live."

With satisfaction, Satan watched as Judas slowly climbed the tree, tossing the rope over an extended branch. It only took a little more encouragement to get him to make a noose and place it around his own neck.

"I'm sorry." The prayer slipped past the Evil One. He couldn't stop it. He knew God heard. Then Judas jumped.

At first, the man dangled, choking and kicking.

Satan scoffed, "You were never good with your hands. You can't even tie a noose that will do the job quickly!" Satan then sent a directive to one of his angels.

Suddenly, the extended limb cracked and fell. Judas landed on the rocks. One sharp-edged boulder pierced his abdomen and his guts spilled onto the ground. Death was not immediate— physical anguish, emotional anguish, mental anguish.

Before his last breath, Judas managed to slip another prayer past the forces of evil. It entered the throne room and went directly to the ears of God.

"I am innocent of this man's blood," Pilate *said* as he brought his dripping hands up, out from the basin of water. *"It is your responsibility!"*

All the people answered, "His blood is on us and on our children!"

Then he released Barabbas to them.[1]

Pilate had no more to say. With a nod of his head, he turned the grim task of execution over to Longinus. Trying to make sense of the injustice he had just witnessed, the commander of the fortress first strode over to Barabbas. With his own hands, he untied the ropes that secured the most notorious criminal in the land. As he worked on the knots, he bent close to say, "A good man— maybe more than a man—is dying in your place today. I hope you appreciate what he is doing." Longinus could say no more. He pushed Barabbas away with an angry shove. Then he turned to a subordinate. "Take the prisoner. Prepare for crucifixion."

As Longinus turned to leave, he saw Herod's royal robe pulled from Jesus's shoulders. It was tossed aside, but then he saw another soldier quickly snatch it and run toward the barracks to hide it among his own possessions. Longinus deliberately looked away. He did not want to see more. It was tradition to let the soldiers entertain themselves and profit from each crucifixion. The practice had always disturbed him, but today, it seemed more barbaric than usual.

Quickly, the Roman commander strode away from the scene, back to his own quarters, where he could wash his hands and declare his innocence before the gods.

The walls of the fortress were not thick enough. Longinus could still hear the muffled drums that called the entire regiment to stand in formation for the final whipping, part of each crucifixion. He knew it was meant to weaken and break the resistance of the convicted one, but in this case, it seemed unnecessarily cruel. Longinus heard the thud of the whip, cutting through already-lacerated flesh. In his heart, he hoped that Rabbi Jesus would die from the whipping. Again, Longinus counted the blows.

In the corner of his room, there was a small statue of Mars, the Roman god of war and the only god Longinus knew. The commander of the fortress dropped to his knees before the statue. "Forgive me. I am a soldier who must obey orders. This man may be one of your fellow gods. I know his goodness, and I tremble to be the one to inflict such a torturous death." The whipping ended, and Longinus thanked his god that it was over.

Taking advantage of the absence of the commander of the fortress, Satan stepped in to give the orders. "Release the prisoner from the whipping post. Strip him in front of everyone! Humiliate this Jewish rabbi. Expose his body to the eyes of my evil angels and these non-Jewish men." Turning to his trembling forces, the Prince of Evil shouted, "Do not fear Yeshua-Jesus anymore! Look at him! He is ours! His angels have deserted him. We are winning this war!"

The men responded to every thought that the Evil One put in their minds. They needed no officer to direct.

Again Satan shouted, "Look at your king! No glory—just mutilated flesh!" Directing his orders toward the soldier in charge, he mockingly announced, "Every king needs a robe. Put the scarlet robe of Rome on his shoulders for he is now in the hands of that unrelenting empire."

The demons howled with glee as a soldier's cape was casually tossed across the bleeding shoulders of their Creator. Satan drew near and whispered. "Yeshua-Jesus, it is not too late. Drop to your knees and worship me. I can make you king."

Looking past his human tormentors into the face of the angel he had once cast out of heaven, Jesus mouthed one word, "Never!"

Angrily, Satan pointed to the crown of thorns that had fallen from Jesus's head during the whipping.

Immediately, a young soldier walked over to that place. He bent down and picked up the wreath of twisted thorns, a painful crown for a convicted king. Amid the taunting cheers of his companions, the soldier jammed this makeshift diadem hard onto the head of the prisoner.

Blood poured down Jesus's forehead, into his eyes. It dripped off his beard. Two more soldiers marched forward. With ridiculing gestures *they put a staff in his right hand. Then they knelt in front of him and mocked him. "Hail, king of the Jews!" they said. They spit on Jesus, and took the staff and struck him on the head again and again.*[2]

Satan turned to Raziel, his second-in-command. "Remember when Yeshua put Adam and Eve out of their garden home, he cursed the ground and caused it to bring forth thorns. Now he carries that curse on his own head."

Raziel laughed. All the other evil angels and demons laughed with him. It was derisive laughter. It traveled through the spiritual airwaves, horrifying the angels of righteousness and breaking the heart of God.

Fully dressed in the battle garb of a centurion, Longinus strode into the courtyard and then stopped, stiff and erect. His stern face and unbending posture demanded an immediate response. It sent a message to every man present: "The games have ended. Now is the time for Roman justice and military protocol."

Even Satan stepped back, quickly returning to the role of an observer.

Without receiving a verbal command, the troops scrambled to fall into formation, leaving Jesus alone, weakly swaying and then slumping onto the bloody paving stones.

"Dress this man properly," Longinus ordered.

One of the soldiers rushed to grab the garments Jesus had been wearing, but he paused in shocked surprise as the beautiful aroma from Mary's anointing reached his nostrils. The fragrance whispered the goodness of the man they had just beaten and mocked.

The soldier felt his heart breaking. Quickly, he handed the clothing to another man, turning his head to hide the unexpected tears that had filled his eyes and were now streaming down his cheeks.

So *after* the soldiers *had mocked him, they took off the robe and put his own clothes on him. Then they led* Jesus *away to crucify him.*[3]

Waiting on the edge of the morbidly curious crowd, Barabbas could not pull himself away from the ghastly drama. He had heard the swish and smack of the whips. He had listened to the cries of sudden pain. He had recognized the rough curses of the two men who had been captured with him, but he had not heard the voice of the rabbi.

Memories swirled through the mind of the man who had just been given an extension on life. This Rabbi Jesus was from Nazareth, a place where Barabbas had once lived in the hills, raiding with a notorious freedom fighter called the Galilean. There was something about the eyes of this rabbi. Barabbas felt sure he had seen the man before. He was certain there had been some earlier contact, moments when their lives had crossed.

The drums began again, muffled and steady. Slowly, the gates to the fortress swung open. The crowd moved back, lining both sides of the road. Four abreast, the drummers lead the procession, followed by soldiers, spears in hand and ready in battle gear. They made two single files, marching along each side of the road. The commander of the fortress followed on horseback.

In the midst of the ranks, three men carried their crossbeams. Barabbas stared at the first two. He knew their names, but he hardly recognized their faces. Teeth had been knocked out. Sections of beard had been jerked from their faces, leaving raw patches of skin. Blood seeped through their tunics from the lacerations on their backs. Both men had eyes that were purple and swollen. Still their anger and defiance remained intact, fighters to the end. Gestas, a loyal son of Israel and hater of everything Roman, cursed the soldier who prodded him along with the point of his spear, while Dysmas, a hard man who had killed many a traveler, spit at the people who lined the road.

Lagging behind these brigands, Barabbas saw Rabbi Jesus stumbling along, falling frequently. His bloody face was ravaged by the effort, but no unkind words escaped his lips. Along the road, wailing women extended sympathetic hands, and at one point, the rabbi paused, leaning heavily against his cedar plank.

Longinus halted the procession, allowing the brief respite.

Between labored breaths, Jesus spoke to the women who were pressing to be allowed to offer a cup of water or a cloth for his bloody face. His voice was weak. Only those who were very close to the road heard him. *"Daughters of Jerusalem,* God has shown me the future of this city. So *do not weep for me; weep for yourselves and for your children. For the time will come* in your lifetime *when you will say, 'Blessed are the childless women, the wombs that never bore and the breasts that never nursed!'* Your children will die in your arms, and you will thank God that their suffering has ended. So great will be the distress of that day that many…*will say to the mountains, 'Fall on us!' and to the hills, 'Cover us!'*⁴ Today, you see the beginning of the end for this city."

Looking up into the face of the mounted centurion, Jesus added, "You will also see that day, and you will remember today." Then, seeing that the Roman commander was ready to move on, Jesus manfully struggled, hoisting his cross-beam up onto his lacerated shoulder. He took three more steps. Then his knees buckled. The heavy cedar plank fell into the dust of the road. Jesus collapsed on top of it, breathing heavily. Once again, the procession stopped.

Longinus brought his horse up to the place where Jesus had fallen. He had seen enough brutality today and did not want to add to the distress of this innocent man. From his mount, he scanned the curious who lined the road, mostly women. He was looking for a strong man.

His eyes fell on a man who was dressed a little differently, obviously a visitor from another part of the empire. "You!" Longinus pointed with his short sword.

Immediately, the man became alarmed. He wrapped his arms protectively around the two young men who were with him. "I have done nothing! I am just passing along on this road. I am with my sons. We plan to spend the day at the Temple."

Two soldiers wrenched the man away from his boys. They propelled him to stand before the mounted commander.

"What is your name?" Longinus asked.

"Simon from Cyrene," he stammered.

"Are you a Roman citizen?"

"No, but my sons were born into citizenship," Simon answered.

"You can be conscripted for temporary forced labor. Your sons cannot." Longinus glanced at Jesus, resting in the dirt, regaining some strength.

With his sword, he pointed first at Simon and then at Jesus. "Carry that man's cross."

Simon gasped, "I'll be unclean!"

Longinus retorted, "You will be alive. Your sons will have a father, and you will return to your home in Cyrene with a story to tell."

One of the soldiers urged the conscripted man into the middle of the road with the point of his spear.

Simon bent to lift the crossbeam. His eyes met the eyes of the man who was going to die that day. Immediately, he knew. Those were not the eyes of a criminal.

Through bruised and swollen lips, Jesus hoarsely whispered, "Thank you."

Simon's heart went out to the mutilated man.

Beneath his breath, Barabbas whispered, "It should have been me." He almost rushed forward. The phrase "I'll carry that man's cross" was on his lips, but Fear suddenly grabbed him. It whispered, "Rome might decide to crucify you, anyway."

Barabbas then slunk back into the crowd. He knew he should flee, but he could not tear himself away from the man who was dying in his place. So, hanging on the edges of the crowd, he moved with the morbidly curious to the place of crucifixion.

Chapter 18

Crucified

Dogs surround me, a pack of villains encircles me; they pierce my hands and my feet. All my bones are on display; people stare and gloat over me. They divide my clothes among them and cast lots for my garment.

—Psalm 22:16–18

Running, stumbling, John led the women down the Mount of Olives, toward the road that circled the city. Ahead, they spotted the evil procession coming out of the gate. Roman soldiers, temple guards, a few representatives from the Temple, three prisoners, and the curious rabble—a peculiar cross section of Jerusalem traveled together toward the Place of the Skull. When Mary the mother of Jesus saw them, she dashed ahead, determined to be with her son, determined to lift her voice to God, his Father.

Surely, God would listen. After all, he had sent his angel to tell her that she would have a son. Her child was to be named Jesus. The angel even said, *"He will be great and will be called the Son of the Most High. The Lord God will give him the throne of his father David and he will reign over the house of Jacob forever; his kingdom will never end."*[1]

The cross? The cross? Mary repeated the same question she had asked the angel many years ago. *"How can this be?"*[2] My son is the Messiah. I have seen him heal the sick and do many amazing miracles."

She pushed and shoved. "Let me through!" Mary demanded, weaving her small body between the moving people. At last, she laid eyes on her son, and she had no words for the pain that ran through her heart like a sword. "God!" She screamed. "Remember your promises to me!"

The mindless crowd pushed her along. John and the other women caught up to her, using their own bodies to protect her from the buffeting of the mob. "I don't understand. I don't understand." Mary said it over and over. "How could this happen? How can we stop it?"

Then Mary saw the Roman commander on his horse. Somehow, she made her way to him. "Sir?"

Longinus looked down into the ravaged face of a graying Jewish woman. She had dropped to her knees in front of his horse.

"Help me!" she pleaded. "This is my son. There must be a mistake. He is a rabbi, a good man. Stop this! He cannot die on a cross."

Longinus took a deep shuddering breath to steady himself. In his heart, he knew the rabbi was an innocent man, but orders were orders, and he was an agent of Rome. Anxiously, he glanced around. There must be someone he could hand this woman off to.

He saw a man and three women, rushing forward to assist. Then he looked down at the mother of Rabbi Jesus. "Good woman, I cannot change what is about to happen. Go with your friends and be comforted by them." Then as Mary fell into the arms of her sister, Longinus spoke gruffly to John. "Take this woman away. She should not see what is about to happen." Then Longinus pulled the reins of his horse so the animal would carry him swiftly away from the emotional agony of those who loved the rabbi.

The last of the procession passed by, leaving Mary in the dusty road surrounded by her friends, her sister, and nephew.

Longinus pushed his horse into a fast trot. He hurried past the procession toward the massive, pock-marked boulder that resembled a human skull. Several soldiers had arrived ahead of him. They were placing the placards on ledges that had been carved into the rock. Each sign would appear above the cross of the victim, advertising his crime in large bold characters for all to see: Thief and Murderer, King of the Jews, Thief and Murderer.

Longinus gave his approval just as the procession arrived. Almost immediately, the representatives from the Temple stepped up to voice their objections to one of the signs.

With anger in his heart, the centurion replied, "Isn't it enough that we are crucifying this man? Take your complaint to Pilate. Those are his words."

Then the centurion turned on his heel and moved on to supervise the execution. First, he inspected the holes. They were deep, free of rubble, close to the side of the road, with the skull shaped rock forming a background. Next, he checked the long beams. A small pile always remained at this site. He selected three and had one placed beside each hole.

Longinus then signaled for the prisoners to be escorted to their places of execution. Dysmas was first. He came struggling and cursing, bound between two soldiers. Longinus stepped up to the man. "For numerous acts of murder and theft along the highways of Rome, you are sentenced to die by crucifixion." With one hand, the commander signaled for the bucket of wine mixed with myrrh. It was a pain killer offered to each man before crucifixion.

Dysmas drank deeply. Then the soldiers stripped him completely naked.

Longinus then stepped over to Jesus. The goodness of this man overwhelmed the centurion, so he just stood there, looking into the eyes of the rabbi. For a long uncomfortable moment, Longinus could not speak. His mind groped for a way to state a crime that had been committed by Rabbi Jesus. But what was this man's crime? Why was he being crucified?

Jesus then spoke very softly. Only Longinus could hear. "I know why I am dying."

Longinus let out a sigh of relief. Then he called for the wine mixed with myrrh. With his own hand, Longinus dipped up the painkiller. He brought the ladle to Jesus's lips.

But Jesus shook his head. "No."

"Please," Longinus tried again.

"No." Jesus was firm, and Longinus respected his request.

With regret in his heart, the centurion turned his back as his own soldiers removed all of Jesus's clothing. Longinus moved on to the next prisoner.

Gestas was standing still between two guards. The centurion announced his crime, "You have been tried and found guilty of murder and theft along the highways of Rome; therefore, you have been sentenced to die on a cross."

As the last word left the centurion's mouth, Gestas spit in the face of the commander of the fortress. Then Gestas snarled, "I'll see you one day in the place that God has reserved for the wicked. You're as much of a murderer as I am."

In his heart, Longinus quaked. How could such truth come from the lips of a convicted criminal?

The crossbeams were attached to the longer beams. One by one, the men were laid on their crosses, positioned and tied. Screams and curses filled the air. There was not enough myrrh and wine in the entire empire to ease the kind of pain that Rome inflicted.

Dysmas was first. Satan watched his suffering, salivating with anticipation. Jesus would be next. Then as the soldiers approached Jesus with the nails and hammer, Satan also approached. "Now, shall we end this ordeal? You can rule this world under me, just like Herod Antipas rules under the Roman emperor."

Instead of replying to Satan, Jesus looked into the eyes of the soldier who held the point of the nail against his wrist. Then he looked into the eyes of the soldier who readied the hammer. Jesus gave a slight nod, permission to continue.

At the crucifixion site, a hush fell over the onlookers. Only the pounding of the hammer on the metal spikes was heard. For Longinus who was used to the cries of tormented men, the silence produced an anguish that he had never experienced before. It was a short silence. The soldiers moved over to Gestas. His screams could be heard all the way to the city wall.

Ichabod, the beggar at the Beautiful Gate, adjusted his bowl so more Passover pilgrims would notice and leave him an offering. Suddenly, there was a small commotion on the wide step where he was sitting. He recognized the participants. Joseph of Arimathea and Nicodemus had cornered the ex-high priest, Annas. He heard both men shouting at the old priest. "It's not too late! If you go with us to Pilate, Jesus can be taken down from the cross. Men have survived after such an ordeal."

"Why would I do that?" Annas cynically asked.

"Because the whole trial was a farce," Nicodemus replied. "Your witnesses lied."

Joseph added, "You lied to Pilate. Rabbi Jesus has done nothing worthy of death."

"This is a Roman matter now," Annas replied. "I do not have any more time. I am on my way to the barley field to oversee the tying of the sheaves so they will be ready for the harvesting of the first fruits."

Nicodemus quickly responded. "Annas, what is more important, the binding and cutting down of a good man or the binding and cutting down of a sheaf of barley?"

"Both are for the good of the people," Annas declared.

Joseph retorted, "This is going to be a matter for the people. When they hear the role your family has taken in killing this man of God, they will protest. Then your family won't have enough money to buy the position of high priest for the next generation."

Ichabod couldn't believe what he was hearing, Rabbi Jesus on a Roman cross! He had hoped that this Passover would be the time when he would somehow get to the healer. He had heard so many stories. And so many times he had imagined his own healing moment. Now his hope was dying with the man on the cross.

He looked up at the three men again. It was easy to read the intimidating stance of the former high priest. "I expect the Temple guard will be making more arrests soon. We will rid the city and the Sanhedrin of his followers. They are all traitors." With that, Annas pushed past the two men.

Outside the city walls, not far from the stone quarry, three crosses stood by the road at the Place of the Skull. Most of the soldiers had returned to the fortress. Only four remained. Longinus mounted his horse again. For now, the worst was over. He and his men just had to wait for each final gasping breath.

In situations like this, the soldiers had expected behaviors. They drank a little wine. Everyone seemed to need something to take the edge off their confrontation with death. Then, as expected, *when the soldiers* had *crucified Jesus, they took his clothes, divided them into four shares, one for each of them, with the undergarment remaining. This garment was seamless, woven in one piece from top to bottom.*

"Let's not tear it," they said to one another. "Let's decide by lot who will get it."[3]

Jesus had clothing that was of better quality than the other two criminals. It also had a fragrance that held each man captive, an unusually beautiful aroma.

Longinus observed the men who had divided the rabbi's clothing. Each man walked off and sat alone, repeatedly bringing the garment to his nose in the manner of a man who contemplates the secrets of the gods.

The road was now full of people, late arrivals for Passover as well as those who were spending each night in the country. Longinus kept a trained eye on the groups that walked by. Most hung their heads and turned away from the gruesome scene, but some were hecklers. Motivated by evil spirits, they *hurled insults at* Rabbi Jesus, *shaking their heads and saying, "So! You who are going to destroy the Temple and build it in three days, come down from the cross and save yourself!"*

In the same way, the chief priests and the teachers of the law, who seemed compelled to become the witnesses of his last breath, *mocked him among themselves. "He saved others," they said, "but he can't save himself! Let this Messiah, this King of Israel, come down now from the cross, that we may see and believe."*[4]

"Yes!"

Jesus immediately recognized the voice of his enemy. It wasn't just coming through the hecklers. It was close and personal. Jesus turned his head toward the voice.

Satan stood beside the cross, allowing Jesus to see all the glory he possessed. In kind and alluring tones, he pressured Jesus. "Now is the time to come down from this cross. If you are the Son of God, show us your divinity. Leap down. Heal your own body. Show us your glory and watch your torturers fall like dead men. All of Israel, and then the world, will say, 'This is our Messiah, the One we have been waiting for!'"

Turning his head away, Jesus refused to acknowledge the temptation. Instead, he focused on filling his lungs with life-sustaining air. Over and over, he struggled to breathe, painfully pushing up so he could fill his lungs before he had to sink back down into a less tortured position.

Between their own struggles for breath, Dysmas and Gestas, the criminals who hung on either side of his cross, also slung vicious taunts.

With only sympathy and understanding in his heart, Jesus responded to those men and to the others who were taking part in his crucifixion. *"Father, forgive them for they do not know what they are doing."*[5]

Then Gestas, the criminal who hung on his left sneered, "If you are the Deliverer, the one who is supposed to free us from Roman tyranny, this would be a good time to do something. Save yourself and us!"

But Dysmas, the criminal on the right, rebuked Gestas. "Soon, we will face the judgment of God. Aren't you afraid? We are both guilty of terrible crimes. But this man has never broken the law. I know he is the One we have been waiting for."

For a few minutes, there was silence as the men struggled to breathe through their pain. Then Dysmas said, "Rabbi Jesus, I know you are the Messiah. When your kingdom is established, call me from the grave. I will be one of your loyal supporters."

Jesus answered him, "I assure you, in my Father's home, there is a place for you. You will not remain in the grave. You will be where I am."

From the road where John and the women had huddled over the mother of Jesus, protecting her from the gruesome scenes of crucifixion, John could see that now was the best time to bring the women close to the cross. He wanted his Aunt Mary to have a final word with her son so he urged the women forward until they could almost touch the rough wood and bloody feet.

Heartbreakingly, *near the cross of Jesus stood his mother.* She was supported by *his mother's sister, Mary the wife of Clopas, and Mary Magdalene. When Jesus saw his mother there and the disciple whom he loved standing nearby,* he tried to give them a little smile. But he could not hold it for long because he had to breathe. Between strangled efforts to fill his lungs, *he said to* his mother, *'Dear woman, here is your son."* With his head, he nodded toward John. *And to the disciple,* John, *"Here is your mother."*[6]

Mary immediately collapsed into uncontrollable sobs, and John, with the help of the other women, moved her away from the cross.

At that moment, a terrible darkness rolled across the sky and shafts of lightening flew from black clouds toward the earth. Around the crosses, most of the onlookers departed, quickly and fearfully. The soldiers, along with a few who remained, huddled next to the boulder called the Skull. From the ominous sky, heaven railed against the fallen angels and puppet men who had dared to engineer the torturous death of Yeshua-Jesus.

Still struggling to place this morning's act of injustice in a mental compartment with many other haunting memories from his past, Pilate strode into his living quarters in the fortress. His wife sat there, quietly stitching. It was the first time she had seen him since she had sent the message. Procila looked up. Her eyes asked the question, "What did you do?"

Before Pilate could come up with a response that would placate her, the room became dark as midnight.

In the blackness, Pilate heard his wife scream. He groped for a flint and found the oil lamp. After a few tries, he managed to light the wick. By its flickering flame, he could just make out the form of his wife, standing rigid by her chair.

Lightning suddenly flashed. The room was momentarily illuminated. Briefly, Pilate could see the wide-eyed terror on Procila's face. "What have you done?" she screamed. "In the middle of the day, the sun hides its face and the gods throw their bolts of fire to the earth."

Procila's fear was contagious. Pilate dropped to his knees and covered his face with his hands. With a trembling voice he replied, "I sent the son of the Great God to the cross."

While darkness engulfed the city, both Pilate and his wife remained in immovable terror.

As the time for the late worship service approached, the darkness gradually lifted. In the Temple, preparations for the evening sacrifice began. The lamb was chosen, inspected, and washed. It was brought to the place where it would lay down its life, penned between two cedar posts. A final drink was brought to the animal.

At the place of crucifixion, the darkness had dissipated except for a cloud that seemed to hang over the center cross.

Satan studied that darkness. Then he said to Raziel. "Yeshua-Jesus has taken on the sins of all men. He has become the serpent that Moses lifted up in the wilderness."

Raziel asked, "Has he become like us, sinful outcasts?"

"Never to see the face of God again," Satan slowly stated. "God cannot look upon sin without destroying it."

From the shelter of the boulder, Longinus watched the men hanging from their crosses. He heard their groans and their struggled breathing. Unnerved, he watched the darkness swirl around the center cross. What did it mean?

Suddenly, out of the darkness he heard. *"Eloi, Eloi, lama sabachthani?"*

Longinus understood enough of the language to know that Jesus was speaking to his Father in the spirit realm. *"My God, my God, why have you abandoned me?"*[7]

Some of the bystanders misunderstood and thought he was calling for the prophet Elijah. For a moment, they talked among themselves, amazed at the strength of his voice after all he had been through. *One of them ran and got a sponge. He filled it with wine vinegar, put it on a staff, and offered it to Jesus to drink.*[8]

The rest scoffed. "Wait and see if Elijah comes to save him."

Then Jesus shouted out again, "It is finished! Father, I release my spirit into your hands." Then he exhaled. It was his last breath.

At that moment, an angelic hand grasped the curtain in the sanctuary of the Temple. At the command of God, it ripped the multi-layered partition from top to bottom.

The priest with knife in hand, ready to slay the lamb for the evening sacrifice, dropped the knife. The lamb suddenly leaped and slipped away from between the wooden posts. But the animal was quickly forgotten as all eyes stared at the gaping hole where the curtains always hung. Then unbelievable fear hit every man who served before the Lord in that place.

The ground heaved and shook as the spirit-being that was Yeshua-Jesus flew toward the gates of Sheol, the place where all deceased men and women rested in spirit form.

In Pilate's quarters, the walls trembled and the lamps swayed. One lamp fell over, spilling oil and fire across the floor.

Pilate responded with military reflexes, quickly beating out the flames with his bare hands. Then with the fortress still shaking, he crawled over to the window that looked down into the Temple courtyard. To his amazement, he could see through the great doorway of the Jewish sanctuary, all the way back into the tiny dark room where the Jewish god was supposed to dwell.

Tremor after tremor rolled through the city. While Procila remained in her chair, holding tight to its arms, Pilate gripped the frame of the window. When the next tremor nearly threw him to the floor, he turned to his wife and stoically admitted, "I should have listened to you. I made a big mistake today. But for now, I am still the governor, and I must see to the needs of this city." Holding onto the wall, he staggered out to deal with the aftermath of the earthquake.

At the crucifixion site, every man that was standing was thrown to the ground. Rocks split apart; fissures instantly appeared around the crosses.

With a jolting crash, the sinless spirit of Jesus hit the Gates of Sheol, bursting them open.

Around Jerusalem, close to the city wall all the whitewashed gravestones trembled. Some *tombs broke open. The bodies of many holy people who had died were raised to life.*[9]

At first, Satan was angry. Sheol was his domain, and he had not expected an invasion. Behind its gates, he held both the good and the evil captive. All had sinned. Every man and woman had been imprisoned by the spirit of Death with no hope of release. No one was supposed to escape. Then he saw that Jesus-in-spirit-form lay just inside the gate, and Satan breathed a sigh of relief. Yeshua-Jesus was the one he really wanted. If he held the life of the Creator, he could bargain with God.

At the Place of the Skull, Longinus could not believe his eyes. The three crosses were still upright. When he looked toward the city, it appeared that shrouded figures were now wandering through the tumbled gravestones. He shook himself and walked over to look closely at the body of Rabbi Jesus.

To his amazement, the rabbi was dead. Still looking up into the face of Jesus, Longinus spoke the truth that resonated in his heart, *"Surely this man was the Son of God!"*

Some women were watching from a distance. Among them were Mary Magdalene, Mary the mother of James the younger and of Joseph, and Salome. In Galilee these women had followed him and cared for his needs. Many other women who had come up with him to Jerusalem were also there. [10]

John was the first to notice the Roman runner. He left the women and hurried to the crosses to hear the news. It was an order from Pilate to hasten the death of the criminals by breaking their legs so they could no longer push up for air.

With a grimace that revealed his distaste for this practice, Longinus passed the order on to his men, adding, "Leave the rabbi alone. He has already passed into the realm of the dead."

Before the order could be carried out, another runner arrived with a question, "Can you certify the death of Rabbi Jesus so the governor can release his body?"

John watched the centurion in charge to see how he would respond to this request.

The commander of the fortress quickly picked up one of several spears that had been tossed on the ground. Roughly he pressed it into the hand of the closest soldier. "Make sure the rabbi is dead."

The soldier turned toward the center cross.

John felt his stomach tighten. The bile rose in his throat. For an instant, he closed his eyes. Then when he opened his eyes he saw a double stream, blood and water pouring from a freshly made wound. It ran down the upright beam of the cross and puddled in the hole that had been chiseled deep enough to support numerous crucifixions.

Beneath the rock and rubble of centuries, the glory of heaven filled the small cave where Jeremiah had secretly stored the furniture from Solomon's Temple. The Ark of the Covenant, the seven branched lampstand, the table of showbread had all been waiting, preserved by guardian angels, for this moment. Now with wings extended like the images of seraphs from the early Tabernacle, they watched as the blood of their Creator flowed from the base of the cross, through a fissure in the rock to drip from the ceiling of the cave onto the gold-plated surface of the Mercy Seat.

At that moment, Ophaniel flew into the chamber with a beautiful vial from the heavenly sanctuary. Swiftly, he collected some of the falling drops. Then shouting, "Life is in this blood!" he flew back to the throne room of heaven.

This was no longer a symbolic ritual performed once a year with the blood of a bull and the blood of a goat. This was the blood of God who had become a man. Tempted beyond what any man had ever endured, he had lived and died without yielding to temptation. The awesomeness of this sacrifice left the guarding angels speechless.

Chapter 19

Three Days

For Christ also suffered once for sins, the righteous for the unrighteous, to bring you to God. He was put to death in the body but made alive in the Spirit. After being made alive, he went and made proclamation to the imprisoned spirits.

—1Peter 3:18–19

The sun hung low over the rugged horizon. Around the crosses, the soldiers began their grim clean up. Except for John and the women, all the curious had moved on, back into their own lives. Among the huddled women, worried whispers and fragmented plans flew back and forth. How could they provide a proper burial for their beloved teacher?

Wagon wheels and plodding hooves drew John's attention away from the concerned women. He looked toward Jerusalem, surprised to see a loaded wagon leaving the city when Sabbath would be upon them shortly. With his eyes he followed its progress. Amazed, he recognized two prominent men, Rabbi Nicodemus and Joseph of Arimathea, both well-known members of the Sanhedrin. They walked ahead of the wagon accompanied by a few servants.

Without hesitation, both men approached the crucifixion site. The centurion met them and then respectfully stepped aside, allowing them access to the crosses.

As John left the women to approach the men at the cross, he heard the mother of Jesus. "Thank you, God. I knew you had not deserted me."

Two roughly constructed ladders were quickly placed against the back of the cross. When John arrived, Joseph was on one ladder holding a long supporting length of linen while one of the soldiers stood on the other ladder pulling the nails, dropping them to the ground, possibly to be used again.

Immediately, John lent his hand, helping Nicodemus catch the body as it dropped into the linen sling, to be gently lowered to the ground. When John touched the cold limp body of the man he loved more than any other, he collapsed into heartbroken sobs. "I don't understand. I don't understand." John repeated the phrase as waves of emotional pain racked his body.

Nicodemus responded, "Evil reigns this Passover season like never before."

Then they *wrapped* the body of Jesus *with the spices, in strips of linen. This was in accordance with Jewish burial customs. At the place where Jesus was crucified, there was a garden, and in the garden a new tomb, in which no one had ever been laid. Because it was the Jewish day of Preparation and since the tomb was nearby, they laid Jesus there.*[1]

Keeping a respectful distance, Mary and her supporting companions observed the men as they carried Jesus into the tomb. The women could not see past the walls of the burial cave, but through their tears, they did see that large quantities of ointments and spices were carried into the cave.

The sun had already slipped behind the hills when John, Joseph, and the servants rolled the huge stone over the opening of the burial cave. It fell into place with a finality that sent sobs and gasps through the grieving women on the hillside.

Mary from Magdela reached over and grasped the hand of the mother of Jesus. "We should go now."

Jesus's mother replied, "But I must come back with my own ointments for his body."

Mary urged the older woman to her feet. "I will take care of that for you. As soon as Sabbath has ended, I will purchase what is needed. I will bring everything to the tomb at first light. But for now, we need to return to the city."

Around the garden tomb, the archangel Michael set a guard. He knew that only the flesh of Jesus lay within that burial cave, but God had told him that within three days that flesh would come to life, glorified and immortal. "Remain vigilant!" Michael directed. "Our enemy desires to hold Yeshua-Jesus in death."

Just inside the shattered gates of Sheol, the spirit being of Yeshua-Jesus remained as unresponsive as any deceased mortal. Satan stood over his spirit form, gloating yet wary. In single file, his own evil ranks marched by, viewing the fallen Son of God.

When one third of all the angelic beings ever created stood in formation around their captured Creator, Satan ordered, "Move him into the bowels of Sheol. Put him in the farthest, darkest corner. Then close it off."

"No one in the ranks of evil moved to respond. All took fearful steps backward. The memory of Yeshua the Creator as they had known him in heaven could not be erased. Recollections of his power, authority, and majesty sent electric chills through each angelic body.

Reactionary rage rolled through the Evil One. "Yeshua is just a dead man now! God rejected him on the cross." Angrily, Satan scanned the faces of his high-ranking angels and demons. "Death?" He called forward the principality who held the keys to Sheol, the realm of the dead.

For a long moment, uncomfortable silence seemed to be the only response. Then Death stepped forward. The keys that hung around his waist clanged ominously.

"Move him," Satan repeated his order.

"I fear this may not be as it seems," Death cautiously responded. "While Yeshua-Jesus walked the Earth, he often said that he would die and then live again after three days."

Raziel, Satan's second-in-command, stepped forward, and confirmed the concern.

"Set a guard then, here and at the tomb." Satan growled. "Make sure he does not escape. We can move him after three days."

"It's over." Longinus repeated the phrase as he dipped beneath the water again and again, trying to remove the blood of numerous crucified men from his tortured mind. During his military career, he had supervised more crucifixions than he could count. But the Rabbi's crucifixion—he could never forget this one.

Wrapping himself in his long red cloak, he made his way from the bath to his quarters. Before he had finished dressing, there was a knock on his door, an order from Pilate. "Send a squad to guard the Rabbi's tomb."

Longinus rolled his eyes. Would there ever be closure for this execution? With a nod of his head and a wave of his hand, the commander of the fortress complied with the governor's directive. As he turned away from the door, his eye caught the little statue of Mars. Somberly, he spoke to it. "We know that dead men do not leave their graves, but gods cannot be held in death like men. Every soldier and every civilian who had a part in the crucifixion of the Rabbi has a little to fear because he did not die like most men. I hope he does what those Jewish politicians fear most. I hope he comes out of his tomb and lives." Then Longinus shook his head. What an absurd thought!

It was dark when John brought Joseph of Arimathea and Rabbi Nicodemus to the upper room where those who loved Rabbi Jesus were gathering to support each other in their grief. By Jewish law, all three men had been made unclean by touching a dead body, but no one in that room gave it a thought. They kissed the hands of the men who last touched their beloved Jesus. Then they fell into each others' arms, sobbing over the events of the previous day. The brothers of Jesus arrived—James, Jose, Jude, and Simon. They brought their mother, weak and trembling.

Andrew stood up and began to pray as Jesus had taught them. "Father, holy is your name. Our hearts still long for your kingdom to come."

Peter quietly slipped in. His eyes were red and his face was puffy. He dropped to his knees beside his brother as the prayer continued.

"Forgive our sins."

"Yes," Peter echoed. "Forgive me. I denied the Messiah of Israel to save my own worthless flesh."

Andrew paused. For an uncomfortable moment, there was silence in the room.

People looked up through their tears, seeing Peter for the first time since the beginning of Jesus's trial.

John came forward and stood beside Peter. "While Jesus was alive and with us, I heard him speak to Peter. He said, 'Peter, Satan has asked to send you a challenge.' I also heard him tell Peter that he would fail that challenge and deny any association with him before the cock completed a series of morning calls. This happened."

Simon the Zealot then stood beside John. "Jesus also said that we, his disciples, would desert him, running away, fearing for our own lives. This happened."

With a strong determined voice, Andrew picked up the prayer. "As Jesus taught us, we forgive every person who has sinned against us."

Everyone in the room repeated the phrase, adding, "Forgive our leaders both Jewish and Roman. They were deceived. And forgive us. We allowed Fear to control our responses, and we failed, unable to prevent the death of your son."

Throughout the night, the prayers continued. Under the cover of darkness, more friends and family arrived. Toma came from Bethlehem, bringing Mary an extravagant gift from their old friend, Khetti. After clearing their campsite on the Mount of Olives, Zebedee and Salome, along with Jairus from Capernaum, climbed the stairs to the upper room to sit with Mary and share her grief. Manaen, accompanied by Cuza and Joanna, slipped out of Herod's palace to mourn with the followers of Jesus.

Just before dawn, Lazarus of Bethany slipped into the room. He was not alone. His two sisters and their husbands were with him.

It was a night filled with prayers and tears.

A long blast, the silver trumpets announced dawn on Passover Sabbath, a day filled with sacrifices and ceremony. For the commander of the Roman fortress, it was another day to keep peace and order in a city that thrived on ancient scenarios of oppression and deliverance.

With crisp military demeanor, Longinus strode into the governor's chamber to deliver the morning report. Purposefully keeping his face non-expressive, he saluted, fist to chest.

Pilate was being assisted through his morning routine, appearing like a man who had slept little while drinking much.

Longinus knew better than to comment on the governor's condition so he began the report. "Earthquake damage was minimal. The veil in the Temple tore from top to bottom. Temple authorities have put up a temporary covering."

Pilate growled, "I don't care what happens to their Temple."

Longinus continued, "At the quarry, some old underground passages collapsed." Longinus paused, remembering the tunnels in the quarry and the unusual events the night they had captured Barabbas. Then he continued, "There was one small break in the aqua duct that runs from the hills of Bethlehem into the city. Crews worked on it all night by torchlight. There should be no disruption to the city's water supply."

"Good," Pilate responded as he sat heavily in his chair, fixing Longinus with a dull stare. "The guard at the tomb?"

"Placed as requested," Longinus answered. "The tomb remains sealed. There have been no problems."

"Caiaphas and his father-in-law, Annas, are two of the most annoying men I have ever dealt with," Pilate groused. "A guard for a dead man! And I did it just to get those men out of my line of vision." He shook his head. "If I had had a spear, the temptation might have been too great."

"Pax Romana," Longinus cautioned.

"I know," Pilate grumbled. Then he moved on. "What can I expect today?"

"The usual Sabbath fanfare with extra large crowds, then at sundown, a procession begins. It goes to the barley field just outside the city wall. They will cut a few sheaves and carry them back to the Temple. The Temple will be illuminated throughout the night while the barley is beaten and ground into flour for a special morning offering."

Pilate responded, "I suppose their choir will sing. Their trumpets will sound and throughout the night the voices of thousands of people will drift through the windows of my sleeping chamber."

"Most likely," Longinus affirmed.

Pilate reached for his cup of wine. "This Jewish festival cannot end soon enough for me."

It was late afternoon. Throughout the day, happy, excited voices drifted from the street into the upper room, clashing with gloom and scattered sobbing. On this High Holy Day, all of Jerusalem, citizens and visitors, seemed to be in the streets, joyfully making their way to the Temple.

Peter looked out the window, staring sadly at the setting sun. Then he commented, "The First Fruits' procession will begin shortly."

Several in the room responded by glancing curiously at Rabbi Nicodemus and Joseph of Arimathea. Their eyes seemed to ask, Will you be leaving to participate with the other important men in the high court?

Nicodemus answered their unspoken question. "We are separating ourselves from that corrupt governing body."

In heaven, Michael blew three long blasts on a silver shofar. God stood. Then Gabriel proclaimed, "The Feast of First Fruits is in progress!"

Every heavenly being focused on a small barley field, close to the northern wall of Jerusalem. The standing barley had been gathered and bound into upright, rooted sheaves.

Gabriel announced, "Yeshua-Jesus was bound and separated from the population."

Above the throne, the angelic choir responded, "It was done! Amen!"

There was a moment of silence while heaven watched the leadership of Israel as they surrounded the field. Designated reapers with polished sickles in hand approached the bound sheaves.

Gabriel's voice rang out. "With his hands bound, our Creator was cut down."

Again, heaven held its breath, while on Earth, the sheaves were cut and then ceremoniously paraded back to the Temple. When the procession arrived at the base of the altar, Caiaphas stepped forward, lifting and waving his sheaf, sanctifying the natural grain before it became a fine-grain offering.

In heaven, God responded to the ceremony on Earth. "I certify that my son, Yeshua-Jesus, was a worthy sacrifice. As a man, he met all the requirements of my law. Never once did he displease or alarm me. I accept his sacrifice on behalf of Adam and all his descendants."

Above the throne, the angelic choir burst into song. "*Who has believed our message and to whom has the arm of the* LORD *been revealed?*"[2]

Then from the Sea of Glass, another choir answered.

> His arm was stretched and nailed to the wood
> For the children of Adam, chained by Death;
> For the sons and daughters of Eve
> who presently walk the Earth,
> And for all of humanity, yet to be born.
> They will believe our message!
> Even the legions of the Deceiver will bend the knee.

Immediately, another choral response came from above the throne,

> Praise Yeshua-Jesus!
> *He,* like the wave sheaf, *grew up before* God
> *like a tender shoot and like a root out of dry ground.*
> *He had no beauty or majesty to attract* men *to him,*
> *nothing in his appearance* that they *should desire him.*

In the Court of the Priests, the threshing began, the repeated beating, grinding, and sifting. Through the hours of the night, the wave sheaf was brutally reduced to an omer of fine flour. In heaven, both choirs sang.

He was despised and rejected by mankind,
a man of suffering, and familiar with pain.
Like one from whom people hide their faces...
Surely he took up their *pain and bore* their *suffering,*
yet they *considered him punished by God,*
stricken by him, and afflicted.
But he was pierced for their *transgressions,*
he was crushed for their *iniquities;*
the punishment that brought them *peace was on him,*
and by his wounds they *are healed.*
The sons of Adam, *like sheep, have gone astray,*
each one *has turned to* his *own way;*
and the Lord has laid on Yeshua-Jesus
the iniquity of all humanity.[3]

In the predawn darkness of Earth, an omer of fine barley flour was carried to the Altar of Burnt Offerings. Solemnly, it was lifted and waved.

In heaven, there was an alarmed response. "Oh, how Yeshua-Jesus suffered!"

Within the broken gate of Sheol, the heavenly lament reached the ears of Satan. Slowly, his lips curled into a sadistic smirk. Yes, he had intended to inflict suffering on the Beloved of God. Gloating, he looked down at the lifeless form of his Creator. Lifting his right foot, he brought it down hard on the chest of the spirit form of Yeshua-Jesus. "In death, you're mine!" Satan announced. "I hold you just like I hold Adam and all his descendants."

In the Temple at the base of the altar, two priests approached. One poured golden oil over the fine flour while the other sprinkled frankincense into the mixture.

In the throne room of heaven, God lifted his right hand and gestured to the Holy Spirit.

Immediately, the Spirit responded. Like a fiery liquid, he poured himself out, flowing undetected over the walls of the New Jerusalem and through the gulf that separates the realms of good and evil. This thin stream of divine fire slipped through the broken gates of Sheol, steadily trickling into the unresponsive spirit form of Yeshua-Jesus.

At first, there was a fragrance, not the usual smell of decay. It was the perfume of heaven's flowers and aromatic spices.

Agitated and alarmed, Satan quickly looked in every corner. His principalities joined him. This magnitude of sweetness could only mean one thing. Their security had been breached! "Find the source of this fragrance!" Satan shouted.

Chaos ensued. Demons and fallen angels darted in and out of dark tunnels and twisted passages. The spirit form of Yeshua-Jesus was ignored.

Drop by golden drop, divinity poured into Yeshua-Jesus. At first, his spirit being warmed. Then it glowed. His eyes opened, and they were like burning coals of fire.

Death stumbled by, still searching for the source of the heavenly aroma. Suddenly, Yeshua-Jesus reached up and ripped the keys from his waist. Leaping to his feet, he loudly proclaimed, *"I am the Living One; I was dead, and now look, I am alive for ever and ever! And I now hold the keys of death and Hades."*[4]

The forces of Satan froze, terrified and trembling. Only their evil leader had the boldness to approach. "I know how you got in, but why have you come?"

A mighty shofar blast suddenly shook the walls of Sheol.

"Your army!" Satan gasped.

Yeshua-Jesus nodded. Then he said, *"Because of the blood of my covenant with* Adam and his descendants *I will free your prisoners from* this *waterless pit."*[5]

At that moment, Michael with his warrior angels burst on the scene. Yeshua-Jesus directed, "All those who have died believing in the blood of the covenant and hoping for the seed of the woman have been sleeping in the passages on the other side of the chasm. Bring them out!"

"Where are you taking them?" Satan demanded.

Emphatically, Jesus answered, "I believe they *would prefer to be away from the body and at home with the Lord.*[6] From this time on, for those whose names are recorded in my Book of Life, I have prepared a place in heaven. They will wait with me until the day that God declares a total end to all the evil on Earth."

Michael put his sword flat against the chest of Satan, pushing him away from Yeshua, back against the black walls of his lair. "If God would allow me to end your life now, I would!" The mighty angel who had taken the position that once belonged to Satan glared into the eyes of his evil counterpart. "God is giving you a little more time. When you hear my shofar again, it will announce your end!"

Yeshua-Jesus left Michael holding Satan. Eagerly, he led his angelic troops across the great chasm, down the first passage, naming and pointing out his friends, the ones he had come for.

"John, my cousin!"

An angel swooped in and lifted the spirit body of John the Baptist, immediately carrying him up to heaven.

"Joseph, my father! Abraham, my friend! Daniel, my brave servant! Esther, my courageous queen!" On and on, Jesus went through tunnel after tunnel, naming and touching each resting spirit, then handing each person over to an angel.

His glory drove the darkness away. It made the demons flee and the fallen angels hide. As he went from passage to passage, his angels sang antiphonally.

> Yeshua-Jesus *pursues* his own *and moves on unscathed,*
>   *by a path his feet have not traveled before."*
>   *"Who has done this and carried it through,*
>   *calling forth the generations from the beginning?*

Yeshua's voice then rang out.

> *I, the* Lord—*with the first of them*
>   *and with the last—I am he.*[7]
> I *say to the captives, 'Come out,'*
>   *and to those in darkness, 'Be free!'*[8]

It seemed that the passages had been emptied, but still Yeshua-Jesus kept looking, deeper and deeper, breaking through the cobwebs of time. Finally, he began calling, "Noah! Methuselah! Seth! Where is my son, Adam and my daughter, Eve?"

Near the entrance to Sheol, Satan smirked sadistically. Then he muttered, "They are well hidden, in a chamber that has been closed off for centuries."

Suddenly, the walls began to shake. On the other side of the chasm, at the end of a long dark passage, a giant boulder split, and Yeshua-Jesus rushed into the once-sealed chamber. Angels followed, swooping up the patriarchs who had carried the seed of the promise.

In the farthest corner of the chamber, Yeshua-Jesus knelt by the spirit forms of a majestic man and a beautiful woman. "Adam, my son." With hands marred by jagged holes, Yeshua-Jesus stroked the face of the first man. "I kept my promise. I died so you will live." An angel then swooped in and took Adam.

Then Yeshua turned to Eve. He lifted her spirit form in his arms and carried her to another waiting angel. Briefly, he stroked her hair. Then he whispered in her ear, "I have paid the price for your mistake. Your children will live with me forever."

In heaven, the angelic choirs were singing again.

He brought them out of darkness, the utter darkness,
and broke away their chains.
Let them give thanks to the Lord for his unfailing love
and his wonderful deeds for mankind,
for he breaks down gates of bronze
and cuts through bars of iron.[9]

In the heart of Jesus, joy was mixed with sadness. Many remained on the other side of the great chasm, *in the* *darkness* of Sheol, *in utter darkness.* They were *prisoners suffering in iron* *chains,* waiting in the abode of demons *because they rebelled against* *God's commands and despised the plans of the Most High.*[10]

With strong strides, Yeshua-Jesus once again crossed the great divide between the resting place of the righteous and the resting place of those who belonged to Satan. Shouting, he approached the broken gates where demons and fallen angels fearfully waited for their Creator to either leave them or destroy them.

"Your accusation no longer stands!" Yeshua-Jesus faced Satan. "The laws of God are good and fair. As a man, *the boundary* *lines have fallen for me in pleasant places; surely I have a delightful* *inheritance* from my Father. *I will praise* God, *who counsels me.*[11] I have not been shaken. My body waits in the tomb, secure, because God has not abandoned me. My flesh will be glorified. It will not decay. The sons and daughters of Adam will also experience glory instead of decay. To this end, I have taken control of the place where men wait for the completion of all things. Next, I will establish my kingdom among the living."

Without flinching, Satan responded, shouting past the archangel who still held him at sword point. "Don't forget the great principle of free choice! Each human must have the opportunity to choose between my government and yours."

Graciously, Jesus nodded. "So you have a little while longer."

Yeshua-Jesus then raised his hand, and Michael stepped away from Satan. Immediately, both Michael and Yeshua dissolved into shimmering glory, melting into the rock walls.

Shaking the foundations of Earth, they traveled to the tomb where Yeshua reunited with the flesh that had been the crucified body of Jesus. With a mere touch, Michael rolled the stone away from the tomb. Fully in the flesh and glowing with immortality, Jesus sat up within the tomb. He swung his legs over the side, stood and carefully folded the face covering that Nicodemus had provided. Then he walked out of the tomb.

Around him, the Roman soldiers lay motionless, struck down, sprawled across the rocky ground. The forces of Satan had made a terrified exit. Only his own angelic guard waited to greet him. Ophaniel led their cheers, *"Death has been swallowed up in victory!"*[12]

Chapter 20

Jesus Is Alive!

Very early on the first day of the week, just after sunrise, they
were on their way to the tomb, and they asked each other,
"Who will roll the stone away from the entrance of the tomb?"

—Mark 16:2–3

Mary from Magdela, Salome the wife of Zebedee, Mary the mother of a young disciple named James, and Joanna the wife of Herod's finance minister suddenly dropped to their knees. The ground was rolling again like it had rolled while Jesus hung on the cross. Each woman fell across her bundle of burial spices, preventing their loss. Hugging the ground, waiting for the tremors to cease, the women watched the sunrise.

As the earth calmed, Mary from Magdela stood. She picked up her bundle and renewed her determined trek. The others followed her lead. Nothing was going to come between them and this final act of devotion. Mary felt frustration swelling within. The men who had been close followers of Jesus were afraid to be seen near the tomb. Some were leaving the city today, making hasty plans to hide out in Bethany, Emmaus, and other towns. No one would come and help with the large stone that covered the entrance to the garden tomb. Mary huffed loudly as she thought about the well-muscled disciples, confused and cowering in the upper room. She had tried, but there was no reasoning with those hard-headed men!

Fueled by her frustration, Mary moved ahead of the other women. With quick steps, she crested the hill and looked down into the small enclosed garden. She gasped. Someone had moved the stone! The tomb was open!

Dropping her bundle, Mary darted down the steep incline and rushed to the open tomb. With a steadying hand on the outer wall, she thrust her head through the open entrance. Sunlight from the small window in the upper wall allowed Mary to clearly see that there was no body within. Without delay, she darted back out of the garden and began running toward the city. Passing the other women she yelled, "His body has been removed!"

Salome, Mary, and Joanna quickly dropped their bundles. Lifting their long robes, they broke into a run, down the hill, and into the enclosed garden. Gasping in amazed breathlessness, the three women then cautiously entered the tomb. Speculation flew from woman to woman. "The high priest with his Temple guard? Pilate and his Roman soldiers? Grave robbers?"

While they were wondering about this, suddenly, two men in clothes that gleamed like lightning stood beside them.

In their fright the women bowed down with their faces to the ground, but the men said to them, "Why do you look for the living among the dead? He is not here; he has risen! Remember how he told you, while he was still with you in Galilee: 'The Son of Man must be delivered over to the hands of sinners, be crucified and on the third day be raised again.'[1] He has risen! He is not here. See the place where they laid him. Now go, tell his disciples and Peter, 'He is going ahead of you into Galilee. There you will see him, just as he told you.'"

Trembling and bewildered, the women went out and fled from the tomb. They said nothing to anyone on the road, because they were afraid.[2]

"Peter! Open the door!" Mary pounded on the heavy wooden door to the upper room. "John! Are you in there?" Mary pounded again. "Someone! Let me in!"

Slowly, the door opened, just a crack. One eyeball peeked through the narrow opening.

Mary did not wait. She gave the door a hard shove, knocking the responder back from the opening door. Bursting into the room, she frantically announced, "Someone has taken the body of Jesus. It is no longer in the tomb! I don't know where they have put him."

"What?"

"Who?"

"Nonsense!"

A room full of scornful male eyes focused on Mary from Magdela.

"Come, see for yourself!" Mary hotly retorted.

At first, no one moved. Then Peter jumped to his feet. John followed. Both men pushed past Mary, breaking into a run on the stairs.

Refusing to waste her time with the other men, Mary turned and hurried after Peter and John.

Both men were running, but John outran Peter and reached the tomb first. Cautiously, John bent over and looked in.

Then Peter came along behind him. He went straight into the tomb, stopping short when he saw the strips of linen as well as the cloth that had been wrapped around Jesus's head. Cautiously, Peter touched the grave clothes. Then he turned to John who stood in the entrance. "How was the body removed without disturbing these strips of linen? It seems to have melted away leaving the cloth behind!" Peter gestured for John to come in and take a look.

So John went inside.

Then both disciples believed everything Mary had reported. Filled with questions and fear, they hurried back to the upper room where the other disciples waited.

But Mary from Magdela remained at the entrance to the tomb, full of despair and crying. As she wept, she bent over and looked into the tomb one more time. Suddenly, through her tears, she saw two angels dressed in white. They were seated, one at the head and one at the foot of the place where Jesus's body should have been.

They spoke to her. "Woman, why are you weeping?"

Pointing to the stone slab where the grave clothes were precisely laid, she said, "My Lord, the Master Rabbi Jesus of Nazareth—his body has been removed! Who would do such a thing and where have they taken him?"

Without receiving an answer, she stepped back into the garden, and there she saw a man.

Kindly, he said, "Woman, your sorrow is great. How can I help you? Who are you looking for?"

"Sir," Mary said, "I know you must be the caretaker for this garden. Have you seen anyone near this tomb? Do you know who removed the body of Rabbi Jesus? If he should not be buried here, then I will find another place." Mary waited for an answer.

The man took a step closer. Then he said to her, "Mary."

Sudden recognition flooded every cell in Mary's body. Overwhelmed, she ran to the man, throwing her arms around his neck. "Rabboni! Jesus!" For a long moment, she clung to Jesus, tears of joy streaming down her face.

Then Jesus took Mary's hands and stepped back. He held her at arm's length and said, "Don't you remember? I told you that I must die, but I would come to life again after three days. You asked me to promise that I would return to you." Jesus smiled at Mary. "I have kept that promise."

In his eyes, she saw the familiar warmth and the twinkle that she loved. In his hands and feet, she saw the jagged holes, evidence of his crucifixion. Slowly nodding her head, she recalled their conversation on the boat docks at Magdela. Then Mary threw her arms around his neck again.

But Jesus said, "Do not cling to me, for I must return to my Father, and there are others I must visit. Now go to my disciples and tell them I am alive. I will see them soon." Then, while Mary still clung to his neck, he vanished.

Immediately, Mary from Magdela ran back to the disciples. "I have seen the Lord!" she shouted. Then she repeated every word he had spoken. While she was talking, the other three women arrived at the upper room. They shouted wildly, talking over each other, laughing and crying. "We have seen the master! We kissed his feet and, with our own fingers, touched the nail scars."

Joanna added, "Jesus said, 'Tell my disciples, I will see them when they return to Galilee.'"

Peter was the first to respond. "What are these women talking about? Have their imaginations gone wild?"

Matthew added, "Females can come to hysterical conclusions when faced with difficulties."

"The tomb is empty. The body is missing," John stated.

"But there must be a more logical explanation," Matthew suggested.

Around the room, masculine heads nodded in agreement. Then the younger James looked directly at his mother and carefully added, "I'm sure there is a rational explanation."

Mary the mother of young James quickly countered, "There is only one explanation. Jesus has risen from the dead!"

Immediately, all the men were talking. Skepticism and fear-filled speculations rolled through the room, but Mary from Magdela did not let it last. With fire in her eyes, she brought her hand down on the table with a resounding smack. "Didn't you men listen when Jesus was with you? He told all of us that he would die and then rise on the third day. Now, it has happened!"

John stood. "Men, many of us were witnesses on the day that Jesus called our friend Lazarus of Bethany back from the resting place of the dead. We saw him walk out of his tomb. It should not be difficult to believe that Jesus could also return to us." Then John turned to the women. He pointed to Salome. "My mother has always been a woman of sound mind, not full of gossip or exaggerations. I believe her report and the report of the other women."

Andrew quickly suggested, "Then we must hurry to Galilee so we can meet him."

But Peter countered, "We cannot leave today. The road to Galilee is being watched."

Mary from Magdela was quick to inform Peter. "Many followers of Rabbi Jesus have already scattered to the small towns around Jerusalem."

Peter insisted, "Those who were his close followers, eleven of us now, will wait in this house until the days of mourning have been observed. Then we will return to Galilee."

"Days of mourning?" Mary protested. "Jesus is alive!"

Waves of comment and speculation rolled through the room again.

With a choked voice, Peter responded, "None of the eleven have seen him."

Obviously frustrated, Mary left the room. The other women followed her.

There was a knock on the door to the armory. Longinus looked up from the open scroll that contained the inventory of weapons for the fortress. Two quick strides and he was opening the door to see one of his officers and a squad of six men behind him. With a casual gesture, he brought them into the room.

Silently, they lined up around the table. Each man then placed a bag of coins on the table.

Curiously, Longinus waited for an explanation.

The ranking soldier began. "We have just come from a meeting with Caiaphas, the Jewish high priest and Annas the former high priest. They pressed gold and silver coins into our hands to tell an untrue story."

Longinus peeked into the closest bag. Eight to ten coins per bag, he estimated. "A bribe—let's hear the whole story with details." He sat heavily in the closest chair and fixed his men with an unwavering stare.

"Just before midnight on Saturn's Day, we relieved the guard at the rabbi's tomb. The seal was intact. All was quiet. There had been no incidents."

"The rabbi's tomb," Longinus repeated while leaning forward to catch every detail.

"We never slept—not one man!"

"Why would anyone think that you slept?" Longinus curtly inquired.

All the men answered at once. "The body is gone! The tomb is open. The crucified rabbi is missing!"

"How?" Longinus growled. "Roman soldiers do not lose prisoners, especially dead ones!" He turned to the officer in charge of the squad, expecting a response.

"Just before dawn, there was another earthquake."

Longinus nodded. He had felt the early morning tremors.

"Then there was a bright light. It just suddenly appeared."

Another man spoke up. "I saw a tall glowing man, taller than any man I have ever seen. *His appearance was like lightning, and his clothes were white as snow.*[3]

The officer continued, "The strength drained from our bodies, and we all collapsed like dead men. But what we saw was amazing! It was like one of the gods had come to Earth. With one hand, he rolled the giant stone away from the entrance. Then he shouted in a language we did not understand."

Longinus looked from man to man. "Is this what happened?"

They all nodded affirmatively.

Then Longinus asked, "What happened next?"

"Rabbi Jesus came out. He was dressed in blazing white. His face was like the sun. Suddenly, the entire garden was filled with those tall, glowing men. They raised fiery swords and saluted. Then everyone disappeared except for two. Those two sat on top of the stone that had been rolled away like they were waiting for someone."

The Roman commander leaned into the face of one of the men. "How do you know this was Rabbi Jesus, the one we crucified? Was he the one who came out of the tomb, or was it someone else?"

"I saw the holes, Sir. In both feet and in his hands close to the wrist, I put those nails in, and I know how I placed them."

For a long moment, Longinus was silent, remembering the way the rabbi had died. Then he softly said, "We crucified the son of a god." After another contemplative silence, he asked, "So, why the bribe?"

The officer spoke again. "It seems that the Jewish leaders do not want anyone to know what happened. They want us to tell the people that we slept on our watch and while we were sleeping, his disciples came and stole the rabbi's body."

Longinus shook his head. "Annas and Caiaphas should fear the wrath of the gods."

"You believe us?"

Longinus nodded. "The governor will want to question each of you."

All eyes went to the bags of coins. "What about the money?"

Longinus shrugged. "Keep it. Tell their story to Jews if you must, but within this fortress, we know the truth."

Longinus stood and took a step toward the door. Then he paused and turned back to the grinning men. "But let me caution you. If this is a fabricated tale, if I discover any evidence that you slept and allowed the body to be stolen, I will personally remove your heads from your bodies, one by one." Longinus then left the room.

In the throne room of heaven, God stood. "I have received the gifts, those once held by Death. I have examined the blood of Jesus. It is life-giving. There is no sin in it. Now, my eyes and my arms long for Yeshua, my son."

Suddenly, from the gates there came a shout!

> *Now to* Yeshua-Jesus,
> *The King eternal, immortal, invisible,*
> *The only God, be honor and glory for ever and ever!*
> *Amen!*[4] Amen! Amen!

Instantly, the atmosphere of heaven filled with flying angels, soaring beings, and herald trumpeters. The beautiful throne of God rose and glided on the backs of mighty cherubim to the royal entrance of the New Jerusalem. From above the throne of God, an angelic choir sang.

> *"Lift up your heads, you gates;*
> *be lifted up, you ancient doors*
> *that the King of glory may come in."*

Angels, lining the entrance to the heavenly city, sang their response. *"Who is this King of glory?"*

The answer came from above the throne.

> *"The* LORD *Yeshua,*
> *strong and mighty,*
> *the* LORD *mighty in battle.*[5]

He fought for the sons and daughters of Adam.
He reclaimed the creation of his hands
that he once filled with the breath of his mouth!"

Then the herald trumpeters brought forth numerous staccato trills followed by a mighty blast. Accompanied by angels from Earth, Yeshua-Jesus soared through the central gate, straight to his Father who welcomed him with open arms. After a long embrace, God pointed toward the empty seat at his right hand. "It is yours again."

Confidently, Jesus took his royal place. Another herald trumpet sounded. Then an angel announced, *"The earth is the Lord's, and everything in it, the world, and all who live in it;*

for Yeshua-Jesus *founded it on the seas and established it on the waters."*

Another angel flew forward asking in a loud voice, *"Who may ascend the mountain of the LORD? Who may stand in his holy place?"*

Every angel in heaven responded, "Yeshua-Jesus! He is *the one who has clean hands and a pure heart, who does not trust in an idol or swear by a false god.* The sons and daughters of Earth *will receive blessing from* God *and vindication from* Yeshua-Jesus who is *God their Savior."*[6]

Yeshua looked over at his Father. "My work is not complete. My kingdom is on Earth, but it must have time to grow. Every human needs an opportunity to choose, but most do not know there is a choice to be made." Slowly, Yeshua shook his head. "My closest followers remain confused. I must work with them a little longer, another forty days. Then"—Jesus nodded toward the Holy Spirit who burned like a ring of fire around the throne—"we will send you to be with each of my followers with the same intensity that you were with me."

With a glorious burst of fire, the Holy Spirit eagerly agreed, and the plan was confirmed.

Throwing a civilian cloak over his uniform, Longinus left the fortress on foot. Compelling questions burned in his heart. Who was Rabbi Jesus? Had he gone to the realm of the dead and then returned to the living? What evidence could he find at the garden tomb? With his own eyes, he had to make an investigation.

From the top of the hill that overlooked the enclosed garden and the open tomb, the Roman centurion studied the site. Within the sweep of his gaze, no one was present. Longinus noticed that a few spears and some camping equipment remained at the site. He made a mental note to make his soldiers responsible for those items.

Alert and curious, Longinus then progressed down the embankment, into the garden. First, he examined the stone, puzzling over the fact that the Roman seal appeared to have been burnt, melted—not just broken. Then he put his shoulder to the stone, attempting to move it, but it would not budge; the size and the weight being massive.

Next, he moved into the twilight of the tomb where the air was heavy with aromas from the burial spices. From the small window, one golden beam of sunlight fell upon the stone slab where a body would normally lay.

The Roman centurion carefully examined the stone table, checking to see if it was hollow or solid, movable, or anchored. Nothing about the tomb seemed out of the ordinary except for the burial linen. How strange?

Longinus realized how abnormal and difficult it would be for grave robbers to unwrap the corpse and then leave the linen so neatly aligned. Cautiously, he touched the fabric. Then he quickly withdrew his hand and moved to crouch in a dark corner of the tomb. He heard voices, and he planned to listen.

"Peter, do not be afraid and filled with remorse."

At the sound of that beautiful voice, chills ran through the body of the commander of the Roman fortress.

"Lord! You're here!"

Longinus recognized a Galilean voice. Then it seemed that the same man was sobbing and wailing. Puzzled, the centurion moved closer to the entrance so he could see into the garden.

One man sat on a stone bench with his back to the tomb, and another man knelt on the ground, face in the dirt.

"I'm so sorry…I said that I never knew you. I should have gone to the cross with you, but I was afraid." Sobs obscured the rest of his words.

Longinus could see the seated man, pulling the sobbing man up from the dust, cradling his head in his lap. Finally, the weeping man gained control of his emotions. Longinus heard his question. "Why? Why did you allow those men to take you? Why didn't you disappear or resist?"

Then the answer, warm and confident, reached his ears. "It was the will of God, and you know I obey my Father in all things. But it was more than just obedience. I had to keep my promise to Adam and Eve. Someone sinless had to pay the price for Adam's sin. So I suffered *once for sins*. I became *the righteous* dying *for the unrighteous, to bring* all men and women *to God. I was put to death in the body but made alive in the Spirit. After being made alive,* I *went and made proclamation to the imprisoned spirits— to those who were disobedient long ago.*[7] Now I have gone back into heaven and have received my reward. It is a seat *at God's right hand—with angels, authorities and powers in submission to* me."[8]

Gradually, the details emerged. Longinus found himself drawn to the conversation. Step by step, he left the tomb, moving into the garden, closer and closer to the conversing pair. Then the man doing most of the talking turned and looked directly into his face. It was the Rabbi!

Longinus gasped—those kind brown eyes—he could never forget their intensity and fearlessness. Then while the centurion watched, Rabbi Jesus vanished.

For a long moment, the two men remaining in the garden seemed confused, studying the place where Jesus had been and then mutely staring at each other. Finally, each man turned away, returning to his individual life.

It was past noon when Jesus materialized on the dusty road from Jerusalem to Emmaus. Ahead, he could see two of his followers, Cleopas with his son Joseph. They walked with plodding footfall, leaning heavily on their walking sticks. Their bewildered and remorseful conversation hung like a cloud of sadness over their journey.

Excited for the joy he was about to bring into their lives, Jesus began to walk briskly, moving up behind and then beside the pair. "Shalom!" he greeted both men. Then pretending to be blissfully unaware, he asked, "What are you talking about?"

Two sad faces stared back at him without a response.

Grinning, ignoring the gloom of his fellow travelers, Jesus cheerfully announced, "This Passover was the most satisfying experience of my life. For everyone in Jerusalem, I believe this holy festival has surpassed all others in significance! Don't you agree?"

Forward progress ceased. The men stood still, obviously upset.

Cleopas finally said, "Are you the only man from Jerusalem who does not know the terrible things that have happened?"

"What things?" Jesus replied.

"Rabbi Jesus of Nazareth has been crucified. He was a powerful man of God, a prophet, and many of us believed him to be the Messiah."

Joseph added, "He healed cripples and lepers, even raised a man from the dead."

Angrily, Cleopas said, "He had not committed any crime. His death was manipulated by the rulers of the Temple." The men began walking again.

Jesus kept pace with their sad steps, listening to every word. "It has been three days since all this happened."

Joseph inserted a puzzling comment. "Just before we left the city, some of our women made an unbelievable announcement. They told us they had found his tomb empty, the body gone. Then they said angels were in that place announcing that Jesus was no longer dead. He was alive!"

Cleopas quickly picked up the story. "Two of our companions ran to the tomb—it was empty. They did not see Jesus or angels."

"We do not know what to believe," Joseph added. "The testimony of women can be quite unreliable."

"I don't understand how all this happened! I was certain that Jesus was the Messiah—then he died."

With a lighthearted smile Jesus *said to them, "How foolish you are, and how slow to believe all that the prophets have spoken! Did not the Messiah have to suffer these things and then enter his glory?"*

"What?" Both men appeared confused.

Patiently, Jesus began to explain. "In the wilderness, Moses made a serpent of brass and raised it on a cross. All who had been bitten by the venomous serpents of the desert only had to look and believe. Then they lived. It was a foreshadowed picture of Messiah raised on a cross and taking the curse of sin upon himself. Both King David and the prophet Isaiah detailed the Messiah's death. Isaiah wrote about the whippings and the healing that would come to all humanity because of those stripes."

Deeply engrossed in conversation, the men approached Emmaus. At the turnoff, Jesus casually waved and continued down the road. But Cleopas and Joseph protested, "It is evening. Spend the night in our home and continue your journey in the morning."

So lightly shrugging, Jesus complied, and he went into their home. At the evening meal, he did not wait for his host to bless the bread. He reached into the basket of unleavened bread and took a piece. As he lifted it, his sleeves dropped to his elbows revealing deep, fresh scars in his wrists. Then looking toward heaven, he began, chanting the Hebrew blessing.

Cleopas and Joseph heard the familiar words, the beautiful melody. The voice—it was the voice of their master!

Then Jesus broke the bread, and with joy and graciousness, he gave each of them a piece.

Simultaneously, both men knew. "Master!" they exclaimed. Eagerly, they reached across the table trying to touch the one they had conversed with all afternoon.

But Jesus nodded his head and then raised his hands in blessing as he vanished from the table.

Astonished, both men stared at the vacant place at the table. Then they asked each other, "Didn't we feel the fire of the Spirit when he spoke to us on the road?" Without eating, they quickly got up and hurried back to Jerusalem.

In the upper room, they found the eleven, with a number of other followers. Obviously, a meal had been served, and some food had been eaten but much of it remained untouched. Everyone was conversing and exclaiming, "It is true! Jesus is alive! He appeared to Peter."

Cleopas and Joseph quickly silenced the men. Then the two told their experience on the road to Emmaus, and how they had recognized Jesus at their meal.

Suddenly, while everyone was talking about this, Jesus stood among them. "Peace to you."

Fear washed over the men and women in the upper room. Certainly, they were seeing a ghost.

But in a reassuring voice, Jesus said, "Do not be alarmed. I am your master in the flesh." He stepped up to Matthew and Andrew who were standing together. "See my hands, my feet. My face is recognizable." He moved over to Philip and James. "Touch my body. It is solid flesh and bones." Then he walked around the room, allowing each person to experience the reality of his resurrection.

Some touched. Some wept. Others laughed hysterically. A few took fearful steps backward. Then some of the women triumphantly proclaimed, "We told you! Do you believe us now?"

And while many still did not know what to think, Jesus said, "I would like something to eat."

One of the women quickly found a piece of broiled fish.

With a gracious smile, he sat at the table and began to eat, picking out the bones, chewing the flesh, and enjoying every bite.

Then he said to them, "Remember the things I taught you— all that has been written in the law and the prophets about me had to be fulfilled." Then he stood and began teaching them in the same manner that he always taught, and so *he opened their minds so they could understand the Scriptures.*

He told them, "This is what is written: The Messiah will suffer and rise from the dead on the third day, and repentance for the forgiveness of sins will be preached in his name to all nations, beginning at Jerusalem. You are witnesses of these things. I am going to send you what my Father has promised, so when you return to Jerusalem for the next feast, *stay in the city until you have been clothed with power from on high.*[10] I will see you again in this room and in Galilee."

Slowly, Jesus raised his hands. Then *again, Jesus said, "Peace be with you! As the Father has sent me, I am sending you." And with that he breathed on them and said, "Receive the Holy Spirit. If you forgive anyone's sins, their sins are forgiven; if you do not forgive them, they are not forgiven."*[11]

And once again, Jesus vanished, leaving excited men and women speechlessly looking around the room.

Chapter 21

Forty Amazing Days

We are witnesses of everything he did in the country of the Jews and in Jerusalem. They killed him by hanging him on a cross, but God raised him from the dead on the third day and caused him to be seen. He was not seen by all the people, but by witnesses whom God had already chosen.

—Acts 10:39–41

With the captain of the Temple guard, Caiaphas strolled slowly through the shadowy torchlit chambers of the Temple, checking the gates, overseeing the nighttime rituals. "It's been quite an eventful day," the captain observed. "This morning, my men gathered and buried the bones of the informant, Judas."

The high priest grimaced as he asked, "Dogs?"

The captain nodded. "They devoured most of the body. The man was almost unrecognizable."

Caiaphas then suggested, "We need to rid Jerusalem of the rest of the close followers of Rabbi Jesus. We have to put a stop to their resurrection story. Bribing the Roman guards will not be enough."

With a few quick steps, both men rounded a corner. Suddenly, they gasped, then took two fearful steps backward. An old priest blocked their path. He stood there, immovably fierce with dark accusing eyes.

The captain of the guard was the first to find his voice. "What do you want? Who are you?"

Boldly, the old priest spoke. "I am Zecharias, an elder in the priesthood when you were both in your apprentice years. The angel of the Lord came to me while I served at the altar of incense and the voice of the Messiah recently called me out of my tomb."

"Out of your tomb?" Both men shook. They tried to turn and flee, but their legs would not obey.

Then, raising both arms and making the sign of blessing with both hands, Zecharias repeated the prophetic words he had spoken over John, his infant son. "*Praise be to the Lord, the God of Israel, because* Jesus our Messiah *has come to his people and redeemed them.*[1] Our prophets foretold this event. I stand before you, proof of their inspired words. '*But your dead will live, LORD; their bodies will rise—let those who dwell in the dust wake up and shout for joy—…the earth will give birth to her dead'.*[2] This has happened to a few of us because Jesus of Nazareth who you crucified is the Messiah. He lives! Around Jerusalem, a number of tombs have opened, and we are now in the city to spread the good news. You will not be able to suppress the truth."

Immediately, the once-dead priest vanished, leaving both Caiaphas and the captain of the Temple guard shaken.

In Bethlehem, just half a day's walk from Jerusalem, Mary sat with James her second son and with Toma, her husband's cousin. They had been to Jerusalem. From both Peter and John, they had heard the details of the empty tomb and two post-resurrection appearances. Toma and James, naturally skeptical, were still offering alternative explanations, but Mary, the mother of Jesus, believed every detail of the resurrection story.

In her heart, a song welled up, a gift from the Holy Spirit that linked this terrible Passover experience with the Passover season when Jesus had been born.

"My soul glorifies the Lord!"

Mary stood. She began to dance as she sang, at first with the solid steps of a mature woman and then with the light skips of the young girl she had been when the angel had visited her and the Holy Spirit had overshadowed her.

"And my spirit rejoices in God my Savior,
   for he has been mindful of the humble state of his servant."

Mary lifted her arms and twirled. She remembered the stable where Jesus had been born, the shepherds who spoke of a heavenly visitation, Joseph's protectiveness during their flight to Egypt and the slaughter of babes and dear friends. In happiness and in suffering, she had surely been favored by God. She shouted,

From now on all generations will call me blessed,
For the Mighty One has done great things for me,
Holy is his name.
His mercy extends to those who fear him,
From generation to generation![3]

Mary made another excited turn; and, wonderfully, she was in the arms of her son Jesus. He was holding her, whispering in her ear, "It's true! It's true! I have returned to you for a short time. Then I will go live with my Father."

Tears came and Mary wept into his chest.

Jesus kept whispering to her. "My Father knows how you kept his promise in your heart, even while I was on the cross. He knows how much you suffered."

Jesus moved his mother back to a bench. Breathlessly, she fell onto the seat. Her eyes never left the face of her son. "It was nothing. I'd do it all again for the joy of this moment."

Toma and James now rushed forward, examining his hands and his feet. Jesus sat and talked with his closest family members until nearly dawn. As the sun touched the rugged horizon, Jesus disappeared and all three dropped to their knees to worship the Creator and Savior of the world.

One by one, the days of unleavened bread passed. In Herod's Jerusalem palace, behind closed drapes, Cuza shared with Manaen the exciting events that his wife Joanna had witnessed. Then Manaen relayed reports that the dead from open graves near the northern wall were making appearances in the city, announcing that Rabbi Jesus lives eternally!

"We must find his disciples," Manaen stated. "Surely, there is more to be said."

Cuza quickly replied, "Joanna tells me those men who were closest to him are staying in the upper room in the house that belongs to Peter's brother-in-law."

Both men took quick steps to exit their office, but brisk footfalls on the tiled hall near the private quarters of the king called them back to their responsibilities. A quick glance, and they knew Herodias was headed directly toward their offices. They waited, bowing respectfully when she faced them.

Speaking with royal directness, she informed her husband's financial counselors that her brother Agrippa was on his way from Rome. She had obtained permission from her husband, the king, for her brother to live with them and to be supported from the resources in the king's treasury. Cuza and Manaen were to comply with his every request.

Cuza quickly responded, "Even Antipas must live within the limits of his treasury."

Manaen was more tactful. "We will work out the details with your husband. Please excuse us."

Both men bowed again and then hurried to leave the palace and find the disciples of Rabbi Jesus. Moving through the narrow twisted streets, they entered the working class area. At the local well, they stopped to drink the water and listen to more amazing reports of the once-dead walking in the city.

Cuza spotted a man passing by and called out, "Thomas?"

The man paused, looking nervously over his shoulder.

"Thomas!" Both Cuza and Manaen ran to converse with him. Surely, this man—one of the twelve—had more details about the resurrection story.

Recognizing Cuza and Manaen as two of the seventy that Jesus had commissioned and sent out, Thomas relaxed and warmly acknowledged them.

Immediately, Cuza and Manaen began an excited barrage of questions. Had Thomas seen Jesus? Where was Jesus now? Had he been to the empty tomb? What did his fellow disciples have to say?

At first, Thomas was speechless, then angry. "Is this a joke?" he roared back. "From a distance, I watched Jesus die. Then I left the city to mourn the loss of all my hopes and dreams for this nation. Your questions do not amuse me."

"So you do not know the things that have happened?" Both men responded with growing comprehension.

"I know that Jesus was nailed to a Roman cross and that is where he died," Thomas replied.

"Come with us," Manaen directed as he and Cuza began walking toward the house where many of the followers of Jesus had gathered.

John opened the door to the upper room, embracing Thomas and greeting both Cuza and Manaen. As soon as Peter laid eyes on Thomas, he shouted the good news, "Our master lives. I have seen him. We spoke."

Others in the room added, "He visited us in this room!"

"He sat and ate at this table!"

"Death could not hold him!"

"On the first day of the week, he came out of the tomb!"

Thomas's face became red, and he shouted over their excited voices. "I do not believe you! Have you lost your minds?"

"We have seen the Lord!" They all shouted back.

But Thomas *said to them, "Unless I see the nail marks in his hands and put my finger where the nails were, and put my hand into his side, I will not believe."*⁴ Then he turned and left the room.

Manaen and Cuza remained, hanging onto every word as each disciple told and retold their post-resurrection encounters with Jesus.

James the brother of Jesus arrived admitting that for most of the ministry years, he had been very critical of his brother, never once believing that Jesus could be anything more than an ordinary man.

"Forgive me." James knelt before Peter and John and the other disciples. "I openly scoffed and ridiculed all of you, but now, I know that you had obtained wisdom from heaven and I had not. I had to become a witness to his death and resurrection before I could fully believe."

Then James stood and addressed all the men in that room. "My brother told me to exhort you to prayer, to pray for the gifts that his Father wants to give you. *Is anyone among you in trouble? Let them pray. Is anyone happy? Let them sing songs of praise. Is anyone among you sick? Let them call the elders…to pray over them and anoint them with oil in the name of* Jesus. *And the prayer offered in faith will make the sick person well; the Lord will raise them up. If they have sinned, they will be forgiven. Therefore confess your sins to each other and pray for each other so that you may be healed. The prayer of a righteous person is powerful and effective.*

"Several times, Jesus has blown on you and said, 'Receive the Holy Spirit.' He did that to me. Through the Holy Spirit, he is giving us greater power than what was exercised by Elijah. Remember, *Elijah was a human being, even as we are. He prayed earnestly that it would not rain, and it did not rain on the land for three and a half years. Again he prayed, and the heavens gave rain, and the earth produced its crops.*[5] So let us begin."

From one of the towers, Longinus looked out over the city. Once again, every highway was filled with travelers, leaving the city, going home to harvest their barley, and tend their gardens. On the Mount of Olives, most of the campsites had been cleared. Jerusalem was returning to normal. In the courtyard, below, Pilate's wife entered her sedan chair, and Pilate mounted his horse for their return trip to the royal residence in Caesarea. Longinus hurried down the stairs to pay proper respect at the gate.

Once again, Thomas climbed the stairs to the upper room. He knew many of Jesus's disciples, his closest friends, would be leaving Jerusalem, returning to their homes. He just wanted to say good-bye and hear their plans.

When he entered the room, he could see that a meal had been prepared. He was offered a place next to Matthew. The women finished serving and left the room. Then James locked the door behind them. Peter lifted one of the round loaves of bread. Breaking off a chunk, he began chanting. "Blessed are you, O Lord our God, ruler of the universe, who brings forth bread from the earth."

Before he could taste the bread from his sister's oven, Jesus appeared in the room and said, "Peace to you!"

Then he turned to Thomas. "You came here with unbelief and sadness in your heart. I came to remove those thoughts from your mind." Jesus motioned for Thomas to come and stand by his side. Then he said, "Touch the nail holes in my feet and in my hands."

Jesus reached out, turning both hands from front to back so the jagged red scars were easily visible. Then he moved his garment to the side so everyone in the room could see the place where the Roman spear had pierced his heart. It was a deep gash, yet healthy skin covered all sides. "Put your hand into the gash in my side." His eyes were directly on the face of Thomas. "Allow yourself to believe."

Dropping to his knees, Thomas exclaimed, "My master and my Messiah!"

Then Jesus said, "You have seen me and believed. But many will believe without this proof. These are blessed with great faith."

Jesus then sat and ate with the men. He taught, "I am the one who spoke the Earth into existence."

"God the Creator!" John echoed.

"Yes," Jesus affirmed. "I am the Word!" Jesus looked at John as he spoke. "You have seen me with your eyes and touched me with your hands." Then with a piercing gaze, he swept the faces gathered around him. "Do not be surprised. Many will scoff when you share this news. Just know that my enemy, Satan, still lives and works against my kingdom. *Every spirit that acknowledges that Jesus Christ has come in the flesh is from* the Kingdom of *God, but every spirit that does not acknowledge Jesus is not from* God's kingdom. *This is the spirit of* Satan, *the antichrist, which you have heard is coming and even now is already* working feverishly *in the world.*[6] He wants all of humanity to deny that I am God the Creator, who became a man of the Earth and then gave my humanity to die once for the sins of every man and woman."

Jesus stood and emphatically warned, "Satan knows more about the Kingdom of God than anyone here. He knows that people must choose citizenship. My Father will not force it on them. I have commissioned you to offer that choice. Return to your homes. Tell your family and your friends the things that have happened in Jerusalem." Then Jesus disappeared.

Chapter 22

Feed My Sheep

Then the eleven disciples went to Galilee, to the mountain where Jesus had told them to go. When they saw him, they worshiped him; but some doubted.

—Matthew 28:16–17

In the dark of Earth's night, Yeshua-Jesus left heaven to walk along the rocky shore of Galilee. Out on the midnight waters, his closest friends hauled in their water-logged nets—no reward for a night's labor.

At the water's edge, Jesus slipped off his robe and undressed to his loin cloth. He picked up a small net, then waded into the chilled fresh water of Israel's inland sea. Swishing the net through the water, he enjoyed the sensations of earthly life—cold water on his skin, his own warm breath making misty clouds in the predawn air.

The casting net in his hand took on additional weight as it soaked up the water. With an experienced feel for the net, Jesus lifted and swung it in steady circles. Every muscle in his body coordinated to release at the precise moment.

With a soft smack, the flared and knotted hemp hit the dark surface of the water. Then it silently sank beneath the murky wavelets. "Fish!" Jesus called to the edible creatures of the sea.

Immediately, the circle of the net filled with thrashing tails and fins. Quickly, Jesus pulled the cord to close the net, hauling his catch back toward the shore with a strong, steady effort.

The rising sun painted the horizon red and gold. Against that glowing background, Jesus could see the sails of many fishing ships homeward bound. His eyes rested on the one ship that carried his heart more than the others. It was Peter's boat. His own stomach growled, reminding him that his friends were in need of nourishment.

Before Peter's boat sailed into hailing distance Jesus had a fire started, fresh fish roasting and flat bread baking. Then as the fishing boat tacked to catch the wind that would take it into Zebedee's mooring, Jesus called across the water, "How was your fishing?"

They answered, "It was a bad night for fishermen and a good night for fish."

Full of encouragement, Jesus called back over the water. "In the spot where you are floating, drop your nets on the right side of the boat. There you will find fish."

Immediately, the men on the boat responded, throwing their heavy nets over the side. As soon as the nets sunk below, the surface they filled.

"There are too many fish for one net!" John exclaimed. "Philip! Throw another net!"

"Thomas! James! Jump in the water and grab the lines!"

In the midst of the chaos, John stopped hauling and said to Peter, "It must be Jesus! Remember, he did this once before."

As soon as Peter heard the name "Jesus," he dropped his section of the net, grabbed his robe, and threw it around his neck. Then he jumped into the water, quickly wading to shore. The other disciples manned the oars, towing their full nets to shore.

When they landed, James looked at the roasting fish and freshly baked bread. A grin spread across his face. "Ah, Master, this brings back memories. When we were younger, you used to meet our fishing boats in the morning with a meal like this."

Andrew added, "Then, while we ate, you taught us from the scriptures."

Jesus quickly pulled the fish off the coals and said, "Bring some of your catch. I'll cook another batch. We'll eat well this morning."

So Peter and the other disciples dragged the nets closer to shore so they could fill their baskets with the fresh catch, large fish.

Then Jesus called, "Come, breakfast is ready."

None of the disciples delayed. More than food, they desired to hear what Jesus would say to them.

When all had gathered around, Jesus took one of the loaves of flat bread. He lifted it toward heaven while he chanted the blessing. Then he broke off chunks, personally serving each man.

It did not take long for the women of Zebedee's fishing business to spot a large catch. They came with their baskets, sorting and taking most of the fish to salt or dry. The men paid no attention to their catch or the nets that needed to be cleaned. Totally focused on Jesus, they remained seated around the dying fire.

When the disciples had finished eating, Jesus motioned for Peter to walk with him along the shore. When they had moved out of earshot, Jesus said to Peter, "Is your love and devotion for me greater than the love and devotion of my other disciples?"

At first, Peter looked a little uncomfortable with the question. In the past, he had frequently proclaimed his great devotion, but now, everyone knew how badly he had failed in the courtyard of the high priest. Still, he managed to look Jesus squarely in the eyes and say, "Yes Lord, you know my devotion for you is greater than most."

Jesus responded, "Then you must become a humble shepherd and care for my lambs."

Peter nodded. He understood the symbolic language. So he replied, "For most of my life, I have been a fisherman, but I can also feed lambs."

Jesus paused, and, for a long moment, he looked deeply into Peter's eyes. "Do you really love me? Is your devotion as great as you have said?"

Vividly, Peter remembered the night when he had denied any association with Jesus, and he shifted uncomfortably. Waves of shame rolled through his soul. But again, with as much conviction as he could muster, he answered, "Yes, Master, I do love you."

Jesus responded, "My sheep must be cared for. It is a job that requires great patience and humility. Will you do that for me?"

"Whatever you ask, Lord, I will do it."

They walked a little further, stopping beside one of Zebedee's fishing boats. Again, Jesus looked deeply into the eyes of his usually brash disciple. "Peter, answer me honestly. How deep and how strong is your love for me?"

Now Peter was worried and hurt because Jesus had not been satisfied with his previous answers. Determined to make his affection and loyalty clear, Peter planted his feet and emphatically said, "Master, you know the heart of every man so you know that I love you. Yes, I did fail to stand beside you. I regret my weakness. At the same time, my love for you is unwavering."

"Well then, will you feed my sheep?" Jesus asked. Then he added. "I am asking if you will give your life for the sheep like I gave my life. You must be certain. I can only leave my sheep with one who will walk the path I have walked and not flee in the face of great danger, even the cross."

Peter nodded his head affirmatively.

Looking into the future, Jesus continued. "When you were a young man, you put on your best robe and went where ever you pleased. Freely, you chose the activities of each day. But when your hair has turned from gray to white, after you have cared for my sheep for many years, you will stretch out your hands on the beam of a cross. Soldiers will bind you with ropes." Jesus held out his own hands. Both the nail holes and the rope burns were still visible.

Peter understood the process of Roman crucifixion—the whipping, the indignity of total exposure.

Jesus continued explaining that Peter was being offered a choice. "I did not want to go to the cross. In the garden, I struggled with submitting to that death." Then Jesus said to him, "Will you follow me by making the choice that I made?"

At that moment, Peter turned and saw that John was standing nearby.

When John saw that he had been noticed, he stepped into the conversation. "Master, what about me?"

"Yes," Peter chimed in. "What about John? How will his life end?"

Jesus answered, "Peter, you must choose how far you will follow me. Many of my followers will take up the cross as they follow me, but others will live long lives and die of old age. The length of John's life has nothing to do with the questions I have asked you."

Jesus did not press Peter any more. He returned to the other disciples, and he heard their whispered assumptions that Peter would die, but John would live forever. Finally, Jesus addressed the speculating group and said, "If I want John to live long, even until I return, that is not your concern. Answer this question for yourselves. How far will you follow me?"

Weeks passed. The Passover crowd dwindled until Jerusalem seemed almost normal except for the daily counting of the days until the next major gathering, fifty days after Passover. The monthly dispatch from Rome arrived by military currier from Caesarea. Longinus tossed the heavy leather pouch on a table and began to sort through the documents.

After breaking the seal of the Minister of Justice, the commander of the Roman forces in Judea was surprised to see that he held in his hand a warrant for the arrest of a man named Agrippa, brother-in-law to King Antipas of Galilee. Agrippa was to be taken into custody and put on a ship to Rome where he would be forced to deal with the enormous debts he had left in that city.

Longinus knew he could not march into the territory that was ruled by Antipas, even with the warrant in hand, but if Agrippa made a trip to Jerusalem, the arrest would be easy enough.

In Galilee, Manaen and Cuza half-heartedly dealt with the financial affairs of King Antipas. Their hearts were drawn to the large hill just outside of Capernaum. Reports had reached them that Jesus often appeared there, meeting his friends and teaching. But for the moment, both men were occupied with the problems that the arrival of the king's brother-in-law had presented. Overnight, they had been inundated with numerous demands for payment, old debts in Rome and new purchases upon his arrival. The total far exceeded his allowance from the treasury. So with armloads of documents, both men stoically approached their meeting with Antipas. They were determined to pressure him into restraining the spending habits of Agrippa.

The sky was cloudless and blue. Jesus settled on one of the boulders near the crest of the hill called the Mount. In town, the market was busy. Near the shore, boats bobbed at their moorings and fishing nets dried in the sun.

A shepherdess was the first to see Jesus. She called to her brother near the boats. He quickly notified the other fishermen. "Rabbi Jesus has appeared again! He's on the mountain."

Those who knew Jesus dropped everything and ran to the Mount. In less time than it took to bake a small loaf of flat bread, more than five hundred people had climbed the hill.

Jesus did not disappoint them. "Many times, I have talked about shepherds and sheep. Those who are wise, those who listen with the aid of the Holy Spirit, understand that I am speaking about myself and people. Today, I am calling each of you to become shepherds and shepherdesses. I want you to tell people everything I have done and said. I want you to gather all those who believe you into flocks that you will care for."

Temporarily freed from their royal duties, Cuza and Manaen made their way up the mountain. They found places to sit beside Peter and Andrew. Joanna and Mary from Magdela joined them, totally absorbed in every word Jesus said.

He said to them, "Shepherding is a dangerous job, full of hardships. You will endure much. Nevertheless, *go into all the world and preach the gospel to all creation. Whoever believes and is baptized will be saved, but whoever does not believe will be condemned. And these signs will accompany those who believe: In my name they will drive out demons; they will speak in new tongues; they will pick up snakes with their hands; and when they drink deadly poison, it will not hurt them at all; they will place their hands on sick people, and they will get well."*[1]

Then Jesus stood. "In just a few weeks, it will be time for everyone to gather in Jerusalem again. I am going there ahead of you. I will see you again on the Mount of Olives near Bethany. Once you arrive in the city, do not leave until you have been filled with power from on high." Before their eyes, Jesus then vanished.

Chapter 23

The Kingdom of God on Earth

After his suffering, he presented himself to them and gave many convincing proofs that he was alive. He appeared to them over a period of forty days and spoke about the Kingdom of God.

—Acts 1:3

Mary from Magdela and Miriam, Peter's sister, slowly cleared the empty dishes and whisked the crumbs from the table. Jesus was with them again, sharing a meal, giving directions for the running of his kingdom. They hung on every word. *Then they gathered around him and asked him, "Lord, are you at this time going to restore the kingdom to Israel?"*

He said to them: "It is not for you to know the times or dates the Father has set by his own authority. But you will receive power when the Holy Spirit comes on you; and you will be my witnesses in Jerusalem, and in all Judea and Samaria, and to the ends of the earth.[1] Stay in Jerusalem. Continue to meet in this room. Pray and encourage each other. You will certainly know when the Holy Spirit has come and released you to spread the good news of my kingdom."

Then Jesus stood. And when he stood, everyone in the room held their breath, expecting that he might vanish as he had done many times over the last forty days.

This time, Jesus just smiled and said, "Walk with me."

Mary dropped her little whisk broom and left the crumbs. Everyone moved with Jesus, out of the upper room, through the narrow streets toward the Sheep Gate. Along the way, other followers recognized Jesus. A few joined the disciples. *When he had led them out to the vicinity of Bethany, he lifted up his hands and blessed them.*[2] "*The* LORD *bless you and keep you.*" His voice trembled with the emotion of the moment. "*The* LORD *make his face shine on you and be gracious to you.*" Gradually, his feet began to lift off the ground. "*The* LORD *turn his face toward you and give you peace.*" Higher and higher, Jesus rose until he hovered above their heads. "*So* as you repeat the things I have taught you and the things you have seen, you…*will put my name on the Israelites* and on all of humanity, *and I will bless them.*"[3]

An angelic escort swooped in. Golden clouds swirled around his feet as Jesus floated up, up, far above the heads of those gathered to hear him, past the treetops, and through the clouds of the sky.

The disciples and many of his close followers *were looking intently up into the sky as he was going, when suddenly two men dressed in white stood beside them. "Men of Galilee," they said, "why do you stand here looking into the sky? This same Jesus, who has been taken from you into heaven, will come back in the same way you have seen him go into heaven."*

Then the apostles, telling and retelling the event they had just witnessed, *returned to Jerusalem from the hill called the Mount of Olives.* It was *a Sabbath day's walk from the city. When they arrived, they went upstairs to the room where they were staying. Those present were Peter, John, James and Andrew; Philip and Thomas, Bartholomew and Matthew; James son of Alphaeus and Simon the Zealot, and Judas son of James.* Remembering the instructions of

Jesus, *they all joined together constantly in prayer, along with the women and Mary the mother of Jesus, and with his brothers.*[4]

From his place at the right hand of God, Yeshua-Jesus remained constantly observant. He knew that his kingdom in its infant state was as vulnerable as a newborn. Immediately, he commissioned the Archangel Michael to keep the forces of Satan away from his kingdom citizens. Each man or woman was provided with an angelic guard and the upper room, which was their place of prayer, remained surrounded by heavenly forces.

The Holy Spirit was sent, each day in greater measure until the morning of the Feast of Weeks. Then soon after daylight, the Wind of God blew forcefully through the upper room and burning flames appeared on each head. Heavenly joy filled each person. Gifts of wisdom, knowledge, and spiritual understanding flooded the room. All the gifts of the Spirit were poured out—faith, healing, miraculous powers, prophecy, supernatural love, and endurance.

Immediately, each person exclaimed over their experience with the Holy Spirit, and they were amazed at the sound of their own voices for they were speaking in the languages of the nations.

Peter was the first to speak understandably. "Men and women, today is the anniversary of the day when God spoke the Ten Commandments from Mt. Sinai. We have always been taught that the thunder that accompanied each statute was that law spoken again in all the languages of the world. Today, God is speaking the good news of Jesus through each of us! He is speaking in all the languages of the world!"

Laughing and babbling, John suddenly ran to the door and threw it open. About 120 wildly excited men and women then hurried down the stairs and into the street. Shouting in various languages about their experiences with Jesus, they mixed with those who were coming from all night Torah study in the Temple

Now there were staying in Jerusalem God-fearing Jews from every nation under heaven. When they heard this sound, a crowd came together in bewilderment, because each one heard their own language being spoken. Utterly amazed, they asked: "Aren't all these who are speaking Galileans? Then how is it that each of us hears them in our native language.⁵ We hear them declaring the wonders of God in our own tongues!" Amazed and perplexed, they asked one another, "What does this mean?"⁶

However, some observers were open to the suggestions of demons. Those men made fun of the followers of Jesus who were pouring out of the upper room. Pointing and laughing they announced, "Those foolish people are drunk."

Then Peter stepped up where he could be seen. "Citizens of Jerusalem and Jews from around the world, we are not drunk. You are seeing what was predicted by the prophet Joel: *In the last days, God says, "I will pour out my Spirit on all people"*⁷

Pilate looked up as Longinus entered with the morning report. "What is the mood of the city for this feast?"

"Calm," Longinus replied.

Then Pilate asked, "What about the aftermath of the story of Rabbi Jesus coming to life?"

Longinus took a deep breath. "More stories of dead men living and walking through the city. I even heard a report about ten days ago that these resurrected people were rising from earth and disappearing in the sky."

"Could it be true?" Pilate asked.

"Longinus shook his head. "I don't know, but a few weeks ago, the centurion at Capernaum reported seeing Rabbi Jesus and listening to him teach from a mountaintop."

"Do you believe him?' Pilate asked.

Longinus hesitated. Then he answered, "Yes."

"Why?" Pilate demanded. "Why do you believe such a tale?"

"After the report from our guards, I went to examine the tomb, and with my own eyes, I saw Rabbi Jesus, alive."

Pilate paled, and Longinus changed the subject.

"I received a warrant for the arrest of a man named Agrippa, brother-in-law and nephew of Antipas. If he comes to Jerusalem for this feast, I expect to arrest him and send him back to Rome."

Pilate grunted. Then he mused aloud, "I wonder if Antipas has enough clout to save him?"

A disturbance at the draped entrance made both men turn to see two messengers. The first one announced a riot in the southern section of the city. The second one informed Longinus that King Antipas was approaching the northern gate with a large entourage. Agrippa was believed to be with him.

Pilate gave Longinus a smug nod, and Longinus turned to give the orders. "Arrest Agrippa. Send a squad to break up the riot without violence."

That evening, Pilate shared a cup of wine with the commander of his fortress in Jerusalem. He asked, "Is Agrippa sitting in a jail cell?"

Longinus nodded. "He is very angry because Antipas did nothing to dissuade me."

"And about the riot?"

Longinus said, "It seems that some of the followers of Rabbi Jesus were telling the story of his death and resurrection."

"Did you put an end to it?" Pilate asked.

"It had already broken up. My men just reported that the pools throughout the city that are used for ceremonial washing were full of people, ducking beneath the water and wildly praising their god."

Pilate shook his head. "My wife says Jerusalem is the center of the spiritual forces that govern this world. She is certain that the death of Rabbi Jesus and the events of last Passover changed the course of Earth's future. I don't really know what that means. I don't know how it will affect my life or yours."

For the remainder of the evening, both men were quiet and contemplative.

The books of heaven were opened. In one day, more than three thousand names were added to the Book of Life, the record of kingdom citizenship. And as the days passed, the population of the Kingdom of God continued to increase rapidly.

Joy filled the heart of Jesus as he watched his kingdom grow under the guidance of the men and women he had left in charge. All of the new citizens sat under the teaching of the apostles in the Temple courts and in homes. Miracles occurred daily. Praise was continual, and the people of Jerusalem were amazed at the power of those who remained loyal to Rabbi Jesus. Their numbers increased rapidly.

The community of believers shared everything so no one suffered in poverty. They fellowshipped together—going from house to house, blessing each other with prayer and kind words.

From the right hand of the Father, Yeshua-Jesus watched over the growth of his kingdom.

Ichabod, the beggar, sat by the Beautiful Gate curled up in his worn leather chair, waiting for someone to drop a coin. He wondered what had happened to the man who periodically sent him a replacement chair, often at the Feast of Weeks. This year, there had been no new chair. This year felt more hopeless than any year in his life.

In heaven, Jesus knew it was time for Ichabod to receive more than a chair. It was time for an old prophetic word to be fulfilled. Through the Holy Spirit, he urged Peter and John to go to the evening sacrifice at the Temple and then to his old teaching place on Solomon's porch. There, they were to tell everyone the good news of his kingdom. Almost chuckling, Jesus imagined the reception they would receive after they followed the instructions he was entrusting to the Holy Spirit.

With practiced eyes, Ichabod surveyed the faces of the men and women entering the Temple. Most were rushed. Many refused to make eye contact with him. But when he saw Peter and John, he lifted his bowl and made eye contact.

Peter returned the direct stare as did John. Both men heard the Holy Spirit say, "Tell this man to stand and walk."

Then Peter and John hurried over to the beggar. "Look into my eyes," Peter said.

So the beggar gave them his undivided attention, expecting a substantial gift.

Then Peter said, "Silver or gold I do not have, but what I do have I give you. In the name of Jesus Christ of Nazareth, walk." Taking him by the right hand, Peter *helped him up, and instantly, the man's feet and ankles became strong. He jumped to his feet and began to walk.*[8]

In heaven, Jesus jumped to his feet and cheered. Angels burst into song, overjoyed that John and Peter had followed the instructions of the Holy Spirit without hesitation!

Then the healed beggar ran with them into the Temple, walking, leaping and praising God. Through the Court of the Gentiles, into the Court of the Women, up the steps and into the Court of the Israelites, Ichabod was seeing all the places he had only heard about.

Heaven held its breath. Warring angels were dispatched. The Kingdom of Jesus of Nazareth was about to confront the religious spirits of Satan's kingdom.

The initial response was positive. When all the people recognized the beggar, they were filled with wonder and passed the story from person to person.

A crowd quickly gathered. Still following the directions of the Holy Spirit, Peter seized the moment and began to preach.

The priests and the captain of the Temple guard and the Sadducees came up to Peter and John while they were speaking to the people. They were greatly disturbed because the apostles were teaching the people, proclaiming in Jesus the resurrection of the dead. They seized Peter and John and, because it was evening, they put them in jail until the next day. But many who heard the message believed; so the number of men who believed grew to about five thousand.[9]

Shouts of joy filled heaven again as more names were added to the Book of Life.

The next day, the Sanhedrin was called into session. These were the men who had sent Jesus to Pilate, forcing his execution. Now Peter and John faced the same court.

Empowered by the Holy Spirit, Peter gave a fearless and faultless defense. In that courtroom, warrior-angels raised their swords and advanced. The powers of darkness fell back, bound and gagged by the Holy Spirit power of the words that Peter spoke.

The first battle in the war between the Kingdom of God and the kingdom of Satan had been engaged. There would be many more battles. Angels of light would fight angels of darkness. People would blindly struggle for and against both sides.

All the while, Yeshua-Jesus sits at the right hand of the Father, watching, directing and waiting for a ground-swell of loyal sons and daughters of Adam. Only Father God knows the number that will cause him to stand and say, "Yeshua, the Book of Life has been filled. Return to Earth. Take possession of your kingdom!"

Epilogue

I am Coming Soon

*"Look, he is coming with the clouds, and "every eye will see
him, even those who pierced him"; and all peoples on earth
"will mourn because of him." So shall it be! Amen.*

—Revelation 1:7

Sunshine sparkled on the green-blue waters of the
Mediterranean. It was the day of the week that Christians
called the Lord's Day in honor of the resurrection of Jesus and
in defiance of the Roman gods who had each been given a day of
the week.

From the roughly constructed prison colony on the
Island of Patmos, John looked across the water that kept him
confined. White-haired and wiry, he sat in quiet contemplation,
remembering personal moments with Jesus both before and after
he had come out of the tomb. The aging disciple glanced down at
his weathered skin. Shaking his head in amazement, he recalled
that day in Rome's Coliseum when he had been thrown into a
vat of boiling oil only to climb out unscathed. "Jesus, you were
with me."

Then John burst into laughter. "We dealt Satan a blow that
day! After I crawled out of that boiling pot, I stood there and
preached in the power of your Holy Spirit. What a call for
salvation! Every man and woman in the stadium stood to be
admitted into your kingdom."

From where he sat, John could see ships moving from port to port, but none were coming to the rickety dock on this prison island. "Jesus, I'm the last witness, the only disciple still alive. I need to leave this island. I need to keep telling your story. I need to bring men and women into your kingdom so you can write their names in the Book of Life before you return."

Suddenly from behind, a voice, like a clear trumpet announced, "I am the Alpha and the Omega, the One who is alive now, the One who was alive with you in Galilee and Jerusalem, and the One who has promised to come and live on Earth again."

John jumped up and turned around. *And when* he *turned* he *saw seven golden lampstands, and among the lampstands was someone like a son of man, dressed in a robe reaching down to his feet and with a golden sash around his chest. The hair on his head was white like wool, as white as snow, and his eyes were like blazing fire. His feet were like bronze glowing in a furnace, and his voice was like the sound of rushing waters. In his right hand he held seven stars, and coming out of his mouth was a sharp, double-edged sword. His face was like the sun shining in all its brilliance.*

When John *saw him, he fell at his feet as though dead. Then* the glowing man *placed his right hand on* John *and said: "Do not be afraid. I am the First and the Last. I am the Living One; I was dead, and now look, I am alive for ever and ever! And I hold the keys of death and Hades.* You know me."[1]

"Jesus!" It was an awed whisper, a confident recognition.

Jesus responded, pulling the disciple that he loved to his feet and saying, "Write the things I will show you and send them to the seven churches. *Look, I am coming soon! My reward is with me, and I will give to each person according to what they have done.[2] Blessed are those who wash their robes, that they may have the right to the tree of life and may go through the gates into the city."[3]*

Then Jesus smiled at John. It was the smile that John loved.

John smiled back. They were old friends sharing a lifetime of experiences without words.

Then Jesus said, "You and Peter prepared a wonderful Passover meal for me, the last I had. I want you to know that I have prepared a banquet for you and all those whose names are in my Book of Life. It will be in the heavenly Jerusalem. There I will share a cup of wine, a goblet of praise, with my guests.

"Like the last cup of the Passover meal, it will be a cup of joy and victory. I want everyone to be there and to drink it with me. So write the things I am about to show you. They are the last scenes of Earth's history, events that will take place in heaven and on Earth. Together, they will bring about the ultimate destruction of my enemy and the establishment of my kingdom on Earth.

"Rejoice because you will soon see the fulfillment of every scripture that was ever written about me. I will be returning soon."

Index of Characters

Biblical Characters

Aaron
: Brother of Moses, first high priest, father of Eleazar, grandfather of Phinehas (Exodus 6:20–26)

Abraham
: The father of the Jewish race (Genesis 11–50)

Abel
: Second son of Adam, killed by his brother, Cain (Genesis 4)

Abihu
: One of the sons of Aaron (Exodus 6:23)

Adam
: The first man, he was created by God and placed in the Garden of Eden (Genesis 2–4)

God
: God the Father, used interchangeably with God, Abba, Lord, Father, and the Eternal One.

Alexander
: One of the sons of Simon the Cyrene who carried the cross (Mark 15:21)

Andrew
: Brother of Peter, son of Jona, fisherman, one of the twelve disciples of Jesus, later an apostle (Matthew, Mark, Luke, John, Acts)

Annas	High priest during the life of Jesus (Luke 3:1–3)
Barabbas	A criminal who had been sentenced to die on the cross, Jesus died in his place. (Matthew 27, Mark 15, Luke 23)
Bartholomew	One of the twelve disciples, also named Nathanael (Matthew 10:3. Mark 3:18. Luke 6:14, Acts 1:13)
Bartimaeus	A blind man who was healed by Jesus in Jericho (Mark 10:46)
Beggar at the Beautiful Gate	Fictionalized as Ichabod, the crippled son of Asa, the Temple perfumer (Acts 3)
Caiaphas	High priest during the life of Jesus (Luke 3:1–3)
Cleopas	One of two disciples walking to Emmaus when Jesus appeared to them (Luke 24)
Cuza	Officer in the court of Herod, manager of Herod's household, husband to Joanna who was one of the women who went to the tomb (Luke 8:3, Luke 24:10)
Daniel	Prophet (Daniel)

Daughter of Putiel	Wife of Eleazar, daughter-in-law of Aaron, mother of Phinehas (Exodus 6:25)
David	A King of Israel and ancestor of Jesus (1 Samuel, 1 Chronicles, Matthew 1, Luke 3)
Eleazar	One of the sons of Aaron, father of Phinehas, high priest after Aaron (Exodus 6:23–25)
Elijah	Old Testament prophet in Israel who challenged King Ahab and Queen Jezebel (1 Kings 7–2 Kings 2:12)
Esther	Queen who saved her nation (Esther)
Eve	The first woman, she was created by God from Adam's rib. She was Adam's wife and was the first to fall into sin. (Genesis 2–4)
Gamaliel	Important member of Sanhedrin, grandson of Hillel (Acts 5:34, 22:3)
Satan	Once a heavenly angel, he rebelled against God. He is referred to in scriptures as the devil and Satan. In this series, he is also called the enemy or the Evil One

Herod Agrippa	Grandson of Herod the Great, nephew and brother-in-law to Herod Antipas, he convinced the emperor to exile Herod Antipas and to then give him (Herod Agrippa) rulership of Galilee and Judea. (Acts 25–26)
Herod Antipas	The Son of Herod the Great and ruler of Galilee during life of Jesus (Matthew 14:1–11, Luke 23:6–12)
Herod the Great	The King Herod who killed the babies in Bethlehem, hoping to kill Jesus (Matthew 2: 1–9)
Herodias	The second wife of Herod Antipas, formerly the wife of his half-brother, Phillip, sister of Herod Agrippa (Matthew 14:1–12, Mark 6:14–29, Luke 3:19–20)
Holy Spirit	Third person of the Godhead
Isaiah	An Old Testament prophet (2 Kings 19–20, 2 Chronicles 26–32, Isaiah)
Jacob	The son of Isaac who was tricked into marrying the wrong woman, Father of the twelve tribes of Israel (Genesis 29:23–25)
Jairus	A leader of the synagogue in Capernaum, Jesus raised his daugh-

	ter from the dead. (Mark 5 and Luke 8)
James Son of Alphaeus	One of the twelve disciples (Matthew 10:2) Maybe also called James the Younger (Mark 15:40)
James son of Joseph and Mary	The brother of Jesus, later a leader in the early church and writer of the book of James (Matthew 13:55)
James son of Zebedee	Possibly a cousin of Jesus, one of the twelve disciples, the brother of the disciple John whom Jesus loved, a fisherman, later an apostle (Matthew, Mark, Luke, John, Acts)
Jambres	One of Pharaoh's magicians who opposed Moses and Aaron (2 Timothy 3:8)
Jeremiah	Old Testament prophet and priest, tradition holds that he removed the ark and the furnishings from Solomon's Temple before it was destroyed. He wrote the books of Jeremiah and Lamentations.
Jesus	Son of God and Son of Mary, Yeshua in his heavenly person (Gospels of Matthew, Mark, Luke, and John)

Joanna	Wife of Cuza, supporter of Jesus, associated with the court of Herod Antipas (Luke 8:3, Luke 24:10)
Job	A man who was tested by Satan (Job)
John Marc	A young man, possibly the nephew of Peter who later wrote the Gospel of Mark and went on missionary journeys. (Acts 12:12, 24–25, Acts 15:37)
John son of Zebedee	Possibly a cousin of Jesus, one of the twelve disciples, the brother of the disciple James, a fisherman, later an apostle, writer of the books of John and Revelation (Matthew, Mark, Luke, John, Acts, 1–3 John, Revelation)
John son of Zechariah	John the Baptist, a cousin of Jesus, the prophet of the desert (Mark 1:1–11, Luke 1: 36–80, Luke 7:18–23, Mark 6:14–29)
Jona	Father of Simon Peter and Andrew, fishing partner with Zebedee (John 1:42, KJV)
Jose	Brother of Jesus, son of Joseph and Mary (Matthew 13:55, KJV)

Joseph	Deceased carpenter of Nazareth, husband of Mary, earthly father of Jesus (Matthew 1:18–24)
Joseph of Arimathea	A wealthy man, member of the Sanhedrin who was able to approach Pilate and assist with the burial of Jesus (Mark 15:43)
Jude	A brother of Jesus, a son of Mary and Joseph, his name is sometimes spelled Juda or Judas. Probably the author of the book of Jude (Jude 1:1, Matthew 13:55, Mark 6:3)
Judas Iscariot	A disciple of Jesus, the one who betrayed him (Matthew, Mark, Luke, John, Acts)
Lazarus	Friend of Jesus who lived in Bethany, fictionalized as the elder brother in the parable of the prodigal son. (John 11)
Lazarus	Rich man in the parable that Jesus told (Luke 16)
Malchus	Servant to the high priest, when Jesus was taken prisoner, Peter cut off his ear. Jesus restored it. (John 18:10)
Manaen	Childhood companion to Herod Antipas, his mother was most likely

the wet nurse for Antipas, later he was an important member of the early Christian community (Acts 13:1)

Martha	The sister of Mary and Lazarus of Bethany (John 11)
Mary	The mother of Jesus, wife of Joseph (Matthew, Mark, Luke, John, Acts)
Mary of Bethany	The sister of Lazarus who lives in Bethany, one of two different women who anointed Jesus (John 11)
Mary wife of Clopas	One of the women at the cross with the mother of Jesus (John 19:25)
Mary of Magdela	A follower of Jesus, Jesus cast seven demons out of her. She was the first at the tomb. (Matthew 27–28, Mark 15–16, Luke 8, 24, John 20)
Matthew	The tax collector at Capernaum, one of the twelve disciples, author of the Gospel of Matthew (Matthew, Mark, Luke, Acts)
Methuselah	One of the men who lived before the flood, the oldest man (Genesis 5)

Michael	A prince of angels who fought the forces of evil to bring a message from God to Daniel (Daniel 10:13)
Moses	A deliverer chosen by God to lead Israel out of Egypt (Exodus, Numbers, Deuteronomy)
Nadab	One of the sons of Aaron (Exodus 6:23)
Naomi	Woman who lost her husband and sons, mother-in-law of Ruth (Ruth)
Nathanael	One of the twelve disciples, also called Bartholomew (John 1:43–49)
Nicodemus	A rabbi in Jerusalem (John 3, 19)
Noah	An ancestor of Jesus, builder of the ark (Genesis 6–9)
Peter	Simon Peter, son of Jona, brother of Andrew, fisherman, one of the twelve disciples of Jesus, later an apostle, writer of First and Second Peter (Matthew, Mark, Luke, John Acts, 1–2 Peter)
Philip	One of the twelve disciples, later an apostle (Matthew, Mark, Luke, John, Acts)

Phinehas	Grandson of Aaron, son of Eleazar, high priest after Eleazar (Exodus 6:23–25)
Pontius Pilate	Governor of Judea, probably appointed by Sejanus (Matthew, Mark, Luke, John)
Rufus	Son of Simon of Cyrene who carried the cross, member of early church (Mark 15:21, Romans 16:13)
Salome	The sister of Mary and the wife of Zebedee (Mark 15:40, Matthew 27:55–56). This relationship is theorized by comparing the two scriptural passages about the women who were with Mary at the cross.
Seth	Third son of Adam and Eve (Genesis 4–5)
Simon	Brother of Jesus, son of Mary and Joseph (Matthew 13:55)
Simon of Cyrene	Man who carried the cross for Jesus (Mark 15:21)
Simon the Leper	A citizen of Bethany, fictionalized as the older brother of Jonathan who was married to Mary the sister of Lazarus (Matthew 26: 6–7, Mark 14:3)

Simon the Zealot	One of the twelve disciples of Jesus, fictionalized as a childhood friend of Jesus who moved to Cana (Acts 1: 12–14)
Thaddaeus	One of the twelve disciples (Matthew 10:3, Mark 3:18)
Thomas	One of the twelve disciples (Matthew, Mark, Luke, John, Acts)
Yeshua the Creator	Yeshua is the Hebrew name for Jesus. In this story, it is used as the heavenly person of Jesus.
Zacchaeus	A short man who was a tax collector in Jericho. (Luke 19)
Zebedee	A fisherman married to Salome, his sons are James and John, possibly an uncle of Jesus (Matthew 4:21–22)
Zechariah	A deceased priest, father of John the Baptist (Luke 1)
Zechariah son of Berekiah	Author of the book of Zechariah (Zechariah 1:1)

Fictional Characters

Bohan	Deceased father of Lazarus and Nodab, father in the parable of the prodigal son
Casper	Fictional name for the young son of Cuza and Joanna, healed by Jesus
Deborah	Shepherdess, granddaughter of Baruch, wife of Jose, sister-in-law to Jesus
Enos	Eldest son of James the brother of Jesus, Jesus's nephew
Ichabod	A fictional name for the beggar by the beautiful gate, later healed by Peter and John
Jonathan	Husband of Mary of Bethany, brother to Simon the Leper, perfumer
Joseph, son of Cleopas	One of two disciples walking to Emmaus when Jesus appeared to them
Kheti	Egyptian owner of a trading caravan, Toma and Nodab are his trading partners, a lifetime friend to Mary and Joseph.
Miriam	Sister of Peter, mother of John Marc, owner of the upper room where Jesus had the Last Supper

Nodab	The fictional name for the prodigal son and fictional younger brother of Lazarus of Bethany, works the trading caravan with Toma and Kheti
Raziel	Fallen angel, second-in-command to Satan
Seth	Adopted son of Toma
Shira	Fictional name for the daughter of Jairus who was healed by Jesus.
Toma	Joseph's cousin, co-owner of a trading caravan, lives in Bethlehem. His first family was killed when the infants were slaughtered.

Historical Characters

The Galilean	An infamous self-proclaimed messiah and freedom fighter
Hillel	A famous rabbi
Judah Maccabee	The hero of Hanukkah who defeated Antiochus Epiphanes
Procila	Wife of Pilate (slightly altered spelling to make pronunciation easier).
Sejanus	Roman ruler under Tiberius. He became too powerful, and he was killed by Tiberius. Then many of

those Sejanus appointed to government positions were also executed.

Simeon son of Hillel	President of the Sanhedrin, possibly at the time of Jesus
Tiberius	Emperor of Rome
Yonatan	A Jewish Rabbi, a student of Hillel, also known as Jonathan ben Uzziel He was from the region of Galilee and his tomb is in that area today.

Traditional Characters

Dysmas	One of two thieves crucified with Jesus
Gestas	One of two thieves crucified with Jesus
Longinus	Centurion at the crucifixion
Ophaniel	An angel, a seraph

Biblical References

Prologue

1. Exodus 6:5–7
2. Exodus 5:1
3. Exodus 5:2
4. Exodus 5:3
5. Exodus 5:4-5
6. Exodus 5:6–9
7. Exodus 9:13-14
8. Exodus 9:18–19
9. Exodus 10:24-26
10. Exodus 10:28–29
11. Exodus 11:4
12. Exodus 12:13

Chapter 1

1. Romans 6:23
2. Genesis 28:14
3. Psalms 24:7–10
4. Isaiah 54:16–17
5. John 1:29
6. Numbers 6:24–26
7. Psalms 93:1–2
8. Luke 12:1
9. Luke 12:6–7
10. Luke 10:10
11. Luke 12:11–12

Chapter 2

1. Mark 10:14–16
2. Hebrews 11:6
3. Mark 10:5–9
4. Proverbs 16:18
5. John 11:41–43
6. John 11:49–50

Chapter 3

1. Exodus 20:3–6
2. Ezekiel 28:13–17
3. Psalm 89:48
4. Isaiah 40:9–10
5. Isaiah 40:28
6. Isaiah 40:29–31

Chapter 4

1. Psalms 67:1–3
2. Matthew 20:25
3. Matthew 20:27–28

Chapter 6

1. Luke 18:10–14
2. John 12:8
3. Matthew 26:13

Chapter 7

1. Job 20:2
2. Job 20:5
3. Job 20:12-15
4. Job 20:18
5. Job 20:27, 29
6. Psalms 22:12

7. Psalms 22:13–15
8. Luke 19:38
9. Luke 19:40
10. Matthew 21:5
11. Luke 19:42
12. Luke 19:43–44

Chapter 8

1. Exodus 12:17
2. Exodus 12:19–20
3. Malachi 1:10–11
4. Malachi 1:14
5. Matthew 21:12–13
6. Malachi 2:1–2
7. Psalm 27:4
8. Matthew 21:42
9. Mark 12:10–11
10. John12:28–32
11. Ezekiel 11:22–23

Chapter 9

1. Exodus 6:1
2. Exodus 6:6–7

Chapter 10

1. Mark 11:22–24
2. Matthew 22:14
3. Luke 20:25
4. Luke 20:27–33
5. Mark 12:26–27
6. Mark 12:30–31
7. Psalms 113:4–6
8. Isaiah 6:1
9. Psalms 113:7–9

Chapter 11

1. Luke 21:3–4
2. Matthew 23:13
3. Matthew 23:37–39
4. Matthew 24:29
5. Matthew 24:30–31
6. Matthew 24:36–37
7. Matthew 24:42
8. Matthew 25:31–36
9. Matthew 25:40
10. Zechariah 13:7

Chapter 12

1. Luke 1:31–33
2. Luke 22:15–18
3. John 13:4–5
4. Psalms 45:7
5. John 13:12-15
6. John 13:17
7. Luke 22:19
8. Mark 14:22
9. John 13:21–29

Chapter 13

1. Luke 22:19
2. Luke 22:20
3. Isaiah 53:7
4. Isaiah 53:12
5. John 14:1–4
6. John 14:12–14
7. John 14:16–17
8. John 14:28-29
9. John 14:30–31

10. Psalms 115:1
11. Psalms 116:12–19
12. Psalms 118:10–11
13. Psalms 118:15–16

Chapter 14

1. John 15:1
2. John 15:2
3. John 15:5
4. John 15:7
5. John 15:9–10
6. John 15:18–20
7. John 16:32–33
8. John 17:5
9. John 17:6, 8–9, 11–12
10. Luke 22:41–42
11. Luke 22:42

Chapter 15

1. Mark 14:60–65
2. Mark 15:1

Chapter 16

1. Luke 23:2–5
2. John 18:29
3. John 18:30
4. John 18:31
5. John 18:33
6. John 18:34
7. John 18:35
8. John 18:36
9. John 18:38
10. John 18:39-40

11. Matthew 27:19
12. Mark 15:9
13. Mark 15:11 -14
14. Ps.22:9 -11
15. John 19:9-10
16. John 19:11
17. John 19:12
18. John 19:13-15

Chapter 17

1. Matthew 27:24–26
2. Matthew 27:29–30
3. Matthew 27:31
4. Luke 23:28–30

Chapter 18

1. Luke 1:32–33
2. Luke 1:34
3. John 19:23–24
4. Mark 15:29-32
5. Luke 23:34
6. John 19:25–27
7. Matthew 27:46
8. Matthew 27:48
9. Matthew 27:52
10. Mark 15:39–41

Chapter 19

1. John 19:40–42
2. Isaiah 53:1
3. Isaiah 53:2–6
4. Revelation 1:18
5. Zechariah 9:11

6. 2 Corinthians 5:8
7. Isaiah 41:3–4
8. Isaiah 49:9
9. Psalms 107:14–16
10. Psalms 107:10–11
11. Psalms 16:6–7
12. 1 Corinthians 15:54

Chapter 20

1. Luke 24:4–7
2. Mark 16:6–8
3. Matthew 28:3
4. 1 Timothy 1:17
5. Psalms 24:7–8
6. Psalms 24:1–5
7. 1 Peter 3:18-20
8. 1 Peter 3:22
9. Luke 24:25–26
10. Luke 24: 45–49
11. John 20:21–23

Chapter 21

1. Luke 1:68
2. Isaiah 26:19
3. Luke 1:45–50
4. John 20:25
5. James 5:13–18
6. 1 John 4:2–3

Chapter 22

1. Mark 16:15–18

Chapter 23

1. Acts 1:6–8
2. Luke 24:50
3. Numbers 6:24–27
4. Acts 1:10–14
5. Acts 2:5–8
6. Acts 2:11–12
7. Acts 2:17
8. Acts 3:6–8
9. Acts 4:1–4

Epilogue

1. Revelation 1:12–18
2. Revelation 22:12
3. Revelation 22:14